STAKES AND BONES

SEATTLE SLAYERS

KEN BEBELLE

JULIA VEE

CONTENTS

1

THE WITCH IN 43B

The air inside of the witch's kitchen was dank, thick with humidity and the heavy scent of herbs bubbling away in the massive cauldron stung my nose. The heavy iron cauldron hung over the coals on creaking chains pinned to an arch of stones that was the main support for the roof. This area was the key to my plan today. I needed it to work and I just had to get my timing right *and* somehow get over the pile of glowing coals under the cauldron.

Waves of heat baked off the hot metal and clutched at my attention, dragging me down into drowsiness. It made me glad I'd tied my long hair back. Even so, the heavy strands stuck to the sweat on the back of my neck. I rubbed at my eyes and told myself to stay focused on the plan. Today I was going to get this witch to make a deal.

I moved into the back of the kitchen, ducking under a mesh bag of apples, dried into wrinkled stones. Plants filled the space above me, riotous green vines snaking low and brushing against my cheek. Instead of something normal like wood flooring or vinyl plank, the floor was packed earth. The low ceiling in this ancient building looked ready to collapse any minute now, but I wasn't going to hunch over–I wasn't going to telegraph my plan to the witch in 43B.

Laila the Enchantress stood with her back to me, turning her critical eye to the clothing I'd given her. At barely five foot tall, she was more than a head shorter than me. Like all in her coven, she wore rich blue robes that almost swept the floor.

When she held out my dark leather duster, the hem of the garment trailed on the packed dirt floor. When I'd tried it on it had fallen past my knees. As tall as I was, it was the closest thing I would find to full body protection if I could convince Laila to enchant it for me.

I'd expected someone older. Enchanting items was a rare specialty. But Laila was no crone. Her lively hazel eyes sparkled against her dark skin. Her long hair was shiny and black as a raven's wing. The almost tropical humidity of this kitchen made me sweaty while the witch glowed with vitality.

The fragrant steam pricked at my eyes and I resisted the urge to rub at them. I'd scoped out Laila's place last week and I had liked what I'd seen. If I could make this work, we would both benefit. Laila sighed and rubbed the leather between her fingers.

I tapped my foot. "What?"

She turned, her dark curly hair snagging on the ivy leaves that dangled everywhere in this jungle of a room. "The spells would last longer if the leather was better quality, but if this is all you have..."

I took the duster back and cradled it in my arms. I really loved this duster. "I traded a lot to get this. Can you still enchant it?"

Life behind the Twilight Veil had been quite an adjustment for me. Boston possessed a wonder of technology driven convenience whereas Seattle was stuck in the trappings of the century before. Residents behind the Twilight Veil had braved much to cross over, and gained much in return, such as longevity and magic. But sourcing items was a constant struggle here. Most of us in Seattle relied on the Caravan, which pulled through Seattle because it was the biggest settlement in the Twilight. The Caravan traded and restocked at the northern farms.

It had taken me a month and negotiating a three-way trade to source the duster, something I could have had in my hands in under an hour back home in Boston.

Laila straightened. "I can enchant a bathrobe. The bigger question is can you pay for it?"

Witches. Can't live with them and can't get them to do a measly enchantment without giving up a kidney.

I shoved down the feeling of desperation that I felt rising deep in my chest. The Slayer Trials were going to be difficult. Even the slightest upgrade to my gear would increase my odds of success. I couldn't panic. I reminded myself I was here to make a deal. "What will it cost me?"

The witch hooked her thumbs into her apron. "If you can't get me a better quality garment, I'll have to make up the difference in the runes. Demon horn is best for enchantments. I also need fresh akkoro squid ink, at least a pint, maybe two, a stinger from a Deathstalker scorpion to embed the ink into the leather, of course for such a large garment I'll need at least six stingers, eight to be on the safe side. Normally I'd use silver dust to bind the runes, but if you really want them to last it's best to blend the silver with black pearl powder which can be tricky to find this time of--"

I raised a hand and cut her off. "It's going to be expensive. I got it. How much?"

"Forty-three ounces. No, actually forty- five due to the extra length. Forty-five ounces."

I nearly dropped the duster. "What?!"

"Hey, if you want protective runes that are going to buckle under a werewolf's bite, you're more than welcome to take your business across the market. But you came to the Blue Rowan Coven because you know you need the best. Our price is more than fair for what you're asking for."

Today had started as a marginal day, one more day of waiting around for word from the Slayers. I was starting to worry that they wouldn't send for me. Laila's pricing just threw the day into the toilet. I didn't have that much silver. I'd sent the bulk of it for my mom's last treatment. The little silver I had remaining was already allocated between the rent for my little apartment and buying enough food to keep me conscious.

I had two ounces of silver and a rock in my pockets. The rock was shaped like a wedge of cheese. I had big hopes for this rock.

I did some more mental math: If I skipped dinners for the next month I would barely have half the amount saved. I'd have more silver eventually, but only after the Slayers took me on.

I let my eyes drift around the room, my vision filling with an almost holographic map of lines as my magic kindled. My magic scored pale green lines of light stretched across the walls and ceiling, drawing a diagram of force and stress. Those lines told a story that I read as easily as any book. Laila's little building had structural issues. My fingers itched to touch the arches.

To save my mother I needed to get into the Slayers. To get into the Slayers I needed to survive their legendary Trials. An enchanted duster was just the thing I needed to help me survive what could be the most brutal week of my life.

Looking at this relic of a place, I could tell Laila needed me too. She just didn't know it yet.

I slipped the duster on, enjoying the feel of the supple leather across my shoulders. It wouldn't do much if I got attacked, but at least I would look good as I got mauled.

Now it was time to execute part two of my plan. Hopefully I'd gotten the timing right.

"Well, thanks for taking the time."

Laila took a step towards me as I turned to the door. "You're leaving?"

I shrugged. "Too rich for my blood."

As I walked out, I shortened my stride deliberately. One thing I enjoyed about the Twilight, everyone here loved to deal and hated to walk away from one.

Laila hurried out from behind the counter and stopped between me and the door. "Okay, hold on. We're just getting started. I haven't even discussed what discounts you might qualify for."

Now we were getting somewhere. "Go on..."

"Well, most of the cost in a working like this is in the materials. If you were able to procure the raw materials on your own, then I could simply charge you for the working itself."

She flipped through a massive worn tome and showed me the page. "Here, these items."

I read the list and nodded. I wandered back towards the cauldron, pretending to examine her plants. Akkoro squids and Deathstalker scorpions sounded like a pretty tough find. Demon horn sounded impossible. I doubted I would be saving time or money by procuring them on my own. "Sourcing these could take me some time. Is there any way we could do a payment plan?."

Laila wrung her hands. "I'm sorry, but the Blue Rowan Coven isn't a bank, we require half up front and..."

My timing had been a little off, but close enough. With a groan, the chains suspending the cauldron slipped and a rain of dust fell on me. Laila cried out as the heavy iron pot tipped and the bright red liquid within sloshed dangerously close to the edge.

I reached up and brushed aside a knotty vine. The pale green lines in my vision coalesced into a bright point of white light just above my head, the failure point. I reached up and put my palm on the capstone of the arch supporting Laila's roof and locked out my elbow. With my other hand I pulled out the vine, revealing the hole its roots had dug into the space between the stones.

The cauldron swung in place gently now, its contents calming. I dropped the vine at Laila's feet. Her eyes were big as saucers.

"These vines are a nuisance, aren't they? Looks like this one cracked the mortar around the capstone."

I reached into my pocket and pulled out the rock. The rock slid into the hole vacated by the vine roots. The white point in my vision faded to pale green. I relaxed my arm and let go slowly. The arch held.

"Maybe we could work out a barter for my services?"

Laila knotted her hands into her apron. "You'd have to speak with Maven Ana Victoria for that."

"Maybe you could introduce us. The coven's building could use a little more tending to. I help out other property owners here in Seattle with their maintenance needs."

Well, I helped one owner—my current landlord, Mrs. Chu. But if the Blue Rowan Coven took me on too, then it would actually be multiple property owners.

Curiosity sparkled in her eyes. "Well, maybe I could do that if you tell me how you fixed that."

I tucked my thumbs into my pockets. I wasn't keen to share my magic so I settled for the basic explanation. "Sure. The answer is science. Capstones work because of geometry and gravity."

Laila waved a hand dismissively. "Science doesn't work the same behind the Veil."

Fair point. "Gravity still works here. Look, assuming you add no further ivy, the capstone should hold even longer."

"If you say so." Laila did not look convinced.

I needed the duster first. That would help me win the Trials. Once I was in the Slayers, silver would cease to be a problem. I tried to keep the desperation off my face.

"So, how about it? Can we work something out?"

Laila tapped a slender finger on the arch as she pondered the capstone. "I do appreciate this fix. If you can get me half the ingredients, we can do twenty-five ounces."

I winced. "Maybe you could see if the Maven could use some work from me?"

Her smile fell briefly and reignited. "Oh. The Maven is very busy. But perhaps you are associated with one of the Guilds? We offer a professional discount to all of them. The Fae Conclave, the Templars, the Slayers..."

Ouch. It was like she knew exactly where to kick me while I was down. If I had wanted to get beaten up like this I could have just jumped in front of the Caravan. The cramped confines of Laila's kitchen pushed in and the ceiling seemed to be crushing down on me. I had to get out of here.

"Let me think about it and I'll come back another time."

I brushed by her and pushed out the door.

Twenty-five ounces wasn't as impossible, but I would have to somehow survive the start of the Slayer Trials until then. Outside the air was lighter and fresher, although still heavy with humidity. At least I didn't have to smell whatever it was that Laila had been cooking in her pot. I squinted unnecessarily as I looked up to the violet sky. Six months here and I still wasn't quite used to the unending twilight that gave this region its name. The Twilight Veil hung over the city like a dark mist, obscuring the sky. Most of the stars were gone, blotted out by the Veil. The moon only showed up as a pale afterimage, and only when it was full. I hadn't seen the sun since I'd crossed over. People who'd grown up here only heard about the sun in stories.

Streaks of orange lit the fog from underneath like the glow from the world's biggest campfire.

Though I couldn't see it from this street, to the west was the Pacific Ocean, post-Rift. When I'd first arrived, I used to go out to the shore and stare at the Tarim Pyramids that jutted out of the ocean. The pyramids gave off an eerie orange glow, their crystalline structure pulsing with inner fire.

The Tarim had made all of this happen. The Rift, the drowning of Seattle, and the cloak of eternal twilight that created the Veil. It had lured all the otherworldly creatures here where they no longer had to hide in the dark of night. The ones who fed off the surge in magic. Which left the rest of us humans to fend for ourselves. Humans got a boost too. Certainly, I hadn't been a Breaker back in Boston.

I loved it here. I hadn't expected to. But being here where my father had made his mark brought out the same yearning in me.

I stood outside the witch's flat and tried to figure out how to earn some more silver.

The trek back to my apartment in the old International District wasn't long from here. It would take me through the east side of the Market. If the Slayers weren't calling me up then I had yet another day to kill. Maybe I'd spend the little bit of silver I still had, buy some flour, sugar, and yeast. Donuts always cheered me up, and I could always sell a few as well. Would that get me to twenty-five ounces? No. But I would keep working on how to earn extra scratch. Maybe my neighbor Jimbo could use an extra hand at his bike repair business.

I was so lost in thought about my plans for tonight that I nearly lost an eye when the carrier pigeon flew into my face.

The bird smacked into me and my vision filled with an explosion of gray feathers. I went to my knees on the wooden planks of the sidewalk and pawed at my face, digging feathers out of my mouth.

When I'd gotten myself sorted out I was sitting on the sidewalk with the carrier pigeon standing next to me, its beady eyes staring at me with unspoken judgment. I jerked to one side as something clicked loudly and someone knelt next to me.

Laila's billowing blue robes spilled around her knees as she crouched. She supported herself with a staff of gnarled pale driftwood. The top of the staff ended in a bulbous twist and several polished wooden rings had been artfully crafted into the wood. Her eyes were focused on the pigeon.

"Do you see the orange tag on the left leg? That's a carrier pigeon from the Slayer's Guild!" Her voice held a note of curiosity.

She turned to me and her eyes widened. "Someone from the Slayer's Guild wants to tell you something!"

Well. It was about time. I reached out slowly to the bird, wary of its sharp beak. The bird held still until my hand was under it and I untied the tiny brass cylinder from its leg. I unscrewed the top off the container and a tiny roll of paper fell into my hand. I closed the container and reattached it to the bird's leg.

Laila leaned in closer, nearly salivating as she looked between me and the scrap of paper. "Well?"

I leaned away from the nosy witch and unrolled the paper, squinting in the dim light. My uncle Samuel's tight handwriting filled the bit of paper from edge to edge.

Denny Park

Five bells

Don't Be Late

The smile on my face threatened to split my cheeks. I could

hardly pull my eyes off the paper. "How much is that discount for the Slayer's Guild?"

The witch grinned. "Twenty percent."

I tucked away the paper. It would be harder but that had never stopped me before. I would just have to survive the Trials without the duster. "I'll be back in a week. Then we can talk about appropriate discounts for members of the Slayer's Guild."

I got to my feet. Five bells. I had plenty of time to go home and pack my meager belongings and get ready for the hardest week of my life.

2

THE FANGS

The quickest way out of the Market and to my apartment took me through The Fangs, a neighborhood of entirely legitimate business enterprises run by Seattle's two vampire perils. The Mist and Mind vampires ran a collection of pleasure houses. The Shadow's Den owned all the nightclubs. Smaller perils of vampires had long ago pledged fealty to one of these two factions, and they operated the other businesses in The Fangs, under the careful purview of their king or queen.

When people were looking for a good time, they came to The Fangs. If they were lucky, they made it out with their minds intact, their bodies whole.

It was a common mistake. Many who came to Seattle assumed that the Market, which operated under the auspices of the Oceanic Pact, was a safe zone. As if anything within the Twilight Veil was safe.

The Oceanic Pact, the most sacrosanct of contracts, codified over a century ago, outlined the structure within which Seattle's factions jockeyed for power and influence. One of the chief benefits of the Pact was Market Freedom. None of Seattle's factions brought their grievances to Market. This relative safety ensured a brisk and steady trade that kept Seattle flush with supplies.

It was this relative safety that led some to relax their guard. While the Pact forbade outright murder of humans, when vampires were involved, there were many options worse than death. Mist and Mind vampires could mesmerize their prey, drain them willingly, and leave them addicted to the euphoria that came from their bite. They were considered the "nice" vampires.

The Shadow's Den members were not so nice.

And yet, Seattle was lucky these two big players--the Night Queen of Mist and Mind, and Pierce Yang, King of the Shadow's Den, had carved up the vampire territory this way because the alternative was worse. The alternative was why Slayers existed in the first place.

The alternative was swarms of rogue vamps wreaking havoc in Seattle. Rogues draining their victims to death and turning more rogues. This was an outcome that even the Night Queen and the Vampire King agreed was bad for business, and jeopardized their feeding grounds.

Rogues were something that aligned the Mist and Mind and the Shadow Den together with the Slayers, which made for odd bedfellows.

But I wasn't a Slayer yet.

The Fangs wasn't an easy area to navigate. Go one way, you could end up traipsing into the Pleasure District, a high-end neighborhood with bistros, salons, and the Queen's own mansion deep in the heart of the district.

Go another way, and you hit the Dens. The Dens were sketchy, and people with higher risk tolerance levels might go there to gamble and otherwise procure less savory experiences.

If I hadn't been in such a hurry, so excited by the arrival of the Slayers' pigeon, so stupidly distracted, I would have circled around The Fangs and taken the long way home. I was halfway into Dens territory before I realized my mistake. Not an auspicious start to my career as a Slayer.

I kicked harder, building up speed on my skateboard. I just needed to get through the Dens as fast as I could to avoid an unpleasant encounter.

I wasn't worried by the Mist and Mind vampires, but one in particular had taken an alarming interest in me and I wasn't in the mood for--

"Oh look, a lost little lamb."

I skidded my skateboard to a stop, just in time to avoid crashing into three nattily dressed vampires who materialized out of the darkness in front of me. A pit opened in my stomach as the vamps spread out and surrounded me, each one of them dressed in slim dark suits with red accents. Fair-haired and pale-skinned, they had the kind of generic good looks you find on glossy fashion slicks, but their prettiness was just a thin veneer. If you looked carefully, you would note the hollowed cheeks and darkened eyes. These vamps weren't just cruising–they were hungry.

The uniform marked them as thugs from the Shadow's Den who'd sworn fealty to the King of the Vampires, Pierce Yang. This was bad. I was a good fighter, and that was helpful, but not a guarantee against just one vampire. *Three* vampires posed a serious problem.

I wasn't an idiot. I knew Market Freedom would keep me alive, but there was a lot of room between not quite dead, and dead.

I made a quick scan up and down the narrow alleys in all directions as the vamps circled me. I didn't see anyone around with the bright orange armbands that denoted their Slayer patrol status. That meant I was on my own. Just me, my skateboard, and my little bit of breaker magic.

I watched the group warily, trying to discern which one was

the leader. Vampires only wanted one thing, so bargaining with them was out. But that didn't mean I couldn't talk myself out of trouble. The tallest of the three drew my eye, but that was more because of his reach. His arms were so long that the sleeves of his jacket sat high above his wrists. Just behind Stretch was a vampire who wore his platinum hair shaved close, the lack of contrast between his hair, eyebrows, and white skin unnervingly ghostly. To the left of Ghost was the shortest of the three, his blocky shoulders filling out his black jacket with a little more heft. Over his left eye, he wore a patch, which told me that he had that before being turned because the thing about vampirism was it healed most things short of a beheading but some pre-existing issues persisted.

My eyes narrowed slightly as I pulled lightly on my magic, scanning for weaknesses. I paid special attention to Patch and his pre-existing conditions.

The vamps danced around me, weaving back and forth, making it harder to keep track of them. All vampires were a problem for a human like me, but some of the Shadow's Den members had the ability to transform and fly, which made them even more disturbing.

Pierce Yang didn't bestow his gift of flight on all of his vampires, but it was a fair bet that the leader of this little peril was one of Pierce's favored. I needed to figure out which one he was, so I could stay focused on the biggest threat.

Outnumbered three to one, my best bet was a passing Slayer patrol. I needed to stall until one came within earshot. The Slayers maintained the peace of Market Freedom. Maybe invoking them would buy me some time.

I kicked my board up and swung it across my back for safekeeping. In a pinch, it would also protect my blind side. I flipped back the tails of my duster and planted my hands on my hips. Sweeping back the duster revealed the twin hammers riding on my hips, Thor and Loki, with polished heads of cold steel and fire-hardened handles turned and sharpened into ten-inch stakes, perfect for dispatching unruly vamps.

Below my hammers, silver-chased daggers rested in sheaths on both thighs. At my back, tucked into my vest and out of sight, more knives, short and perfectly weighted for throwing. I might not be a Slayer yet, but I knew how to kit myself out like one.

"Evening, boys. What business do you have with the Slayers tonight?"

The vamps laughed, an ugly, grating sound. I clenched my fingers down, willing my hands to stop shaking.

Stretch growled. "The lamb thinks she's a Slayer. Don't see no ink. Don't see no bandana."

I crossed off Stretch as the leader. Too talkative. Too brash. Down to Ghost or Patch, then. I put my money on Ghost, with Stretch and the third guy shooting him quick glances before turning their hungry gaze back on me.

"You think every Slayer needs to wear their ink where you can see it? How have vamps as stupid as you survived this long?"

That jab earned me a deadly glare from Ghost. He didn't like being cut down in front of his subordinates. Of course, only the glare was deadly. They weren't planning on killing me. Not under the Pact. No, they were going to enslave me and turn me into cattle. Anything short of killing me inside the bounds of Market was fair game--a truly devious contract worthy of fae approval. It hardly mattered that vampire enslavement turned you into a mindless zombie, the Pact only concerned itself with true deaths. The only exception was for humans, because we were all outmatched so we could stand our ground or save a life. A human life. Today I aimed to save my own.

Ghost took a step towards me, pushing aside Stretch roughly. When he spoke his voice was a hoarse whisper. "You might dress like a Slayer but you smell like a blood donor. You're coming with me tonight."

That was definitely over the line. At least, it was over the Slayers' line. If a Slayer on patrol were present, they would be instantly adjusting Ghost's attitude. But despite my attempts to stall, no convenient patrols had come within sight of my little drama. While Ghost talked, the other two vamps moved to cut off my escape.

My options were disappearing quickly. I dropped my weight into my knees, getting ready to move in any direction. Lessons from my dad buzzed through my head and my eyes darted left and right, scanning for exits. My mouth kept talking, almost on its own. "Do the math guys, this is not going to end well for you."

The vamps laughed again, and in the midst of that laugh, Ghost lunged for me, blurring into a pale smear of color.

My nerves vanished like mist in a volcano as adrenaline took over. I already had my weight leaned towards Stretch. As the leader of their small peril, I knew they'd give Ghost the first strike, so I only needed to decide which of the other two to eliminate first. When Ghost disappeared I pushed off and launched myself at Stretch, vampire of long limbs and weak knees.

Muscle memory led the way and both of my hammers came out. Heads out, sharpened stake side down--I didn't need to attract the attention of Pierce Yang for killing his goons unless I had to. Against vampires, I could go all out with my hammers and see if that discouraged them first.

Stretch had half a moment to register a look of utter surprise as I came straight at him. He probably wasn't used to being the center of attention. I like to make people feel important. Thor likes to make an impression, too, and he did as the twenty-ounce stainless steel head whipped through the thick night air and connected with the side of Stretch's wonky left knee.

As the hammer slammed home I sparked the active aspect of my breaker magic. Vampires are tough. Any extra edge helped. The tracings of light that illuminated Stretch tugged at my mind like an itch. I followed the sensation to the point where the green lines faded to pale white inside the vampire's knee. In my mind the taut knee ligaments were like aged, brittle rubber bands. I pushed with my mind and Broke them.

Bone splintered with a crack that echoed off the brick facades of the vamp clubs. In my magic sight, the bright white point of his knee ligament shone like a tiny supernova as the tissue ripped in half. Stretch's knee caved inwards at a forty-five degree angle and the vampire gave a scream of surprise and pain as he went down and landed on the destroyed knee. His knee would heal within moments of him feeding. Too bad for Stretch it would always return to its original gimpy nature.

In the next moment a wave of...wrongness...rolled across me, the recoil from using my active magic. I'd Broken something, altering the world in a small way. Like dropping a pebble into water, the shockwaves of my magic spread out, then returned, collapsing into me. It felt like chewing tin foil and running my hands through broken glass. The sensation rocked me back but I shook it off, the sensation fading as quickly as it had appeared. I'd done this before, and thankfully I hadn't overdone it.

At the instant Stretch hit the asphalt, a rush of rotten air blew past me, whipping the tails of my duster. I'd just dodged Ghost as I'd taken out Stretch. Nothing like a little luck to grease the skids. I prayed my luck held up.

One down, two to go.

Where were the Slayer patrols?

I spun on the ball of my foot, both hammers up. Patch stared stupidly at me, his one good eye wide and round. Probably not used to their cattle fighting back. I had to take him out quickly. In a one-on-one I had a sliver of a chance. It would take Ghost another second to turn around at the speed he was going. I thrust Loki in a straight jab, aiming for Patch's solar plexus.

Or at least, I tried. A cold hand grabbed my back leg and yanked me back. My balance disrupted, I windmilled and crashed to the asphalt. Patch grabbed me by the wrist, his bony fingers crushing my tendons. Loki fell to the ground.

From the ground, Stretch had me by the ankle, his face twisted in pain as his knee snapped back into place. Patch pulled in the other direction until my shoulder felt like it was going to pop. I bit down on a scream. Where were the patrols?

Ghost walked back to me, looking at me like a roast on a spit. "There, now, that's better, isn't it? This is the Twilight, where the strongest survive. Sorry, lamb, you just weren't the strongest tonight."

The vamp's mouth hinged open, huge, too wide for a human mouth. His fangs extended, curved tips glistening with saliva. I pulled and twisted, but the hands holding me were like ice-cold iron. My heart hammered against my chest and bile threatened to climb up my throat. The scream in my chest burst out but all that came out was a high, thready whisper. With my free hand I drew one of my knives. Ghost's hand lazily slapped my wrist, sending my blade clattering to the concrete. My arm went numb to the elbow.

Ghost placed his cold hands on my face and shoulder and exposed my neck. I bucked, wrenching my body, trying anything to get them off of me. He hissed in anger and his hands clenched. Patch growled, a feral, animal sound, and pulled harder on my arm. A burning star of pain exploded in my shoulder as Ghost's fingers dug into the joint and I nearly passed out.

He bent down to feed. I closed my eyes and silently begged

my family, my mother, and my uncle for forgiveness. I'd failed them.

The vamp's fangs stopped within an inch of my neck, the scent of his foul breath cascading over my face. I sensed a very large presence above me, someone who hadn't been there the instant before. The agony in my shoulder relaxed as my arm and leg were released and I dropped to the ground. I caught the barest scent of pine, woodsmoke, and coffee. It was familiar, alluring, and problematic. *Oh no.*

Goddess. Relief warred with dread in my gut. I didn't want to be a blood slave to the Den but I also didn't want to owe my rescuer.

"Roxy, really? The Den? And after I invited you to dinner at Delightful Distractions."

I rolled over and tried my best not to wince. The vamps pulled back, except for the one currently being lifted off his feet by the neck. The strong hand wrapped around Ghost's neck belonged to Tyee Wilder, the lazy vampire princeling who "managed" the Mist and Mind pleasure houses. He was a royal pain in my ass. He was also saving my ass right now, which only irritated me more.

Tyee filled out his indigo wool blazer to the perfect amount of stretch, his tailor clearly an artist. His broad chest was swathed in a silky expanse of silver cloth, the perfect foil for the inky waves of his shoulder-length hair. With his arm outstretched, holding up the offending vampire, the t-shirt had come untucked, exposing a tantalizing slice of smooth, dark abdomen just above his belt buckle. He was handsome, witty, and charming and had taken an inexplicable interest in me.

I took a moment to steady my breathing and calm my racing heart. With his enhanced senses, Tyee knew how close I'd come to being culled, but I'd be cursed if I'd show weakness in front of the prince. After I got myself collected I forced my eyes up to Tyee's face, not that it was any less distracting than his belly. "I had to decline your invite since it wasn't clear if I was dinner."

His fine brow arched. "Drinks, perhaps?"

Tyee dropped the vamp. I braced myself, but Ghost merely goggled, looking back and forth between me and Tyee before scrambling away from us. Stretch and Patch followed and in a moment they disappeared into the darkness.

Nearly culled by Shadow's Den vampires, only to become indebted to a vampire of Mist and Mind. Could my day get any worse? "No, Tyee. Same problem."

Tyee bent and picked up my hammer and handed it to me. He held the hammer with two fingers, like he was holding a dirty dish rag. I snatched it out of his hand.

His smile was infuriatingly alluring, with a ridiculous and unfair flash of dimple. "Yes, of course. Allow me to clarify, *ma bichette*, I'd like to offer you drinks, on the house, of course, as well as my much sought-after company. I'm told my company is quite entertaining. We can celebrate your...victory."

His pet name for me, "doe" made me wince. Maybe he meant it in a playful way, a reference to my long legs and dark eyes, but instead it reminded me that vampires were predators and humans were prey.

He leaned close. "I am more than happy to show you all that Delightful Distractions has to offer."

I put a hand on his chest and pushed him away. It made me perversely happy to have an excuse to touch him. "Just like last time, and the time before that, I must regretfully decline the invitation. No thank you, Tyee."

Tyee backed away and laid a hand over his chest, his eyes sad. "Alas. Until next time then, *ma bichette*."

A cloud of dark mist swallowed him. Before he disappeared he gave me a wink, and then he was gone.

Jerk.

3

GHOST

My apartment sat on the northern edge of the old International District, in the shadow of the hulking remains of the 5 Freeway super bypass. On my skateboard the mile and a half from the Market to my apartment only took ten minutes, leaving me at two hours to get my meager belongings together.

I pushed hard, using the skateboard time to settle my nerves. The incident at the Fangs had shaken me badly. In minutes, I had gone from elation at my Slayer Trials invite to almost being a blood meal for the Shadow Den.

Carelessness could lead to a fate worse than death here in the Veil. Sure I had solid fighting skills, but I was still just a human and no match for three hungry vampires. The Oceanic Pact only protected me so far. I had to rely on my wits for the rest, and my wits and fighting skills had failed me today.

Instead, the vampire prince had saved me, which was galling.

I didn't want to owe Tyee Wilder anything, but now I did. I hated that and I hated myself for getting into a fight I couldn't finish.

I needed to be smarter if I wanted to be a Slayer.

"You have to be the best, Roxybear."

I hadn't been the best today. I kicked harder on my board, letting the thump of the pavement under the wheels work its rhythmic magic.

Halfway back to my apartment I passed the old King Street Station, an expansive red brick building that had once been adorned with a two-hundred foot clock tower. While the main structure had survived the Drowning, the clock tower had fallen victim to the earthquakes and came crashing down.

When the Pacific Ocean receded, leaving Seattle a kelp-ridden wreck, the wreckage of the clock tower was revealed. Covered in junk, sea plants, and dead fish, the jumble of bricks and concrete drew a massive cross pointing at the old station.

Few people in the Twilight would ignore such an obvious sign. It had taken only days for a new crop of true believers to congregate at the old bus terminal. In another month they had all pitched in and cleaned out the station, turning it into one of the first inhabitable buildings after the Drowning. They opened their doors to any and all.

To gain entry you only needed to swear fealty to the Church of the Sharpened Cross.

The cross on the grounds in front of the building had long since been cleaned, each brick lovingly scrubbed and kept in its place of reverence. The church maintained continuous vigil over their cross, protecting it from newcomers who might view the cross as simply another pile of neglected building materials.

As I passed the church a familiar young man in the plain white smock of a Supplicant ran to intercept me. "Good day, sister! How can the church protect you from evil today?"

Gods save me from zealots. I kicked harder, putting on more speed to pull away from him. After my fracas in the Fangs, the last thing I needed was a dustup with the Church. The Supplicant slowed, his footsteps falling behind me. "Until tomorrow, sister!"

Despite the Supplicant's painfully awkward sales pitch I didn't miss the crude wooden cross tucked into the hemp belt cinched at his waist. Nor the larger cross strapped to his back. Both hammered together from scavenged wood, the ends whittled down and blackened from fire hardening. Last week I'd witnessed a handful of Crossies take on a rogue in the wetlands to the south. It hadn't been pretty, and they'd lost a few of their own, but the vamp had ended up skewered all the same. What the Church of the Sharpened Cross lacked in skilled fighters they more than made up for with blank-eyed passion. Or craziness.

Probably just crazy.

My place was thankfully safely far enough away from the Church and as always, I felt a rush of gratitude for my uncle finding me this place. The landlady, Mrs. Chu, had worked out a sweetheart deal for me where I had not only a studio apartment to myself but use of the shed out back. Well, she called it a shed but I think it would have been more fair to characterize it as a carriage house. It was a two story building with a loft above a small garage. I got the use of the tools and the only other tenant who used the shed was Jimbo, who kept his bike repair gear there.

In exchange, I kept Mrs. Chu's building in tip top shape, shoring up every little weakness and making sure the tenants all had hot water and whatever else they needed. In a place where magic had reigned for the last century, technology had become a rare art and one where my talents had proved valuable.

I unlocked the iron gates and shuffled down the hallway past the mailboxes and rickety entryway way table. Nobody really had mail these days so the mailbox area had become sort of a bulletin board area of sorts where we posted notes for each other.

I took the stairs to my unit two at a time then came to a crashing halt.

The ghost was back, a pale, floating apparition on the landing. Its sad eyes were locked on my front door.

As I stood there, Mrs. Chu came up the stairs, waved at me and then walked by the ghost on the landing like he wasn't even there. Could she not see him?

Why was I so special?

Maybe he had lived in my unit. I sidled around our ghostly guest and entered Unit 3. I looked around the modest studio, taking in the cracks and the faded yellow paint. The centuries hadn't been kind to it but the building had withstood the tempests unleashed by the Veil. That was all that mattered. Still, I had tried to make it cozy and secure. Fairy lanterns were strung along the ceiling, giving off a soft gold light that pushed the darkness back into the corners and underhangs.

For security I'd hung a bagua mirror over my door. The bagua had been blessed by the temple monks, and the eight sides were gilded and trimmed with red paint. Since I wasn't sure how good the threshold was when I'd moved in, the bagua was a little extra protection against vampires.

In a place like the Twilight, it was always wise to take added precautions against vampires.

Soon I would be locked in the Slayer Trials. I didn't have time for much, but my mother had taught me to always pay respects to the dead. I opened the cupboard, pulling out a small white rice bowl trimmed with pink flowers. From last night's pot, I scooped out some long grain rice. On my way to the door I selected a tangerine from the fruit bowl.

Balancing the offerings, I opened the door with one hand and peered out. Yup, Mr. Ghost was still there. Though we were indoors, his clothing fluttered from an invisible breeze.

I set down the rice bowl and the fruit, and looked at my undead visitor. He stared back at me, hollow cheeks and empty eyes.

I pointed to the offering and made a small bow. "Please eat."

"Roxy! What are you doing?"

Mrs. Chu stood above us, peering down over the railing. My landlady might have looked like someone's tiny grandma but she bellowed like a truck driver. Clearly, those werewolf lungs were going strong. Also, she was a bit hard of hearing.

I gestured helplessly to the ghost, who was now kneeling by my offering. I didn't have any joss sticks so I would have to get some from the shop on the corner next time.

Mrs. Chu hmmphed. "You shouldn't feed the ghosts."

So she could see him!

The ghost in question had started eating, his skeletal fingers scooping from the bowl, his gaunt cheeks working as he chewed. As I watched, his outline seemed to fill in, the wavy edges now gaining dimension. I hadn't been expecting that. It wasn't like I was a necromancer or anything.

The bowl was empty now.

I looked up at Mrs. Chu and she shook her head at me, her exasperation clear.

"Just you wait. First you feed them, then they start asking you for things."

Ghost boy now manifested more identifiably as a young man, with dark hair standing in shaggy tufts. He was no longer colorless and his tattered cloak took on a distinct deep green. It looked like what the Herbal College students wore.

Number 4, the door next to my apartment opened up and the peeling white paint flaked off into tiny bits of snow into the hallway. Jimbo peeked out, his long red locks slicked back. He must have just taken his bike helmet off. Whenever I saw Jimbo, it was usually with his bike in tow and a slightly dented helmet covering most of his head.

"What's all the yelling...oh, hello Ernest." Jim stepped out, his face perplexed as he studied the ghost.

"You...you know him?"

"Sort of. It..used to be Ernest Wong. Ernest lived in No. 3, before he..ah...you know."

Jimbo made an awkward gesture at his neck. I gathered that meant Ernest had been ganked by a rogue vampire. It did explain the ghost's initial withered state. Although after that bowl of rice Ernest was looking quite a bit more substantial now.

Ernest ignored us, apparently focused on the tangerine.

Rogues were the bane of Seattle. It was the one reason that the Night Queen's Mists and Mind co-existed uneasily with Pierce Yang's Shadow Den. Vampires under their control meant the city kept the Twilight protection the vampires craved. It was part of the Oceanic Pact. But more rogues crossed the Veil daily, drawn to this nirvana of endless Twilight. The Night Queen and Pierce Yang demanded their fealty and if the rogues declined, they were put down. If the perils failed to keep the rogue problem under control, the Slayers stepped in.

That's what I was looking forward to–putting down rogues who killed hapless residents like Ernest here.

Jimbo turned to me. "Roxy, would you be able to take a look at the kitchen faucet? Henry has been complaining about it."

I shook my head. "Tell him I'll have to check it later. My Slayer pigeon came in."

Jimbo gasped. "Is it today?"

"Woo!" Mrs. Chu cheered from above.

I nodded. "Yes, I have to be at the Slayer's Hall by five bells."

"Wonderful. Break a leg! I mean, well, you know." Jim bobbed his head.

I grinned. "Thanks."

"Knock 'em dead!" Mrs. Chu hollered.

Knowing my landlady, I think she meant that literally. I waved up at her. "Will do."

As I turned to head back inside my unit, Ernest set the tangerine peels in the bowl. "Slayer?" His voice was papery thin, like the rustling of dry leaves.

"Uhh...yes. That's the plan anyway."

"Slayer." Ernest pointed at me.

"If all goes well after the Trials, yes."

Ernest nodded, his ghostly hair bobbing. "Slayer."

He sounded pretty certain for a dead guy. I couldn't believe I was getting a pep talk from a ghost. Well, I guess I had to take my encouragement wherever I could. Couldn't hurt.

I held out my fist for a fist bump with Ernest. He returned it, the cold chill of his hand passing through mine. I resisted the urge to shiver. "Thanks, man. Catch you later."

Now came the packing. I opened the oven and pulled out the granola bars I'd made last night. I wrapped them in wax paper and shoved them in my waist pouch. I slid out the other tray and studied the Apple cider donuts. They probably wouldn't travel great. I shoved one

in my mouth and took a heaping bite.

Apples from dryads packed a punch. The tart and sweet cinnamon goodness rolled across my tongue. I chewed with appreciation. I'd gotten this recipe just the way I liked it now. To hell with it, crumbled donuts were still going to be delicious later. I packed two of the donuts and filled my canteen.

I yanked open the top drawer of the dresser. This is where I usually I kept my two hammers, Thor and Loki in all their polished and pointy glory. I'd sanded the ends until they were the perfect stakes--ideal for getting up close and personal with a rogue vampire. Since I was already loaded up with my hammers, it was time for additional embellishments.

The knives. More knives, that is. I already had several on my person. Now I slid more into straps along my waist and under my duster. A last one in my boot. All the silver I'd brought to the Veil had gone into this artillery. The spelling for the duster had been a lower priority until now.

I picked up the framed photo on top of the dresser. It had been taken during happier times. My mom looked softer, her cheeks full and her lips curved in a warm smile. My dad had an arm around me and another around my younger brother Jasper. My little sister Ava leaned against our mom, her face a miniature replica of our dad's. The same dimples, the slashing brows. I'd gotten his height, but she'd gotten the rest of his genetics.

"Dad, I'm doing it. Just like we talked about."

I could almost hear him answer me. "Just like we trained, Roxy bear."

After he'd passed away, I'd been the sole breadwinner for the family. I'd watched my mom get sicker and sicker. It hurt to see her withering away, to know that we could never afford the care we needed to actually cure her cancer. Instead we could just treat the symptoms, and make her comfortable. But my dad had been sure that the Slayers had another way to heal my mom.

My father and his brother had crossed the Veil, so I knew that we had what it took to make that crossing. That wasn't true for most people. Most people couldn't cross. But once on this side, people enjoyed the benefits of the Veil, which meant more robust health.

I'd made the Crossing. I'd felt stronger and kindled my small magic when I'd gotten here. But now I was finally carrying out the plan.

My eyes stung and I sat the frame back down. I couldn't let him down. I wouldn't let him down. Dad had trained me to fight with the best. Now my mom needed me to deliver.

Gabriel Lim's daughter was getting on the Slayer's roster.

4

DAY ONE

Look up Seattle in any of the old histories and they would all describe the skyline with the Space Needle. The towering structure was built for the World's Fair in 1962, and designed to withstand hurricane force winds and 9.0 earthquakes. Unfortunately, it had not been designed to endure both of those, along with a tsunami.

On the day of the Drowning, the Pacific Ocean rose up like a spiteful child and struck the city with the force of an atom bomb. Gale force winds uprooted trees and blasted windows out of buildings. A wall of seawater twenty feet high barreled into Seattle like a runaway freight train. The bedrock of the city bucked like a wild animal trying to shake off the city. Under the combined assault of wind, earth, and water, the Space Needle's architecture failed. The saucer atop the Needle tilted as one of the upper supports buckled. No one had been up to the saucer since.

Of course, I'd seen pictures of the old Seattle skyline. The news shows loved showing old footage of old Seattle whenever the anniversary of Drowning Day came around. From First Hill, where the Seattle Slayers had founded their headquarters, the

Space Needle was visible in the distance as a bright set of spindly legs that rose up and disappeared into the dark purple mist of the Veil. It was hard to make out at this distance, but a Slayer watch tower sat in the crook of the legs, halfway up the structure. From that vantage point, the Slayers kept watch over the center of Seattle.

When I was younger, Dad had described the Slayers' HQ to me. I'd treasured those times because it meant he was in a good enough mood to talk about his days behind the Veil. I had soaked up his stories like a sponge, enamored with the idea of an entire city hidden away behind a wall of magic fog and threatened on all sides by bloodthirsty vampires and evil fae. I eventually learned to bring dad an extra beer, which would earn me stories of the Seattle Slayers, warriors of legend who defended Seattle from those who would try to tear the city down. To elementary school me, it had all sounded incredibly exciting.

"You really fought vampires and demons, Dad?"

"The vampires were easy, Roxybear--it's the demons you really had to watch out for!"

My right hand dropped to the hammer swinging from my gun holster, the comforting weight easy on my hip. I slipped my fingers around the haft and my memories blurred until I was handing the same hammer to my father in his shop, an engine dismantled on the floor in an artful mechanical dissection. With his elbows deep in something mechanical, my father was most prone to waxing nostalgic about Seattle and his dreams of going back. The arrival of me and my brother had put those dreams on hold. When he'd gotten his diagnosis, he'd redirected that energy towards training me on the weekends, pouring that dream into me.

Now I was here. Finally fulfilling dad's dreams and taking control of his Legacy, just like he wanted. I was up to the challenge. I had to be.

I squeezed down on the smooth wood of Thor's handle and whispered under my breath. "I got this, Dad. I got this."

As I rolled up to Denny Park, I was struck again by the harsh reality of Seattle colliding with the romantic vision I had envisioned as a child. In my fantasies, Denny Park had been enclosed by a neat barricade of heavy vertical logs, with stone towers set at the corners to house guardsmen. Instead the wall was an amalgam of heavy stones and broken chunks of concrete and asphalt enclosing an area to the west of the park. Guards armed with long bows and crossbows paced along the top of the wall. What little wood had been available anchored a massive set of gates in the southern wall. The gate itself was a faded patchwork of battered sheets of metal, held together with a maze of welds and rivets. Guards in threadbare black uniforms stood sentry across the gate, each one armed with an eight foot spear topped with a leaf-shaped blade.

The exterior of the Slayers' HQ was much less romanticized magic fortress, and much more ad hoc apocalyptic military base. A loose crowd of applicants congregated around the gates, small knots of bodies forming and dispersing as the crowd pulsed like a living being. Tree-sized towers had been set up across the grassy field that had once been the center of Denny Park, and bright fires danced atop the towers. To the north, low buildings hid in the shadowy darkness beneath a stand of old-growth trees.

It was old, it was imposing, and I loved everything about it. I thought about myself striding into Slayers' HQ–one of them.

Today I would find out if I was good enough.

I kicked my board up, slung it across my back, and made my way into the crowd. My months in Seattle had been truly eye-opening. I mean, my landlady was a werewolf, but walking into the crowd of applicants for the Slayers was like walking into a story book.

The nearest group was a cluster of slender men and

women, all of them several inches taller than me, but for one. They wore glittering armor made of some pearlescent material. The short one drew a curved saber, the blade milky and translucent. The others in her group bent their heads and began murmuring, and the blade glowed with bright light. Her eyes widened and her cat-like irises shrank against the glare.

Wow. Fae. Each of them carried at least one edged weapon, and half of them had finely carved bows slung across their shoulders as well. Heavy cloaks with glittering runes covered their backs and supple leather armor shielded their limbs. The short fae with the milky sword bowed to the others and sheathed the sword at her hip. Her golden eyes found mine as I approached them.

Everyone knows this rule. On your first day on the playground, you establish your space or you get eaten. I held her gaze as I walked by. Nothing too intimidating, but I didn't drop it until I'd passed beyond them.

The fae's cloak swished and her leather boots squelched on the wet turf as she turned on her heel and fell into step beside me. I kept my eyes focused ahead of me and kept my gait steady. For several steps she simply kept pace with me.

She broke the silence first. "Is this all your patron sent you with?"

I turned to look at her. Close up, she had supermodel good looks. Eyes that seemed to glow with golden otherworldly sparks, cheekbones that would cut your knuckles, and full lips that quirked in amusement. Her eyes came to the level of my chin, and she struck me as really short for a Fae.

Her shining golden eyes traveled up and down my rig. I felt the judgment in her gaze. "Was there not better armor available for you?"

Watching the faerie's cloak trail behind her made me wish that I'd had the silver to get the duster spelled before everything started. She looked right despite her smaller stature, like she was ready to go on the Slayer's roster tonight. This fae warrior had the easy confidence of someone who knew they outclassed everyone else in the room.

I tried to match her breezy confidence. "I like the freedom of movement."

Her lips curled up again into a half smile. "Look around you, girl. Do you see any others who prefer 'freedom of movement'?" She gave a little chuff of laughter as she asked the question. My lips tightened in annoyance. Her curiosity seemed genuine and not malicious though, which made it feel even worse.

Closer to the gates now, the crowd was denser, and everyone around us had the hard edges you only get from living on the fringes. Over shoulders and on hips, swords decorated nearly everybody. Spears and halberds came in a close second. Armor glittered on most as well, either firelight dancing off battered metal, or the glow of enchantment. One lion of a man, sporting a mane of fiery red hair, carried a mighty battle axe that looked like it could slice a piano in half. For those without armor or giant weapons, I was leaning towards shifter. They might look human, and the only reason for not carrying weapons was that your body *was* the weapon.

The press of the crowd around me started to nibble away at my confidence. I'd arrived in Seattle with my training and my wits. All around me the chipped swords and dented armor spoke of real experience slaying real monsters.

How would my time against my practice dummies hold up? Ghost's pale face flashed across my eyes, and my nose stung at the memory of his stinking breath.

I took a deep breath and made a show of studying the crowd. I was the daughter of Gabriel Lim, fabled Breaker of Seattle. His shoes might be big, but I was going to fill them. Somehow. "No, I don't. I figure that means I'll be the fastest one here."

The fae arched one delicate eyebrow at me. She looked like she would be more at home at a dinner party, but she carried herself with the air of someone who had thrown her fair share of punches.

She seemed to come to a decision and extended her hand. "I like you. You may call me Cordelia."

She made it sound like some kind of honor. "I'm Roxy."

I took her hand and we both squeezed briefly. Despite her glamorous looks, her palms had the tough calluses born of endless hours with a blade. While most fae I had met so far had been aloof and cut-throat, my instincts said Cordelia was something else. If nothing else, her short stature made her less imposing than her brethren. She also smiled more than most fae. It made her easy to like. I hoped that wouldn't become a problem later.

Metal screeched and groaned, the noise sending shivers up my neck. The guards in front of the gate pulled back until they had lined up on either side of the gate and cleared the area in front. The crowd hushed and backed away as the gates cranked slowly open, sweeping massive arcs across the wet turf.

The bell rang once.

Then twice.

My heart pounded as the endless time between rings stretched out.

At last, the fifth bell rang.

Three figures marched out of the Slayers HQ, flanked on both sides by two columns of men carrying torches. As they got closer the flickering orange firelight threw dancing shadows across the grass. I let out an involuntary gasp when I realized that my uncle Samuel was in the middle, and the smallest one of the three.

We Lims were big people and my uncle stood a couple of inches taller than my six feet. But between the other two Slayers, he looked like the runt on the team. My uncle wore scarred fighting leathers and a battered vest of lacquered scale that left his arms free to move. The grip of his enormous katana bobbed at his hip.

The woman on Samuel's right towered over him by almost a foot. Like other fae I'd seen, she was tall and long-limbed, and she moved with an inhuman, liquid grace. While my uncle looked dressed for war, this woman's clothing straddled the line between combat and party finery. A cloak of some sort of shimmering material draped over her shoulders and seemed to be trailing sparkles of light as she walked. An ornately carved bow of silvery wood was strapped across her chest and two machetes inscribed with silver runes rode on her thighs. Her hair was silvery moonlight and fell in a straight sheet that ended just past her shoulders. Large golden eyes looked out on the crowd and when they passed over me a shiver ran up my spine.

If the fae made my uncle look short, the beast of a man on his left made him look scrawny. He was wide like a tank and half a head shorter than my uncle, but had to outweigh him by a hundred pounds. His short, dark hair came down his neck and blended into dense, pale fur with dark spots covering his broad shoulders and barrel chest. Shifter. He wore a light t-shirt and loose workout pants and didn't seem to be carrying any weapons. While my uncle and the fae had stern expressions, the meaty shifter seemed to be telling a joke and laughing riotously at his own story. A half-empty bottle swung in his left hand, clear liquid spilling out of the neck as he walked alongside the other two, his arms waving as he cackled.

My uncle frowned at the clowning man next to him. The fae woman looked like she was doing her best to ignore both of the men. When the trio reached the center of the gates the guards fanned out in front of them. Uncle Samuel slapped the big man on the shoulder, which seemed about as effective as slapping a building, but it did get him to settle down. The shifter raised his head to the dark sky and let loose a great, coughing roar like a thunder clap. The remaining voices in the crowd died off instantly.

"Form up!" Samuel bellowed.

The crowd shook itself to life, metal clanking and ringing as bodies moved forward into the open space in front of the gates. I dodged through the crowd, hoping to find a place towards the front where I might catch my uncle's eye. In my periphery, Cordelia made her way through the crowd as well. She seemed to be keeping an eye on the fae that had walked out with my uncle.

The crowd around me was a cesspool of amped adrenaline. I bobbed and weaved between hulking men, fae, and shifters in everything from leather, to scale, and even one man who'd managed to cobble together a half set of plate. Only the shifters went without weapons but nearly everyone bristled with weapons and I noticed more silver than I'd expected.

One man, like me, wore a mishmash of modern tactical armor from the other side. Where his vest would have carried guns and ammo he had several combat knives. Something about him screamed former military, and it wasn't just the regulation crew cut and urban camouflage shirt. It was the eyes, and the way he kept watch on everyone around him, his hands always hovering near his weapons. Instinctively, I took a half step away from him.

To my left were two women who stood out. There was the curly-haired brunette with the double swords crossed on her back. Another slim woman with a shaved head clad tightly in black fighting leathers. She carried silver knives all over her person, along with cruciform stakes at her belt. She might as well have a sign on her that said, "Assassin."

As the crowd settled into a loose square I let my magic kindle and focused it on the armor around me. As I had suspected, most everything here was cobbled together. Loose seams and weakened joints flared all around me. Only a select few had protection that was worth its weight. Cordelia's armor was a nearly solid mesh of green that covered her from the neck down.

Uncle Samuel yelled, "Settle down! Aislinn and Altan will take a count."

I tried to catch my uncle's eyes but failed. I knew he couldn't show me any favoritism but a nod would have been nice.

Anything to remind me that I was in the right place.

Three teams of horses appeared beyond the gates pulling large wagons that bounced and bobbed over the ruts in the turf. The fae woman and the shifter moved ahead of my uncle and drifted through the loose formation of candidates. They both moved through the crowd without saying a word, only stopping here and there to give one of the candidates a more thorough looking over.

The ground trembled under my feet as the massive shifter stopped in front of me, his face inches from mine. I guessed this was Altan Altai, one of the famed Freaks of Seattle. The others around me took a step away and gave us a little space. How considerate.

Altan's eyes were a dull yellow and bloodshot. He leaned in closer and sniffed at me although I wasn't sure what he would smell over the stench of alcohol and sweat that surrounded him like a thick haze. My eyes watered as I stood still, steeling myself from leaning away from him. I focused on the pattern of dark spots that marched up his neck. Was he a were-cheetah? Jaguar?

His bushy eyebrows arched up and he bared his teeth into a disturbing grin, his canines huge and yellow. He gave me a slow wink and wandered off into the crowd.

What was that about? I wasn't asking for any favoritism but if this was the encouragement I got, then I would take it. From the looks of this crowd, I was going to need every bit of my training and a dash of luck to rise to the top.

On the other side of the crowd, all eyes were on Aislinn. She had stopped in front of Cordelia. I had thought she was a little short, and now next to Aislinn, Cordelia looked downright pixie sized. But she kept her back straight and did her best to look the fae woman in the eye without tilting her head back. Aislinn shook her head and walked on. Cordelia's chest deflated a little.

As Altan and Aislinn continued to survey the crowd a new figure appeared in the open gates. This new figure caught my eye because I was pretty sure he caught everyone's eye. Even at a distance anyone could see that his arms and armor were exquisite. His chest plate was polished to a mirror shine. Finely lacquered scales covered his joints as smoothly as snake skin, reflecting a dark rainbow of colors. A straight, two-handed long sword hung at his belt, the cross guard glittering with what looked like sapphires and rubies. The scabbard was decorated with an iridescent inlay of mother of pearl. He wore knee-high riding boots of supple leather and carried a half helm under one arm.

He drew closer, drawing murmurs throughout the crowd. As if the fantastic cost of the arms and armor wasn't enough, he was also fantastically good-looking. A strong jawline with just a hint of pale stubble. Thick waves of light brown hair trailed to his shoulders, cut far too long to be comfortable under his half helm.

"Samuel! I'm sorry I'm late. It looks like we have a good turnout for the Trials!"

I caught a brief twitch in my uncle's eyebrow as he turned. That was odd. Samuel usually had all the emotive qualities of a boulder. "Good evening, Tanner. Glad you could join us."

Tanner smiled, his teeth flashing at a thousand watts. "Of course! I wouldn't miss this for the world!"

He sighed with satisfaction and moved through the crowd, taking a moment here and there to shake a hand or clasp an arm. With a lucky few he spoke quietly and those candidates were left starry-eyed. He passed within a few feet of me and I caught a whiff of something like lavender soap and oiled metal. Who was this guy?

Tanner seemed to have seen all he needed to because when he finished his circuit he returned to my uncle and clapped him on the shoulder. "They look great, Samuel. I'm sure you'll find the best of the bunch, as always."

Samuel nodded, perhaps a bit stiffly. "Yes, of course."

Tanner waved and smiled at the group. "Best of luck to you all!" He turned and walked back to the gates. His shiny boots gleamed in the gray day, making the rest of us look filthy.

The wagons stopped off to the side of the crowd. Since I'd made my way to the front of the formation I wasn't closest to the wagons, but I was at least closer than most. Were we going somewhere?

Altan howled and smashed his bottle against one of the wagons. "Good haul of blood donors this year! Glad to see so many of you show up. How many did you count, Ash?"

Aislinn crossed her arms and appeared annoyed. "Sixty-seven."

Altan scratched at his chin. "Hmm, that's quite a few, isn't it? The thing is, we need to get you lot up to the Farm for the first round. Also, Ash and I have seats so...But there's ... sixty-seven of you and only..."

He made a show of counting the seats on the wagons. "...only thirty seats."

Altan's smile widened. He seemed to be having the time of his life. "The fastest way to the Farm is on the wagons. If you're not at the farm by seven bells you're out. You guys can sort it all out."

Aislinn huffed. "The rules, Altan."

The big man growled in annoyance. "You're no fun, Ash." He raised his voice again. "No killing! No maiming! At least, not on purpose. And don't hurt the horses, or I'll kill you."

With that, my uncle, Aislinn, and Altan mounted horses that had been brought out of the compound. Aislinn reached under her cloak and pulled a delicate sphere that looked like a frozen soap bubble. A spot of dull orange light pulsed in the center of the bubble. The fae woman lifted her slender arm and the bubble rose from her hand and drifted over the crowd, hovering over our heads. When she spoke, her ethereal voice sounded like it was right beside me. Several people around me jerked at the sound of her voice.

"This first test begins when my bauble ignites. I will know if you start early and I will punish you."

She smiled and the expression was cold, distant, and devoid of humor. "But first, you all must swear to keep what you learn during the Slayer Trials secret."

The crowd went still. Very still. A fae geas was a serious thing. It bound one for life. The nerves in my stomach went tight with anticipation. This was it. I was finally doing it. All my senses lit up until I felt like my skin was electric and I could taste the cold iron and steel of my weapons.

The fae gestured to the street. "Anyone among you who does not wish to be bound by the geas may depart now."

Heads turned in the crowd. After a shuffling movement, two people left. The rest of us watched the fae expectantly.

"You shall not reveal anything you learn or are shown by or from the Slayers during these Trials."

My lips silently made the vow and a strange silvery light circled my head, making me light-headed.

"So you have all sworn, may the Moon bless your Trials."

With that, Aislinn turned to Altan and Samuel. The trio cut an imposing swath to their horses and rode off to the north, leaving sixty-seven candidates standing in the middle of Denny Park.

Cordelia materialized near my elbow again. Her sword was still on her hip but she held a thick length of silvered rope taut between her hands. "This does not look good for you."

She wasn't wrong. I'd trained to fight against my dad, never in a brawl with so many people. He hadn't been able to tell me specifics, but I'd had some sort of idea of what the Trials would be like based on little pieces I'd put together. This was nothing like any of that.

The hair on my neck stood on end and a flush of heat raced down my back as everyone around me put their hands on their weapons. "Oh, I don't know, like I said, I'm pretty fast."

I dropped my weight into my knees, my blood thundering in my ears, my mouth suddenly dry and sour. My eyes darted between the nearest wagon and the people surrounding me. Swords, spears, a mace, a crossbow. My left hand crept to the small of my back for my fighting knife before relaxing and dropping back to my side. My right hand drifted down to Thor, my sweaty palm sliding down the haft.

All eyes in the crowd were focused above us now. The light in the floating sphere throbbed like a heartbeat quickening before a fight. The light grew in intensity as the rhythm sped up.

Cordelia pivoted a little until our backs were almost touching. Even with my height, the two of us together didn't weigh as much as some of the men around us, even before all their armor. I had known I was going to fight for my spot on the Slayers, but I hadn't imagined the fight would start so fast, or that I would be fighting every candidate all at once.

As irritating as she was, Cordelia was probably good to have on my side. If I could get her on my side.

"You might be right. I might be over my head here."

"Finally, she sees some sense."

"Even you wouldn't be able to get me a seat on the wagons."

"Now you're just being ridiculous. Getting you on the wagon would be the least challenging thing I'll do all day."

Wow. I needed to take a page out of her book. I also needed to fight at her side rather than against her in this crowd.

I let my gaze roam around the crowd. Everyone watched the timer. I used the lull to scope out the competition and steady my hands from all the adrenaline coursing through me. My eyes locked on a skinny kid slouching under an oily backpack, his eyes hidden under dirty brown bangs. Like me, he had a skateboard tied to the small of his back. Unlike me, he looked like he'd taken a wrong turn on the way to the skate park. Well, at least that meant I wasn't the least prepared candidate here.

It was a minor strain to keep my magic up, but it was going to be worth the effort as the timer blinked ever faster. I made note of rust-weakened armor, stretched knee ligaments, and dry rot eating away at wooden weapons. My magic would help me carve through the crowd like a cake, but could I cut my way all the way through?

My dad's voice whispered in my brain. "Roxybear, you have to be the best."

What if I wasn't the best? Then what? I still had to get through this first hurdle to make it to the Farm. If I didn't make the cut here, I'm not sure I could bear to see Uncle Samuel's disappointment or even look at myself in the mirror tomorrow.

I focused on the wagons. I had to get there and I had to use everything I could to do it.

The fae tilted her head, her voice coy. "What do you say we make this interesting?"

The fae loved their bargains. To be fair, I enjoyed a good haggling myself but right now the stakes were too high. "This isn't interesting enough for you?"

She sniffed. "Getting a seat on those wagons will be child's play. I warrant I could get two seats if I wanted."

I'd planted the seed earlier, but I wasn't sure if it would bear fruit. I gave her a tight smile. "I'd have to see it to believe it."

Aislinn's bauble flared, the orange light bathing the crowd in light like the sky was on fire. The pulsing reached a fever pitch, the light stuttering and strobing over us. People raised arms and fists against the light. Breath rasped, leather creaked, boots and feet squelched in the wet turf for purchase. The world seemed to hold its breath.

I caught Cordelia's eye. "So? You going to show me how good you are?"

The gleam in her eyes sharpened and I could almost hear her ego leaking out her ears. "Watch me."

Aislinn's bauble swelled until the flickering orange light was an oppressive dome of radiance cowing us into submission. It exploded with a thunderclap and the light vanished, leaving us in the perpetual dim of the Twilight again. Silence and shock flowed across the crowd like a wave.

Then someone screamed and everyone was running.

5

SCRUM

Hammers or blades? The chaos around me quickly reached a deafening crescendo, nothing I had ever encountered in all my training. My nerves jangled like live wires and I flinched as a hatchet flipped past me. I went with my gut and grabbed Thor and Loki since they gave me slightly longer reach. Also the last thing I wanted was to break too many rules on the first day.

As one, the crowd of candidates surged toward the open wagons. I got all of three steps in before someone kicked me in the small of my back. I tucked my shoulder and turned the momentum of my fall into a roll. I came up in a crouch with my hammers up in front of me.

It was no good. The crowd was a swelling tide of people and weapons. There was no way to know who had hit me, or if it had even been on purpose. I did the one thing my dad told me never to do. I froze.

"Never stop moving." That had been dad's first piece of advice when I'd started training. When he'd been fit and healthy, bouncing on the balls of his feet, dodging around me as he threw lefts and rights at my face. The sound of his voice in my head shook me out of my daze. *Keep moving.* It was a smart tactic when I had one opponent. It had to apply here too.

I dodged out of the way of a scrawny looking were-tiger in a jogging suit and turned back to the wagons. The fight wasn't the priority here. I had to get on the wagon and get a seat.

At my left, Cordelia made her way slowly towards the closest wagon. She wielded a silvery whip in her hands with graceful efficiency, using it between her hands to parry, then snapping her wrist and sending it out to attack at a distance. Her movements were precise and fluid, the crack of the whip the tempo of some music only she could hear. She'd managed to clear a small area around her as she advanced.

I gritted my teeth and fell in behind her. The long afternoons and weekends spent training with my dad were only a marginal help. Fighting one person was not like fighting twenty. I dodged and weaved, my hammers swinging around me in short arcs, blocking incoming strikes on the hardened wood and clubbing people to keep them back.

A hand clamped onto my shoulder and I screamed, twisting and swinging my left arm, Loki whipping around at head level. Cordelia ducked at the last moment, my hammer passing harmlessly through a fine spray of her golden hair.

I pulled Loki back. "What are you doing?!"

"What are *you* doing!?"

A burly woman with a baseball bat launched herself at us, yelling at the top of her lungs. The wide end of the bat crackled with orange streaks of energy. I panicked. A little. I screamed, braced, and launched a front kick, planting my booted foot in her belly at a weak seam in her chain mail. I didn't even need to Break it. The shock jolted up my hip and the chain mail split open like a gourd. The woman went down gasping and her bat fell to the turf, orange energy dissipating into the ground.

I caught my breath, my heart hammering in my ears. "I'm fighting! What else?"

Cordelia looked...distressed. "Your fighting is horrid! You! Have! No! Style!"

With each exclamation she lashed out with her silver whip, striking people in the face and neck, punctuating each statement. Oh, this woman was a treat. We were in a melee with homicidal maniacs and Cordelia thought it was ice dancing.

I grabbed Cordelia and shoved her towards the wagons. "The fight isn't important. Getting on the wagons is."

As I pushed forward I stretched up to see over the melee. The nearest wagon was bedlam. A handful of humans had managed to take control and they flung wind and fire magic in short bursts, keeping the crowd at bay, but a knot of werewolves in the crowd looked like they were about to make a run at them.

No good. There had to be lower hanging fruit.

The next wagon was also occupied, but the situation seemed to be more stable. A handful of big fae warriors in armor trimmed with fur held the wagon, protecting their claim with raised bows. Cordelia was still near me, scoping out the wagons as she ran.

I twisted up on tiptoes and found the third wagon. And my stomach dropped into my feet.

A pack of shifters, mostly wolves and bears, had taken the wagon. The field around them had been churned into pulp and a ghostly blue spectral bear at least a dozen feet tall loomed over the wagon. A man in mismatched fighting leathers bolted for the wagon, stepping lightly over the mud and fallen bodies. He jumped, leaping impossibly high, screaming as he brought a two-handed sword down like a headsman's axe.

The spectral bear roared, the sound like a toppling tree, and swiped a massive blue paw at the man in midair. Ghostly claws ripped across the man's body and a blood-curdling scream tore out of him. As the claws raked across him, his body blurred and doubled until a faint blue image of the man stretched away from his body. Then the claws were past and the blue outline snapped back into place. The man fell to the mud like a stone and landed without a twitch.

Definitely not the last wagon, then.

I squirmed through the press of bodies, dragging Cordelia with me. Her whip snapped left and right, keeping a tiny perimeter around us clear.

A tall fae wrapped in silvery furs charged through the crowd, his iridescent sword held at high guard. His eyes blazed with arrogance and his lips curled into a lazy smirk. He was probably already imagining how he was going to smash me into the dirt. His dirty armor presented a solid mesh of green protecting his body, including cleverly fashioned gloves and a patchwork cloak of hides with multiple layers of enchantment. To anyone else looking on, the fae was set to crush me to a pulp.

But my talent showed me the flaw in his weapon his swordsmith had missed. Cordelia had her back to the fae, her whip holding back what looked like a bear shifter in half-form. I stepped up and instead of raising my hammer to parry the blow, I swung Thor to meet it.

The cold iron of my hammer met the brittle fracture line in the crystalline structure of the sword, striking at the precise angle and force needed to cleave the sword in half. The sword broke with a sound like a bell, the broken stump of the blade passing harmlessly by. The fae warrior's stunned expression morphed into sputtering rage as the shattered bits of his sword rained down. With a keening scream, he launched himself at me, wielding his broken sword like a crude dagger.

I backpedaled but the muddy ground sucked at my feet, robbing me of any speed. Overbalanced, I pitched back onto my butt, landing on a pile of unconscious bodies. The broken sword whistled down at my head and I twisted away from the fae's manic attack. He fell over me, the broken sword plunging into the mud. Eyes wide and crazed, the fae scrambled after me, his other hand clawing at me, both of us sliding across the mud-slicked ground. He lunged at me again, all but foaming at the mouth now, broken sword swinging through wild arcs.

"Hey! No killing! No maiming!"

The fae's eyes sharpened, golden irises burning with inner light as hot as the lower levels of hell. He raised a hand to the sky, fist clenched tight enough that his nails drew blood that trickled down his wrist. The ground rocked and twisted under me and I felt myself sliding down.

"Get down!" Cordelia yelled.

I wasn't one to ignore timely advice. I curled into a ball as Cordelia's silver rope lashed out over my head and caught the fae warrior right between his haughty eyes. A violet spark of electricity cracked as the rope made contact and the fiery light in the fae's eyes vanished. His frenetic attacks stopped and a second later he keeled over like a felled tree.

The fight seemed to be winding down, the grassy plain littered with unconscious bodies and scattered weapons. The action was now centered around the wagons and the last few vying for seats. My seat.

Cordelia stopped next to me, breathless. "And really? Hammers? Could you not have equipped yourself with something that has more range?"

I clambered to my feet and tried to wipe the mud and turf from my jeans. Damn. They'd been clean this morning, too. I pointed a finger at Cordelia, hand still clutched around Thor. "Hey. These were my dad's hammers."

I nodded to the unconscious fae. "What the heck was his problem?"

Cordelia's face stiffened. "Mountain fae."

Her eyes widened as she took in the scene around us. Cordelia crouched and pointed to the shattered sword remnants. "Mother in the moon. Roxy, his sword was a Legacy."

I had no idea what that meant but we had bigger problems to focus on. I eyeballed the truck closest to us. There were four open seats and five candidates between me and the truck. One of those candidates was Red Lion and his giant axe. The brunette sword fighter had both long swords out and both she and the assassin from earlier were slogging through the mud to the wagon. From out of nowhere a man in black and blue robes loped ahead of us, his feet barely touching the muddy ground. Daoist monk?

Endless night, my odds did not look good against this bunch. Cordelia on the other hand seemed to be just hitting her stride.

Cordelia's rope whipped out in a shimmering lash and the brunette went down with a shriek of outrage. The skinny assassin stepped on her, smashing her into the mud, and kept running. I guess they weren't friends or allies.

The Daoist monk put on a burst of power and took to the air, his robes flaring around him. In a blink, he had vaulted into the wagon and grabbed a seat just behind the Red Lion.

Two seats left.

I palmed one of my throwing blades and snapped it out, aiming for the assassin's thigh. Non-lethal, I promise. The soft mud under my feet gave way on my follow-through, angling the blade low. Instead of landing in her thigh, my blade sunk halfway into her calf. She stumbled but didn't go down. She didn't even yell, but she turned to give me some serious stink eye. Shattered skies, was anything going to go my way today?

As I pressed forward, Cordelia jerked beside me when Camo Guy yanked on her cloak. Her sword gleamed in the light as she drew and reversed it, smashing the pommel down against his knee. He bellowed in her face and she kicked him in the chest. Cordelia could hold her own.

I made for the wagon, hoping to overtake the assassin.

The wiry woman yanked my blade from her calf and threw

it in the mud.

Goddess in the moon she was still going. I had to get past her.

The assassin snarled at me and pulled her feet out of the mud, struggling forward. Cordelia was right, I really needed to add a ranged weapon to my kit.

I fumbled through the mud to retrieve my throwing knife and slid it back in my thigh sheath. She was only a few yards away from the back of the wagon now. I ran towards her, or tried to, the mud sucking at my legs.

Cordelia sailed past me, vaulting off the back of Camo Guy as he let loose a rush of wind magic. Her booted feet kicked the man in the face and he went down with a strangled cry. A burst of wind carried her up and over the battlefield. She flung her rope down and in a blinding flash of purple, it attached itself to the side of the wagon. Like a swinging vine, her rope carried her onto the back of the wagon where she landed like a bee on a flower.

Cordelia unwrapped her rope and yelled, "Roxy!"

There was only one seat left. It was now or never. I'd have to try the fae bargain. "One silver ounce says you can't get me on that seat!"

Cordelia gave me a beaming smile and whirled her rope like she was in a rodeo show.

I leaped for the assassin, counting on my bigger mass to give me the advantage. I hit her in the back and wrapped my arms tight around her. We both grunted and went down hard, which was better for me than it was for her. Oily mud squelched and slimed my hands, making it impossible for me to stay centered. In moments she bucked me off. The mountain fae on the wagon hooted and shouted encouragement. I dug my elbows into the muck and dragged myself towards the wagon and the screaming fae. I would make them eat this mud when I got on board.

Assassin army-crawled a few feet and then flipped over just as I passed her. She had surprisingly long arms and grabbed my ankle in an iron grip. I hopped up onto one leg and cursed.

I kicked out at her but she proved to be an evasive target even at close range. My heart pounded hard in my ears, drowning out the sounds of the melee around us. I needed to get that last seat on the wagon.

I called out to Cordelia. "So can you get me to that seat or what?"

The rope lashed out, missing my cheek by a millimeter and the woman on the ground howled in pain and outrage.

My leg broke free and I clutched at the wagon, my hands slick with mud. I yanked myself up and clambered into the wagon, mud sliding down my face and neck, down into places it would take me days to find and clean. I fell into the last open seat next to Cordelia. As my weight touched down a shimmering dome of orange-tinted light sprang up around the wagon. Outside the dome of light the remaining conscious candidates cursed and howled, throwing their weapons at us. The objects bounced off the aegis harmlessly.

I slumped into the bench, heart hammering in my chest. Relief sent a cool wash of sensation down my spine. My jaw relaxed and my face ached.

I'd made it. Barely. If Cordelia hadn't intervened, that assassin might have been sitting on this very seat. My dad's training had only taken me so far in this initial Trial. What would happen on the next Trial, which was sure to be more challenging?

I didn't like the anxiety that was rising to the fore. I needed to pull myself together.

"Get your head in the game, Roxybear."

I will, I told myself. I am. I ran my fingers over the cool steel of my hammers. *I made it*, I reminded myself.

It doesn't matter how close it was, I made it.

6

WELCOME TO THE FARM

No matter how much I wiped my face, mud still dripped down my neck and onto my duster. Cordelia had somehow managed to stay clean. Also the robed man didn't have a speck of mud on him either. I'd thought he was a Daoist priest before but now up close I pegged him as a Shaolin fighting monk.

I dug my fingers around my ears and under my chin. Gods, the muck was everywhere. How had Cordelia kept herself so clean?

The suspiciously clean fae smiled primly. "You owe me an ounce of silver."

I scowled at her and dropped another clod of mud on the floor of the wagon. "You never said when it was due."

Cordelia pouted, making her look like a sulky toddler.

I wondered how old she really was. With fae, it was hard to tell.

The wagon bumped along, finding every rut on the road. My body ached all over and my lower back felt like one giant bruise. The adrenaline of battle drained out of me, leaving me hollow and exhausted. I sipped from my canteen and studied the other occupants of the wagon as my mood turned somber.

We'd gone from sixty-seven down to thirty candidates in mere minutes. If I hadn't had an assist from Cordelia, I wasn't sure I would have gotten the last seat on the wagon. I thought I'd have an edge being trained by a former Slayer but my dad had never prepped me for anything like this.

Cordelia was a clear shoe-in to make it on the roster. The three mountain fae looked strong and mean and I couldn't discount them either. There was one big one and the other two red headed fae appeared to be twins.

Hard to tell what was going on with the fighting monk on the bench across from us. So far he had ignored everyone else on the wagon, silently staring out into the distance and giving me a view of his smoothly shaven skull.

Maybe I stared too hard because he turned to catch me.

I smiled, sheepish now. "Hi. I'm Roxy."

He gave me a small nod. "Wen."

He was older than I had first thought. Though his skin was smooth and unlined, his dark eyes gazed at me with the wisdom of one much older than he looked. I made a little walking gesture with my fingers to mimic stair stepping.

"Good moves back there."

"I took the simplest path."

Couldn't argue with that. It had looked like a cakewalk for the monk. I didn't have that luxury since I couldn't leap that high or walk in mid-air like him.

"Have you done the Trials before?"

"Yes, a few years ago."

"So did they have you fight to get on the wagon last time too?"

"No. Last time the first trial was hand to hand combat there in Denny Park."

That was what I had been expecting. Looks like the Slayers

had changed things up a little. Any insights my dad had passed on to me were going to be of limited help. I didn't know if the mad dash to get on the wagon was better or worse for me than hand to hand with one of these contenders on the wagon would have been.

Red Lion guy sat next to Wen. He was enormous and intimidating for sure, but strength alone couldn't be the only way to every challenge. Dad had assured me that the Slayers valued a fighter's wits and ingenuity as much as their raw strength of arms. I had to believe there was a way through this for me. For dad. For mom. They were counting on me.

Next to me and on the other side of the Red Lion sat three people dressed in matching leather armor, two women and a man. They kept their voices low as they spoke to each other, avoiding eye contact with anyone else on the wagon. Not fae, but based on the amount of weaponry and armor on them, not shifters either. Beyond them, at the front of the wagon, sat the three mountain fae Cordlia had been studiously ignoring ever since we stepped aboard.

The floorboards creaked and the wagon pitched to one side as the biggest of the mountain fae stood and took the two steps to stand in front of me.

He was massive, maybe a touch smaller than Red Lion, his broad chest covered with a coarse hide vest trimmed with what looked like bear pelt. Heavy leather pauldrons, also trimmed with fur, capped his shoulders. The ensemble left his arms exposed, arms covered in taut, ropy muscle, his skin pockmarked with scars and covered in crude tattoos. An iridescent sword hung at his waist. It looked distressingly similar to the one I'd shattered on my way onto the wagon.

The fae looked down at me, his golden eyes almost glowing. His face was not standard fae-pretty, but the harsh angles and asymmetry of his nose somehow lent a regal air to him. The front of his vest was a maze of shallow cuts. The hide had clearly been spelled to resist blades. This fae had risen to power the hard way, and he was holding onto it the hard way.

He must have had a little luck though, because the shoddy spellwork around his right shoulder pauldron stuck out to my eyes like a flashing target. Even one of my throwing knives would pierce the leather like soft butter and disable the deltoid group on what was probably his dominant arm. Stupid.

When he spoke, his voice was the deep rumble of an oncoming avalanche. "Sven is my sworn brother. By rights he should be here at my side."

I didn't know Sven but I gathered it was the fae who I'd left in the muck with a broken sword.

I shrugged. "He had the only right any of us had--to fight for his own spot on the wagons. Maybe he should have had a better sword."

Cordelia gasped next to me. Fury kindled behind the big fae's golden eyes. "You dare!?"

I squinted at him. I was dead tired and not in the mood for his posturing. "Look, I don't know who your armorer is but you've got a problem with a spot on your pauldron and Sven had a weakness in his blade. Not a good idea when going into battle."

He took a heavy step towards me that rocked the little wagon precariously. "This armor was crafted a millennia ago by the Dark Smiths of the Upper Crescent! Sven's sword was passed down from his grandfather's grandfather. You little--"

Red Lion put out one meaty fist, shoved the mountain fae and rumbled. "Sit down."

Mouthy fae's muscles strained but Red Lion didn't budge. Wow, he really was strong. Not all human then. Maybe he had a little giant or ogre blood.

Mountain Fae grunted. "Release me!"

Red Lion growled, and shattered skies I was pretty sure I felt the vibrations through the bench. It was a growl filled with menace and now even I felt sorry for the mountain fae that was ready to chop my head off.

The mountain fae backed off and sat back down, resentment clear on every line of his body. I didn't know what I had done to gain the welcome intervention of Red Lion but I was grateful. I didn't want to plunge a knife into the shoulder of mouthy fae's armor but I would have. Not that we were going to be friends anyway since he was all broken up about that Sven guy.

"Thank you." I bowed my head to Red Lion.

He grunted without bothering to look at me. "The guy was blocking my view."

I looked out across the scenery. Red Lion was right–it was a nice view.

The wagons followed the ruins of Interstate 5 to the north. We were about to leave the spelled gates of Seattle proper and enter the Wild. The northern limit of Seattle was marked with a pair of sentinel stones, massive granite constructs that had been raised from the earth by the Founders. As we rumbled north the sentinel stones crept into view, straddling the route of the old interstate. The stones themselves were nondescript, just ordinary chunks of west coast granite standing on end like crude obelisks.

The plain look of the stones belied their extraordinary nature. My dad had recounted the story to me several times. How the stones had been raised and enchanted when the Slayers had tamed a small plot of land around the center of the city. Using magic that no one had seen in generations, the Founders had anchored a massive protection spell on the sentinel stones. The spell connected to two more pairs of stones at the eastern and southern borders of Seattle, drawing a semi-circle that ended at the coast. It was this spell that pushed back at the Wilds of the Twilight and allowed the Slayers to carve out an island of sanity.

On the other side of the stones, past a hazy field of translucent violet energy, lay the Wilds. The Wilds were lands made strange and wondrous by the Twilight, a foreboding wilderness filled with wild magic, dark fae, packs of feral shifters, and if my dad's stories were to be believed, demons.

Over the course of a hundred years, the wilderness had reclaimed the Pacific Northwest with a vengeance. Fir, spruce, and hemlock trees reached high enough that the canopy of the forest disappeared into the murk of the Twilight. Under the Twilight, trees somehow found enough light and energy to grow to massive size, and the forests outside of Seattle had grown to dizzying heights. The forest approached to within a stone's throw of the border. Something about the energy of the border kept the Wilds at bay, including the trees. On the other side of the stones the work of many Slayers kept the path to the Farm free of trees and brush.

The sentinel stones towered over our little cart as we approached and the buzz of the border magic set my teeth vibrating. More than a few of us looked around in confusion, but it seemed the horses had been well trained. They gamely stepped forward and through the protection field. The aegis magic covering the wagon flashed briefly as we passed through and then we were in the Wilds.

I hadn't been out here since I first came to Seattle. Seeing it now and knowing it was because I was this much closer to getting into Slayers put a lump in my throat. I wished my Dad could see this.

The spelled gates served to keep the wild magic elements out of the city proper. Things like dark fae, certain demonic denizens, and other unsavory elements that I would not like to encounter on my walk home.

But for certain magic users, leaving the gates and going to the Wilds meant a freedom to use their powers to their fullest extent. The Slayers had wisely commandeered an abandoned farm for their secondary training post. My magic was much like Dad's and he had never been stationed at The Farm.

The Slayers who got stationed at The Farm? The heavy hitters. Elemental magic users, check. Shriekers, check. Boomers, check.

I was none of those.

On the other hand, most of the folks on this wagon weren't heavy hitters either. I eyed the blustering mountain fae. I could take them. Maybe not all at once, but in a one on one setting, sure. I assessed the twins. One had two braids and one had a single braid, but they really did look identical, from their fiery hair to their leather gauntlets. All the mountain fae were taller and had longer reach than me, but I was fast and they were overconfident.

I was starting to get hungry. I pulled out one of my cider donuts and unwrapped the waxed paper to inspect my baked goods. A little squashed but still edible. I shoved a chunk in my mouth and the hit of sugar and cinnamon made me sigh with pleasure.

"Is that apple?"

Cordelia was staring at my donut.

I swallowed and then pulled out the second donut from my satchel. "Yeah, dryad apples. I ferment them a little too before I work them into the yeast dough."

Cordelia's eyes followed my hand as I waved the donut around. The scent of apples, cinnamon, and sugar trailed my hand. Fae did love their sweets. Maybe this would get me out of my debt to her.

"Smells good."

I took another large bite and chewed deliberately. "Yes, gives a great texture, cakey but not heavy."

I watched as Cordelia's throat worked. Perfect.

"Would you like a donut?"

She didn't hesitate. "What cost?"

"One silver ounce."

It was ridiculous. I was asking for an ounce, which could buy ten dozen donuts. But I was the only game in town and Cordelia looked hungry. Plus, her armor and sword told me she was loaded.

"Done." She snatched the donut from my fingers and I suppressed a smile before I went back to polishing off my own donut.

Now we were square and I didn't have to worry about my earlier fae bargain. I watched with satisfaction as Cordelia bit into the apple cider donut with a look of pleasure. My cooking and baking skills had only earned me a minimum wage on the other side of the Veil but here they were more highly valued.

The Farm was up ahead and it was almost seven bells. The aches and pains from bumping along in the wagon faded as excitement rose in its wake. I was at The Farm. Me, Roxanne Lim from North Dorchester and I would soon be facing off against Seattle's leanest and meanest.

Neat fields of crops divided the land into tidy squares. Behind shimmering mesh enchantments, cattle wandered slowly in small herds. The central structure of the Farm was a two story building built from rough hewn logs. Low barracks lined up on the back side of the main building and watch towers built onto existing trees stood at the corners. If it weren't for the perpetually purple twilight and fairy lights along the barn, this could have been a photo from centuries ago.

The wagon slowed to a halt. I used the respite from movement to arch my back and tried to stretch out the kinks. I hadn't been out of Seattle since I arrived and even the air smelled different here--earthy and rich.

Without the noise of the rolling wagon, the sounds, or lack thereof, were the first thing I noticed. The hustle and bustle of Seattle was an hour away and here there was only the rustle of tall grass and the low nicker of the horse. I scanned the grounds. It was actually too quiet. Where was everyone?

A loud rap against the side of the wagon jarred me out of my study of the Farm.

"Up and out."

My uncle Sam moved quietly for such a big man. I'd missed him walking to our rear. Our eyes met across the wagon and he tipped his head in a curt nod.

I'd made it and now he knew it, and knew I was my father's daughter.

We hopped out of the wagon and I resisted the urge to groan when my feet hit the ground.

Overhead, the skies darkened. I peered up and gasped.

A massive lion flew overhead, its wingspan the size of my entire studio apartment. The lion swooped in low and alight on its back was a slight person, a wisp of black against the twilight. In two more sweeping passes, the lion landed next to the barn, a majestic beast that seemed very out of place on this farm. Its passenger slid down slowly and gave a quick pat on the rippling mane of the lion before turning to hobble towards us.

The lion flew off and found myself mesmerized by the sight. I'd seen so many things in Seattle but nothing like this.

As the slender figure drew closer, I felt a sinking sensation in my gut. It couldn't be. What were the odds? The black fighting leathers, the crucifixes at the belt. Yep.

It was the assassin from earlier. She'd gotten a ride here after all.

The bells started ringing, the sound startling in the still night air. The assassin had made it before seven bells.

UNCLE SAMUEL GAVE the thirty-one of us the lowdown. They were divvying us up in smaller groups and we would be assigned a number of tasks. Then the tests would come. We would have little warning what the tests were or when they would take place. It was all to gauge our battle readiness. Or something like that.

"Any questions?"

The obnoxious mountain fae from my wagon moved forward, his mouth curled in a cocky half smile. "I am Harald. My brothers and I travelled a great distance. We heard much of the mighty force that is the Seattle Slayers. Where is this mighty force?"

He swept an arm out at that, indicating the seemingly empty grounds.

Uncle Samuel regarded Harald stonily. "Right. Since you were coming today, we gave them the day off. No sense having extra bodies just sitting around doing nothing. Group up by color and find your team leader. Each team has tasks assigned to them today and every day of your stay at the Farm. You will each earn your keep here these coming days."

The mountain fae looked offended. "This is a joke?"

Samuel shook his head. "No Harald, this is work. Work you will all perform without complaint. You will work with your teammates and take instructions from your leader."

The skinny kid with the skateboard raised his hand. "Is the work part of the tests?"

"First test is in three days. You all have three days to prepare."

I couldn't help myself. "For what?"

Uncle Samuel speared me with his dark eyes. "For anything."

7

MUCK

The town of North Dorchester where I'd grown up wasn't a big city like Boston, but it wasn't exactly rural either. This meant I was not particularly well acquainted with farmwork. Or horses.

The Slayers kept a huge, immaculate horse barn that should have required its own small army to keep clean. As I looked over the row of shovels awaiting us, I understood how they kept it so clean. They used the recruits as free labor during each cycle. The drab gray exterior gave no clue to what we would find inside. Stepping inside revealed a high vaulted ceiling that was freshly painted. The stalls were built with golden hued lumber and topped with iron bars. The horses within were all different shapes, sizes and colors.

Cordelia's eyes sparkled with delight as she identified the horses. "Pegasi, Friesians, Andulusians, ooh, and look over there–a Mongolian steppe horse!"

At least one of us was happy.

A tall slim man with inky black curls clapped to get our attention. If I hadn't prepped in advance, I wouldn't have known he was a Slayer. Nothing but his orange armband signaled his status. Instead of armor or weapons he was dressed as a humble farmer, with patched and worn overalls and heavy work boots. His hands were long fingered and nimble, like hands used for creating art. Nothing like mine or Harald's, calloused and rough with scar covered knuckles. Akhil Anand, Lightbringer, brought his hands together sharply and golden light sparked from his fingertips like tiny shooting stars. A good talent to have in a city infested with vampires.

Akhil introduced himself as our team leader. Each wagon had been assigned to a different Slayer. He gave rapid fire directions, pointed us to the shovels, and divided us up to muck out the stalls. To my dismay, I got paired with Harald, the burly mountain fae. Harald who had threatened to pummel me back on the wagon.

I studied my shovel and looked down at my grimy boots. At least I wouldn't get much dirtier. There was no sense delaying. I put my back into it and soon my boots were covered with not just mud, but horse manure and hay. Sweat beaded in my hair and ran down my face, stinging my eyes. My face itched and my eyes watered which was so distracting that the smell stopped bothering me.

The horse was none too pleased to have us in her stall either.

The assignment sounded simple. Replace soiled hay with clean hay. But it was slow going. Possibly because I was too busy trying to avoid getting a hoof to the skull. Maybe that was the first test–dodging crabby Agnes before she stomped me to death. Also, who named a huge chestnut Friesian who stands at fifteen hands, Agnes? I gritted my teeth and vowed to finish the assignment. I was going to become a Slayer. I could handle a little horse manure.

Harald was more vocal in his complaints.

"Shoveling horseshite! How can I prove my worth with a shovel? Give me a sword. Or an axe," he grumbled.

I was just relieved that he had now directed his animosity to Samuel and Akhil as opposed to me for "stealing" his sworn brother Sven's seat on the wagon.

Also, I was having a slightly easier go of it because I'd taken the sturdiest shovel. I'd spotted weakness in the others, which was now causing them to jiggle. You did not want a jiggling shovel of "horseshite" like Harald was dealing with.

Cordelia and Red Lion worked in the neighboring stall with Smoke, a handsome black Friesian male with powerful sloping shoulders and a long silky mane. Smoke seemed to have fallen madly in love with Cordelia, nickering gently while she cooed at him. I wondered if she'd have the same luck with Crabby Agnes. As the temperature rose and the itch on my neck intensified, Cordelia hummed a quiet little tune and pranced about her stall like a princess while Red Lion bent his massive frame and shoveled manure

Harald cursed and threw down his shovel in disgust. "I will not tolerate this! I am Harald of the Reach, son of Sten--"

In my annoyance, I wasn't paying attention to my surroundings, and got a little too close to Agnes' hind quarters as I tried to ignore Harald's bloviating. Agnes did not like that at all.

The massive horse reared and I stumbled back, smacking Harald with my shovel. My manure covered shovel. Harald roared in anger as my shovel jabbed him in the gut. He drew back an arm to punch me. I ducked and his swing went wide, landing on Agnes' rump.

Agnes screamed and bucked. Harald lost his balance on the hay strewn floor and slid, arms pinwheeling. He slammed into the wall and a shower of hay fell on his head. He landed with his ass into the muck. I threw myself aside as Agnes' massive hooves came down where my feet had been. The horse's flailing forelegs smashed into Harald. I heard the sickening crunch of bone and Harald howled.

With a lurch, he launched himself at the Friesan, his leg drawn back to kick her.

Oh no.

Akhil ran into our stall and stomped his boot down in front of the horse. "Agnes!"

He didn't raise his voice but the horse immediately stilled. Agnes snorted and settled into a high alert stance, head up and nostrils flaring. She tossed her mane and ground a hoof into the straw on the floor.

Harald stood, clutching his broken arm to his side. His eyes blazed and spittle flew as he screamed at me. "You useless coward! I'll have you hung by your ankles over--"

Akhil took a single step towards Harald and clapped his hand over Harald's eyes. Brilliant light leaked through his fingers and Harald's screed cut off with a high-pitched cry of pain. The burly fae dropped to his knees, tears streaming from his eyes. Akhil caught his broken arm by the wrist on the way down and yanked upwards.

Harald shrieked, his voice cracking and going hoarse mid-scream. Akhil studied the fae's hand and the heavy ring on his middle finger, tarnished silver worked into a set of curling ram's horns. One of the horns was smeared with blood.

Akhil placed a delicate hand on Agnes' flank where Harald's ring had torn a scratch into her flank. Warm light glowed under his hand and Agnes nickered. In a moment the light faded and when he removed his hand the scratch was gone.

The Slayer's voice was quiet and calm, and yet thick with terrible authority. "You struck a horse."

Harald had been reduced to a blinded cripple on his knees at Akhil's feet but he was still unrepentant. "She struck first. An unprovoked attack! I am owed recompense!"

I could not believe this guy. "It was an accident! I was only trying--"

Akhil held up his other hand. "I will have silence. From both of you."

Once again his quiet voice carried more authority than Harald's hoarse ravings. We both shut up and waited to hear our fates.

The Slayer dropped Harald's arm, eliciting another hiss of pain from him. "You struck a horse, one of our prized companions. Agnes is worth more than you will ever be to the Slayers. Your punishment will be decided by Altan. Go to the infirmary and see the healers about your arm."

Amazingly, Harald rose and left the horse barn with barely a grumble. That left me with the Slayer and the annoyed Agnes.

"Master Akhil, it was an acci--"

"You were careless, and your carelessness resulted in injury to your fellow initiate, as well as one of our animals."

"But--"

"On a hunt, this kind of carelessness would get you and your team killed. There is no place for it here. Your punishment is to clean the remainder of the barn without assistance. If I see so much as a scratch on another animal, you're through." With that, he made a sharp pivot out of the stall.

I heard him tell the others to go wash up and head in early to dinner.

The unfairness of it stung and my throat tightened up. I ducked my head, my face hot with shame. I would never hurt an animal and Akhil's words echoed in my ears.

I can't be through, I just got here.

My dad had passed away three years ago but I could feel his judgment from the afterlife. I thought about Uncle Samuel and how he would be ashamed of me if he knew how I'd almost just blown it. My fingers curled around the shovel.

Cordelia poked her head into my stall. "Roxy, I'll keep your stuff with mine."

I lifted my chin and willed my eyes to stay dry. I didn't want the other recruits to see me crying. "Sounds good."

She tossed me a little pouch. "Here."

I caught it on instinct, and the smell from the small muslin bag made my eyebrows lift. Bergamot and sugar. Cordelia smiled. "It's my tea stash."

She pointed at Agnes, who was giving her the side eye. "That one needs a bit of sugar."

My spirits lifted. Maybe that was the key to getting through this. Thanking the fae wasn't a great idea so I worded things as best I could. "I really appreciate the tip and you sharing your tea stash."

Cordelia's eyes twinkled at my wording. "Have to make sure you stay in the game long enough for us to have a go."

"Don't worry, I'll give you a run for your money."

"Exactly, I'll expect another wager with you." With a smirk, Cordelia flounced out of the stall. How one managed to flounce while wearing fae armor was beyond me but she'd obviously had years of practice.

I leaned the shovel against the wall and took off my gloves. Opening the drawstring bag revealed wax paper wrapped around sugar cubes and a few sachets of fine tea. Of course a fae princess like Cordelia would carry around tea along with her weapons and armor.

I shook out a sugar cube and put the tea kit into my vest pocket. Crumbling it a bit so that I had two smallish pieces, I held it out to Agnes.

Her nostrils flared and she ducked her head. With a long swipe of her tongue, the Friesan gobbled up the sugar. I snatched my hand back with a yelp when Agnes tried to chomp down on it.

"Look, Agnes. I'll give you the other sugar bit when we are done here. So please let me finish, ok?"

Agnes rolled her eyes and tossed her mane. But she stopped fussing. We had a deal. Hopefully the other horses would be easier. I counted the stalls. Nineteen more to go. I sighed. It was going to be a long evening.

8

A RIVER RUNS THROUGH

The ache that had started between my shoulder blades had spread until my entire back felt like a solid brick of flaming ice. I set down the shovel and willed my fingers to unclench and actually let the tool go. I braced the shovel against the wall and straightened, my spine popping as I tried to undo hours of torture. Hay and grime flaked off my gloves as my fingers stretched open for the first time in hours. Shocks of pain ran up my forearms as I wiggled my fingers and stretched my wrists.

All in all though, I'd done pretty well. And the pegasi had been really cool.

I looked around, or at least, as well as I could look around with my neck in a permanent kink. All twenty stalls were clean and stocked with fresh hay. The thick smell of manure from before had faded, replaced with the earthy scent of hay and animals. I was no horse whisperer like Cordelia but I could swear the animals looked happier. I rapped my knuckles on the gate in front of Agnes.

"There. That wasn't so bad, was it?"

Agnes bumped her nose against my hand, her tongue

flicking out and questing against my hand. Cordelia's sugar had done the trick. I wondered if I would need the sugar cubes every time.

"Sorry girl, no more sugar cubes. Maybe next time."

The horse nickered softly and turned to the clean hay instead. I stowed my tools, exited the barn and headed up to the main building, trying to stretch some life into my back as I went. If I never saw another clod of horse manure in my life it would be too soon. The air outside the barn was sweet with the scent of running water and night flowers. I took a deep breath, trying to rid my nose of horse smells. Whatever other tests the Slayers had for us, I hoped that mucking the stables was done for now.

I'd had plenty of time to think as I worked and I hadn't liked my conclusions. Those horse stalls were not meant for two people to be in there mucking. It had actually gone faster for me with Harald gone.

Clearly a stable master like Akhil knew perfectly well it didn't take two recruits per stall to get it clean. It had been a setup for disaster from the start. It had to have been a test. And I'd failed.

My mood had not improved when I thought about how I'd almost gotten booted out before I'd even really started over something so mundane as ranch chores.

Sorry, Dad. I'll try harder.

My steps quickened as I approached the main house.

The main house was a sprawling ranch structure that housed the inked Slayers who were here to train the initiates, and those who worked the farm. Rough cut timber logs a foot thick dominated the architecture, their heavy beams mortared together with clay and mud. A passing glance told me whoever had built the structure had done it well. The walls were sturdy enough to withstand an earthquake, and sealed tight against the Pacific Northwest winters.

The smells of the barn faded and the scent of grass and cool night air brushed my face.

From the path to the barn I could see glowing yellow fire-light shining through picture windows on the near side of the ranch. Shadows flitted back and forth across the windows and the faint sounds of lively conversation drifted down to me. Perhaps I hadn't missed dinner after all.

The path branched ahead of me, the left fork to the ranch. The wind shifted as I approached and the thick odor of horse manure assaulted me again. I stopped and nearly gagged. I looked down at myself and all thoughts of dinner fled my mind.

I was a mess. Mud, manure, and who knows what else caked my boots and my pants up past the knees. Hay was stuck all over me, glued in place by the lovely mud and manure mixture. I took off my gloves and ran my hand through my hair. It was nearly stiff with dried sweat and accumulated dust.

However my fellow initiates might feel about me, my first impression could not be walking into the dining room smelling like...this.

I took the right fork in the path, following the smell of fresh water and eventually the sound of a running river. I shucked my gloves and jacket as I went, shedding mud and hay along the path. By the time I reached the water I was down to my boots and underwear. I dropped my clothes in a heap, kicked off my boots and waded into the river.

I hissed as the cold water hit my feet. Once I was out to my knees I held my breath and plunged deeper into the water. The shock nearly drove the breath from my lungs but I held on and stayed under, scrubbing furiously at my skin and hair. I swam upstream a bit before resurfacing. The water and night air felt like cleansing fire.

My skin felt clean at last and then I was done bathing, just swimming for its own sake. That was one thing about being in Seattle proper. I took quick showers, but it's not like there was anywhere to swim. There were things in the Puget Sound best avoided.

I needed to get out and forage for some food soon but I took a few more strokes in the water and worked the kinks out of my back and legs.

I lifted my head from the water and stared up at the moon. It was a hunter's moon, low and fiery. Away from the city, the eternal twilight looked less hazy and the moon more vivid through the purple veil.

A hoot of laughter rang out, followed by the pounding feet of several people. Looked like my time alone was up.

With a howl, someone launched up to the nearest tree with the agility of a cat. The moonlight glinted off her pale skin and she dove buck naked into the water. It was Cordelia, of course.

When her head popped up from the water like a slick otter, I skimmed the side of my hand across the water's surface like a blade to fling water at her.

She dodged and laughed, a light rippling sound.

"Roxy! Finally done with the horses, I see."

On the river bank the skinny kid with the deck on his back slouched out of the trees, his hands deep in his pockets. When he reached my pile of clothes he squatted down. I froze for a moment until I saw that his hands stayed in his pockets, but his eyes stayed glued to worn boots. I wondered how he'd gotten onto a wagon. He certainly didn't seem very intimidating.

Cordelia swam close, her hair glistening in the moonlight. "If I'd known you would be done already I would have brought you some food."

"And I would have politely refused food from a fae."

She made a moue. "That's only when you're in a fairy mound."

Sure. I arched an eyebrow at her. Every fae I had ever encountered was always working some kind of angle. That assumption had already saved my butt a few times.

A petite woman in dark clothes exited the trees behind the kid with the skateboard and stopped next to him. The two of them spoke in quiet voices, their heads bent together. When she turned I caught a glint of light off the silver crucifixes strapped to her thigh. Ah, the woman who'd flown in on the eagle, then. I swam closer to shore, Cordelia following me.

They were standing by my clothes. Which was kind of a problem. I mean, I wasn't modest or anything but I didn't want to be nearly naked and weaponless in front of strangers. Especially one whom I stabbed in the leg a few hours earlier. Call me paranoid.

I needed them to move.

"Hey, how's the leg?"

She looked up and scowled at me, her face a study in angles. Dark brows drawn into a point. Sharp chin jutting out in annoyance. Maybe I shouldn't have reminded her that I had thrown a blade in her leg.

Cordelia treaded water next to me, barely making any waves. It seemed like she was just standing in the water. "Roxy, this is Haruto and Marnie."

I gave a small wave. "Hi."

Marnie turned her face away from me like my face offended her. Well, I suppose I should have expected that. But hey, she got here by winged lion anyway. Bygones? More importantly, I needed her to move away from my clothes.

Haruto gave me a bob of his head, his dark bangs covering his eyes. "How do you ride your board with those boots?"

I blinked in confusion.

He pointed to his shoes, nearly pristine checkered skaters with thick flat soles and alternating laces in vivid colors. "These are skater shoes. Your boots are..." He shuddered and made a disgusted face.

"I guess I just make do."

Haruto's face bore a look of horror at my lack of attention to good footwear. He rolled up his pants, exposing pale, skinny legs. He took off his shoes and set them carefully to the side and away from the water as he walked down to dangle his feet in the water.

I kept my eyes on Marnie, who hadn't moved from my clothes. I nodded off to the side. "Do you mind?"

She looked down at my clothes and her lip curled in disgust. She pulled a stiletto as long as her forearm from a sheath strapped to her thigh. The blade flashed in the moonlight as she flipped it over her knuckles and caught the leather-wrapped handle between her fingers. The guard was dull gray and worked to resemble a crucifix. Marnie stooped to my clothes, her nostrils flaring. She stabbed at my clothes with her blade and flung them to me.

Cordelia yelped and ducked under the surface just as my filthy clothes hit the water right in front of my face. I spluttered as water and muck smacked me in the face.

Marnie flipped her blade again and made it disappear into her thigh sheath. "Oops."

Cordelia popped up, decidedly upstream from me. I grumbled and gathered my clothes. They would have needed washing anyway, and if Marnie was satisfied that we were even, I figured I would take this as a win. I guess if I were in her position, I'd have the same attitude. Cordelia drifted closer as I started scrubbing my clothes.

"How was Agnes?"

"Fine. I...She...appreciated the sugar you left for her."

The fae's eyes twinkled as she smiled. "Well, I'll be sure to let her know I appreciate the sentiment."

I was still learning all the rules on this side of the Veil and it went against my upbringing not to say thank you. But those rules needed serious modification when dealing with the tricksy fae. My clothes slowly returned to their normal color, and a murky cloud stretched down river from me. Marnie had found a spot on the riverbank a few feet away from Haruto and sat with her knees pulled up, idly spinning a blade across her fingers.

"Where is everyone else?"

"Oh, they're off plotting their strategies for the rest of our time on the Farm. Alliances are being formed, and plans are being made. The future of our cohort is being written!"

Cold that had nothing to do with the river water stole into my belly. Cordelia seemed far too chipper. "What? What are you doing here then?"

Marnie called out from the riverbank. "We're plotting, too. The fae forgot to mention that none of the other factions wanted anything to do with the likes of us."

I nearly sank into the river. This was unbelievable. I almost got myself booted out on the first day, and now I was stuck here with the rejects? Then I was offended. It's not like the rest of that lot were any better than me. I mean, maybe they were better at mucking out horse stalls or other farm chores, but even that worthless lout Harald was there.

I sneered, "As if those mountain fae could plot their way out of a paper bag."

Cordelia gasped, then started giggling. Even Haruto's lips quirked up a tad, erasing his sullen expression. Marnie snorted. "Indeed. A box of rocks would be more clever."

If Marnie had been closer I would have high fived her.

After a moment Cordelia regained her composure and lifted her nose in the air. "Harald of the Reach, son of Sten, and Guardian of the Northern Pass, is of highborn blood and upbringing. He is reputed to have keen intellect and battle prowess. Also his compatriots Gorm and Ulf, sons of Skarde and Hilda are valiant fighters as well."

Marnie's blade stopped spinning, pinned between her knuckles. "Liar."

I had to agree. Harald exhibited the intellect of a tree stump and that was insulting the stump.

Cordelia tilted her head, her lips curled into a sly half smile. "You know we cannot lie."

Ha! Fae said they couldn't lie but it's amazing how they managed to work around that. Cordelia had been careful to say Harald had a reputation for keen intellect, but she didn't say it was true or that she agreed.

Marnie scowled. "The mountain fae might not be the brightest, but they are likely more prepared for the next task than we are. Does anyone know what we should expect?"

Everything was a test. I almost said it but I bit down on the words. I didn't know these people, didn't know if they were assets or liabilities. My father had taught me that I had to be the best to get through the Trials, but after the skirmish to the wagons, I wasn't so sure any more. I hadn't been the best. If anything, I had been at the bottom of the barrel, but I was still here. And I was still here because Cordelia had made me a wager.

I didn't know anything about Haruto, but what I knew about Marnie told me she was a contender.

I took a deep breath and decided to risk sharing a little intel with them. Samuel had been fairly cagey, but I'd been able to glean from him some sense of the structure.

Finally I settled on what I could offer. "They need to whittle us down. Like in Denny Park. They need recruits, but the Slayers can't train that many at once. First challenge will be team based."

Haruto's eyes peered out from behind his curtain of hair. "And the losing team...?"

I shivered, even though I had acclimated to the water's cold. "The losing team goes home."

"Excellent." Cordelia did a lazy backstroke towards the

riverbank. "That means when we pass the next test, we'll all go through at once!"

A low whistle pierced the night. Akhil stepped out from the trees and walked up Marnie, his feet silent on the dirt path. "Tomorrow we will have an early start."

Cordelia called out, "We will return shortly, stable master."

Then sotto voce, she whispered to Haruto, "Now that Roxy's cleaned up, we don't have to worry about her stench waking us."

I splashed her again. As infuriating as she was, her performance in Denny Park was more than enough to prove her worth. I'd given her a donut in return but truly, I felt I owed her more than that.

Akhil turned to leave. "Be on your guard. We may be on the Farm, but we are still out in the Wilds."

I slogged out of the water and wrung my clothes out. Cordelia walked out behind me, naked as a jaybird, and headed to the treeline where I saw another small pile of clothes. Fae.

Marnie sat up as if something had just occurred to her. "Does being so short make it easier for you to pass as human?"

Cordelia paused, a wrinkle creasing the smooth, pale skin between her brows. Then it disappeared and she smiled. "No, the ears and eyes always give it away." She disappeared into the trees without another word.

Marnie nodded. "Unlike shifters. Never can tell with them since they pass for human."

Haruto hunched up his shoulders. "Shifters are human."

Marnie shook her head. "No, only humans are human."

Haruto frowned. He opened his mouth and then shut it without saying anything.

I struggled into my sodden clothing. "So what's happening tomorrow? What's with the early start?"

Cordelia's voice called out from beyond the treeline.

"Kitchen prep! We are tasked with preparing a meal for everyone!"

Would kitchen duty be some sort of test as well? Maybe a teamwork exercise? I'd already learned the hard way how teamwork could work or not work in the stables.

Haruto kept his face carefully averted as I got dressed, so I had to strain to hear his already quiet voice when he spoke. "Why are you all here?"

The question struck me as odd. I knew why I was here, but I had never considered why anyone else would test themselves this way.

Cordelia returned from the trees and answered smoothly, filling in the dead air. "I have been tasked by my liege to render aid to the Slayers. It is a most noble endeavor."

Even Haruto scoffed at that one, his thin shoulders shaking with amusement.

The skinny kid laughed when Cordelia pulled a face. Then she cut him some slack and gave him a sunny smile. He had the good grace to repay her with a respectful nod.

Cordelia wasn't letting him off the hook, though. "And you?"

He swept his hair out of his eyes, an unconscious gesture. "I lived on the outskirts, just at the edge of the Wilds. I got to know one of the Slayers who did patrols out there, a big werebear. Nice guy. He taught me a few things, just stuff to stay safe so far from the city. When I got old enough he suggested that I should try."

Aha. Haruto had been something of a mystery until now. "So you're a shifter, then?"

His eyes slid sideways to Marnie. "...something like that."

Cagey. I could appreciate that. I didn't recall seeing him fight at the park, and I hadn't noticed him on any of the wagons. How had he earned his way in?

Three sets of eyes now turned to face me and I realized that the last thing I wanted to tell them was that I was related to Samuel, or that my father had been a Slayer. I told a half-truth that would make any Fae proud. "My father always wanted this for me. I'm doing this for him."

Cordelia's eyes narrowed at me. "Only for him?"

I shrugged, uncomfortable now. "My family could use the extra funds I'd earn as a Slayer."

I had to keep this conversation from delving into my family. "Marnie? How about you?"

She'd been quiet as we'd answered, her eyes staring off into the middle space. Now her blade started dancing over her knuckles again. "I'm here for blood."

That killed Cordelia's playful mood. She leaned ever so slightly away from Marnie. "Whose?"

Marnie lifted her eyes to us. "Any vampire I can get my hands on."

The blade sped up, glittering dangerously as it played over her hand. "The Church took me in when I was a babe. They found me in an encampment in the Wilds, just to the south."

As she spoke, her voice took on a hoarse, dry quality. She spit out her words like bitter poison. "I was the only living thing in the camp. The vampires...they had gorged themselves on my family and gone to sleep. They were saving me for later. Like some kind of snack."

"The Church always travels with a contingent of guards. They staked every one of the vampires in their sleep and brought me back to the city with them. They fed me, raised me, trained me. I owe them my life. I'm going to repay them by cleansing this city of as many vampires as I can."

Her eyes focused on me and then on Marnie and Haruto in turn. "This isn't about money for me, and this isn't a game. This is my mission."

A shiver crawled up my back. It wasn't a game for me, either, not with my mother's life on the line. I had only shared my plans with my brother and sister, so that they understood what I was doing, and why. No one on this side of the Veil could know. Not before I had everything I needed.

Cordelia nodded, her face somber. "Yes, we really should turn in. Tomorrow will be challenging, I'm sure."

She was right, of course. Things were only going to get harder, and the further we progressed, the tougher the competition would be. Would we still be so friendly with each other in a few weeks?

Cordelia looked like she was going to say something else but before she got a word out her eyes went as big as dinner plates and I spun on instinct. Haruto had already clambered back from the water's edge and he was dragging Marnie with him.

Glowing, blood red eyes emerged from the dark waters of the river. A set of horns that curved in, ending with wicked points, bracketed the bulbous, bovine eyes. Water sluiced off wiry black hair sprouting off a pebbly black hide. As the monster rose up its mouth became visible, a hellish maw filled with jagged yellow teeth. It crawled towards us and six crab-like legs crested the water behind it, scissoring back and forth. Its body was bloated and heavy, like an insect thorax, and covered with black, matted hair.

Haruto's voice was a bare whisper. "Ushi-oni!"

Great, a water demon. My father had warned me. He said that fighting demons had always been the hardest. So much for turning in early. My first day on the Farm was just getting better and better.

9

USHI-ONI

This beast looked like it could eat three of the horses in the stable for an appetizer. Between me, Cordelia, Haruto and Marnie, we probably weighed as much as one of its six legs.

The ushi-oni blinked its blood-red eyes. Its hind legs skittered back and forth as it took in the the four of us. Not fighting. Not running. Just staring.

The slow, deliberate blink of its eyes warned me that this was a predator, not a mindless demon. Cold, dead eyes that were the eyes of a predator, meant to intimidate prey. It was almost beautiful, in a hideous, grotesque kind of way, like it was carved from a piece of onyx.

Cordelia's voice was a low, raspy hiss. "We need to scare it away."

Making a concerted effort not to move a muscle, I snuck a glance at her. "Why?"

"This is a river demon. And it's hungry. If we don't scare it off it's going to cut through us and make for the horses."

Haruto knelt next to Marnie. "Don't stare into its eyes."

I didn't want to because they were terrifying but I had to ask, "Why not?"

"Because it will suck out your soul."

Ok, that sounded bad.

I picked a spot beneath its hairy chin. There. A safe place to look. The demon opened its mouth, revealing fangs as long as my arm, dripping with thick saliva streaked with bright green... stuff. Its head rose from the water and the mouth dropped open even wider, hinging open like some hideous snake. The demon straightened its forelegs, raised its head to the night sky and roared, green-streaked spittle spraying from its throat. Charming.

Cordelia was wrong. Nothing would scare this yokai. We had to kill it. My magic sparked and an intricate web of green lines covered the demon. I scanned up and down, looking for some weakness, anything we could use to defeat this monster.

"Cordelia, use your rope whip chain. Go after the legs." I whispered.

The fae nodded and uncoiled her rope from around her waist, twitching her wrist left and right. I reached to my low back, drawing two small throwing knives in each hand. I cursed the fact that my hammers were safely in my dorm room and swore to the moon to never take them off again.

I pointed to Marnie. "We need to attack the hind legs. Go for the joints."

Marnie stood and two gleaming stilettos appeared in her hands. Her wrists flicked and her blades spun. "You don't defeat a killer by taking out its legs. You go for its eyes."

Fine. Whatever. Haruto was still sitting on the riverbank with his shoes in his hands, carefully picking away bits of dirt from the uppers. Other than his statement about the ushi-oni's eyes, he seemed to have decided to ignore the river demon.

The ushi-oni reared up on its hind legs, waving its front legs at us. Legs that ended in deadly sharp points. Its mouth opened and closed, fangs scraping against its teeth, making a chirping noise, a macabre rasping cricket song.

And then it lunged.

Its mouth was wide enough to swallow half my body. I jumped to the side, diving under its jaws and slicing into the water at its legs. I kicked, propelling myself to its rear legs. I came out of the water next to one of its legs and stabbed my throwing blade into its...do river demons have knees? I fell forward as my blade skipped off the leg.

Dark skies, this thing had skin like hardened leather! Cordelia yelled something from the other end of the demon. I planted my feet and threw my shoulder into the knee. Pain flared in my shoulder at the impact. I might as well have tried to knock over one of the sentinel stones. In my magic sight, the beast was a solid wall of green, with no seams, no cracks for my power to worm its way in.

Cordelia screamed again, her words punctuated by snaps of her whip. "Roxy, why aren't you helping?"

My hands slipped off the demon's slick legs and I fell onto my butt in waist deep water. Cordelia stood in the shallows, peppering the ushi-oni's forelegs with her whip, keeping it from advancing onto land. Her rope cracked through the air, biting into the demon's leg. The ushi-oni howled, the sound becoming a crackling buzz that made the hair on the back of my neck stand up.

Marnie prowled behind the fae, looking for an opening. Goddess, we were all going to die at this rate.

The ushi-oni saw its opening and moved forward again, lifting its rear leg. I grabbed hold again, the hairy hide biting into my hands. When the demon took its weight off the leg I shoved forward, pushing the leg towards the creature's abdomen. The demon roared as I tipped it off balance. I straightened my arms, locking them out and planting my feet in the muddy riverbed.

The web of green light around the ushi-oni's knee faltered and turned pale as the creature's weight gave me the leverage to break its leg. I hung on for dear life, my hands burning from the creature's rough hide, and prayed the demon's leg would snap.

The ushi-oni thrashed and pain shot down my arms and through my shoulders. My feet sunk deeper into the mud and the cold crept up my legs, leeching my strength.

Footsteps ran towards me. Marnie pelted down the river-bank and across the shallows, both her knives flashing as she ran. Her calm eyes never strayed from the ushi-oni. Marnie jumped at the last moment and launched herself right at the demon's maw. Her eyes were cold and emotionless as her arms swung up and she brought both her stilettos down in vicious arcs towards the demon's eyes.

With a sound like tearing paper a gout of saliva like a fire-hose erupted from the demon's mouth. Marnie flipped in the air, graceful as a falling leaf, and dodged the spray. She landed lightly on the ushi-oni's head, spun, and brought both knives down at the demon's eyes.

The demon lunged forward and nearly tipped Marnie off her perch. Her strike went wide, blades skipping off the bony ridges around the eyes. I screamed with effort and pushed up. The green lines around the demon's knee faded to silvery white and the leg snapped with a sound like a gunshot. The ushi-oni roared. Hot ichor spewed from the shattered limb and sprayed my arms and chest. My arm went numb.

I slipped and fell into the water, my hands raw and burning from the demon's skin and blood. The ushi-oni turned, its eyes glowing like burning coals, fangs clicking. It opened its maw and dripping yellow fangs descended on my head.

A glittering silver rope lashed out and wrapped around one of the fangs. Cordelia yanked and the demon's head swerved away from me and plunged into the river. This time Marnie lost her grip and she disappeared into the dark water. Cordelia leaned back, digging her heels into the dirt. I scrambled back, putting distance between myself and the demon.

Cordelia screamed. "You're still not helping!"

The fae pulled another rope from around her waist and lashed it around me. With a heave she dragged me through the water to the riverbank. I landed at her feet and she loosed the whip. She threw out her second whip and wrapped it around the demon's foreleg. She wrapped both ropes around her wrists and leaned back, keeping the demon from moving.

Wow, for a short little fae she had some guns on her.

A thundering roar erupted behind me. I spun in the mud and my jaw dropped open.

A fifteen foot bear made of ghostly blue energy stood above me, its legs thick as tree trunks, forepaws ending in shining claws, its ragged muzzle dripping bright blue saliva through a row of sharp white teeth. At the bear's side, set atop a clean river stone, were Haruto's skaters, the laces neatly tied and tucked inside the shoes.

Goddess in the moon, that was Haruto? The bear's outline glowed like he was backlit by blue starlight. Between one breath and another, the bear flickered and I could see Haruto as a pale outline within the bear's chest. But the scrawny skater boy with the shaggy bangs was gone. In his place was a thin man dressed in crude animal skins. He had the same sheaf of dark hair partially covering his eyes, but he looked rangy and mean, a far cry from the kid who had teased me about my boots minutes ago.

The massive bear stood on his hind legs and a primal fear froze me in my tracks for a split second before I remembered we were on the same side. I hoped.

Haruto-bear fell back on all fours and jumped into the river. He slammed a massive paw into the water and swept a huge wave towards the ushi-oni. The demon rocked up and the bear got his shoulders under the demon's belly, lifting it out of the water. The remaining legs snapped down trying to stab him but they passed harmlessly through the bear's glowing blue light.

A dark shape emerged from the water around Haruto's feet and scrambled for the demon. Marnie grabbed a hold of the demon's pelt and began climbing its thorax. The bear heaved and pushed the demon further back into the river.

Cordelia yelped as she was yanked forward by the force. I scrambled to my feet, and ran to her, wrapping my arms around her middle and lending all my weight. Feeling was returning to my arm in a wave of needles that ran down from my shoulder. I dug my heels in, and my arms screamed from the strain as the demonic bull yanked and thrashed.

Haruto-bear roared and clamped his jaws around one of the demon's hind legs. The skinny leg snapped like a twig in the bear's mouth. The ushi-oni screamed, a high-pitched, chittering cry like nails on a chalkboard. Haruto stood, dragging the demon out of the water by the broken leg. The bear's paws swung and worked over the demon, ripping off chunks of hide and flesh out of the demon's underbelly. Marnie made it to the demon's head and this time when her blade flashed out it hit home, piercing the demon's left eye. The orb exploded in a shower of gore and blood.

The demon screamed and twisted, shooting a stream of poison at Haruto-bear's torso. The stream of liquid passed through the ghostly bear, but Haruto's form was knocked back as it passed through. The bear stumbled, his jaws opening and the demon crashed back into the water. Marnie leapt off the demon before it hit the water. She landed in the shallows and collapsed.

The demon's roar was deafening, its rage tangible. Dark, malevolent magic pressed in around me. I panted from the exertion of shutting out the demonic waves emanating from the beast. Even Cordelia was sweating, her golden hair damp and plastered to her forehead. I focused my magic on studying the beast.

Even with two legs maimed, the demon was still incredibly strong. I had the horrible feeling that this would go on until it, or one of us, died. Haruto hauled himself out of the water, his bear form shaking and retching as his body did the same inside him. Marnie groaned, her arms and legs scrambling in the mud. Blood streaked Cordelia's ropes, her hands shredded from the friction.

Cordelia looked back at me and smiled through the effort of restraining the ushi-oni. Her words were a little breathless. "It's going to be fine, Roxy."

It's what my dad always used to say. I heard dad's voice add the 'bear' to the end of my name. He was right. I was going to be a Slayer. This was why I was here. I felt my father's gaze upon me and knew we couldn't let this demon get past us. We had to stop it here and now at the river. The ushi-oni bellowed its awful chittering scream again. My magic sight covered the demon in a glowing web of lines that showed me everything I needed to know.

Cordelia was right. It was all going to be fine.

I patted Cordelia on the back. "Hang on. I'll be right back."

"What?!"

I ran back into the water and dove under the roiling surface, kicking hard to send myself to the muddy bottom. The demon's remaining legs stabbed down, kicking up mud and debris. I dug my hands into the mud, searching for what I knew had to be there.

When I broke through I coughed and gasped, vomiting black river water over myself. Lovely. Cordelia was nearly horizontal, tendons on her neck and arms straining as she held her weight against the massive demon.

Cordelia's voice clipped around the strain. "Awfully nice time to take a swim, but you're still! Not! Helping!"

"I think this will do it."

I had the section of the demon's hind-leg that I'd snapped off at the knee. In my hands it resembled a short spear, ending with a single, needle tipped talon that glistened an inhuman black.

"Great! What do we do with that?"

I trudged back into the water. "Keep it from moving!"

"What does it look like I'm doing?!"

I yelled up at the spectral bear and prayed Haruto could hear me. "Haruto! Keep it busy!"

The bear roared, the blue glow intensifying to near blinding and it brought both paws down in a crushing strike to the demon's back.

I pushed forward, my legs burning as I forced my way through thigh-deep water. The ushi-oni screamed again and I ducked, keeping to its left and avoiding the spray of poisonous saliva. The creature's mouth hung open, fangs exposed and dripping, along with the bright white star that showed me the soft spot on the roof of its mouth.

Marnie had been almost right. Not the eyes, the mouth. I braced the broken end of the leg in my right hand and thrust up with my left, guiding the needle tip home. The point pierced through the demon's soft spot and I rammed it hard. The sharp end went in easy for a few inches and then stopped, the chitinous ridges of the leg catching and getting stuck.

I screamed in frustration and reached out with my magic, trying to Break through the demon's skull. It was too big, too fast. My magic slipped off the weak point, unable to gain purchase.

Two arms wrapped over mine and added weight behind my makeshift spear. It was Marnie. She braced against me, her body quivering with effort. Veins bulged on her forearms and she shrieked with fury.

Marnie wrestled the spear from me. My shredded hands let

go and I fell into the water. Marnie hopped on my bent thigh and dove upward. I grunted from being used as her springboard but pushed the bottom of her feet upward as she climbed into the maw and forced the spear all the way home.

The ushi-oni screamed, its chittering cries speeding up until it was a high pitched, keening whistle that raised gooseflesh all over my body. The beast fell to the water and the wave pushed me back to shore where I crawled back to the relative safety of the sand. I collapsed next to Cordelia and moments later Marnie joined us in the mud.

The blue spectral bear faded out and Haruto dropped to the water with a splash. He stumbled to the shore and collapsed face first into the sand.

I crawled towards him until I managed to roll him over. "Haruto. You alive?"

His voice was muffled by the sand. "...sleep..."

And then he was snoring, out like a light. I lay back down.

Marnie said, "Do you think we passed the test?"

It would have been funny if I wasn't so tired. I raised my fist to her in salute. She stared at my hand for a long moment before hesitantly bringing hers up as well. When she didn't close the distance I reached out and bumped our knuckles. "Yeah, I'm pretty sure we passed."

"Oh. Good." Then she closed her eyes as well.

I rolled to my back and stared into the night sky, my chest heaving, a sharp stich of pain at the bottom of my lungs. The beast was dead at last. I sobbed with relief. If we had failed I would have died the victim of this demon, never to fulfill my calling.

It was a sign of how exhausted I was that the sound of pounding of hooves didn't even make me flinch. I rolled over and lifted my head. Akhil appeared, riding on Agnes. I never thought I would be happy to see that cranky Friesan again but the night had done wonders to change my perspective. Akhil brought Agnes to a skidding halt in the mud and dismounted with a graceful leap. As he strode over to Haruto light sparked in his hands and bathed us all in a gentle glow.

Oh gods, we looked like hell. Marnie was covered in mud from head to toe. Haruto looked even worse than Marnie, his chest barely moving with each breath. Cordelia's pants were crusted with mud to the knees and her hands were a maze of blisters and friction burns.

Akhil waved his arm in an arc and a cascading sheet of fiery effects revealed the corpse of the ushi-oni in all its glory. The Slayer's golden light reflected off the shining black eyes of the demon and I finally got a good look at the full scale of it. Fangs as long as my arm. Horns on either side of its head as long as my leg. The leg I'd used to kill it had exited the top of the ushi-oni's head, the sharp point smeared with bright green ichor.

Akhil smiled. "Nicely done. Cordelia, please assist Haruto back to the main house."

The fae nodded and gave me an apologetic smile. She roused Haruto and the two of them limped up towards the main house.

What about me? I also wanted to go to the main house. If nothing else I could use another shower at this point.

"Master Akhil, I wonder if I could--"

"You, Ms. Lim, and you Ms. Black, are not going anywhere just yet."

Frustration seared my fatigue away and I bit down on my tongue to keep from mouthing off to an inked Slayer. "Sir, I think--"

Akhil turned, ignoring me, and pulled two massive cleavers from Agnes' saddle bag. "I require your assistance."

I bit my lip and took one of the cleavers.

Marnie picked up the other one. "Stablemaster, what do you require of us?"

"You vanquished the demon and to the victors go first pick of the spoils."

Marnie sneered. "I want none of this demon corpse."

The stablemaster gestured to the expanse of the ushi-oni. "The river demon is an invaluable resource, and we will not waste this bounty."

Marnie set down the cleaver. "With all due respect, I would set it afire so it may join its brethren in hell."

She pivoted sharply and stalked off toward the ranch house.

I gulped and hefted my cleaver. "Where would you like me to start?"

10

BAD BLOOD FOR BRUNCH

Akhil seemed to think of the ushi-oni like a side of beef. Did demonic water buffalos taste like regular water buffalos? It had to be several hundred pounds of meat. Maybe it just needed a real heavy duty marinade?

He knelt by the corpse and took the cleaver to the neck. Blood did not arc out like a fountain so that was reassuring that it was really dead. He set down the cleaver and fanned out his hands about shoulder width apart. He began humming and I found myself relaxing. The adrenaline of battling that beast slowly dissipated and I was just left with confusion over Marnie dipping out. Now it was just me and Akhil and I wondered how I'd again gotten stuck with yet more work this evening.

Light emanated from his palms, a cool white light and I watched with wonder as the light bathed the ushi-oni corpse. Though the night air was decidedly cold, heat surrounded us as the Slayer's light intensified. Akhil's magic wasn't merely for special effects–he could tune it for other qualities.

Maybe he could singe vampires to ash. His magic was perfect for the Slayers.

Akhil's fingers moved gently, like he was playing a piano

and the light fractured into even slices, and like a swivel, rotated until what had to be two dozen blades of light punched into the hide and split it open. Neat. Totally not what I was expecting either.

"Roxy, please attend me."

I knelt next to the stablemaster and followed his instructions. He moved the entrails out of the way and directed where to hack and cut. His earlier cuts had drained the blood. Akhil explained which parts were nutritious, and which ones were to be avoided. We worked like this for a few minutes, quickly reducing the carcass into neat cuts of meat and offal.

"What about those?" A row of swollen green glands hung along the length of the beast's esophagus.

"No. Those are poisonous and cause paralysis."

Okay, then. Definitely did not want to cut into those. But I did briefly entertain the thought of serving some of that to Harald and his loudmouthed mountain fae buddies. Not a lot. Just enough to paralyze their vocal chords.

Time passed quickly as we worked until Akhil stood and went back to Agnes who had been patiently cropping grass by the river. He set up some kind of contraption for her and then we strapped all of the meat to it. What kind of person shows up with cleavers and a set up to load and carry hundreds of pounds of meat?

Akhil knew.

When he left us at the river, he knew what we would be facing. Either he came back expecting to drag back our dead bodies, assuming the ushi-oni left any behind, or he came back to help us bring home the meat. I liked to think positive, so I chose to think it was a good sign he brought the cleavers.

Everything was a test. Even this.

I looked down at the hulking skeleton before us. Agnes was a big girl but I wasn't sure how this could possibly work.

"What about the bones?"

"The marrow is nice. We'll roast them."

Damn. That meant bringing the bones back too.

When I approached Agnes, the cranky Friesian tossed her mane. Luckily Akhil was here because I was all out of sugar cubes and I didn't think she'd want a hunk of demon meat. Well, who knew what the Slayers fed her? Maybe Agnes was extra ornery from a steady diet of demonic food.

Akhil rubbed his hands together and I watched in awe as he gathered a small spinning circle of light. The ball unfurled until it became a many sided star and with a slash of his hand, the star winged its way through the skeleton.

In moments, the bones collapsed into a heap, sliced into manageable chunks by Akhil's lightblade star. Wow.

Akhil gestured to the horns. "Roxy, these spoils of the hunt are yours."

"Uh, thank you."

I picked up the two horns and sagged a bit under their weight. Each one was the size of my leg, but thankfully hollow. But what would I do with them?

The stablemaster seemed to hear my unasked question. "After roasting, you grind them to a powder. Boosts endurance and strength. Has protective qualities too for your immune system."

Interesting. This would make a lot of bone meal. A lot. But did I mix it with water and drink it like a protein shake? I strapped them together and then hung them around my shoulders like the world's most ridiculous backpack.

Our progress back to the main house was slow as we dragged back several weeks worth of demon meat and bone. Our slow progress gave me extra time with Akhil.

Akhil was not a chatty person, though. He didn't just talk to fill the silence, seemingly content to stay utterly quiet. This was the perfect opportunity to gain intel on the next Trials, but breaking the silence seemed...rude. Finally I asked, "So do you guys eat demonic water buffalo often here at the farm?"

Akhil chuckled. "Usually about once a quarter. Altan likes to make sausage with it. The rest we will salt and cut into very fine strips and smoke. Makes a nice jerky."

Slayer Trials were held every quarter. I had been lucky that the others had decided to take a dunk in the river. I would have been toast if I'd been out there alone with the river demon. I owed them big. Because of them I was still breathing now and still a contender to be a Slayer. Maybe my Dad was watching over me.

"How long were you watching us?" I tried to keep my tone neutral.

A hint of a smile played at his lips. "Long enough to see you and Marnie make the killing blow."

So that was why he'd given me the horns. If Marnie hadn't bailed earlier, she'd have some too. I would have rather had his help during the battle but I guessed I could live with the spoils.

My poker face must have needed some work because Akhil continued on. "Before you think to judge, understand that my only goal is to make the Slayers as strong as possible. The Trials are a series of tests, designed to separate the strong from the weak. Keeping the Slayers strong is the best guarantee for a lasting peace."

I couldn't argue with his goal, but after today, I could spot a few flaws in his methods. For once though, I chose to keep my mouth shut. I hadn't asked him any questions, but he'd still managed to provide some answers. Hard answers, but answers nonetheless.

The main house was visible now and Agnes slowed and gave a soft nicker. That was all the warning I got before someone leapt out at us from the dark shadows.

Altan. The werejaguar lifted his nose high and inhaled deeply. His cheeks billowed out and then he lowered his nose.

"Good haul tonight. I do like me some rare ushi-oni. Especially sliced thin, with a little mustard."

Guess we were having demon carpaccio tonight.

Altan pointed to the horns I was lugging. "You scored, kid.Those are worth a lot."

My spirits lifted at that. How many ounces of silver could I get for these? Surely enough to get my duster spelled. With a spelled duster, my odds of living longer here in Seattle increased substantially.

Altan leaned in close and while the river demon had been terrifying, I rated it a close second to having the werejaguar lean in so close to my neck. I held myself very still and exhaled slowly.

He flicked one of the horns and it thwacked against my thigh. "Good job, Lim. Nice to see the blood runs true."

He knew my father. I couldn't tell from his expression if that was a good thing or a bad thing in his eyes.

I gave him a small nod. "Thanks."

Akhil grunted. " Altan, why don't you bring in the meat? I'll get Agnes settled in the barn."

To my relief, Altan turned his feral gaze to the stablemaster. "Happy to."

While they unhooked the meat sled from Agnes, chatting about marinades, I made my way into the main house. After a quick sponge bath and hunting around, I found Cordelia. She was snoring softly and I was ready to collapse too. I set the giant horns down in our room and bunked down. It had been the most harrowing day of my life and the trials hadn't even officially started. I sent up a quick prayer that tomorrow would go more smoothly.

∼

AT FIVE BELLS they had us up and getting grub together for everyone. Cordelia smiled and hummed as she squeezed bushels of oranges into juice. Her morning cheer grated but I held it together while I sliced the bread. Others had been tasked with cooking eggs and frying river demon sausage so I got one of the easier gigs.

I had no idea when I would get time to roast and grind the demon horn but I wanted to do it as soon as possible. Our "tasks" started soon and we were going to need every advantage.

A grubby hand reached for a slice of bread. I whacked it with the flat side of the bread knife. The hand belonged to one of Harald's compatriots. It was Gorm, the twin with the single braid.

"Hey!"

"You can wait your turn."

The ginger fae made a face, the sulky expression ridiculous on such a big warrior.

"We need sustenance if we are to fight."

"You'll get fed just like everyone else."

"Give me the bread!"

I pointed the bread knife at him. "We're all trying to get the food ready. Make yourself useful and go set out the coffee."

He sneered. "If you had any pride you would not stoop to performing such tasks. I was told this was a test for warriors, not servants."

Cordelia chose that moment to come up behind me with a double armful of ceramic pitchers brimming with freshly squeezed orange juice. If Gorm's attitude towards me was belligerent, it turned downright murderous to Cordelia. His shoulders tensed and his knuckles cracked as his hands balled into fists.

"You." He spit his words out like venom. "Deserter. Traitor."

Cordelia ignored Gorm, set the orange juice carefully on

the table, and picked a fleck of invisible lint from her sleeve before raising her eyes to meet the mountain fae. She tilted her head to the side and gave a tight smile. "Are the mountain fae still wallowing in the pain of the past? Still drowning their failures in weak mead and self pity?"

Gorm's eyes hardened like chips of ice and a growl started deep in his chest.

Cordelia leaned forward, her eyes burning hot, her voice raspy with scorn. "Does Harald of the Reach, Defender of the Northern Pass, still cry himself to sleep every night?"

The growl exploded into a strangled roar that shook the windows. Gorm clawed at his belt and lunged forward.

His hatchet was barely a quarter of the way out of his belt when my hand wrapped around the heavy braid at his neck. It was heavy and softer than I would have guessed. It made a fine handle.

I yanked, putting my weight into it, and pulled the big fae down. His legs buckled as his head slammed onto the counter next to the loaf of bread. I twirled the bread knife in my other hand and stabbed it into the loaf, right beside Gorm's bulging eye.

He didn't spare the knife so much as a glance. Even half-dazed, his wild eyes stayed fixed on Cordelia. "You coward! You Hinterlanders only know how to run and hide, cowering behind your walls as your brothers and sisters burned!"

Cordelia stilled, her soft gold eyes hardening, and the usually friendly features of her face turned to stone.

Harald burst through the far door from the dorms at the head of a loose crowd of people, his voice a sharp bark of laughter. The laughter died when he took in the scene and his eyes darted back and forth between me and Gorm, pinned to the countertop. He unbuckled the sword at his hip. "You! Unhand my sworn brother!"

Gorm's actual brother Ulf ran in behind their leader, his

battle axe already loosed. I snarled at them. All I wanted was my coffee. Couldn't we just have coffee before we tried to kill each other?

The crowd behind Harald surged in as people jostled for a good view of the fight. Voices in the crowd rose in volume and filled my ears with the buzz of bloodlust. I dropped my free hand to the hammer at my hip.

Gorm and Cordelia hadn't moved, their eyes locked in place. Cordelia's fine features were chipped out of pale marble.

With a loud thump, Red Lion set his coffee mug down on the table. When he pushed his bench back, it screeched against the stone floor and he stood, drawing all eyes to his massive frame.

Red Lion tipped his head at me. "When you're done schooling him, would you bring the bread over?"

I gave him a tight smile and moved my hand away from the hammer. "Sure. I'll just be a second."

The door to the kitchen opened with a creak.

"Can we at least have breakfast in peace?"

Akhil's voice was soft, but his absolute authority filled the entire room. Harald stopped mid-stride and Ulf ran into his back. Even Gorm stopped struggling even as I continued to hold him down by his braid.

Akhil stood in the doorway, a steaming tray of eggs in his hands. He moved smoothly to the long communal table and set down the food in the center. He looked at me and raised an eyebrow. I unwound my hand from Gorm's hair and the big fae stood on shaky legs, rubbing at his neck.

Red Lion nodded and sat down, scooting the bench back in.

Cordelia's face relaxed, and her usually cheerful demeanor returned, her cheeks pinking up again. She schooled her expression, but when Akhil couldn't see her she gave me a wink.

With the promise of a fight dashed, the crowd settled down

and with a few grumbles, everyone organized themselves into a semblance of a line for food. This time, hunger had won out over everyone's fighting instincts.

The mountain Fae trio scowled at me and pivoted to head to the opposite side of the room. Fine by me. This way the stink of their furs wouldn't ruin my breakfast.

Akhil smiled and clapped his hands. "Excellent. Now that we've remembered how to be civilized, we can enjoy our breakfast."

11

PICKING SIDES

The rest of the cohort filtered in around the long table. Cordelia and I managed to snag seats far enough away that I couldn't hear Gorm muttering to Harald, but the two of them kept their heads together until most everyone was seated. Then the room went silent but for the scrape of chairs and clank of cutlery on plates. Altan stalked in, his muscular arms hefting two heaping platters of sausage. The smell of grilled meat and roasted potatoes filled the room and everyone visibly perked up.

I poured myself a steaming mug of coffee--finally--as Haruto slid in next to me. Gone was the terrifying spectral bear from last night. Once again he was just a skinny kid with shaggy hair and baggy clothes.

I tucked into my own plate. River demon sausage turned out to be surprisingly delicious. I would've thought something emerging from the river would taste like seafood but this was basically demonic beef. Excellent. Altan was quite the culinary talent, marinating the meat with red wine vinegar and filling the sausage with an earthy blend of herbs. The yolks of the eggs were bright orange and everything tasted vibrant and fresh. Maybe it was the farm or maybe it was just that I was glad to be alive today and amped up for our first challenge.

Haruto shoveled in the food like he had two hollow legs.

I refilled his orange juice. "So, bear, huh?"

"Yeah." His voice was garbled as he chewed yet another sausage link.

"What kind of bear?"

"Higuma bear."

That seemed fitting, given his heritage. Higuma bears were brown bears that terrorized Hokkaido, and could weigh over eight hundred pounds. Second only in size to the Kodiak bear, the Higuma bear was a man eater. No wonder the kid was eating so much. Shifting like that had to burn a ton of calories every time he did it.

The double doors opened again and Samuel and Aislinn rolled in, tall as giants. A cool gust of morning air floated in behind them, carrying the damp scent of turned earth and pine trees. I envied my uncle his long duster. I would have mine soon, hopefully. Upon seeing them, Altan pushed back his bench with a loud scrape and jumped on top of the table with a thump. "Good bread, good meat, right?"

Folks nodded and continued chewing. I set down my coffee. This was it, the werejaguar had to be announcing the first Trial.

"You can all thank Roxie, Cordelia, Marnie, and Haruto for the meat."

Eyes around the room narrowed in speculation and zeroed in on the four of us. The spot between my shoulder blades twitched, and I had to resist the urge to back away until I was standing at the wall. This was not the kind of attention I wanted.

"Today we divide you into four groups and assign your trial judge." Altan gave a broad smile and spread out his arms in a wide gesture to encompass Akhil, Samuel and Aislin.

Of all them, I knew Samuel would never allow the impropriety of being my judge. I hoped for Akhil, judging my odds with the stablemaster to be better than with the fae or the werejaguar.

Samuel thumped his walking stick and then reached into his duster and came out with a fistful of bandanas. My heartrate skipped up a notch. These weren't the orange ones for Slayers working patrol, but the urban camo ones they wore for blood runs. It was happening. My Slayer Trials were going to start.

Samuel tossed the bandanas and as one whipped towards my face, I snapped it out of the air. A second one landed in front of Haruto. From the corner of my eye, I saw Cordelia catch one as well. I didn't see Marnie but assumed she got the fourth. I didn't know where this was going, but I clutched the bandana tight.

Altan cleared his throat. "This year my brothers and sisters in arms decided we would try something new. You're the first class to run through our new and improved Trials."

My stomach clenched. I had prepared and trained for the old Trials. I did not like the sound of "new and improved" which might be a euphemism for "more difficult and deadlier."

"We used to send the losing teams home after this first Trial. But we thought it might be more... sporting if we put you on a points system." Altan cackled, apparently very pleased with himself.

Aislinn rolled her eyes and cleared her throat. "Everyone who made it on a wagon got ten points."

She pointed to Marnie. "You, we gave 11 points for showing up on the winged lion. Plus one for style."

My throat tightened. Not only was Marnie in the lead, but my blunder at the stable yesterday had likely cost me points. Hopefully I hadn't gone negative. On the other hand, Harald had likely lost points as well, so at least I wasn't alone at the bottom.

Akhil, who had been absent during these announcements, stepped into the dining hall, two leashes in his right hand. He gave a soft whistle and two dogs, one gray and one red, trotted in at the end of the leashes. Except, they weren't dogs...they looked more like fluffy raccoons?

Akhil made a gesture and the two raccoon dogs sat on their haunches, their pointy ears high and alert.

"This is Tanuki and Tabi. Each team will be trying to rescue them."

My lips turned down in dismay. Rescue? I had trained to fight vampires and demons. I had expected to face down enemies in combat during the Trials, not rescue cute, fluffy... whatever these animals were.

"Since Roxy, Cordelia, Haruto and Marnie brought in the kill that fed you all today, they will be your four team captains. They also got five extra points each. They will take turns drafting candidates of their choosing to their team."

I tied the bandana on my left bicep with a taut snap. Marnie was at the top of the leaderboard with sixteen points but I didn't need to be at the top. Even if I got the last slot, I would still be a Slayer and get my ink. That was all that mattered.

The draft began. Altan conducted it with the theatrics of an auctioneer. The noise level in the room was deafening, or maybe that was the blood rushing in my ears. I'd spent the first day alone in the stables and missed out on meeting anyone other than the three who helped out with the ushi-oni. I needed to pick a team based on a rescue mission, and I didn't know what anyone's strengths were. Flying blind like this was a pretty crappy way to start my day.

I picked my team members on sight alone, trying to give myself a range of body types, in case the mission required us to be flexible. By the time it was over the universe had thrown a bone to me as I managed to nab the monk and Red Giant from my wagon. At least I'd seen what the monk could do. And a seven foot giant had to have something in the plus column for me.

Samuel and Aislin started grouping the rest of the candidates around their team leaders. I stared at six members that collected in a loose ring around me. Gods save me. Another thing I hadn't planned on was leading a group of fighters. Dad had taught me to fight on my own, not relying on anyone else. When your chips were down and you had a vamp's fangs at your throat, the last thing you wanted to rely on was someone else. I cursed Altan silently for choosing this year, of all years, to change the Trials.

In the opposite corner, a tight ring had formed around Marnie. She had drafted one of the mountain fae, Gorm. If she wanted to deal with that hatchet wielding idiot, that was fine with me. I certainly wasn't picking any of the mountain fae. Harald and Ulf turned and scanned the room, eyes stopping on Cordelia and me. With a scowl, the two made a rude gesture at me and Ulf and Harald ended up on Cordelia's team. I did not envy Cordelia, especially after our little bread incident with Gorm earlier.

Altan tossed a silver coin high in the air. It seemed to flip in slow motion, time stretching as our fates were decided by the toss. The coin landed on the table and rang like a bell. Altan smiled, all teeth, and looked from me to Marnie.

Marnie's stare hit me from across the room like a physical blow, her gaze as hard and focused as it had been when she'd yanked my blade out of her calf. Her team looked tough, anchored around fighters carrying swords of all sizes. Marnie stood in the center of her team, her hand on her cocked hip, fingers playing over the stiletto sheathed there. Her eyes traveled over my team and a slow, wide smile spread across her lips.

The monk stepped up beside me, his hands on the wooden

staff held before him. "Looks can be deceiving. Our talents will be revealed at the Trial."

It was a good thought, but I couldn't help but worry that we were outmatched. After tonight, some of us were going home.

12

TANUKI AND TABI

I spent the rest of the morning trying to coordinate the team, and running back and forth to roast and grind the horns. I settled on the simple method of setting them in a low fire and letting the heat burn away the meat residue. '

While I stood by the grills, I studied the rock wall shielding this seating area. I didn't remember seeing it when we arrived. A bucket and trowels were off to the side, as if the wall was still in progress.

The door from the kitchen slammed and Altan sauntered out with the compost bins.

We worked in companionable silence, me roasting meat and bone, him chopping wood.

Altan tossed a stick at me. "You're going to need more wood for that."

"Thanks."

"Make sure you drink that bone meal to strengthen you for the Trials."

I nodded.

He pointed to the rock wall. "That imbecile Harald built

that overnight. Aislinn wouldn't let me break his femur, which I thought was a fair punishment for hurting Agnes."

My teeth clicked together in annoyance. The upcoming trial had almost made me forget that I had lost points in the barn because of my altercation with Harald. Almost.

Altan grunted. "I'll say one thing for those mountain fae, they are strong. I told him if that wall didn't get done by sunrise, he would be disqualified from the Trials. He got it done and those red headed twins helped him."

Strong, and loyal to each other. I filed that away. The Slayers rarely took more than three initiates at a time. Was I better than those mountain fae? I would have to be.

"Here, you'll need your strength."

Altan reached into his vest pocket and handed me a waxed paper pouch.

I opened the flap and took a sniff. Gamey. "What's this?"

"River demon jerky."

Nice. I didn't know what I'd done to warrant this gift from the jaguar but I was grateful. I was behind on points and I needed every bit of help I could get.

Altan gave me some more pointers for dealing with the smoker and left me to my little protein making project. I'd found a mortar and pestle in the kitchen and worked feverishly, grinding down the horn into a powder.

There were glass jars under the sink and since I'd washed dishes after breakfast, I snagged several jars and started filling them with the demon bone meal. I stashed them in my room, already counting the silver I'd be able to land from the witch coven with these.

Holding my nose, I gulped down the gray coagulating mass of collagen and meal I'd mixed for myself. Yech.

Moments later, a curious warmth surged through my belly. I hadn't heated up the bone meal smoothie but it was as if I'd drunk a bowl of hot soup. Maybe it was psychosomatic but my shoulders loosened up and the heat spread to my hands and feet.

Who knew if it would do anything but I would take any edge I could get. It could make all the difference in this upcoming Trial.

I stared at the jars I'd secreted away in the closet of the room I bunked in with Cordelia. I didn't feel right not sharing the spoils of the kill. What would my dad say about this? He'd always told me I had to be strong to be a Slayer. That the weak ones would be a walking vamp meal. I dropped my head in frustration and blew out a long breath.

I grabbed three jars and stalked out to the common areas to find Cordelia, Haruto, and Marnie.

Cordelia was easy. Of course she was with the horses. I kept a wary eye on Agnes while I handed Cordelia the jar of bone meal.

"Here. Akhil said these would give a boost for strength and endurance."

She unscrewed the lid and took a small sniff. The fae wrinkled her nose. "How quaint."

I shrugged. I mean, I wasn't a healer, what did I know about magical remedies? Regardless, I felt a little better giving Cordelia one of the jars.

"Have you seen Haruto?"

"I think he went to the kennels." Cordelia turned back to Smoke and gave him a friendly scritch. The big black Friesian leaned into her hand, clearly adoring all the attention. I wondered if we would be allowed horses in the Trial or if it was all on foot. If we had the use of the horses, Cordelia would have the clear advantage.

It would be easy to resent her because her gifts were many and she was most certainly the cream of the crop in these

Trials. But I liked her. She'd helped me get on the wagon, she'd been kind to me after my stable incident, and after last night with the ushi-oni, I trusted her to watch my back. It was a strange thing to realize that I trusted a fae, and maybe a foolish move, but I did.

The kennels were just behind the stables and I found Akhil showing Haruto and two other candidates around the kennels. The two little raccoon dogs were there too. I watched the gray one lift its black lips and snarl at Haruto. Guess it didn't like the smell of spectral Higuma bear. The red one yipped, and Akhil threw it a small fish which it lunged up for and snapped up with a loud crunch.

Akhil smiled and tossed another fish to the gray one. "Here you go, Tanuki."

That meant the red one was Tabi then.

Haruto had the right idea, coming here and trying to befriend the pair. But clearly they didn't like the way Haruto smelled. Maybe they wouldn't like any of the shifters, which meant they couldn't be tasked with the actual rescue. Which was fine, given that shifters were better at leading the charge and clearing the roadblocks.

I walked cautiously up to Tabi, and held my hand out, palm down. She didn't curl her lip in a snarl, so that was promising.

"Hi Tabi." I stayed still, waiting for a sign that it would be okay to get closer.

She tilted her square little head, her ears and nose quivering. Then with a lunge, she leaped up and planted her forepaws on my quads. I stumbled and almost fell backwards.

"Whoa!"

For a small creature that was maybe twenty-five to thirty pounds, she was surprisingly strong. Tabi's claws pricked my pants and almost punched through the heavy fabric. Her black nose nudged against my side pocket, and she pawed at it.

"Ow!" I took a step back and gently lifted Tabi off my leg. Patting my side pocket, I realized I'd put Altan's jerky in there.

Akhil came forward and patted Tabi on the head. "Take it easy, Tabi."

Tabi gave a soft woof and then lifted up on her hind legs, her face attentive. Akhil chuckled and tossed her another fish. Tabi snapped up her treat and then dashed off, her fluffy tail waving high.

Haruto walked over to my side. "They didn't like me."

I shrugged. "I think they just like fish."

Haruto grinned and we started walking back towards the stables.

I pulled out a jar of demon bone meal and offered it to him. I gave him the same pitch I'd given Cordelia.

The kid scratched his head. "I'm already really strong in my bear form."

I patted a bony shoulder. "Maybe it will help you in your human form."

He considered this for a moment then put the jar in his hip pouch. "Thanks, Roxy."

That left Marnie for last. After she'd stormed off, I wasn't sure what to say. But fair was fair and it didn't seem right not to bring her some of the spoils.

I made a detour for the river first.

By the time I tracked down Marnie, I was wet, cranky, and tired but I'd obtained what I hoped would be a little insurance for the next part of the Trials.

The main house was a byzantine maze of rooms but I found Marnie in what looked like a trophy room. If trophies meant an array of scary weapons mounted haphazardly across a walnut paneled wall. One of the walls had floor to ceiling books so maybe it would have been more appropriate to call it the library, but nothing about the room felt scholarly or restful.

I followed the sounds of exertion and violence and found

Marnie in the back of the room,throwing axes against the far wall. In order to prepare for the trials, Cordelia had gone to the stables, Haruto had gone to the kennels, and Marnie was taking target practice with axes. What was I doing? I was some kind of magical pony express, delivering jars of ground up demon horn. Most of the morning was gone, and I'd spent the time sharing an advantage with my competitors. We might be friendly now, but that didn't mean I wasn't going to regret this later.

What would my father say? He would have told me to keep the demon horn. Who knew how much I would need to pay for the spells on the duster. The fae were a mystery to me. The demon horn might be completely wasted on Cordelia. And Haruto wasn't wrong, his bear form was powerful. Maybe I should have kept it all for myself. That would have been the smart play. But it had felt wrong.

Marnie looked up when she heard me approach. I knew what dad would have said, but that didn't make it feel right. Everyone had helped bring down the ushi-oni. Sharing the reward was the right thing to do. "I brought you some of the demon horn. Master Akhil says it helps with strength and endurance."

She tossed the handle of the axe from hand to hand and made no movement to accept the jar. Finally she said with disdain, "I wouldn't defile my body with demon horn any more than I would consume the demon meat they served this morning."

"Are you a vegetarian?"

"No, a child of God."

I looked down at the jar. "Maybe you could use it for barter?"

Marnie held my gaze, her eyes troubled. "I won't profit from that unholy filth. You should consider the consequences of dealing in demonic items."

I blinked. Now probably wasn't the time to tell her I'd already guzzled a mug full of the unholy filth.

Marnie turned away from me and threw the last axe, its head slamming in the walnut panel with a loud thunk and a quiver. She turned and stalked out of the trophy room.

Huh. That went well.

At least I didn't have to worry about Marnie gaining some edge from the use of the demon horn.

Since I was alone it seemed a good time to practice too. Why let Marnie have all the fun?

I yanked two of the axes out of the wall and began throwing. The weight was good, a little lighter than my hammers. It wouldn't have done much against that ushi-oni last night but Cordelia was right, I needed some range weapons. After I made it past this first Trial, I would need to work on my strategy for round two of the Trials. I told myself I would make it through this first Trial. I was fast and I had the Red Lion and the monk on my side. I would task the monk with grabbing the raccoon dog. I would run interference with the other team members to give the monk cover.

It could work.

It had to work.

I pulled an axe out of the wall and strapped it against my leg.

"I should've known I'd find you here."

My uncle's gruff voice startled me and I whirled to face him. We hadn't spoken the entire time I'd been here at the Farm. My spirits lifted at seeing him, the craggy lines of his face reminding me so strongly of my dad that it made my throat hurt.

"Hi Sam. Any words of wisdom for me?"

His lips quirked. "Don't get killed. Grab the tanuki."

Okay. I had figured that much out so far.

I mean, I knew my uncle didn't want to be perceived as

giving me some unfair advantage but I could have used a little encouragement.

He looked at the axes lodged in the wall and grunted. His bushy eyebrows drew together and he seemed to come to some internal decision. Finally he reached into his vest and pulled out a set of keys.

With a jingle, he unlocked the tallest wall cabinet.

My uncle was so tall and wide that he blocked my view as he rummaged around in the closet. Finally he yanked out a long, dark spear, adorned with a black tassel on a metal ring. The blade gleamed with menacing light, made of some dark metal. The base of the blade glittered with orange light, a crystalline lotus. Ooh. A classic qiang, augmented with crystal. Knowing my Uncle's talent, he had likely shaped this crystal. We Lims were a fine pair. Samuel could sculpt and forge while I could smash at any weakness I saw. In short, he was a maker and I was a breaker.

Uncle Samuel's workmanship was fine. This crystal ornament on the spear was perfect for the follow up. Stab with the spear, drink with the crystal.

My heart lifted. Samuel had given me a great gift and just talking to him while he was really seeing me made me realize how much I was missing Jasper, Ava and Mom. Since coming to Seattle, I'd thought I would have more time with Samuel but he'd kept me at arms length. I knew he wanted to show he was impartial, but it had hurt.

Now Samuel was giving me the spear he'd made for my dad. I used to train with spears with my dad. It had been Dad's favorite weapon. My fingers itched to grasp that smooth wood.

Samuel handed me the spear. "Here. I know you love those ridiculous hammers, but you need a weapon with more range."

When Cordelia had said that to me, I'd been annoyed. Somehow it was okay when my uncle said it.

I wrapped my hand around the haft of the spear and tested

its weight. The haft was a little thinner than my wrist, with just a touch of flexibility. The head was edged on both sides and narrowed to a dagger-like point. Good for both thrusting and slashing, then. I dropped my weight into my hips and tried a practice thrust. The ring clinked as the tassel snapped.

My uncle scratched his chin and watched me take a few more lunges. "At least he trained you well."

I straightened. "At least?"

Samuel turned and relocked the cabinet. "My brother left a big hole in the Slayers when he left, Roxy. It made us a target for a long time until we could replace him."

He waved a hand at the cabinet. "And until you decided to come, all of this had just been sitting here. A waste."

The disgust in Samuel's voice was plain and shocking. Dad had never even hinted that he had left the Slayers on bad terms. "Dad wanted to come back, uncle. It's just…"

With mom's diagnosis, so many of our plans had fallen apart. Now I was down to my last option, and I had to push in all my chips to do it. I didn't dare tell Samuel what I intended to do when I passed the Trials. Not now. Maybe not ever.

My uncle sighed and pinched the bridge of his nose. "I know, I know."

He smiled, and this time I saw a little of my father in him. "You remind me of him, you know."

I grinned. "Tall? Good looking? Confident?"

"Ha! Cocky, more like. Headstrong."

"Well, then I truly am suited to step into his boots and continue his legacy."

My uncle's head snapped up. "His legacy?"

"Sure, I mean, I don't know if I'll rise to become one of the Freaks, but I'll do my best to live up to his name."

I pointed to the cabinet Samuel had pulled the spear from. "Is the rest of dad's gear in there? His armor? His weapons?"

Samuel nodded.

"I'll earn them, uncle. I promise."

His eyes studied me for a long moment and flicked up to the head of the spear. Then he turned and walked out of the room. He spoke without looking back at me. "Pass your Trials, Roxy. Then we'll talk."

13

ONE TEAM

I twirled the spear and then tucked it under my arm. It was flexible and light, perfect for extending my reach. My hammers were great but had limitations. Between the spear and the hammers, I could now cover more range. But that left some logistical issues for carrying back the Tanuki.

The spear would be handy in fending off the opposing team. I rolled the spear between my palms, enjoying the heft. The points for these next trials gave me two options—I could aim big for a team win to sweep all the points or I could just go for the Tanuki myself and gain individual points. I didn't like that option. Slayers fought as a team. But I could hear my dad's voice telling me to do what it takes.

I couldn't be a Slayer if I didn't make it through the Trials. I needed to keep my options open.

I set down the spear. I needed my hands free for carrying the Tanuki, just in case everything went sideways.

My thoughts raced as I grabbed a long sleeve shirt and pulled it on over my head. I needed to be on the forward squad. I had to have a clear shot at grabbing the Tanuki myself.

I checked my gear one last time, patting my pockets,

touching all my weapons. One free pocket so I stuffed some Ushi Oni jerky in there. I wasn't sure how long I would be out there. A little protein never hurt.

With a grimace, I guzzled the last of my river demon smoothie and then made my way to the team meeting area.

The Red Lion made it really easy to figure out where my team was.

I pointed at the six of them. "Sound off with your name."

"Wen."

"Axel"

"Yvonne"

"Augusto"

"Minji"

"Dario"

Axel and Wen had been on the wagon ride with me. Axel was about the size of an oak tree and three times as wide. With his fiery red curls and beard, it was pretty obvious why I'd nicknamed him the Red Lion in my head. I didn't know if Axel had any special abilities but he could squash heads like a grape so he was a good one to leave behind as a defender.

Wen was the monk I'd watched leap above the fray like he was running up an invisible staircase in the sky. I wanted the monk on the forward squad.

I studied the rest of the team and suggested we reveal our abilities and figure out how we could help the team. "Show us what you've got."

Yvonne stepped forward, her movements quiet but assured. She moved like an ambush fighter, all sinuous movements and silent footsteps. Her long dark hair was tied back with a red strip of torn cloth, tiny braids woven into a smooth larger braid. A stout oval shield made of hardened animal hide was strapped to her back, and she carried a knobkerrie, a seven foot walking stick made of red wood. It ended in a large knob that was polished to a mirror shine and looked like it would cave in a skull with little effort. She spun the knobkerrie once, the wood whistling through the air, then caught the shaft and pointed it at me.

"Why should we show you? You're not a Slayer. You are not in charge of us."

Her words were abrasive but her tone was gentle.

I shrugged. "I went to meet Tanuki and Tabi. Didn't see any of you there."

A couple of heads turned. I had their attention now, which was good because I needed this to work. I needed this team to win so that I could put more points on the board and stay in the Trials.

"If we don't have a plan, we are all going home. How many of you made a plan?"

No one said anything but I saw their body language. Wen and Axel stepped closer to me. I took that as a good sign. I just needed to persuade the other four people.

Minji stepped forward and laid her hand on Yvonne's upper arm. She came up to Yvonne's shoulder. Where Yvonne was muscular, Minji was slight. Wispy bangs framed a heart shaped face, the rest of her dark hair shaved high and tight. Her street clothes were sleek and stretchy for movement. The only concession to these trials was a form fitting yellow vest. Minji's eyes connected with Yvonne's and a brief flash of silent communication passed between them.

Those two would fight back to back, and they likely had made some plan that involved only the two of them.

That wasn't going to work for me. I needed a plan that I could control.

"Slayers fight as a team. We will have to do the same to win this round."

Minji tilted her head. "What are you suggesting?"

"Look, I'm sure some of you are fast."

Minji grinned and her eyes danced. Okay, she was probably very fast.

Dario, who had the stocky build of a sprinter also nodded. He crossed his arms, his body telling me that he was not receptive to what I had to say. His dark brown hair was a mass of tight curls that he wore down to his shoulders. I couldn't place his age, but I would hazard a guess that he was the oldest among us, his eyes revealing a man who had come through life the hard way. I needed to convince him, and maybe Augustin would fall in line too since he seemed to be copying Dario's pose.

I gestured to Wen. "Well, while you two are trying to get across the field, you'll have to deal with all the terrain and the other team members who will fight you every step of the way. But Wen here is probably able to outdistance all of you because he practically walks on air."

Minji blinked and Dario turned to scrutinize Wen, who bore all the stares with equanimity.

Dario cleared his throat. "What did you have in mind?"

I pointed at Augusto's hunting knife, the carved bone handle peeking out from his braided leather belt. "That's for up close fighting. It tells me that he's comfortable confronting people face to face. It also tells me he doesn't shift into anything or else he wouldn't carry something he might lose in the shift."

Augusto put a protective hand on the knife handle.

I swiveled to Dario. "But you carry nothing. No weapons, just a lightweight armored vest. That tells me that you are a shifter and not only that, you can shift just your arms."

Dario's bushy eyebrows drew down in displeasure, a heavy vee of wrinkles in his forehead. I'd nailed it. Partial shifting to a warrior form meant he was an exceptional fighter.

Minji tapped on Yvonne's bicep. "Roxy's right. We're already outnumbered by the other side. We shouldn't be going in blind."

A gust of air blew across my cheek and in a blink, Minji appeared at my side, her elbow resting on my shoulder. The sweet smell of fruity shampoo followed the breeze. Her impish smile reminded me of my little sister, dimples and everything. "Is this what you had in mind?"

I nodded. "Yeah. If we know what our strengths are, we can figure out how to divide and conquer. We can't leave our own prize unguarded and all run down to the other side."

Red Lion grunted. "It's a time trial. I'm strong but I'm not fast. We need the faster ones up front."

I held up a finger. "One catch, I saw that Tabi and Tanuki didn't like Haruto. He's a spectral bear."

Dario snorted. "Small raccoon dogs wouldn't like a bear, would they."

"Will they like you?" I asked.

A light golden sheen rolled over his eyes. Dario didn't shift but something about his body language sent a visceral message to my hindbrain telling me to run. The forward tilt of his shoulders, the way he scented the air with his mouth as well as his nostrils. Whatever he shifted into, it was going to be big, and an apex predator.

His answering grin only made things worse. "Yes, they are like my little cousins."

My eyebrows lifted up. "Okay cousin, let's see how they react when we go meet them."

In agreement for now, if not exactly unified, I got the group to agree to head past the stables and be assessed by the very discriminating Tabi and Tanuki.

The results made it clear who would be on the forward squad and who had to stay to guard home base. I drew in a deep breath and ran my fingers over the Slayers bandanna tied around my bicep. I had a grand plan to sweep the points, keeping our own home base safe while liberating the other side's treasure and returning home in the time allotted. I had to assume that Marnie was working along the same vein.

I shoved some ushi-oni jerky into my mouth and chewed hard, the gamey flavor coating my tongue. I swallowed and chewed some more willing my body to absorb every bit.

May the best Slayer win.

14

THE FIELD

At six bells, we were led to our starting positions. My team was led to Black Base and Marnie's team to White Base. We had our Tabi on Black. We had to grab Marnie's Tanuki and bring him back to Black Base.

No killing. No maiming.

The field might have been an actual field once, but now it was a nightmare of sharp edged rock formations jutting randomly from the land, looking disconcertingly like giant teeth.

If the Farm was where some of the Slayers with elemental talents came to practice their magic outside of city confines, it was clear that this field was their laboratory. I didn't have that kind of talent and hadn't witnessed it either. But that would change now that I was in the Trials.

The wind picked up and whistled through the stones with an eerie rising shriek.

Aislinn stood perched atop a tall outcropping of rocks ahead. The tall fae seemed to blend into the rocks, her silvery braids whipping in the wind. Aislinn waved her right hand in a small circle and swirl of heavy fog began rising from the ground, as thick as chowder. Soon, we wouldn't be able to see our hands in front of our faces.

The tall fae reached into her robes and pulled out another sphere, like the one she used before in Denny Park.

The sphere glowed with an inner orange light and then distorted, the shape morphing into an hourglass, with grains of orange sand. It rose above her, a beacon not unlike a north star to guide us. Instead of telling us direction, it would count down our ten minutes.

Somewhere on the other side of Aislinn's rocks lay our target–White Base.

To my left was Wen, his blue and gray monk robes fluttering. He and I had a brief conversation about sweeping all the points.

"Wen, you are our best shot at getting to Tanuki."

He raised a brow. "Perhaps you or Minji are the better option."

"Well, that's why we're part of the forward team, but I have a plan."

Once he heard my plan, both eyebrows went up.

Basically it came down to strength. The raccoon dogs had to weigh about thirty pounds, if not more. Minji didn't look like she could lift more than a pencil, let alone a squirming raccoon dog. Yvonne was strong, but not particularly fast. That left me and the monk.

Wen could grab Tanuki, hand it off to me where I would placate it with the ushi-oni jerky. Then Wen could slingshot me back to our home side. We'd be over and above the fighting, and we'd get Tanuki back to our side before the other team could even get near Tabi.

No fuss, no muss. We'd sweep all available points on the field.

Assuming everything went perfectly, which was a big assumption.

On my right stood Minji, who shivered in the fog. Her teeth chattered and I'm sure she wished she had on more than workout clothes and a vest. On the other side of Minji was Yvonne, who twirled her staff in small circles as we waited for the starting call.

"When are they going to start?" Minji grumbled.

Yvonne stopped twirling the staff and looked down at her. "Why don't you run around to warm up?"

Minji's lips flattened as her eyes scanned the fog. I wondered how much stamina she had for her speed moves. Was she trying to keep something in reserve? After a moment, she began to do jumping jacks, or at least the first one looked like a jumping jack. After that, all I saw was the blur of the fog and the faint ghost image of Minji's yellow vest.

If she could see and not hit a giant boulder while zipping over to Tanuki, this thing would be over in a blink. A part of me was excited at the prospect of a guaranteed sweep of the points, but the part of me that wanted to be the one to carry Tanuki back made me envious of Minji's speed. It would be nice to be that fast. To be able to move so fast that no one could see.

Unfortunately, I didn't think it would be that easy.

Something about the way Minji leaned on Yvonne told me that there was a reason they fought back to back and it wasn't only trust. They needed each other. Something about Yvonne's magic acted like a shield and a torch for Minji. Together they would be slower than Minji alone, and faster than Yvonne alone.

I glanced over my shoulder at the home team.

For all the Red Lion's size, the raccoon dogs had liked him just fine. We'd agreed upon Red Lion staying with Tabi's crate, ready to pick up the crate and run if he couldn't bash the heads of anyone who got close.

Contrary to Dario's assertion that the raccoon dogs were like cousins, Tabi and Tanuki had hissed at him, their hackles rising visibly. They were smart. They knew a terrifying predator when they smelled one.

Dario and Augusto would create a secure perimeter around Red Lion and Tabi.

Yvonne and I would be the muscle on the forward squad, buying cover for Wen and Minji to get ahead to Tanuki and liberate him from his crate and run back to our home base with him, getting us all the points.

The rules were simple.

If one team ended up with both Tabi and Tanuki back at their home base, every member of that team would score 40 points.

If we ended up with their Tanuki and got him back to Black Base but lost our Tabi, each team member would receive 25 points.

For any individual who procured the other team's raccoon dog, that individual would score twenty points.

We had ten minutes.

Ten minutes was an eternity in a fight, but hardly seemed long enough to slog through this terrain and come back. That meant the likely scenario for either team was to get to the other base, but not be able to get back to their home base in time.

Part of me resisted letting Wen or Minji grab Tanuki. If I got the raccoon dog I had the possibility of sixty points. It would be more than enough to get me to the next round, but I wasn't as fast as Wen or Minji. They were our best shot at a team win, which would get me through. I couldn't help but feel like my dad wouldn't appreciate how I'd set up two other people for the scoring run.

Behind me, Red Lion knelt down to bring his face closer to Tabi. She gave a soft woof and curled up in her crate into a tight circle of gray fur.

"Here." I pulled a small waxed paper package out of my pocket and handed it to Red Lion.

"What's this?"

"A fish."

Red Lion made a comical face as he realized the squishy bag I'd handed him held a fish in it. I'd used the spear to nab a fish after seeing how Tabi and Tanuki had snapped up the treats from the stablemaster.

Augusto and Dario had already spread out. I couldn't hear them or see them but I had to trust that they would stick with the plan and keep the other side from getting to Tabi.

I pointed at the crate. "Akhil feeds them fish all the time. Show her the fish and she'll want to stick close to you."

Understanding dawned in the big man's eyes. "Will do."

Aislinn raised both hands in the air and clapped, calling down lightning that speared down and struck the ground before us in a dramatic flash. A moment later, thunder boomed around us and echoed off our rocky canyon surrounds.

"Begin!"

Wen grabbed my hand and my stomach turned over as he pulled us up and over the rocks, our feet barely making contact.

I couldn't see them, but I imagined Minji and Yvonne en route as well. Minji's natural speed would be greatly diminished while pulling Yvonne along but they would still be faster than most of the competitors.

Lightning flashed around us, casting tall shadows from the canyon below and illuminating forms of the four footed and the two as they raced in opposing directions. The movement was about all I could see. I knew Tanuki lay further north but I couldn't tell where their base was.

Wen set us down and his robes blended into the fog and gray stone. We paused in the heavy fog, the sound of my own racing heart loud in my ears. I couldn't see anything now, not even the rush of bodies. I wished I had my spear, which would have given me a way to forge ahead and poke things before I ran into them.

Between the fog and the drizzle of rain, I should have been freezing. The duster was good but my blood was running hot and the skin of face felt hot. Adrenaline could explain some of it but I suspected the ushi-oni bone meal effects were kicking in.

I hoped it would be enough.

An eerie howl echoed in the rocks. Some of our competitors had shifted to their four legged form. That would surely give them an edge in these conditions.

"Wolf?" Wen asked.

"Wolves," I responded quietly.

Sure enough, a couple of other yips followed. I leaned closer to Wen, grateful for the monk's surefooted leaps that had taken us above the fray. I thought about Marnie's team, how they already had the advantage of an extra player and now some of them had four legs instead of two. Hopefully Dario would be a sufficient equalizer for us.

Wen and Minji had the hops that could get us over to White Base. I had to make sure I handled the rest. I patted my pockets, an almost compulsive movement.

We could do this. I could do this.

Then it started to rain.

My foot slipped on the rock and Wen grabbed my elbow.

From the west a bird call sounded, its shrill sound rising and falling. At the familiar signal, I exhaled in relief.

"That's Yvonne. Let's move." I braced myself for Wen to take off.

Wen leapt into the gray haze of fog and rain, carrying us over the nearest boulders. In two steps the wolf sounds faded behind us. In two more the fog parted as we descended onto a wide, flat clearing. Wen landed like he was stepping off a stair, his feet sure and silent. His robes fluttered as he drifted to a stop. I hit the ground and took the shock through my knees, then bled off the rest of the momentum with a forward roll. I popped up with my hammers out.

Yvonne stood on the far side of the clearing, her hip cocked at a lazy angle, her staff resting across her shoulders. Between us, in the center of the clearing, Marnie cradled Tanuki lightly in her arms. A rumbling, contented purr emanated from the raccoon dog, its snout resting on her shoulder.

Wen slid to my left on quiet feet, and I moved to the right, keeping our spacing even around Marnie. I scanned the clearing, trying to pierce the haze of fog at the edges. By the sound of it the wolves were still moving away from us and it seemed like we were alone for now. A faint blur passed between the boulders, carrying the scent of strawberry shampoo. "Just the one?"

A rush of wind pushed into my back. I spun and found Minji behind me, her eyes bright and cheeks flushed. She spoke in an excited whisper. "That was fun! No one else around! I wonder where they all went?"

Yvonne rolled her eyes and sighed. She pointed her knobkerrie at Marnie. "You sent everyone else up and stayed back all by yourself? Seems like a bad plan."

If Marnie felt any dismay at facing off against the four of us, she didn't show it. In fact her face remained flat and impassive as we spread out and surrounded her. "I am a Child of God. I will not stray from my Path. Though I may be tested, my faith will never fail me."

She tilted her head slightly towards Tanuki and murmured a few soft words I couldn't pick up. Tanuki scrambled out of her arms and clambered onto her back, grabbing her over the shoulders like a little monkey.

Marnie had missed the wagons but made it to the Farm on a winged lion. Now the little raccoon dog was taking her commands. Marnie had to be a beast talker. My jaw clenched. She'd been standing in my way to get the last seat on the wagon and now she was standing in my way to getting through this trial.

I had to get Tanuki away from her.

Her arms free now, Marnie reached down to her thighs and pulled out two ten-inch stilettos, the handles worked to resemble driftwood crosses. She drew the blades slowly, reverently. She kissed each blade lightly, then reversed her grip on the left, laying the blade along her forearm. Tanuki rode calmly on her back, not even making a sound.

Marnie assumed a fighting crouch, her eyes flicking left to right, tracking our movements. "Come, unbelievers. Come test yourself against me."

Yvonne swung her knobkerrie off her shoulders and cracked her neck. Her knees went loose like she was standing on a listing ship. Wen's robes fluttered around his ankles, and he smiled at Marnie.

Minji hopped up and down, her clapping hands a blur. "Ooh! Ooh! Are we starting now?"

I twirled Thor, then Loki, limbering my wrists. I should have brought the spear, giving me more reach, but we had four to one odds.

Easy peasy. Sixty points were as good as mine.

15

TICK TOCK

Fighting with a raccoon dog hanging off your shoulders should have been ludicrous. The kind of anxiety fueled nightmare that would plague you before a big fight. It should have been impossible.

Marnie made it look effortless.

Minji was the first of us into the center, a blur of fruit-scented color and wind. Her high, chirping laugh warbled as she passed me. Marnie turned to one side and in a smooth motion dropped to her knees and rolled. Minji's laugh cut off as Marnie took her out at the knees and sent her careening toward the edge of the clearing.

Wen jumped. His robes flared around him and he collided with Minji in midair. The monk wrapped his arms and legs around the smaller woman just as the two of them slammed into a boulder, taking the brunt of the impact on his back instead of Minji's head. Minji squeaked and the two of them fell unconscious to the dirt.

I swept to my left, staying across the clearing from Yvonne. We started a slow, counterclockwise rotation. Marnie got back to her feet and presented her profile to both of us, trying to keep us both in view. Tanuki seemed to have gone to sleep on her back.

The wolf howls in the distance were now intermingled with human shouts and cries of pain. Marnie twitched her head in the direction of the sound. "You should go help them. They are hopelessly outnumbered."

The nerve of this one. "You should talk about being outnumbered."

Marnie laughed, a sound completely without humor and her eyes fixed on mine. "Roxy, I could fight a hundred of you. You're in this for money. I'm in this for justice."

Before she'd finished her last sentence Yvonne closed the distance, the gnarled head of her knobkerrie swinging around in a vicious arc aimed at the back of Marnie's head. Marnie pivoted to her left, a subtle motion that brought the sleeping Tanuki in line with the descending club.

Yvonne's eyes went wide and her shoulders tensed as she tried to arrest the inexorable momentum of her weapon. Under the shifting torque her footing gave way on the muddy ground.

I launched myself forward. I couldn't save Yvonne but I knew an opening when I saw one.

Marnie pivoted back towards Yvonne as the witch-warrior fell to the ground. She drew back her right hand. "Your concern for innocents is duly noted, and appreciated."

The cruciform stiletto swung down and the butt of the handle connected with Yvonne's temple with a sound like splitting wood. Yvonne's eyes rolled up and she collapsed into the mud.

My legs propelled me up into an overhead strike. My right arm came down, Thor's polished steel head whistling through the damp air. Marnie twisted at the waist, brought both her knives up and caught the head of my hammer in the crotch between the blades, stopping my strike an inch from her face.

Her arms held as firm as steel and the shock of the impact blasted up to my shoulders.

She raised one eyebrow to me, her eye framed between her blades. "Hammers? Truly?"

Everyone was a critic. "They were my dad's hammers."

I twisted Thor, but now Marnie tilted her blades together, trapping my hammer. She jerked down with her arms and nearly pulled me to my knees. Her voice dripped with condescension. "The Twilight is no place for a child playing with her father's toys."

She pulled, yanking me to the right but I hung onto my hammer. Marnie snarled through the rain dripping down her face. "You don't have the conviction to be a Slayer."

Heat flushed up my back and I snarled back at her. "My father was a Slayer and I will take his place among them!"

I swung Loki up from behind me. Marnie jerked back but now I pulled with Thor, and her stilettos came with me. Loki came up underneath, between her hands and I locked the heads of my hammers together. I twisted and brought both hammers with me like I was swinging for the fences. The force pulled the stilettos from Marnie's grasp and flung them across the clearing where they landed in the mud with a plop.

Marnie hissed, the sound like a wounded animal. "You are unworthy!"

She reached down and pulled out two hatchets from her boots. Both with curving blades and handles of polished driftwood. "This is your last chance, Roxy."

Rain pelted down on us and ground melted to sludge beneath our feet.

I was a full head taller than Marnie, I had longer reach, and I wasn't carrying a squirming creature on my back. I knew all this intellectually but I couldn't shake the feeling that Marnie was going to slip through my fingers. I couldn't let her outplay me. I hooked my hammers back onto my belt and pulled out my throwing axe and piece of jerky.

I squinted through the sheets of rain and let the lines of my magic narrow in on my opponent. Her vest had weakened from Tanuki's weight. With a little encouragement it would rip easily.

The hatchets were a problem.

I feinted to the right, then dove into the mud, tucking into a forward roll aimed at her ankles, nearly identical to the move she'd used to take out Minji. With a grunt, Marnie tipped backwards. As she folded she slammed down and the handle of her hatchet found the back of my thigh.

The pain was a sharp bite, then a spreading fire before leaving behind a trail of numbness in its wake. Tears stung my eyes and I blinked as I slashed at the side of her vest. Marnie's eyes went wide as my blade passed within inches of her torso. The keen edge of my hatchet parted the straining cotton and her vest fell apart.

Tanuki screeched and clambered down the shreds of Marnie's outerwear. Once the raccoon dog was clear I flipped the hatchet and smashed the butt into her ribcage.

A part of me hoped I broke a rib. But all I needed was for her to get off me, which she did, instinctively putting distance between me and my weapon. We rolled away from each other, both of us covered in mud and slime. I wiped the sludge from my eyes as we circled. Tanuki ambled near Marnie's feet, shaking the water out of his fur.

Lightning flashed again, bathing the clearing in blinding light. When my vision cleared Marnie wasn't looking at me. She was looking up.

I dove to my left just as Wen landed. His robes were filthy and sodden, but his expression was still the calm of a placid lake. His feet touched softly on the mud and a pair of whip chains fell from his sleeves. He flicked his wrists and the whip chains danced like writhing snakes.

He didn't take his eyes off Marnie. "Roxy. Get Tanuki."

Wind and rain swirled around Wen and his whips flew out in a whirling dance. In a flurry of twisting movement, the whips snapped out and nailed Marnie, one in the ribs, one cracking across her ankle.

She screamed in pain and fell back into the mud. I couldn't lie, I felt a moment of satisfaction watching her take another hit in the ribs.

I backed away and turned back to our primary objective–retrieving the target.

Tanuki scrambled in the mud and I went after him, sliding on all fours. "Here, boy!"

I waved the jerky and prayed the pouring rain didn't erase the scent of the ushi-oni jerky. He halted and sat back on his rear. Even sopping wet, he was pretty adorable.

I tore the jerky and tossed a bit at him. He lunged for it and then dashed towards me. "Good boy!"

I threw a couple more bits of jerky and forty pounds of wet, muddy raccoon dog crawled into my arms, wet, icy cold claws popping through my duster. I sucked in my breath and winced at the pain of his slicing claws.

From my peripheral vision, Wen's twirling whip chains churned up a thundering cyclone of water and mist. Tanuki took all my concentration because thirty pounds of raccoon dog trying to eat through your pockets is demanding that way. But the glint of silver in the mud still grabbed my attention. Marnie's stiletto's lay half buried within arm's reach. I wrapped my arm tighter around Tanuki and stretched for the blade.

Marnie screamed, "Yield!"

With an ear splitting shriek Marnie flung a hatchet at me. I chose discretion over valor and twisted away, throwing myself and Tanuki into the mud. Wen launched up, his leg stretched out in an impossible lunge. His whip chain lashed out and knocked the hatchet off course. So instead of spinning at my head, the hatchet swerved off course and drew another white hot line of agony across my thigh. I screamed, burying my face in Tanuki's side.

I tensed, sure that the next blow was coming for my neck. My magic lashed out, panic driving it from me in reckless waves until it latched onto the granite stone behind Marnie. I could Break it, bring tons of stone down on her head, bury her in the rubble. My magic wormed into the ancient stone like a greedy child, searching for faultlines, however small. A scream built in my chest like a growing tide and power flowed into the stone, swelling it to bursting from within.

The stone cracked with a sound like a cannon shot. The stone was ancient, raised in the time of the Drowning, and heavy with the inertia of history. A scream in my gut burst forth. Then the recoil landed on me with the force of a bomb, rocking my head back.

My scream faded to a whimper and I collapsed, the cold mud soaking into the holes that Tanuki had made in my coat. A frisson of broken glass crawled across my body, raking all my nerves with icy fire. If I could have controlled my hands I would have clawed my eyes out. My grip on Tanuki relaxed and everything became muted and distant. No, no. *Dad, I tried.* My eyes closed as pain drowned me. The world tilted and then all I could see was the throbbing orange light of Aislinn's timer. With each second the light pulsed and grew until it filled my world.

THE ORANGE LIGHT SHRANK, the fuzzed out edges slowly fading back into sharp focus until it became the alert light on dad's IV monitor at his bedside. The machine beeped, a shrill sound that demanded attention. A kinked line, an empty bag, or time for medicines.

Dad groaned and wiped a skeletal hand across his sunken cheeks.

"Roxy, shut that damn thing off."

I hurried over, careful to step around the supplies piled at the foot of the hospital bed. Bottles of meds that solved symptoms, but not diseases. My shaking hands needed three tries to find the right button to cancel the alarm, then two tries to pop open the machine and install another vial of meds. Only when I finally managed to get the door shut and the meds flowing did dad relax into his pillow, a soft sigh escaping his lips. I brushed away the layer of empty takeout containers and collapsed into the folding chair and checked the time.

Jasper would be home soon. With mom's diagnosis, we had taken to splitting shifts, going back and forth between home and the hospital. My brother was a good kid, but the strain was starting to show. He'd missed too much school, and he was falling behind, even though I knew he'd never mention it. Ava wouldn't be home until late. She'd managed to pick up some extra shifts, and the money helped us limp along, if only for another day or week. It didn't matter. I couldn't think or plan beyond the next day anyway.

I must have dozed off because the next thing I knew, dad's hand was wrapped around my wrist, squeezing with surprising gentleness. His fingers were long and bony, his nails turned yellow from the side effects of the meds. But this time when I looked at him, his eyes were clear and sharp.

His grip tightened, and when he spoke, his voice was stronger than I'd heard in weeks. "Roxybear, I need you to do something for me."

I'd been doing everything for him for months now. "Sure, dad. Sure. Anything. What do you need, a pillow? Some juice?"

My wrist ached as his fingers clenched down. "Promise me you'll take care of your mother, Roxy. Promise me you'll do what I couldn't."

"What? Dad, mom's..." The words stuck, even though I knew I had to say them. "Mom's just working late, she'll--"

"I'm not so far gone that I can't see what's happening. I know you're trying to protect me, but I don't need it. Your mother does."

Tears welled in his eyes and his voice broke. "I wasn't strong enough, Roxy. I wasn't strong enough for any of you. I wish... I wish..."

His eyes clouded over and I watched the haze of the meds seep across his consciousness like a blanket pulled over his face. I clutched his hand in mine, a small part of me horrified at how brittle it felt, like I could snap his bones with my fingers.

I brought his hand to my face and kissed his scarred knuckles. "I promise, dad. I'll do whatever it takes for mom. For all of us."

Dad's clouded eyes seemed to pass through me. "Don't break your promises... Don't break... I was the Breaker, Roxybear, did I ever tell you? I broke the world once..."

THE RECOIL SLOWLY FADED. As it passed, sound and light returned. The first sensation I was aware of was another hand on mine, fingertips pressed gently into the inside of my wrist. Tension and pain seemed to flow down my arm, draining away. My mind cleared enough for me to see Wen, kneeling at my side. His eyebrows lifted as our eyes met.

"That was unwise, Roxy."

I coughed, the spasms bending me over. I half expected to find blood in my hands. "I didn't mean to do that."

Then I remembered why I was lying in the mud and I jerked up. The world swam but Marnie was nowhere in sight.

Wen steadied me with a hand on my shoulder. "I was able to chase her off, but we can't stay here."

Marnie was headed for Tabi at Black Base, I knew it. Given the way she had charmed Tanuki into cooperating with her, I didn't doubt now that she could lure Tabi away from Red Lion. We wouldn't be able to sweep all the points.

Our only chance now was to get Tanuki back to Black Base before Marnie made it back to White Base with Tabi.

I flattened two hands against a nearby boulder and got up on one knee. A hairline crack emerged from the mud and ran up the center of the stone, splitting off into tiny tributaries as it rose above me. I had barely cracked the stone, and the effort had nearly killed me. Blood soaked my pants and ran pink in the rain. I swayed.

Wen got an arm around me. Even with his help, the added weight of the squirming raccoon dog was too much. My right leg gave out and I stumbled. Wen hoisted my right arm over his shoulder and we made a sad three legged man progress to where Yvonne was slumped.

A few yards away, Minji's petite form lay deathly still and her skin had taken on a blue tone.

I looked up at the timer, its glowing shape pouring sand faster and faster to the bottom.

We were running out of time.

I looked at my leg, in no condition to run back. My throat tightened and it had nothing to do with the pain in my leg, or the recoil still fraying my nerves. It had everything to do with the sickening nausea of failure rising in my gut. I looked down at Yvonne and Minji. Someone needed to stay with them and try to revive them. Between me and Wen, I was the smart choice to stay behind. Assuming I could slow my bleeding down.

I forced the words out and they were bitter ash on my lips. "Wen, you can still make it." If he made it back first, the team could still score enough points to put us through. To put me through. I just had to trust that he could do it.

He shook his head. "No, we all can still make it. We can stick with the plan. You can take Tanuki back to get the points."

"I propose a new plan, Roxy, one where we all bring Tanuki back."

I didn't have it in me to argue with him. Finally I said, "I'm going to need a piece of your robe."

16

BLACK BASE

For the record, carrying an excited raccoon dog wasn't as much fun as you would think. First, they have claws. Sharp claws. Second, Tanuki didn't listen at all. And thanks to my treats, he was amped up on demon jerky, just to make things extra interesting. Add the fact that I had only one good leg, and I had the makings of a comedy except for the part where I was sobbing from frustration and pain.

I used ribbons of Wen's robe to bind my wound and tie my wrecked leg to his. We were now literally the three-legged man. The tourniquet did a good job of slowing the bleeding. But I knew the more time I spent with one, the worse it was for my leg.

The Veil had many amazing aspects to it, but good medical care was not one of them. I needed stitches, and soon. But I tried to take it one hobble at a time, relying on Wen's calm voice to keep me focused.

I had lost a lot of blood and wasn't thinking straight. Wen had taken over and for once, I was glad to no longer be in charge.

Wen used some amazing acupressure to revive Minji and

Yvonne, both of whom were a little groggy but otherwise only bruised up. Then Minji tried to run back to Black Base and ended up sprawled back in the mud, her face a mask of confusion.

One way or another, we had to get back. Wen nodded into the mist. "Yvonne, take Minji with you. Scout ahead and make sure she doesn't run."

Minji scowled. "Awww..."

Wen looked down at the mess of my leg, tied to his. "We'll do our best to keep up."

Yvonne nodded. "Listen for my call." She dragged Minji out of the clearing, keeping a firm hand on the smaller woman's hand.

Wen turned to me. "Ready?"

"Not really--"

Wen launched us out of the clearing and into impossibly thick fog. By some miracle we didn't smash into a rock face or leap out over a sheer cliff. Maybe Wen was really good at listening to the voice of the universe. I concentrated on not passing out and keeping Tanuki from squirming out of my arms. Between leaps we paused to listen for sounds of our teammates. Grunts and shrieks echoed and the clash of steel bounced off the rocks.

Ahead of us, Yvonne's faint whistles beckoned us forward. We bounded from boulder to boulder as I struggled to keep Tanuki under control. Flashes of pain flared up and down my leg, turning my leg icy cold and burning hot in alternating waves. Yvonne's next whistle was much louder and Wen directed us down. When we hit the ground my leg gave way and the cloth binding me to the monk parted. My breath rushed out as I hit the ground and Tanuki scrambled out of my grip.

Minji squealed and tackled the raccoon dog. "Tanuki! Who's a good boy?"

Yvonne materialized out of the mist. "The path is clear from here to Black Base. No sign of Marnie."

Cold sweat slicked my hair down to my neck and I choked back the urge to vomit. Dark stars danced across my vision and I swallowed what was left of my battered pride. "I'm not going to make it back. Take Tanuki back with you. Make sure the team wins."

Minji's eyes widened. "What about you?"

Goddess, was she going to make me say it? I gritted my teeth and got to my feet, closing my eyes as the landscape seemed to tilt and sway. "I'll make my own way back. Give the dog to Wen. Cover his back."

Strong hands grabbed my arms and two sets of shoulders tucked in under me. I opened my eyes to find Yvonne and Minji holding me up. Wen had a surprisingly docile Tanuki held close to his chest.

I squinted at the raccoon dog. "Faker."

Tanuki panted, his tongue lolling out. Yvonne tipped her head. "Get the raccoon dog back to base, Wen. We'll get Roxy home."

"Hey..."

Wen gave us a quick bow, turned, and leapt, disappearing into the mist without a sound. Yvonne and Minji supported me as we limped off in the same direction. I clamped down on the pain with every step that jostled my injured leg.

The hourglass in the sky pulsed an ominous, dark orange, with only a small pile of sand in the upper glass now. "We're not all going to make it. You should leave me."

Yvonne blew out her breath. "Not with that attitude we're not."

My experience in the Twilight had so far shown me that my father had been right. Nearly everyone who came here was looking out for themselves. I had included Yvonne and Minji in my plan to maximize my possible points in this exercise. Their best play right now was to leave me behind as the dead weight I'd become.

"Why are you doing this?"

Yvonne shifted her shoulder under mine. "You didn't leave us behind. That counts for a lot in my book."

I couldn't. "That was Wen. He needed you to scout the way back for us."

"Mmm." She didn't sound convinced.

Another ten painful meters forward and Yvonne jerked to the right as if something had caught her eye. I squeezed her shoulder. "What is it?"

We veered right and shapes materialized out of the mist. Gray, shaggy shapes the size of . Wolves, at least four of them, lay bloodied and unconscious around a small clearing between the stones. Near one of the larger stones, Dario lay with his arms in a death grip around the neck of another wolf. They were both unconscious.

Minji whistled as she surveyed the carnage. "He did all this? Himself?"

Yvonne smiled. "Apparently."

Something about her smile hinted at history between the two of them. Yvonne knew more than she was letting on. I pulled my arm off her shoulder and Minji sagged under my weight. The witch warrior turned to me in surprise.

I nodded towards Dario. "Go. Get him. We'll bring him back with us."

Yvonne held my gaze for a moment. "That counts, too." In two steps she was at Dario's side, pulling the werewolf off him with seemingly little effort. Yvonne knelt at Dario's side and shook the young man lightly. He roused and she whispered a few quiet words to him.

Dario rolled to his feet and moved across the clearing. With one muscular arm he picked up an unconscious werewolf, revealing Augusto buried underneath. The big man was almost unrecognizable, his face and chest covered in slash wounds and dried blood. Dario grabbed his friend by the waist and hauled him up onto his shoulder. As he trudged by under his load he winked at me.

Goddess.

Yvonne got her shoulder back under mine. I caught the hint of a smile in her voice. "Do we need him to scout ahead, too?"

I scowled. "Let's go. Wen's probably wondering what's taking us so long."

Yvonne found Axel partially trapped under a boulder that had been tipped over on him. Despite the size of the massive rock, Axel only seemed merely perturbed at being pinned. Yvonne used her knobkerrie, and with Dario adding another shoulder, they levered the stone up enough to let Axel scramble out from underneath. If Yvonne noticed my none-too-furtive glances at the dwindling hourglass in the sky, she didn't comment.

The six of us limped back to Black Base. Well, four of us limped, Augusto was carried, and I hobbled between Yvonne and Minji. My leg had turned into a constant, cold throb of pain from hip to toes. But the pain was good. The pain reminded me I still had a leg. The pain kept me upright when I wanted to lay in the mud and cry.

If Aislinn was watching, I was sure we were the sorriest bunch of Slayer candidates she had ever seen.

Until we reached the clearing for Black Base and my vision tunneled down to the wooden cage in the center of the clearing. Rather, the shattered remnants of the cage that had once held Tabi. Behind the cage was something new, a lone maple, its big leaves dark gray in the mist. A glowing mesh sphere of orange light sat high in its branches. Wen and Tanuki were nowhere in sight.

My arms slipped from Yvonne and Minji's shoulders and I went to my knees in the mud. I barely registered the shock of impact, or the stab of pain that shot up into my lower back.

We'd lost. Not only had we failed to return with Tanuki, we had also failed to protect Tabi. We were washing out right here, right now, and it was on me.

Dario dropped to his knees as well, setting Augusto gently on the ground. He punched a fist into the mud and cursed softly.

Minji moved ahead of me. "Tanuki? Where are you buddy?"

Behind me, Yvonne sighed, the sound thick with regret. "Roxy, I'm--"

Minji squealed.

The mist above the clearing swirled and split open. For a fraction of a second, clear, violet sky was visible in the break. A silhouette of flapping robes appeared in the slice of clear sky. Wen dropped out of the clouds with Tanuki on his back and landed softly at the base of the maple tree. He dropped Tanuki next to the tree and turned to us, sketching a quick bow.

"Apologies. Marnie was here and I did not wish to risk Tanuki."

Tanuki scrambled up the tree, nosing through the branches until he reached the glowing orange sphere. I recognized my Uncle Samuel's style. He had formed this construct–perfectly sized for the raccoon dog to enter but not for us to tamper with. Tanuki barked in delight and dived headfirst into a little bucket of fish perched on the branches within the glowing sphere. When the raccoon dog entered the sphere the tree lit up in glowing light, banishing all shadows from the clearing. The rain stopped falling above the tree and a growing circle of clear night sky expanded from there to cover the field below.

I sagged in relief at the sight. We had done this one thing right. Or at least Wen had.

Above us more light showered the sky.

I turned to look behind us. From White Base, the rain clouds had parted and beneath that clear bit of night sky radiated the same glowing orange sphere. Marnie had set little Tabi scampering up their tree as well.

The pain gnawing in my gut came back and I felt sick with despair. Had she made it to White Base first?

17

WHO GOES, WHO STAYS

The blood loss proved too much and left me laid out on my back in the mud. I struggled to keep my eyes open. At least this way I didn't need to expend any effort to keep myself up. The wound in my leg had morphed into a cold, pulsing throb of pain and my foot was completely numb. That was bad.

I didn't think the Slayers would let me die from blood loss. Maybe someone could stitch me up. But the longer I waited with this tourniquet on, the more the risk went from losing function, to losing my leg entirely.

I remembered Akhil's terrifying lightbringer magic, the way his magic has seared through the ushi-oni like a high-powered laser. The thought of him cauterizing my wound forced a whimper escaped my lips.

"Please, Dad. If you're watching, I could use some help."

I stared at the sky, blinking hard, and tears streaked down the sides of my face, hot against my icy skin.

Thankfully the fog had dissipated and Aislynn had turned off the rain spigot, so at least I wouldn't drown as I stared into the violet night sky. Unfortunately, my clothes were still soaked and the warming effects of the demon jerky had worn off. I was freezing.

But now there was a show in the sky that would tell me my fate, a good distraction from the pain and cold.

Sometimes I missed the huge holo screens that peppered the night sky over Boston, blanketing the city with news and advertisements. Sometimes. Maybe someone else missed them as well because they'd found a way to make a magic version here in the Twilight.

I missed my family, but I didn't miss much else about life on the other side.

If my little sister Ava were here, she'd be dazzled by the show. I didn't know who on the Slayers was in charge of the light show, but they certainly had a flair for the dramatic. If Jasper were here, he'd tell me tech light shows were better and at least we knew how those worked. He was all about under-standing stuff.

Me, I didn't need to understand how the magic worked. I just needed it to work *for me*. For my plan. For my mom.

Next to me Wen sat cross-legged. Minji and Yvonne sat together, heads tilted together. In companionable silence we watched the results. I didn't know that many people and I certainly didn't know their real names. But I knew Cordelia and I knew Haruto and I cared about what happened in their matchup.

Only one of their teams could advance.

Names started scrolling across the purple sky in curly script:

Cordelia of the Hinterlands

Harald Stenson, Guardian of the Northern Pass

Ulf Skardeson of the Reach

Serafina Trentini, of New Jersey

Pawat Darawan, of Thailand

Frank Elliott, of Oregon

Mason Macnamara, Eastern Ice Pack of Canada

Ilya Kirillovich, of Florida

I was happy to see Cordelia's name. She was a natural and the Slayers would be all the better for her joining it. I couldn't say the same about the mountain fae Harald and his sworn brother Ulf.

Flourishes followed, like some kind of celestial intermission and my stomach twisted as I waited for our results. We had gotten the other team's raccoon dog back to Black Base but had we done it in time? What about the fact that we had lost Tabi?

The pain of my wounds had initially distracted me from the sinking realization that I was likely going home–my time with Slayers over before it even really started. My time here behind the Veil a waste, going home a failure, and worse, empty handed, with no cure for my mother. I might as well head home and pull the plug on her myself.

My eyes stung with tears and I pawed at my face, my breath catching in my chest. The staggering enormity of my failure was a crushing weight above me. I barely registered Wen's hand on my wrist. Only when he gently pulled my arm away did I turn to face him.

Wen pointed up. "Roxy. Look."

Against the dark sky the orange and yellow flourishes had disappeared, replaced by another listing of names.

Marnie Black, of Washington

Wen Luck, of New York

Minji Kim, of California

Yvonne Peterson, of Missouri

Dario Direwolf, Lone Wolf of Brazil

Augustin Bravo, of Mexico

Axel Walsh, of Ireland

Roxanne Lim, of Massachusetts

I sagged into the dirt and sobbed now in earnest. I had made it. Somehow, what I had done, what *we* had done, had been enough. My body ached all over. My back felt like someone had ridden Agnes over it. Where Marnie had cut me, my right leg alternated between fiery pain and numbness. Neither of which was promising. But I was going to live to fight another day.

Wen patted my shoulder.

I wiped my eyes and swallowed hard. I had gotten this far, and I had another shot. I tried not to let bitterness at Marnie's ranking overshadow this win. Because this was a win. It hadn't been pretty and it hadn't been certain, but none of that mattered now. The only thing I needed to focus on was the next trial. Sixteen of us were going in, but only three were getting a place with the Slayers. I needed to be one of those three.

Dad had prepared me for this. Mom was counting on me.

"Sweet!" Minji jumped to her feet, whooped and spun in a tiny circle. Then she grabbed her head and sagged against Yvonne who wrapped her arm around Minji's waist and pulled her in tight.

Augustin was leaning on an enormous gray wolf. He limped slightly and held his ribs as they made their way over to me and Wen. Wen leaned down and looked at the blood-soaked shreds of his robe that adorned my leg.

"You've lost a lot of blood."

"Probably."

"I'm concerned."

I was too but I gave Wen a tiny smile. "It will be okay."

I hoped.

Wen abruptly stood up and moved his arms, gesturing vigorously. What was he doing? The wolf's ears rose, tips quivering. Then Yvonne smiled. "Fortune is smiling upon us."

Samuel and Akhil appeared at the edge of the clearing. As usual, my uncle was scowling, his face cast in thunder. In contrast, Akhil had an easy smile and his calm demeanor put me at ease.

Akhil knelt at my side. "Let's take a look at that leg."

I strained to get up to my elbows. My back screamed from even that much effort. Akhil placed his hand on the side of my head, his palm glowing with soft gold light. I flinched but Akhil's hand didn't pause until he cupped my cheek. Warmth spread from the Slayer's hand, pouring into my head and melting away the icy cold that had dragged my thoughts to a crawl. My arms tingled, my nerves jangling as life rushed back into my limbs. I bit down on a scream as feeling returned to my leg and the cut across my thigh lit up like a red hot poker laid over my skin.

Akhil grunted. "Samuel. Now."

My uncle opened his fist and brilliant light spilled from his fingers. My team gasped and luckily for me, the blinding pain in my leg saved me from trying to keep my poker face.

In my uncle's palm was a glowing orange Crystal about as big as his thumb, delicately carved in the shape of a rose. A small hole had been bored into one side through which a length of fine silver chain was threaded and secured to my uncle's wrist. The Crystal shone with brilliant light, the petals so razor edged they looked sharp enough to cut skin.

This was Samuel's Midnight Rose, the only thing that truly separated a full fledged Slayer from those who might pretend to the name. A tiny vial made of pure Crystal, forged by a sect of monks whose existence had been wiped from the earth decades ago, then enchanted by a coven that the Night Queen had drunk down to the bones she wore on her wrist. No one knew how to make these any more and Roses were the only known means of safely transporting and preserving the most vital substance in all of the Twilight, vampire blood.

The massive wolf at Augustin's side melted away and Dario appeared at Augustin's side, both their eyes glued to the Rose. This was how the Slayers had built their power in Seattle, how teams of Slayers could march into a den of wolves, a circle of witches, or a rove of vampires and still be assured of victory. It allowed mere humans to stand toe to toe with those who had been strengthened by magic. It cured all physical wounds and blood disorders.

Samuel knelt next to Akhil and looked around, making sure to make eye contact with everyone around us. "Just so you all know, there's no favorites here. Aislinn is patching up some of Cordelia's crew. And we're fixing up the rest of Marnie's team as well, even if they didn't make the cut. The Slayers stand together."

Akhil echoed quietly, "Stand together."

My uncle lifted the Midnight Rose into his fingers. "You kids have probably heard endless stories about this, nearly all of them untrue."

His eyes hardened to stones. "This isn't some fairy book magic. This is the real power of the Twilight, and power always comes with a cost. Always."

With a stroke of his finger the Crystal shuddered and the center of the Rose bloomed open, darkness swirling within. In one smooth motion he shoved the Rose into my mouth and clamped his big hand over my lips.

I couldn't help it. I swallowed reflexively. Thick, oily blood coursed over my tongue and down my throat. The taste of copper and salt overwhelmed me. It didn't matter that I'd swallowed, it felt like the blood ran down my throat of its own accord, leaving a drying, itchy trail of salt in its wake. I tried to cough but Samuel kept his hand clamped over my mouth.

"Hang on, Roxy. You will live to slay another day."

Stupidly, I tried to say something around his big hand, until the vamp blood finally hit and I stopped trying to make any sense of anything. The vamp blood lit a fire in my belly and traced its way out to my limbs.

When Akhil's magic had revived me from my cold and

numbness, it had felt like a soothing heat, like warming myself next to a camp fire.

The vampire blood ignited a raging inferno in my core that raced down my nerves and set my arms and legs tingling. Every cut and bruise on my body lit up like a signal flare, but where there had just been aches and pains, there was now only sensual, liquid warmth.

I held out for as long as I could, about another second, before a gasp of utter ecstasy escaped my lips. My eyes flew open and stars chased my vision as my head whipped back and forth in the mud. Pulsing heat rolled up and down my body like a lover's caress, driving my senses wild. It was mind-blowing sex and world-class food and warm hugs and punching your enemy in the mouth, all rolled into one seamless sensation that poured over me like a scalding hot shower.

When the feeling passed I was spent. I had all the backbone of a wrung-out dishrag, gasping in the mud, trying to hold tight to the last wisps of the feeling as the vamp blood dissipated through my body.

My breath came in panting gasps and my heart hammered in my chest like an animal trying to get out. As my breathing slowed I was able to focus again on the clearing around me and the rest of my team.

And what had apparently been an embarrassing healing session. Samuel and Wen stood a bit off to the side with the werewolves, their faces studiously turned away from me. Axel sat with his back against one of the large boulders, his eyes closed, ignoring the rest of the world again. Akhil had disappeared.

Only Minji stood close to me, in fact she was staring intently at me, her hands on her knees, her eyes wide and bright.

"Oh, wow, Roxy, that looked amazing! I can't wait to try it!" She gave a little squeal.

From behind, Yvonne cuffed Minji lightly on the ear. "Enough with that kind of talk. The Slayers only use their Roses for deadly injuries. Count yourself lucky, jackrabbit."

I didn't know how to explain, but I finally understood the Midnight Rose. It was how the Slayers could honor their motto–Live to Slay Another Day. And now I wanted it even more, to get my ink, get my Rose and save my mom. It was everything that I had hoped for and nothing and no one was going to stop me.

Minji pouted and then smiled like we were sharing a secret. "I bet it was totally worth it. It was worth it, wasn't it?"

Before I could answer, a gasp of breath caught my attention. Marnie appeared between two of the stones at the edge of the clearing, her eyes focused on me. With a growl Marnie stomped over the muddy field, making a bee line for me.

Minji pivoted to stand over me. "Uh-oh. Someone looks unhappy."

Samuel peeled himself away from the boys and smoothly intercepted her. My uncle placed his considerable bulk between us and simply held up a hand to stop Marnie. She stopped and pointed an accusing finger at my uncle. Her voice was hot with outrage.

"We are supposed to be ridding Seattle of vampires, not partaking of their unholy blood. Are the Slayers so weak as to debase themselves like this?"

My uncle bore the verbal assault with equanimity. "Roxy lost a lot of blood. At your hand, I might add. Unless you know of a convenient blood bank for transfusions--"

Marnie cut him off. "She's weak and unworthy."

I guess Marnie wasn't holding back her feelings for me anymore.

Samuel put a hand on Marnie's shoulder and turned the young woman around. "Until you prove yourself worthy to get your ink as a Slayer, you have no say in how we treat our own. If you had been as badly injured, we would have healed you as well."

Marnie swung her arm up and batted Samuel's hand away. She hissed. She actually hissed. "I would rather die than be sullied by vampire blood!"

She swept the clearing with flinty eyes. "You think you're strong, but your lust for the vampire's power makes you weak. And weakness has no place in the Twilight."

Her eyes zeroed in on me. I tried to get up on my elbows and at least make a show of standing up to her, but my arms felt like wet noodles and my hands still weren't obeying my instructions. Instead of sitting up to look Marnie in the eye, I ended up flopping around in the mud like a dying fish.

Marnie finally pulled her eyes from me and looked up at my uncle. If she was at all cowed by the fact that he towered over her by at least a foot, or outweighed her by at least a hundred pounds, it didn't show. She turned on her heel, giving me another disgusted look before she left the clearing.

I flopped back into the mud. "I guess I gave her a reason to hate me?"

Minji smiled cheerfully. "More. You gave her a reason to hate you more."

Great.

18

DELIGHTFUL DISTRACTIONS

W here there had been a gaping wound from Marnie's axe, I now had a shiny pink line to remind me of how I'd almost bled to death. I also had a heightened sense of awareness of everything around me, the air on my skin, the scents and sights all felt dialed up. Did vampires feel like this all the time? I'd had a thimble full of vamp blood and felt incredibly alive. There was good reason it was called Cure. Even a little Cure would turn mom's treatment around. Instead of spending her days drained from her treatments, if she could have even a fraction of the vitality I was feeling now...

I had to get my hands on a Midnight Rose of my own.

I couldn't let her down.

My resolve hardened and I hefted my bag onto the wagon. Cordelia offered me a hand so I took it and hopped up next to her.

The wagon held half of the winners of the first round of the Trials. Another wagon held the other eight winners, all of us in slightly less cramped conditions than when we arrived at the farm only a few days ago. The other fifteen from our cohort were nowhere to be seen. I was the last one to board the wagon and took an end seat next to Cordelia.

Somehow we'd ended up with nearly the same seating arrangements as when we arrived. Wen and Axel filled out the bench on our side. The two of them sat quietly with their eyes closed. Maybe they were meditating?

Harald and Ulf sat on the other side, and I noted, towards the far end of the wagon, as if to keep as much space between them and Cordelia as possible. Marnie and Dario took the seats opposite me and Cordelia.

Haruto wasn't here, which was sobering.

Thirty one of us had started this Trial, but only sixteen would go through the last Trial.

I easily could have been with Haruto on the earlier wagons leaving the Farm. Marnie's blow had nearly cost me my leg. There was no conceivable way I could have gotten back to Base on my own, or lived to complain about it. Wen could have taken the raccoon dog and finished. Heck, any of them could have. In their place, I would have. But they didn't. Instead, he and Yvonne had bullied me into moving, patched me up and carried me back to the finish.

Maybe the Trials weren't about who was the best fighter. Maybe the Trials were about who could work best together with other Slayers.

The Twilight was harsh, I knew Marnie was right about that. But a solo human fighter could only do so much against a shifter or a vampire or a demon. Dad had taught me to fight alone, but that hadn't worked out so well for me in the first Trial. Only by teaming up with Cordelia had I gotten on the wagon. Only by Wen and Yvonne's efforts had I made it through the second Trial.

Dad had always told me to count on myself, but maybe that wasn't enough.

I looked around me. These guys were it. They could either knock me out of the last Trial, or help me through it.

Which would it be?

I hadn't yet asked Cordelia how her Trial had gone, but from the way Harald studiously stared past the horses, it looked like there was no love lost between those two. Ulf, however, managed to make brief eye contact with the two of us, before dropping his gaze to the floorboards.

As Ulf seemed to study the bottom of the wagon I nudged Cordelia. "What happened with those two?"

She sniffed. "Their pride."

Cordelia seemed to think that was answer enough, and refused to say any more.

Dario leaned forward with his elbows on his knees. His eyes were bright with excitement and took in the three of us.

"So? Who are you hoping for in the next round?"

I'd done my research, but was somewhat surprised to know that Dario had done the same. Even so, I didn't want to give anything away. "Who what?"

The werewolf winked at me. "No need to be coy. Mentors. We each get assigned a mentor for the next round."

He turned to Marnie. "You first. Which Slayer makes the best mentor for a Crossie?"

Marnie's sneer could have curdled fresh milk. "See, this is the difference between me, and all of you. I come to the Trials, trained and prepared to wage war. You are all children. I need no mentor to teach me."

With that pronouncement she turned away from us to stare out at the passing greenery. I had to give her points for confidence.

Dario shifted to Cordelia smoothly. "I imagine you're pulling for Aislinn. I've heard stories about that one that would curl your hair!"

Cordelia's face went still. "If you knew the stories I knew... You wouldn't be speaking about her like that."

I filed that little nugget away for later. Maybe I could pump some information out of my uncle. Of course I'd known what Dario was hinting at. Truthfully, I held out hope that Samuel would be my mentor. It seemed only right. But saying it aloud seemed like a bad idea. "Who are you hoping for, Dario? Altan?"

Dario made a face like he was considering it. "That old man? I mean, I'm sure he's seen a lot of action. But you know what they say, you learn best from someone better...or bigger... than you."

I rolled my eyes. "You want someone bigger. Than Altan."

The werewolf smiled, all sharp teeth. "How about you?"

I played it casual. "I'm just happy I made it through the first round. Any of the Slayers would be a unique learning opportunity."

I'd thought Cordelia had drifted away but she broke back into the conversation. "Not all of them. Not Kotori."

Dario's smile faded. "Right. Not Kotori."

I looked between the flirtatious wolf and the short fae and wondered how they'd suddenly found common ground on this issue and why I didn't have the same kind of intel. My time in Seattle had been peppered by moments like this where I felt a day late and a credit short.

"Why not Kotori?"

Dario shuddered dramatically, his shoulders hunching.

Cordelia's eyes went back and forth, as if checking to see who else was listening in. "She hasn't mentored a candidate in years," she whispered. "They say she and her candidate were ambushed and nearly drained by a peril of rogues."

As she spoke, Cordelia's eyes trembled. "Kotori used her Rose to save herself, and then staked her candidate to prevent her from rising."

Dario grunted. "Yeah, I don't know about you, but I'd hope my mentor would have a few other options in mind before staking me through the heart."

I scowled at both of them and turned back to watching the countryside. The Slayers' reputation was sterling. Whatever stories had spread about Kotori had to be wild rumors. Still, I kept my fingers crossed that I would have Samuel as my sensei.

I KICKED HARDER to propel my skateboard and zoomed past the two Supplicants from the Church of the Sharpened Cross who hollered at me, "Repent, sister. We can save your soul!"

I was more worried about my body at this point. I was starving.

My apartment was just a few blocks away and I felt the need to rush home. Mrs. Chu had been watching my pigeons, Dumpling and Noodle. I was sure they were fine, but I couldn't help feeling a bit anxious, having been away for so long. I finally had some good news to share with my family on the other side of the Veil. Jasper and Ava didn't totally understand my zeal to get into Slayers, but I hadn't shared my full plan with them. I wouldn't share my plan by pigeon, but I still wanted to let them know I'd passed the first Trial.

A bell tinkled behind me and I turned to see Jimbo barreling towards me on his minty green Peugeot bicycle, the basket in front loaded with groceries. Food. My stomach growled, reminding me that my last meal at the Farm had been a while ago. The thought of another bite of demon jerky locked my throat up.

"Hey Jimbo."

"Roxy! How'd it go?"

I slowed my skateboard, scooping it up and strapping it to

my back. Jimbo hopped off his bike and we walked side by side back to the apartment.

I smiled and puffed out my chest. "You're looking at a next round candidate for Slayers."

Jimbo high fived me. "We knew you'd make it!"

Jimbo was so sweet. His apple cheeked face was flushed with exertion and was almost as red as his hair. He'd spoken with total conviction about my Trials and I was really touched by the faith he had in my abilities. Then I remembered I hadn't fixed their leaky kitchen faucet.

"Hey, did you guys still need me to take a look at the faucet?"

"Yeah, that would be great. Henry would really appreciate it."

"Sure thing, just let me get squared away and I'll take care of it today."

Between the two of them, Henry was the chef and was no doubt complaining about the faucet. Maybe I'd get some of his famous lasagne out of them when I did the fix. My stomach growled on cue.

The cheery yellow building of our apartment was just ahead and it was such a relief to see the place I called home in Seattle.

My steps quickened and I made a plan with Jimbo to head over to their unit once I had washed up and settled in. My feet pounded up the concrete steps, and then I came to a sudden halt in front of my unit.

I'd forgotten about the ghost.

His tattered cloak fluttered, transparent but vaguely green. Right, he was the kid from the Herbal College. What had Jimbo said his name was? I racked my brain.

"Uhh. Hi, Ernest."

The ghost floated a few inches closer, his hollowed out face uncomfortably close.

"Slayer?" he mouthed.

"Yes. I mean, no. Not yet. Almost. I passed the first Trial."

I was still so happy about it that it didn't get old saying it, even to a ghost.

I gestured to the door. "Do you mind scooting over so I can get in?"

It seemed rude to just walk through Ernest. I mean, it's not like he could feel it, but then what did I know? It's not like I was with the Necromancers Guild. I had no idea how any of it worked.

Ernest obliged me and floated across the stairwell so I could get through. I waved to him in thanks and headed into my place with a sigh of relief. Now that I was home, my shoulders sagged with exhaustion as the adrenaline drained out of me. On autopilot, I put away my things and headed out to my tiny balcony to check on my pigeons.

Noodle and Dumpling cooed from their lofts and I opened the gates. I had converted my entire balcony to a flying pen for them, which extended far beyond what would be the normal barrier of my balcony. Luckily, my landlady didn't mind and as a bit of consideration for the accommodation, I let her use them to send messages on occasion.

Dumpling was white and plump, with a gray ringed neck and a green iridescent sheen to her chest. Noodle was brown and gray, with charcoal tail feathers, his body trim and beady black eyes alert.

Back in Boston, we had a dog named Mochi and while I missed our large labrador mix with her floppy ears and goofy grin I found that the pigeons were surprisingly good company. I'd worked hard on their training and I had a system where they knew to go to the Spokane messenger post and the postal clerks there would get messages through the Veil.

I fed them their favorite sunflower seed mix and while they

pecked away, I penned a short note, rolled it up and stuck it in the small capsule that would go around Noodle's leg.

"Dear Mom, Ava, and Jasper - I passed round 1. Love, Roxy"

The urge to say more was right there, a yearning to share what had happened with my family, until Aislinn's geas clamped down on my arm and my fingers refused to move. Wow. Not even in writing. When my thoughts backed away from revealing more details of the Trials, my hand relaxed. I sighed and loaded Noodle up with his cargo. With a stroke over his head and a soft word he took wing and was gone in an instant.

I opened my bread box and grabbed the half loaf of three-day old sourdough. No mold. In short order, I sliced some smoked ham and fashioned a sandwich. I got the kettle on and brewed some oolong tea. I almost cried at how good it was to eat this simple meal standing in my tiny utilitarian kitchen.

After washing up, I headed down to Jimbo and Henry's unit. After a quick look, it was clear that my toolbox alone wasn't going to do it. I needed a particular part. That meant I needed to head to Market, which also gave me an excuse to swing by the Blue Rowan coven and visit my resident witch to spell my duster. By the luck of fate and the bounty of the river, I'd scored demon horn. Now the witch could haggle with me about whether I qualified for a Slayer's discount!

Jimbo said, "Was it hard?"

"Yeah, I almost lost my leg." I didn't sugarcoat it for him.

He gasped and pointed, "But...you're walking!"

"Yeah, I got lucky that the Slayers gave me..." and then my throat seized up.

It was Aislinn's geas again. The oath forbade speaking of the Slayer's tools of their craft. The Midnight Rose would absolutely be part of the tools of the craft. After a tense moment without air, I gasped when my throat released.

With a gulp, I finally got out, "I can't talk about it."

Jimbo nodded sagely. "Slayers keep their secrets."

The way he said it totally made me feel like I was almost a real Slayer. That I would be getting my ink soon. That I would learn more Slayer secrets.

I had to believe it. For me and for my mom. For dad.

Jimbo gave me some silver for parts since my deal with the landlady was only for my labor. I wolfed down a cold slice of Henry's excellent lasagne and headed off to Market.

THIS TIME, I remembered to avoid going through The Den.

Unfortunately, that meant passing through the Pleasure District.

My skateboard slowed and I passed a mix of bicyclists with baskets filled to mounding with groceries, small carts drawn by horses and donkeys. Two story buildings with shiny glass windows sparkled around me, as fae lights and colorful hand-blown glass lanterns dangled high above.

The buildings went on for three blocks and spread three blocks across. The plate glass offered a tantalizing show of beautiful staff. Vampire staff. Their clientele eagerly awaited the opportunity to experience the charms of the staff. Literal charms. Because the Night Queen's constituents received her gift to mesmerize their prey, and fill them with euphoria. The cost of such bliss was a small measure of blood from the clientele, mostly human, but not necessarily. Not worth it in my view. But the Veil was hard. To many here, giving up a small measure of blood in exchange for bliss was a fair trade. But for me it was a reminder that we were on the bottom of the food chain. I didn't like that one bit.

My eyes landed on the sign for Delightful Distractions, with its lavish gold font swirling across the painted black background. I'd never gone in but the wide expanse of plate glass window showed the bistro style interior, with high backed velvet sofas and Parisian style artwork. If I looked, I knew I would see champagne flowing and people in passionate embraces with clothing in disarray.

"Ready to join me for that drink?"

I nearly jumped a foot in the air. Tyee had snuck up on me, which was unsurprising since he could turn into mist.

I scowled. "Are you following me?"

"Would you like me to?"

The man's lazy smile invited me to join him in a private joke, as if he knew exactly how absurd he was. I had never given him a lick of encouragement. At least, I hadn't meant to. But it wasn't like I didn't have eyes in my head. Even worse, being the predator he was, he could detect the uptick in my pulse.

"I'm a Slayer, and you're...well, you. So, no."

"I don't see any ink, Roxy."

"I'm getting it."

It was true I didn't have my ink yet, but I would. I just had to make it through a ride along with my new sensei the Slayers assigned me, and then the last Trial. Then my first Blood Run. Then I as good as had my ink.

Tyee leaned in close, too close. I did not want a vampire anywhere in the vicinity of my neck but even as I dodged, Tyee's nostrils flared and his eyes widened slightly.

"Why, Roxy...have you been partaking from one of my staff?"

"What?! No." Then it hit me. "No...oh wait."

"Because you smell like you've had a gift from one of us, one that is rarely shared."

Tyee's voice was no longer playful. It had taken on the silky undertone of menace. They called it the Blood Gift, and it was how vampires bestowed favor on trusted humans, or between each other. It was an exchange based on power, loyalty, and in some cases, passion.

Tyee thought I had received the Blood Gift from some vampire sugar daddy. Mortification flushed my cheeks.

I took another step back. I didn't know how to explain about drinking vamp blood. I wasn't allowed to talk about the Midnight Rose due to Aislinn's geas. After the painful reminder in Jimbo's kitchen, I had learned something. I tried to talk my way around it.

"It's not what you're thinking."

"You have no idea I am thinking, *ma bichette*."

"I got hurt. Badly. During the first trial."

I gestured a bit to my leg and feigned limping, a ridiculous pantomime. But a geas knows your intent, so I skirted revealing the Midnight Rose to just talk about my injury.

Tyee's head tilted a slight fraction, his body very still.

"I can't talk about the rest," I concluded lamely.

The tight set of his jaw relaxed a touch. "Slayers and their secrets."

But his dark eyes held more secrets, and knowing. He'd smelled the vampire blood I had ingested. Despite his playboy persona he was also the Night Queen's heir. I had no illusions that Tyee would be unaware of how the Slayers conducted business. Geas or not, I wasn't going to give it to him on a platter.

Resentment and anger seared away my embarrassment. Tyee Wilder was a Prince of the Night and he was the last person in Seattle who should judge me. He walked around every day feeling vital and strong, immortal and secure in his place here.

Some of us didn't have that.

"I don't owe you any explanations." My voice went as flat as his and I matched his hard stare.

I turned on my heel and stalked past Delightful Distractions. This princeling had no hold over me. I had a duster to spell and a faucet to fix.

19

ENCHANTMENTS FOR A PRICE

The Blue Rowan Coven was known for their high quality enchantments. I didn't know what my next trial had in store for me, but I needed a little something extra to protect me. The witches were a mercenary sort, perfectly in keeping with Seattle's free market mentality. The coven's motto was "Enchantments for a Price". Luckily this time I had a pocket full of demon horn and I was ready to spend it.

I could have gone to a more seasoned witch, I'd gone with Laila on the theory she would be young and more willing to haggle than a crone would be, and her unit was on the ground floor of the corner unit which had the most potential for damage and ease for me to heroically shore up.

I mean, I could have let the whole thing collapse around the entire coven but after I met Laila, I'd decided I liked her.

Energy crackled around her here in this damp coven kitchen, and I had felt a comfortable kinship with her. She was trying to rise in the ranks in her coven, and I was trying to get in on the ground floor with Slayers so that someday I could be as legendary as my dad. A Freak of Seattle.

"Wow, that's a lot of demon horn." Laila's eyes gleamed with interest.

"Yeah, I killed one at the Slayer's Farm."

Okay, maybe I was trying to impress her. I mean, I had killed one, but I hadn't done it alone. Technically, Marnie had struck the killing blow. Still, I needed all the leverage I could get with the witch while we haggled.

"Since you don't have the Deathstalker scorpion or the black pearl powder, I'd be happy to do an ounce for ounce exchange on the demon horn."

I tilted my head and pretended to think.

In actuality, I didn't need to think. I'd gotten more information out of Altan before we'd left the Farm. The ushi-oni was a river demon and while there were many lakes and rivers around Seattle, they didn't deign to make an appearance other than at the Farm. Instead, the Seattle covens were used to getting oni horns, as the oni appearances were more frequent in Seattle proper. Oni horn was potent but didn't have the full array of benefits that ushi-oni had.

"That exchange doesn't sound quite right to me. Maybe I should double check with the Wild Rose Coven on their rates."

Laila raised a hand and made a placating wave. "I'm sure we could work something out."

I tossed her my duster, the leather stiff from its recent abuse at the Farm.

"I still need this spelled."

Laila smiled slowly, revealing tiny white teeth straightened by orthodonture from the other side of the Veil. "We can definitely work something out."

We went over the charms and protections I needed her to weave into the fabric of my duster. I left her place several ounces lighter, but with a promise my duster would be ready by three bells in two days.

WHEN I GOT BACK to my place, I found my landlady, Mrs. Chu, had left me a note.

"Soup."

Only one word, but I knew what it meant. The one word was news, an offer, and an order, all in one. She'd made a pot of something she thought I needed to drink and I'd better go up and drink it, or she would bring it down and then she would stand there until I drank it or she would pour it down my gullet. My landlady could shift into a brawny gray wolf with a terrifying warrior half form so I did what she told me.

Sometimes the soup was something innocuous, like chicken and goji berries. Other times it involved things like pig knuckles and lots of XO liquor that left me flushed and drowsy. Every time it had been simmering for hours, extracting all the nutrients possible from roasted bones and meat. She was right about me needing the collagen. Training for Slayers was hard on my joints.

Getting adopted by a Chinese werewolf granny was something I was absurdly grateful for. Uncle Samuel couldn't show me any favoritism but he'd introduced me to Mrs. Chu when I'd arrived in Seattle. She'd given me a low rent and hadn't required a security deposit. In exchange, I fixed everything that needed fixing and sometimes, she made me soup.

No matter how strange it smelled, I always drank the soup.

Today's soup was lotus root, pork ribs, and absurdly bright carrots. It was delicious and while I chewed on the carrots Mrs. Chu grilled me about the trials.

When I mentioned the injury, she set down her ladle with a hard thunk.

Despite her flowery apron and helmet of wiry gray curls, her eyes were as keen as an eagle's. "Did you drink from the Rose?"

I choked on a carrot chunk.

Cautiously, I tested the boundaries of the geas by attempting a small nod. My neck froze up and my head didn't move a millimeter.

I made a gesture zipping my lips.

Mrs. Chu hmmphed. "Slayers and their secrets."

I nodded and, relieved the geas hadn't tried to strangle me, and resumed fishing the final pork bits out of the bottom of my bowl.

Everyone seemed to know something about the Midnight Rose but I sensed Mrs. Chu knew more than most. I avoided her gaze and focused on finishing my bowl before she tried to ask me more.

She held up a bony hand, her wrist looking delicate under a heavy jade bangle. "Whatever you do, never drink from a vampire. The Cure is a last resort, but never take from the source."

I swallowed and wiped my lips hastily.

"Why not?"

"It will tie you to them for eternity."

20

SENSEI

At Nine Bells, my Uncle turned up at my door. He rolled in like a storm, scarred fighting leathers smelling of oil and rain. We Lims were all tall. Uncle Samuel was a few inches taller than I was and I was almost six feet tall in my sneakers. We both had long black hair, his tied back in a practical tail. But where I looked like I could always use an extra char siu bao, Uncle Samuel was built like a northern coastal redwood. Some of it was the shoulder armor and some of it was the way he moved--with menace and purpose.

Today was no exception. He swept into the room, the force of his personality and his magic swirling around him like thunderclouds. His sharp eyes swept my small room for threats with the efficiency of years of experience.

His eyes landed on my family photos. He stopped for a moment and his voice was low and gravelly.

"How's your mom?"

"Getting sicker by the day."

Samuel's lips thinned and he reached inside his duster.

With a heavy thunk, he dropped a fat satin pouch on my dresser.

"For her medicine."

"Thank you."

By the size of the pouch, it was a lot of silver. It would go a long way on both sides of the Veil. I quickly swept the coins into the top drawer and then grabbed my tool belt to sling around my hips.

Once outside, I hurried to keep up with my uncle as his long strides ate up the crumbling asphalt.

"Where are we going?"

Samuel pulled his cloak tighter around him against the chill wind and grunted. "To meet your new teacher."

That stopped me short and then I had to run to catch up with him. "What? But you brought me in. Aren't you going to mentor me?"

Despite my obvious confusion my uncle didn't slow down in the slightest or even deign to look at me as he spoke. "I don't have time, Roxy, and I can't be seen as giving you any special treatment. Which is also why I chose this particular mentor for you."

"That doesn't sound ominous at all."

That earned me a little side eye. "This is no joke, Roxy. She isn't going to like you and she will run you into the ground. But I need you to make this work."

"How can you say she won't like me? I'm very likable."

Samuel's mouth twitched. "Don't take it personally. She doesn't like anyone."

As we walked farther south, the noise of the Market died out and Seattle crumbled into ruin. The air grew cold and damp and we trudged through more puddles than dry land. The buildings here were dark, eyeless corpses, their bones rotted and sagging from years of insidious decay.

I peered down each dark alleyway as we passed, but Samuel

didn't pay any mind and kept walking a straight path. We arrived at what looked like the blasted remains of a flophouse. The one story building was shedding bricks like dandruff and only one door remained in working condition. A lone sentry stood at this door, a hulking shape blocking the entrance as effectively as a tank. A low growl emanated from the dark as we approached. My uncle didn't slow down.

The shape in the door stepped into the street as we came within ten feet of the door. I'm sure my eyes about jumped out of my head. Stepping out from the shadow of the building, the shape resolved into a massive creature with broad shoulders capping a broader chest and arms bulging with thick ropes of muscle. A coat of glossy auburn fur covered the arms and shoulders where a form fitting tank top did not. The werewolf's muzzle was long and tapered, her mouth filled with sharp fangs.

The werewolf held out a hand and spoke in a surprisingly delicate voice. "Stop."

Samuel swept back the hood of his cloak. "Hey, Stef. Busy tonight?"

Stef's shoulders relaxed when she saw Samuel's face. "Hey, Sam. It's just the usual crowd."

Her mouth widened into a frightening grin. "You off duty? Thinking about stepping in?"

"Heh. Way too old and too smart for that."

"Tell that to the Fox."

"You think that would help?"

Stef laughed, a sound that sounded like high-pitched yipping. "No, it wouldn't. Besides, she's good for business."

She turned her eyes to me and I made an effort to close my mouth. "Fresh meat?"

Samuel's voice stayed casual. "She's with me. Just visiting."

Stef looked back and forth between me and my uncle. Our family resemblance would be obvious even if we were covered in mud. "Uh-huh. Right. Well, does she know the rules at least?"

Samuel grabbed my hand and yanked me into motion, walking us towards the door. "She will, don't worry!" He gave Stef a cheery wave over his shoulder as we entered the building.

A rack of torches lined one wall of the first room. Samuel took one and lit it, filling the room with dancing orange light. I thought the exterior had been bad, but the interior of the building was even worse. Holes like gaping mouths dotted the floor, forcing us to weave side to side in order to navigate the narrow hallways. Strips of brittle wallpaper hung in shreds from the walls and ceiling like dead ivy. Samuel batted them away as we walked, filling the air with choking dust and crud. He led me down several rickety staircases, in some places ladders that had been lashed to the floors with rope and wires.

This building must have been in one of the low lying parts of the city, entire neighborhoods that drowned after the appearance of the Pyramids. Down here, the windows were all shattered inwards, broken by the crushing force of the Pacific Ocean. Now beyond those windows there was only tons of dirt and silt brought in by the rushing waters. Huge sections of the building were completely inaccessible but Samuel wound his way through the maze as if he'd been here a dozen times. With each twist and turn we kept heading down. The air grew dank and humid as we went lower.

I coughed on the smell of stale air and mold. "How far down are we going?"

"This building is six stories, but we're going past the basement."

"How do you go past a basement?"

"This isn't the first time Seattle was buried."

With that pronouncement he opened a door. Instead of opening into a wall of muck and dirt as I'd imagined, soft golden light poured in through the door, illuminating an old but serviceable alleyway of poured concrete.

We stepped out into the alley where glowing round fairy lights hung above us. Brick arches joined forces with support struts of metal and timber to support the sagging ceiling. Fairy lights lit a path that ventured off to our right and across the narrow space. Plain storefronts faced the alley, all with decaying windows and doors. Sounds of a raucous party or nightclub drifted to us from the end of the path.

Samuel chuckled at my open-mouthed wonder. "Close your mouth, kiddo. You're letting everyone know you're new in town."

He explained as we followed the path, quickly describing how the original city center had been buried following a devastating fire.

"And then when the Pacific rolled in it just got buried further down. Took a while to dig out a path back down here, but they got it done."

"What's down here?"

My uncle smiled cryptically. "No satellite, no vids, no net feeds. We've got to do something to keep ourselves entertained."

At the building at the end of the path another werewolf in warrior form stood guard but only tipped his head to my uncle as we approached. He opened the door and waved us in.

A wall of sound and heat blasted me in the face. The space we walked into was twice as tall as the alleyway and rows of bleacher seats had been installed on opposite walls nearly to the ceiling. Humans and supernaturals thronged the seats, every one of them standing and shouting at the tops of their lungs.

The cage dominated the center of the room, stretching to fill the space and enclosing an area about twenty feet on each side. The corners of the cage were scavenged metal welded and riveted together. One corner looked like a salvaged telephone pole. The walls of the cage were twined barbed wire. Melee weapons of all kinds hung from the inside of the cage. A few truly massive hammers and poleaxes sagged from the ceiling.

A roar blasted from the cage. A werewolf that could have been Stef's twin sister sprang to attack, spittle flying from her muzzle as she swung her arm in low. Her clawed fist connected with her opponent, a slight, pale-skinned woman dressed in red fighting leathers adorned with bone-white buckles. The impact hit with a low boom and a rush of wind that forced the spectators to shield their eyes. A cloud of dust sprang up from the point of impact, obscuring what had to have been a deadly blow. The crowd screamed in delight.

I felt a little sick to my stomach. "Cage fights to the death? That's your entertainment?"

Samuel snorted. "This? This is just a little fun and games. You'll see."

I eyed the weapons inside the cage. All of them had the heavy look of deadly intent. I remembered what Stef had said. "What are the rules?"

My uncle ticked off his fingers as he spoke. "Anyone can fight. Only one on one fights. No killing. No rules."

"Wait. No rules?"

"Anything goes in the cage other than fatal blows. And no rules from the surface apply here. Grudges, bad blood, all that stays up top. Down here, everyone just wants to see a good fight. You can come down here, beat the snot out of your boss and go back to work the next day without a care in the world."

I raised an eyebrow. "Really."

"If you could beat her."

The crowd hushed as the plume of dust settled and the view of the cage slowly returned. The werewolf stood in a fighting crouch in the center of the cage. She swept her leg in a roundhouse kick and the burst of wind cleared the rest of the dust. The crowd roared as the woman in red clambered up the walls of the cage, apparently unhurt.

My eyes bugged out. Not one woman, but six identical women in red crawled up the cage walls, nimble as mice. The werewolf spun in place, trying to keep all of them in sight. Each one of the women raced to one of the weapons and tore the weapon off the walls by brute force. One of the women finally reached a two-handed hammer hanging from the ceiling. As one they leapt off the walls. The noise from the crowd swelled to fill the room with frenzied cheers.

The werewolf made her choice and jumped to meet the one with the battle hammer. My uncle tsked and shook his head.

I flinched as the werewolf's claws slashed at the woman's midsection ... and passed through with no effect. The illusion frayed to wisps of light and disappeared. With no resistance, the werewolf over swung, her body twisting in the air. She landed on the dirty floor with a shriek of straining metal. The other five women converged and all but one disappeared. The last one held no weapons and landed astride the werewolf's chest, her hand held like a blade to her opponent's neck.

"Yield."

Panting, the werewolf nodded. "I yield."

The petite woman snarled in disgust, drew back and threw a brutal jab into the werewolf's cheek. The crack of bone rang out and echoed off the bare walls. The werewolf gave a pained yip and collapsed, red tongue lolling from her mouth.

The red woman stood and walked calmly to the door set into the wall of the cage. The crowd's cheers and screams morphed into a name chanted in time to stomping feet that set the whole building vibrating.

"Ko-to-ri! Ko-to-ri!"

Samuel grinned and bared his teeth. He grabbed my arm and started for the same door as the woman in the red fighting leathers. "Let's introduce you to your new teacher."

21

HER FATHER'S DAUGHTER

Outside the cage, Kotori looked almost normal. Except for the bloody knuckles. Up close Kotori had delicate features at odds with her fighting leathers. Short black hair with streaks of gray and wispy bangs framed a fine boned face that ended with a pointy chin. Her eyes were striking, black as night, narrow and sharp.

She hunched slightly and shook, like an animal in the rain and her fighting leathers morphed into a sweeping crimson leather cloak, the edges trimmed with luminous white fur.

I blinked. That was a neat trick. I didn't know if this was another illusion in her repertoire or more akin to a shifter's half form type of shift.

When she gave me the once-over, I resisted the urge to look away. The staring made me uncomfortable, like I was in some kind of strange dominance challenge. She was indisputably my superior but did she want some kind of acknowledgement?

Finally I tipped my head into a bow. "Sensei."

My sensei snorted.

Samuel sighed. "Kotori, Roxy will be coming along with you and Bashir tonight."

That brought the woman to a standstill. "Samuel. I have made it clear that I will not be a mentor."

My uncle's eyes hardened. "You will do this. For me."

"Rogue hunts are dangerous enough without forcing me to babysit, neh?"

I wanted to protest that I didn't need babysitting, but knew better to interrupt when the grown ups were talking.

"You know who she is. She's well trained." My uncle sounded exasperated.

Kotori swept her gaze up and down, taking me in. "Mmm." The sound she made was somewhere between agreement and polite disinterest.

She leaned closer and studied my toolbelt. "Are those...are those hammers?"

I pulled my shoulders back. "My father gave me these."

"Of course he did. What do you think you're going to do against a vampire with those? Nail down their floorboards?"

Heat rushed to my face. Before I could do or say something rash, my uncle put a heavy hand on my shoulder.

"Kotori, I've given you a lot of time but every Slayer pulls their weight. As of today you're part of the Trials again."

Her lips flattened in annoyance. "Fine. But get her a real weapon."

Samuel reached into his duster and whipped out a curved blade. It was a karambit, a wickedly deadly blade from Sumatra. My eyes widened. The six-inch blade was chased with silver and etched with intricate whorls and runes. Pinpoints of orange Crystal dotted the handle.

He handed it to me and I hefted it. My fingers folded smoothly around the handle and my pinky slipped into the ring forged at the base of the grip. I twitched my wrist and the blade spun liquidly around my finger until the grip snapped back into my palm. This was a beauty. Was my uncle gifting this to me? I tilted my head and offered it back to him. He shook his head. "It's yours."

Kotori raised an eyebrow, the high arch communicating more than words. She knew this blade and she knew the significance of my uncle handing it to me.

"Thank you."

I had been waiting this whole time for some kind of vote of confidence from my Uncle. That he believed I was truly going to fight by his side like my dad had. This was it and the warmth that rose in my chest from this overshadowed my frustration that he'd paired me with the dreaded Kotori.

If Kotori noticed any of this, she gave no indication. She finished cleaning the werewolf's blood off her knuckles and strapped on the rest of her weapons, a six-foot naginata with an enormous blade that she wore over her shoulder, and a slender fighting knife that she buckled to the small of her back. Before it disappeared under the cloak, I caught the gleam of mother of pearl on the handle of the fighting knife.

Now I felt some chagrin for leaving my spear at home. A spear wasn't the most inconspicuous for walking around downtown Seattle but since Kotori walked around with that giant weapon, I guess being inconspicuous wasn't a priority on this run.

Thus armed, Kotori looked ready to take on the entirety of the Shadow's Den on her own. She gave me yet another skeptical look. "Are we ready to go now, or must we wait for her to get her screwdrivers?"

Hey, that was uncalled for.

Samuel cleared his throat. "Actually, there is one more thing."

~

WHAT MY UNCLE had failed to mention to either Kotori or me earlier was that our little rogue hunting excursion would also include Marnie. Even worse, while Kotori made it clear she was not happy for getting stuck with me but somehow, she seemed fine with Marnie.

Kotori studied Marnie's stance and weapons and gave a nod which I took as approval whereas I'd only gotten a displeased grunt after greeting her.

Marnie was smiling, and that creeped me out more than when Marnie had been cursing me to all the levels of hell for taking the Cure. Maybe the prospect of burning out a bunch of rogues entrenched in a cave was an enjoyable one for her. I guess that made her well suited for being a Slayer.

I tried to remind myself that odds were high I might end up with Marnie as a Slayer and that I should practice some tolerance. Yes, she had injured me badly at the Trial, but if my Breaker magic had worked right, I might have buried her in rubble. Today we were supposed to be on the same team, so I dug deep and I offered her a tentative smile. She snapped her teeth together like an alligator crunching a tasty mammal.

Okay then. So much for my attempt at camaraderie.

I turned back to Bashir, who didn't alarm me quite so much.

The menacing curve of his long pulwar was alarming but Bashir moved with an easy confidence that told me he knew exactly how to handle this blade and wouldn't accidently lop off my head with it. The pulwar was almost three feet long and if he drew it from the beautifully carved leather and rosewood sheath, I knew I would be looking a fine watered steel curved like a dragon's fang.

Bashir was tall and husky, his body rippling with thick muscle under his light gray hoodie and black tactical jacket. Beneath the hood, black curls and the prominent blade of his nose dominated his face. He pursed full lips and whistled a cheery tune. The wind picked up and swirled around Kotori, batting the tails of her jacket playfully.

"Bash. Knock it off." Kotori growled.

Bashir smiled and the wind vanished. Cool talent to be a Wind Whistler. All he needed was a fire source and he could take on an entire peril of rogues alone. When he smiled, the skin around his eyes crinkled and I realized he was older than me, but younger than Samuel. I wondered if he knew my dad. After this raid, I'd have to ask him.

With a gruff rebuke to confirm that everyone was, in fact, ready to go out and kill some vampires, Kotori led our little hunting party further south into the derelict portions of the city.

The building above the fighting pit had at least been upright. The building Kotori led us to now was the memory of a building, at best, a towering mound of crumbling bricks and chunks of concrete. A handful of rotting support beams stuck out from the mound at strange angles like denuded trees. Fuzzy moss and mold covered the decaying wood like a winter coat. Kotori brought us to a halt at the foot of the debris pile.

I tapped my magic lightly and saw, unsurprisingly, a deathtrap.

Marnie's eyes glittered. "Are the vamps under there?"

Kotori gave us both a look that wavered somewhere between disgusted and impatient before leaping into the air and dashing up the mound. Her light feet barely disturbed the bricks. I was about to go after her when I felt a hand on my shoulder holding me back.

Bashir rolled his eyes. "All right, settle down, children. Let Kotori work. She's your mentor, so watch her for cues, and don't do anything other than what she tells you to do."

A sharp whistle drew our attention back to the mound of rubble. Bashir led the way, picking a path that skirted the edges and brought us around the back side. Kotori stood on a nondescript pile of broken concrete, her finger pointed down at her feet.

Bashir squatted down to examine the broken concrete. The chunk was skewered with bits of rebar that had been broken off by scavengers, the stubby ends orange and green with rust and mold. He whistled a low, mournful note and a current of air swirled out of the rubble at Kotori's feet, the air thick with dust and the wet smell of rot. Kotori sniffed once and nodded, the movement sharp and precise.

Bashir got up, dusting off his knees. He drew his blade and sighted down the edge. I had been right, the blade nearly glowed. "Going to be tight in there."

Kotori drew her short fighting knife from the small of her back. It was a graceful arc that looked like a sliver of moonlight. "It would be easier without them."

"Nothing worth doing is easy."

"No, it's not, is it?"

Bashir turned to look at me and Marnie, as if just realizing that they were talking about us. "How do you want to do this? Like last time?"

Kotori nodded again, that almost imperceptible movement. "I do not like that ridiculous pulwar at my back. And I do not like having my fur singed off."

Bashir sighed. "Nobody truly appreciates a rare talent anymore."

Kotori growled, the sound deep in her chest. She stepped nimbly off the concrete and got one hand under the edge. She lifted and the entire block, along with several other jagged blocks, swung smoothly up on hidden hinges, revealing a wide, dark hole in the rubble. Stale air that smelled of dust and decay wafted out, along with a thick, musky animal smell.

With the flat of her blade, Kotori nudged me forward as Bashir approached the entrance. "You're with Bashir. Marnie and I will bring up the rear."

Did Kotori already have a reason to favor Marnie over me? I moved up to stand next to Bashir. Sweat slicked my palms and my mouth was uncomfortably dry. The tunnel opening at our feet was pitch black, and I couldn't see even two feet into the interior. Anything could be down there, already waiting for us to jump into their claws, mouths, or fangs.

I pulled out the karambit and held it in my right hand. I drew Loki with my left. Bashir looked at my weapons and then back to my eyes, his expression unreadable.

I tried to talk, but it came out as a choked whisper. I coughed and found my voice again. "What are we doing?"

Bashir held his sword vertically and put his left arm around my shoulders. "It's very simple. Don't stick me with that knife. And don't die."

With that he pulled me forward and we stepped out into the bottomless abyss.

So, it wasn't a bottomless abyss. We fell for a few seconds before the ground smacked me in both feet, the shock traveling up to my head and nearly making me bite off my tongue. I went down to my knees and just avoided spearing myself on my own karambit. Luckily any embarrassment I might have felt was first shielded by the darkness and then burned away by the fear of slicing my own neck open.

Training in a studio was all very well and good, but nothing prepared you for fighting in the dark, underground with the threat of rogue vampires surrounding you. My mouth was dry with fear and I tried to calm the rapid staccato of my heart.

Bashir landed lightly on his feet just behind me. He grabbed me by the scruff and dragged me to the side with a whispered word to stay quiet.

I crawled on hands and knees to keep up with him. A heartbeat later two more soft impacts landed behind me, Kotori and Marnie. I fetched up against a wall and leaned against it, happy to have some kind of reference in the darkness. The floor sank wetly beneath my feet and felt like damp industrial carpeting, as did the walls.

My eyes finally started adjusting and I could just pick straight lines of low walls that extended into the darkness at right angles from our position. We must have dropped into an office building, now a maze of molding cube walls and worthless technology. Light emanated from patches of the mold that glowed with soft, blue light and cast dim shadows across the floor.

Kotori squatted next to Bashir, her cloak fanned out around her like a pool of drying blood. "Well?"

Bashir closed his eyes. He seemed to be humming a low tune to himself. After a long moment he opened his eyes. "No one in the building. They've gone to ground."

"Fine. We'll do it the hard way, then."

Bashir grabbed me by the collar again and hauled me to my feet. "All right, Donor. Time to see if you're worthy of any of your hype."

That caught me off guard. "What?"

He grabbed my shoulder and turned me down the narrow aisle. He walked steadily into the darkness, following a path accented with more clusters of glowing mold. Just like when Samuel had led me to the fight club, Bashir led us down an increasingly fragile set of stairs. The air thickened into a musty soup and my ears popped repeatedly as we descended. The mold colonies grew into crusting, bulbous growths the size of hedges.

Kotori and Marnie trailed us by about one flight of stairs. I caught brief whispers of conversation between the two of them, but couldn't make anything out but the tone sounded friendly enough. I felt again like Marnie's second fiddle.

I caught up to Bashir and whispered, "Did I say something to offend Kotori?"

"Why do you ask?"

His gaze drifted up to where the others' voices drifted down to us. "Oh, that? I wouldn't worry about that. Kotori has her ways. To her, you are simply another candidate, just like any other."

That did not sound like a ringing endorsement. "Well she seems pretty chummy with Marnie, but I need her as my mentor, too."

Bashir made a strangled sound and I nearly panicked until I realized he was holding in laughter. "I don't believe anyone has ever accused the Fox of ever being...chummy. In due course, she will see to your training as well."

"Fox?"

He ignored me and held up his hand as we came to a stop at a shattered picture window. Beyond the broken glass and twisted frame, a four foot hole had been dug through the dark, packed earth that had engulfed the building. My magic outlined the tunnel in faint lines of pale green that twisted off into the distance. It was narrow, but wouldn't cave in on us.

I peered into the tunnel. "We're going down there?"

He pulled a bandana out and wrapped it over the lower half of his face. "We go wherever the job takes us, no matter the danger."

From his belt he unhooked a delicate silver chain that gleamed in the darkness like it was lit from within. Bashir held it out to me. "You may need this tonight if we get separated. It will immobilize a vampire and give you time to stake it."

He pointed to my hammers. "It's good that you keep those sharp. Do not hesitate to use them tonight."

And with that Bashir disappeared into the tunnel. After his terrifying words, I briefly considered not following but then imagined Kotori's disappointment if she found me here without Bashir, and decided that crawling through the tunnel was likely preferable. I patted the chain for good luck, stowed my weapons, and climbed in after Bashir.

Not content with merely hiding in the old Seattle underground, rogue vampires had taken to digging beyond the treacherous underground, eventually adding an even more deceptive warren of tunnels that sometimes connected to enormous caves. The tunnel we crawled through was mercifully short but just long enough for me to visualize a vamp barreling down on my head while my arms were held cramped and useless by the narrow walls. I fell out of the tunnel exit with a breathless sigh of relief.

The tunnel ended at the narrow end of a large, oval cave. More tunnel mouths branched off the cave at suspiciously regular intervals, each one of them clogged with rock and debris. The tunnel appeared to be a dead end.

Bashir stood by the nearest blocked tunnel, humming under his breath again. He looked up as I crawled out of the entrance tunnel.

"Excellent. I shall need your assistance for the next step in our hunt."

Finally. An opportunity to prove myself to an inked Slayer. I stepped up, my hands itching to pull my hammers, or my new karambit. "What do you need?"

"Your eyes, little breaker. Tell me what you see." He pointed to the rockfall.

I deflated a little, but called on my magic and a web of glowing lines covered the face of the rockfall. Towards the bottom, a rusting length of rebar protruded from the rocks. A white glow came from where the rebar ended inside the rocks. Is this what Bashir wanted from me? To clear garbage?

"If we pull here, we can clear the tunnel." I reached for the rebar.

Bashir held me back with a light touch on my shoulder.

"Ah, yes. So painfully obvious that even one without your notorious talent would at least try, yes? No, this is not the tunnel we want. The next one, please."

We proceeded to make our way down the length of the cave. At each tunnel I found the weak point in the rockfall, and at each one, Bashir lamented that this tunnel was still not the one we were looking for. Through it all, the Slayer kept humming under his breath, a low, tuneless hum that became a buzzing drone in my ears.

After the sixth tunnel I got frustrated. "What exactly are we looking for? And how is your humming helping?"

Bashir broke into a wide grin. His teeth were large and crooked. "Well, at least you're more patient than your father. My humming drove him nuts right off from the start."

The mention of my father derailed my thoughts and made me forget my irritation. "You knew my dad?"

"Of course. I know your uncle, so I knew your father. The Lim brothers were legendary in their time, the Maker and the Breaker. Yes. I've been looking forward to working with you. Can you truly fill your father's rather prodigious boots?"

He stopped in front of the next tunnel and held his hand out to the rockface. A low hum vibrated in his throat and faded away. "This is the passive field of my magic. I sense the flow of air currents around me, and if I concentrate, farther away from me. I've trained to use my passive field to detect others even if they're behind locked doors or around corners."

Wow, that was some talent.

"One's active magic is an extension of the passive field." He whistled softly, the notes sweet and light. The dust and pebbles at my feet swirled around me as a miniature dust devil appeared out of nowhere. Bashir's whistle spiked into a harsh, sharp note and a gust of wind nearly pushed me to my knees. As the sound died the air fell still.

"My father never taught me this."

"If you'd never come to the Twilight, you would never have experienced it."

Something from earlier today twigged in my memory. "So what's Kotori's magic?"

Bashir smiled again and this time the expression was pitying. "A little slow like your father as well then, eh?"

Before I could protest Bashir turned and pointed to the rock face. "Now we will see if you are truly your father's daughter. Break it."

Clammy sweat sprang up in my palms. Goddess. The last time I'd used my Breaker magic was during my skirmish with Marnie. It had gone badly. The broken glass sensation of the recoil was still fresh in my mind, the pain hovering over me like an executioner's blade. I reached out with my magic, tentative, brushing up against the rock fall.

Bashir appeared behind me, his voice close to my ear. "Do not fear the recoil. It is the natural consequence of using your active field. You must learn to mitigate the effects."

Fear warred with my desire to increase my power. "How?"

"Your magic, it changes the world, like dropping a stone into water. Bigger change, bigger stone. The recoil is like the splash of water."

My magic sidled up to the rockfall. This would be far easier than the stone at the Farm, but my mind still shied away from the prospect of the recoil.

Bashir's voice continued in soothing tones. "You must be gentle. Any fool can throw a stone into water. The skilled practitioner knows how to make the change...with subtlety."

He whistled a high, clear note and wind stirred around us. Now that I was looking for it, I could almost sense the recoil building around us as Bashir moved the air.

The recoil never landed. Or if it did, it landed so softly that I couldn't sense it. Bashir's wind magic faded. I reached out, closed my eyes and blocked everything out, stretching my senses ahead of me. Having already seen the force vectors, the image remained in my mind, like a glowing web imprinted inside my eyelids. I knew what needed to happen. That rock there, shaped like a gourd. Multiple lines converged on the fat section of the stone. It was the keystone, much like the wedge of stone I'd used to keep Laila's hut from crumbling. The stone just needed to shift, ever so slightly down, and gravity would take care of the rest.

Prickly hot sweat popped up down my neck and across my shoulders. Bashir was right. Throwing the rock in the pond was easy. How could I do it with more finesse?

Behind me, Bashir made a low sound of approval.

Could I reshape my thoughts, my magic, to fit the rock?

My magic swirled in my chest and flowed down my arm, reaching for the gourd shaped rock. It settled around the rock like a wet blanket, clinging to the unique shape, fitting into every nook and cranny. Why just this rock? Why not the whole rock face? My heart thundered in my chest as possibilities spooled out in my mind. If I worked slowly, gently, how far could I extend my active magic? Could I open doors from across the room? A city block? The whole city?

The floor trembled beneath my feet.

If I could do this here, why not elsewhere? Did the structure need to have a weak point to exploit? Or could I make my own, exactly where I needed it? Was it possible to bring...anything... down? Is that the magic that earned my father his nickname?

It felt like slipping into a trance. My mind had molded itself around the gourd-shaped rock, and now it spread, sliding over the adjacent rocks and rubble like a greedy child. I inhaled, and the breath seemed to go on forever, filling my lungs to bursting. It felt like flying.

Somewhere distant, a rock cracked with a sound like a gunshot. I was dimly aware of a faint line of pain drawn across my cheek.

As my breath slowly released, something clicked inside me, like a hidden latch had been undone. My key, my mind wrapped around the rock, slowly began to turn and the tumblers of the lock began to crash into place. I leaned into the feeling, eager to see what would happen next.

Rough hands grabbed my shoulders and threw me to the ground. The magic disappeared like vapor before a fire, and the sensation fled. My eyes flew open and all I saw was swirling red leather as I fell on my butt. Kotori stormed over me and jabbed a finger into Bashir's chest. Her eyes glittered with incandescent rage.

"What do you think you are doing?"

Bashir seemed unfazed by Kotori's outburst. "Candidate training. You might try it sometime."

"You pompous ass. Always dreaming, never thinking. What if she had brought the cave down on our heads?"

Wait, could I do that?

Bashir drew his blade. "Dreaming of returning the Slayers to our original glory, with a Breaker, no less. I think that is a dream worth nurturing."

Kotori hissed, "She is not Gabriel!"

"No. She is not."

Bashir's calm eyes found mine. "I believe she will surpass him."

"That is pure speculation, and unworthy of you."

Kotori unslung her naginata with a huff. "And none of this furthers our goals tonight."

She stalked back to me and pulled me up by my collar. For a smaller woman she was surprisingly strong. The temporary high of nearly grasping the full extent of my magic withered under Kotori's baleful stare. She pointed at the rock fall. "Clear it. Without using your magic."

Marnie caught my eye as I stepped up to the tunnel entrance. Did I see a trace of smugness in her expression? With

Kotori mentoring both of us, I had the distinct feeling that I was the least favorite student so far. I grabbed the keystone and turned it. The rocks tumbled and in moments we had a large enough space to crawl through to the tunnel beyond. More patchy mold followed the length of the tunnel, giving us the worst kind of visibility. Enough to see and move through the tunnel, not enough to see a vamp until it was on top of your head.

Bashir tilted his head to one side and started humming again. I resisted the urge to put my fingers in my ears. After a moment he raised his head. "This is it."

Kotori took one look down the tunnel and tossed an unlit torch at me.

"Take point with Bashir. He knows what to do."

She jabbed a finger at me. "No. Magic."

My mood soured further.

I unscrewed my flask and tipped the contents onto the linen. The alcohol soaked the fabric quickly. I slipped the flask back into my belt and fumbled around for the container with the matchsticks.

Bashir gave me a slap on the back. "Easy there, or you won't have any eyebrows left when you light it."

He could joke. He was an inked Slayer with years of cred. Meanwhile I was trying to make a good impression on my mentor and absolutely botching it left and right.

Kotori pointed down the tunnel. "Let's get moving."

Behind her, Marnie winked at me, a decidedly smug smile on her face. Goddess, could the night get any worse? The vamps ahead of us were starting to look good in comparison.

22

TAKE NO PRISONERS

After what had to be thirty minutes, the tunnel walls seemed to close in around me, fraying my nerves and nearly making me jump at every dim shadow or hint of movement. The peril had hunkered down deep in the caves, which was both good and bad.

Good because at many points the tunnel was so narrow that only one of us could move through it at a time. This prevented the vamps from swarming us, which was hard to defend against, especially if we encountered vampires who could fly.

Bad because no more than one person at a time could go through which meant I couldn't count on having Kotori or Bashir at my side. Also bad was Marnie behind me, which made me uneasy. And there was the added issue that the ceilings were high, which meant we couldn't rule out an aerial assault. All of this was bad from my standpoint.

I studied the tunnel and let my eyes focus. My magic went to work, precision lines and angles picking out the pressure points in the rocky cave. No need to worry about a cave-in but maybe I could find something that could give us a little insurance for the exit plan.

My grip on the torch tightened as we stepped into the darkness of the cave. Vampires couldn't see any better than we could in this darkness but they would hear our heartbeats. Mine was probably beating the fastest.

Bashir was a big guy but moved just as silently as Kotori. I felt like my every step thundered in the narrow passageway but I kept moving, my eyes adjusting to the darkness. At Bashir's signal I would blast the torch. It would blind all of us but at least we were prepped for it and it would clear the space above us immediately.

Bashir held up a closed fist which I didn't see until I crashed into his back. "Oof."

Marnie grunted in annoyance but didn't ram into me.

I tried to quiet my breath, repeating the practice from the dojo. It didn't work. Something else didn't work either, which was my magic. It was so dark that it felt like a heavy blanket muting all of my senses. I couldn't see beyond the faint mold glow around me and my saving grace was that I also couldn't see Kotori. The force of her glare bored into my back, though. I didn't know which was worse—getting chewed out by Kotori after, or getting ignored by her.

I reminded myself that my job here was simple. I just had to light a fire. The matches were in my pocket and I had a striker I'd jury rigged myself to work with a quick squeeze. It would be fine. I'd get the torch up, it would repel the flying vamps and Kotori and Bashir would take care of the rest of the vampires. Assuming Bashir didn't take my head off in one of his battle moves or that Kotori didn't nail me with her naginata. What could possibly go wrong?

A loud scratching noise echoed through the cave, followed by what sounded like the scrabbling of claws. My breathing got shallow, and if it got any worse I would be panting. Bashir backed up, and I could just make him out, peering into the darkness above us.

"Now!"

I squeezed hard on the trigger and the torch burst into life. It nearly did scorch off my eyebrows. The bright firelight speared my eyes and I staggered back.

Bashir whistled. And I now realized he'd been holding back before. A ton. The sound Bashir generated didn't sound like it could be produced by a human being. His whistle cut through the air like a blade, a shrill, high note that made my ears ache.

The torch bucked in my hands and I scrambled to get two hands on it. I could not drop it now. The torch bloomed into a white hot column of fire that rocketed to the roof of the tunnel. Flames crashed against the rocky roof and crawled down the tunnel, lighting up the tunnel like high noon on the other side of the Twilight. Some who lived in the Twilight had never seen light so bright, so piercing, and so clean.

Especially the vampires swarming down on us from the walls and ceiling. At least a dozen, most of them drawn and emaciated, a sure sign that they were blood starved, but still strong enough to rip a human in two. They all wore dirty, tattered clothing. Some of them were naked to the waist, their ribs jutting in stark lines on pale skin. All of them had eyes like circles of ink, inhumanly huge irises adapted to seek prey in the dark. Ouch.

They shrieked as the flames shot up to the ceiling, their thin, ropy arms coming up to shield their eyes. They clung to the rocky walls of the tunnel, sharp claws ripping through the stone like it was soft clay.

One of the vamps was unlucky enough to be on the roof itself. Another moment and it would have dropped onto my head and torn my throat out. Bashir's excellent timing instead turned the vampire into an impromptu barbeque. The column of cleansing fire engulfed the vampire and reduced it to a cloud of drifting ash.

Bashir stepped forward and his pulwar came down in a

swift, precise arc, hacking into the closest vampire between the neck and the shoulder, cleaving it through to the breast bone. It screamed, a hoarse, guttural noise as the wound began to smoke. The pulwar must have been inlaid with silver. The vamp grabbed Bashir's blade and tried to lever itself away. As it did so, the vampire's hands began to smolder. Bashir lunged and pinned the vamp to the tunnel wall.

"Roxy!"

The torch jumped and sputtered when Bashir stopped whistling. I jerked, as if waking from a dream. This was real. I was really fighting vampires in Seattle. This was what I had trained for.

I pulled Thor from my belt, my fingers slick with sweat curling around the cool steel head. The vampire was too focused on prying itself off Bashir's silver blade to notice my approach. My nose twitched, the air was thick with the rich, sickly sweet smell of the vampire burning alive from the enchanted silver. The screams of the encroaching vampires pressed in around us, smothering my senses in a blanket of rage, fire, and chaos.

My training took over, years of muscle memory in the gym staking straw-stuffed dummies. My arm cocked back and thrust forward, Thor's sharpened end aimed unerringly for the vampire's center mass. I'd lovingly turned, sharpened, and fire-hardened the point to near needle sharpness and now it paid off. My stake struck true, spearing the vamp through its heart. It shrieked again, the sound nearly rupturing my eardrum, and then went limp, its pale skin going ashy as it began to crumble into ash.

I fell to my knees and threw up onto the tunnel floor.

Bashir grabbed the torch before it could roll away. My guts spasmed again and then Kotori's hand was curled into my collar and she hauled me up.

"Get up, or you truly will be a blood donor!"

She threw me behind her and Marnie caught me before I could fall again. Kotori moved up beside Bashir and the two of them waded into the vampires.

I had heard the stories from my father, read his diaries, learned the lore. Nothing prepared me for two inked Slayers in action against a swarm of rogues. Even Marnie seemed awed as we watched Bashir and Kotori stand shoulder to shoulder in the narrow tunnel and methodically cut down vampires as they slowly marched forward. The two of them might have argued before, but in the face of hostile vampires, they were as one, fighting smoothly together as if they were one mind. Blades flashed and swung, each movement precise, with no wasted motion. Not every strike killed, but every strike took off a limb, pushing the vampires back.

More vampires boiled out of the darkness, and suddenly Bashir and Kotori's martial dance looked a lot less like elegant fighting as much as a futile effort in the face of insurmountable numbers. Vampires descended on them from all angles, throwing themselves into their whirling blades if only to buy another half second for their comrades to gain another foot of ground. The vampires were going to overrun us. It was only a matter of time. Very little time, in fact.

Kotori risked a look back at me and Marnie. "Move up!"

She grabbed the torch out of Bashir's hand. "Do it!"

Goddess. I'd been moving forward and then Bashir's whistle ran through my head like a red hot lance. I went down to my knees and dimly noted that Marnie was on the ground next to me. My hands clamped down on either side of my head, trying in vain to block out the sound.

The torch transformed from a mere pillar of flame to a spewing geyser of violent, fiery madness. Flames raced down the tunnel and sucked the air along with it, the gust rolling me forward onto my face. I squinted my eyes against the swirling dirt, ash, and searing heat. Vampires exploded into ash as the wall of flame battered through their swarm like a hot knife through butter.

If Bashir hadn't just showed it to me I would have missed it. The recoil from his magic barreled down on him like a freight train, heavy with potential from the huge expenditure of his magic. And then...it landed on him with the grace of a butterfly and faded into nothingness.

Wow.

Bashir collapsed, his face shining with sweat, his body racked with hacking coughs. The effort still cost him something, but the recoil hadn't incapacitated him. He was able to keep fighting. I had to learn this.

The torch returned to mere human levels of flame and darkness closed in on us again.

Kotori set the end of her naginata on the ground. "Everyone still alive?"

She sounded distressingly calm and not even out of breath even as Marnie and I gasped for air in the wake of Bashir's fireball. I managed to grunt out something that sounded like assent, and Kotori nodded her approval.

"Good. Bashir, get up. We're going after them."

The big man got up on one knee and knuckled the sweat out of his eyes. "I expected as much. No rest for the weary. I propose sending the candidates back. This peril is larger than expected. We needn't overburden ourselves with their care as we finish."

Kotori huffed. "That is what I said at the beginning."

She tossed the torch to me and I managed to catch it without fumbling it or burning my face off. "You two head back. You are forbidden from doing anything stupid."

With that she turned on her heel and stalked off into the darkness of the tunnel. Bashir got to his feet and stretched his back. He pulled out a rag and wiped down his blade.

"Best listen to your mentor. Backtrack our path to the surface and make your way to headquarters."

He winked at me. "Heed your mentor's instructions. No stupid stuff."

And Bashir, too, turned down the dark tunnel, leaving Marnie and me slightly stunned. Our mentor had just left us alone in a puddle of torchlight, in a maze of tunnels crawling with rogues, buried under the mud and bones of Seattle.

THIS HAD TO BE A TEST. I said so and Marnie scoffed.

"All of life is a test. If you didn't know that then your life has been too soft."

She wasn't wrong, but I was a quick student. "All right, let's get--"

Marnie hissed and leapt in front of me, pulling her stilettos on the fly. She landed with a crunch that sounded like cracking bones.

I ran after her and found Marnie stabbing her blades repeatedly into the legs of a vampire that was doing its best to crawl away from her. This one didn't have much fight left in him. It wasn't hard to see why. The vampire's face and chest was a mass of livid black and red burns. His fingers ended in hooked claws that carved away the tunnel wall like soft butter. Marnie's blades were sharp but they weren't spelled silver. The vampire ignored her, intent on tunneling away.

"Roxy! What are you waiting for?!"

I brought the sharpened wood of Thor down on the vampire's back, aiming for its heart.

Too late. Before my stake could ram into its heart, it let out a grating howl and pulled his ravaged legs away from Marnie's knives, and squirmed into the newly dug hole.

With the vampire gone Marnie ducked her head down. "Roxy. Bring the torch."

When I brought it closer Marnie gasped. I squatted down to look. The tunnel branched off from the main one, the floor of the new tunnel showing signs of transit of many feet.

Marnie's eyes glowed with fervent light. "This is how they swarmed us. They came through the walls. I bet the tunnel leads to their lair."

With her knives she began hacking at the wall, enlarging the opening started by the vampire, an idea that, I was betting, Kotori would rank as high on the stupid list.

"What are you doing?"

"What I'm supposed to do. I'm going to be a Slayer. Slayers hunt and kill vampires, Roxy."

The image of the tunnel, filled with burning vamps, was still bright on the inside of my eyelids. "This is a huge peril, Marnie. We can't go after them without backup."

Marnie turned away from her digging. "Maybe you can't, but I've prepared my whole life for this. I thought you said you were ready to be a Slayer."

She was right. This is what I wanted, needed, but I also needed Kotori as a mentor and I didn't want to screw that up any more than I already had. My uncle was counting on me for that.

Marnie gripped my arm. "How else are you planning to prove yourself, if not by staking as many vampires as you can?"

Her eyes burned with fervor and even though I didn't trust her any farther than I could throw her, I agreed with her plan to find the lair. Bashir and Kotori might be running towards a trap. Slayers wouldn't leave one of theirs behind. If Marnie and I could eliminate the surprise factor of the lair, Bashir and Kotori could handle the rest.

I dropped to my knees beside Marnie.

"Keep digging."

THE NEW TUNNEL branched off at a right angle to the main and the floor was littered with footprints and drag marks. Whatever the rogues had been doing, it had been recent, with many of the tracks still wet and fresh.

We followed the vampire's tracks until they veered off the main tunnel into a much smaller, much darker branch. The smaller tunnel turned sharply, creating a blind corner.

Marnie edged up to the corner, her knives out and poised to strike. "Ready?"

Samuel's karambit was in my right hand and the torch in my left. I nodded and we swung around the corner together. I held the karambit high, ready to take an oncoming vampire in the throat if needed.

Lucky for me, the vampire also chose to go high. His pale form materialized out of the darkness as the light from my torch lit the interior of the cave. His healing was working overtime, the skin on his chest already a patchwork of smooth, pale skin. Charred bits of skin and blood flaked away from him as he descended on me.

In the half second it took for him to reach for my throat, I caught the telltale signs of blood starvation. Skin drawn tight over ribs and cheekbones. Dark hollows under the eyes. Lips pulled back to reveal long fangs protruding from gums so dark they were almost black. The healing process was eating him alive.

I locked my elbow out and the vamp landed on the razor edge of the karambit, the blade entering just below the hyoid bone. He was starving, as the wound barely bled. A shock of impact traveled up my arm and into my shoulder as my blade rammed up against his vertebrae.

The vampire screamed, a high, whistling sound that sprayed me with gore-flecked spittle from the slash I'd just made across his neck. His arms swung forward and bony hands wrapped around my throat, his fingers long enough to intertwine on the back of my neck. His icy claws found my soft skin and I knew he was a moment away from tearing my head off.

Marnie rolled around my left and slid her blades into the vampire's neck, just below my karambit. With a flick of both wrists her blades whipped side to side.

The vampire's eyes went wide and then his hands fell slack around my neck. Marnie kicked him in the chest and his body fell back as his head toppled off his severed neck. The head dissolved into ash before it hit the ground.

Marnie cleaned and sheathed her blades. "Thanks for the assist."

I kept my blade in my hand, mostly so I could keep my fingers clenched and keep them from trembling. Marnie took the torch from me and began scouting the cave. It was a round space with a low ceiling. Several small pits had been dug at regular intervals around the edge of the cave and Marnie checked each one with the torch.

There was just enough light for me to check the other side of the cave and meet Marnie on the other side. The pits were deep enough to hold someone, and most of them showed signs of being occupied at some time. Perhaps this was where the rogues imprisoned their blood slaves. A small, disused passage exited the rear of the cave, the opening clogged with rocks and debris.

As I searched the pits I ran my free hand over the back of my neck, shuddering at the memory of the vampire's cold claws. My hand came away with faint traces of blood where his claws had scratched my skin. I had literally come within inches of a grisly death on my first outing with the Slayers. What would Kotori think? Or my uncle Samuel? Or more importantly, my dad?

"Just like we practiced, Roxybear."

I exhaled slowly, willing my heart to stop racing.

A grunt from Marnie wrenched me away from my thoughts, and I cut across the cave to her. She stood over one of the far pits, shining the torchlight into the hole.

Two forms lay huddled at the bottom. One was a plump blonde woman I didn't recognize, dressed in a white frilly dress with puffy sleeves.

The other was turned with his face to the wall. Rusted chains, with links as thick as my fingers, wrapped around his body and arms and terminated in crude manacles at his wrists. The chains were secured to an eyebolt set into the center of the floor in the pit. Even from behind I noted the breadth of his shoulders and the fine cut of his dark wool jacket.

I sucked in a breath. "Goddess of the Moon. That's Tyee Wilder."

"Who?"

"The scion of the Mist and Mind."

Marnie threw me a skeptical look. "Why are you so familiar with the Mist and Mind?"

I hoped the relative darkness hid the flush creeping up my neck. "Because I do my homework. He's the favored son of the Night Queen."

And a distraction I didn't need, but that was neither here nor there. "This is bad. Really bad. We need to get him out of here."

Marnie's voice was flat and emotionless. "No. We don't."

"What are you talking about? We're on a rogue hunt. They're not rogues."

"They're all vampires, Roxy. What's the difference?"

"They're--" And I stopped, because I didn't know what I could say about Tyee that might convince Marnie. Irritating manners aside, Tyee had done me a solid and I would not stand by and watch him die like a trapped animal.

Marnie seemed to take my hesitation as agreement and she

stepped around me. She pulled one of the crucifix blades and kissed the metal. "Just watch, Roxy. They might dress and act like humans, but take off their heads and they all crumble into dust."

I had come to the Twilight to fulfill my father's dying wish, to carry on his legacy and save my mother. Both of those things involved killing vampires, but this was over the line. I hadn't realized that the line even existed until my hand landed on Marnie's shoulder and I pulled her back from the edge of the pit.

"No."

The torchlight danced across her incredulous eyes. "No? Since when have Slayers granted mercy to vampires?"

She pointed an accusing finger into the pit. "Do you think that thing would even give you a thought if it was in a blood frenzy?"

"Marnie, it's not that simple--"

"It. Is. A vampire. You are either its enemy, or its food."

"Are you planning to kill the woman as well?"

Marnie sniffed. "She is cattle."

"Now who's talking like a vampire?"

"She made her choice. You consort with fangs, don't cry when you get bitten."

"I won't let you kill them."

Marnie's eyes narrowed. "If you're not against them, you're with them."

She drew back her stiletto so fast I didn't see it until a hot line of pain flared across the arm I had on her shoulder. I jumped back, just in time to miss the down stroke of her blade. The cut on my arm was shallow, but it hurt, and a trickle of blood slicked my palm. I dropped the torch and drew my hammers.

Marnie sneered. "Still playing with your toys."

She lunged at me. I swept Loki across my body and swatted

the blade away, dancing away from the pit. If I could at least lead her away from the pit, maybe Tyee would wake up and lend a hand.

Marnie chased after me, her eyes hot with fury now. "How many people do you think it has killed? And instead of stopping it, you're going to set it free?"

She came at me again, both crucifixes out now, her blades flashing like lightning. In the dim light of the torch, she was a blur of limbs and steel. I backed away, blocking her strikes with my hammers. If I'd brought the spear I'd have a fighting chance. As it was, I had nothing to turn the tide.

"I knew you were weak from the moment we met!"

I reached out with my magic, desperate now as Marnie closed in. The cave walls lit up in green with plenty of pale points of white light. Whatever the rogues had done to secure the main tunnels, this prison had not seen the same treatment.

Marnie stabbed and I spun away. Too slow. The blade parted my shirt and raked a scorching line across my ribs. I cried out and stumbled. The exit was just in front of me, the archway shining like a constellation of white stars. Goddess, we were lucky it hadn't collapsed on us when we came in.

I scrambled away from Marnie on hands and knees. I panicked now as pain lanced up my side with each movement.

Marnie screamed and jumped on me. I flipped over and caught her by the wrists before she could impale me. Marnie might be a better fighter than me, but I was bigger and more desperate and I was pretty sure I could wrestle her to the ground.

Time to play dirty. I brought up a knee and socked her in the ribs. Her breath blew out in a rush and I took the opportunity to launch a punch at her. Since I was holding her wrist, I ended up clocking her across her cheek with the butt of her knife. She screamed, almost feral now. Oh good, now I had her full attention.

So she didn't notice when my gaze drifted past her shoulder and I sent my magic into the ceiling, molding around the soft clay and damp earth. Marnie writhed, unable to free her hands. She head-butted me and starbursts flared across my vision. I held onto my magic and forced it into the dirt, loosening the structure of the tunnel.

A low rumble shook the cave and clods of wet mud began to rain down on us. One smacked Marnie on the back of her head and she jerked up at the impact. We both stared at the roof above us, tons of dirt and rocks bowing out like a bubble ready to pop.

I got my knee up and planted my combat booted foot in Marnie's chest and shoved. My kick forced the smaller woman off of me and into the little dog leg tunnel. The bubble in the ceiling popped with a sound like a thousand books being ripped in half. I crawled, scrambled, and rolled away as dirt and mud and rocks washed down into the cave. A plume of dirt and dust washed past me and darkness devoured me.

I COUGHED and rolled to my knees. The grating sensation of the magic recoil put me back down on the dirt floor, clutching at my head. I rolled onto my side and controlled my breathing, waiting for the pain to subside. Thick dust clouded the cave, but the torch was still lit, so at least I wasn't in the dark. When the recoil had dropped to tolerable levels I crawled over to grab it.

The entrance to the cave was completely blocked, and dirt filled in at least a quarter of that end of the cave. My magic sight told me in an instant that there was no secret to clearing the entrance. Physics had done its level best to bring the earth in that end of the cave to its lowest energy state.

I jerked at the sound of another coughing voice. The sound was dim and muted.

"Roxy?"

Damn. Marnie, but on the other side of the dirt.

Marnie called out again. "If you're still alive in there, Roxy, I hope you enjoy the last bit of your time. Are the cuts on your arm still bleeding? I wonder how long until the vampire wakes up? Do you think he'll be hungry?"

Footsteps now, fading away. "Don't worry, I'll tell Kotori you fought well. Just not well enough."

23

THE PRINCE

Anger and fear had fueled me in the skirmish with Marnie but now the adrenaline drained away. Solving one problem had left me with another. I had not expected to find the Night Queen's son unconscious and chained to a slab on this rogue mission. At least, I assumed he was unconscious.

I lowered myself into the pit and took stock of the situation.

A vampire at rest was an unnerving sight. They didn't breathe and their hearts didn't beat. So they looked dead. Or perhaps, more dead than usual. Less undead? True death meant dissolving into ashes. So a perfectly still vampire was still a threat, only marginally less so.

There was also the complication of the small blonde woman in white ruffled skirts. Dirt streaked her clothing. Tyee's clothing hadn't fared much better, the once smartly tailored wool blazer now torn in places. I stayed a few steps away before trying to wake him.

"Tyee!"

He blinked, his eyes going black in the torchlight. His lips drew back and his fangs dropped. His arms came up and strained against the chains, which didn't look strong enough to hold him. He hit the limit on the chains and the eyebolt shook in the floor. Yeah, definitely not strong enough. I took a step back and whipped out Loki. I did not want to stake the prince and cause an incident. He was a non-combatant in this rogue operation but I also had to defend myself if he was about to get fangy.

Tyee struggled to sitting position on the slab and the chains rattled ominously. Also not spelled silver. I don't know what those rogues were thinking with such haphazard restraints.

There were two problems with my hammers and Samuel's blade. The first problem was that if Tyee dissolved into his mist form, none of my weapons would work. The second problem was that even if he didn't shift into mist, staking the Prince with my wooden hammer would kill him. I needed to rescue him, not slay him. Despite Marnie's arguments, I owed him. I had to try.

"It's me, Roxy." I kept my voice low and calm.

His head tilted forward, gaze intent on my neck. His nostrils flared and I knew he could scent the blood from the wounds Marnie had dealt me. Wounded vampire prince trapped in a cave with me bleeding was a dangerous combination.

I grabbed the throwing axe from my thigh holster and flung it downward at him. It slammed into his thigh and he looked down with a hiss. In that moment of distraction I flung Bashir's spelled silver chain around him. I looped it tight and hoped fervently it would hold.

The effects of the silver chain were instantaneous. Tyee tensed under the silver, like he'd touched a live wire.

"Roxy?" His voice was hoarse and I could hear the confusion in it. He blinked again and the sclera of his eyes brightened, returning to sanity.

"The one and only."

He looked down at his hands, the manacles hanging off his

wrists, the tendons standing out against his pale skin. "I need blood."

I pointed to the lady on the ground. "Wasn't she with you?"

"Eloise was drugged. That's how they got to us."

They'd drugged his source of nourishment. It also explained why they didn't need to use spelled silver to restrain him–they were counting on his drugged state to last a while. So Eloise was drugged unconscious and Tyee couldn't drink from her or end up even weaker. That did pose a problem since he needed blood to regain his strength.

Tough. I wasn't a donor.

I pointed to my face. "Friend, not food."

Tyee's lips quirked. "How you can make me laugh in a situation like this is..."

"It's a gift."

He shook his head, bemused. "I need you to at least remove all these chains."

I wanted to. But I also wanted to keep my blood where it belonged, which was inside my body. I held up a finger.

"I'd be happy to get you out but first I'm going to need a vow from you that you will not take blood from me or compel me to offer it."

His full lips straightened from amusement to annoyance. "Roxy you have my word that I will not drink from you unless you invite me to."

I heard the qualifier.

"How about you won't drink from me and you will not compel me to invite you."

His brows drew down in anger. "It's not an invitation if I compel you. Invitations have power, Roxy."

"Swear it on your mother's life."

His jaw went taut. All his easy charm was gone and he didn't like me right now. "I swear upon my mother's life that I will not drink from you unless you invite me to, nor will I compel you to offer your blood to me."

I nodded and unlooped Bashir's spelled silver.

Tyee's shoulders relaxed a touch and then I wondered if the silver caused him pain. I'd never considered it before.

"Did it hurt?" I asked softly as I wound the silver into a loop back on my belt.

Tyee stared at me, his dark eyes steady on mine. "Yes, although the burn is likely what roused me out of the drug haze."

He didn't thank me for it but we both knew I was helping him out of a bad jam. He might not like my methods, but my results were on point.

I turned my attention to the heavy chain wrapped around his arms and chest. Tapping into my magic, the green lines of the structures glowed and I picked out the weakness in the manacles. *There.*

Without the threat of someone, ie. Marnie, trying to kill me, I took the extra moment to try and find the stillness and subtlety that Bashir had taught me. I extended my magic gently, folding it over the manacles, letting it seep into the nooks and crannies like a thin film of water. The weak point drew my magic like a lodestone and when it was the metal was fully enclosed, my view of the manacle opened like a book.

Before, I had always seen crude lines that sketched out lines of force. My vision now was like going from grainy black and white to high definition full color. Not only did I see how the manacles would break, I knew exactly where and how to apply my Breaker power to do it. Before I had used my magic like a sledgehammer. This was like using a precision chisel.

My magic struck true and the manacle fell in half with a click. A rush of pleasure warmed my body, suffusing me with satisfaction as I felt the chain break. That was all on the metaphysical level but the sound that the chain made was loud enough that Tyee heard it as he looked down quizzically.

This power was what I had truly come to the Veil for and I hadn't even known it. I felt the recoil coming, and it passed through me like a gentle spring breeze. Bashir's finesse had diffused the impact of his recoil. I had done the same and elation rose in me like a hot air balloon.

Tyee shook off the chains and a waterfall of metal showered the floor. He gave me a considering look, perhaps regarding me as somewhat more of a threat now. That was good. I never wanted him to see me as prey.

"You're welcome."

He hopped off the slab, shifted his weight to his legs, and promptly collapsed.

24

A VAMP, A SLAYER, AND A CHEF

With the drugs still in his system, Tyee would need a lot of help getting out of here. I pulled his arm over my shoulder and got him into a fireman's carry. For cutting such a trim figure he was no lightweight.

He struggled to stand and demanded, "Eloise. Get Eloise."

I looked at the blonde slumped on the cave floor. "Is she your..."

It seemed rude to call her a blood slave, or even worse, cattle the way Marnie had. Finally I settled on "employee."

His dark eyes danced with amusement. "Just so."

"I'm not going to be able to carry both of you."

"You don't have to carry me."

"Really? What am I doing now?"

"I can walk."

"You can barely stand."

"You threw an axe at my leg." He sounded incredulous. Which made me feel a little defensive.

"You were going for my neck!"

He grunted and started to move forward. "Get Eloise, please."

"Fine."

With an awkward shuffle, I got Tyee to the wall so he could brace one hand against it while he walked. Then I turned to the employee unconscious on the ground and sighed. Luckily, the woman looked to be small enough for me to lift.

I tried rousing her first by shaking her shoulders. Nothing. Her pulse seemed normal and steady. I tucked her curly blonde hair behind one ear and called her name. "Eloise!"

The yelling did nothing. I debated slapping her but that felt too rude. This woman had already had a lot of trauma tonight. Batting her around on top of it would make things worse.

I sighed again and bent my knees into a deep squat and scooped up Eloise the way I carried our senior golden retriever back home. It was both easier and harder. The dog always tried to lick me when I had to lift her up into the vehicle. Thankfully, Eloise did not do that. However she weighed more and was not cooperating. I tried to think of her like a giant bag of rice. A package.

Curiously, my package was wearing an apron and smelled like apples. Maybe she really was an employee at Delightful Distractions. Maybe they did serve food. Other than the humans I mean.

In an ungainly move, I hefted her over my left shoulder like a kidnapped bride. It was weird, but this whole evening was decidedly strange.

"Thank you." Tyee's voice was low and I felt something in my chest soften at his tone.

"All part of the Slayer's service."

Tyee had straightened up and he looked a little more alert than he had just moments before.

"This would be easier if I could feed. I can easily transport the three of us through the mist. We can be back home in moments."

Nope, nope, and nope. I was not giving up my blood to a

vampire and I definitely did not want to be *transported* with the Mist. And certainly not to wherever Tyee called home. I shook my head. "That's not part of the Slayer's service. Looks like a nice evening stroll is in your near future instead."

The two of us managed to get Eloise hoisted out of the pit. After I climbed out I pulled Tyee out last. I pointed to the exit I'd found earlier and we made a sorry crew as we kicked our way through the debris and stumbled along. Eloise was small but she weighed more than the family golden retriever and this cave passage felt endlessly long. My quads burned, and I huffed from exertion.

Eloise coughed and I almost dropped her.

As quickly as I could manage, I knelt down so I could set down my now squirming package. I got her down and managed to step back before she could kick me. Eloise let loose a stream of rapidfire French. None of it sounded friendly. My high school French was rusty but I was pretty sure her words weren't in my curriculum.

"Eloise. Be calm." Tyee's voice lowered into a tenor that was otherworldly.

"Mon prince." Eloise stopped kicking.

This exchange creeped me out. Eloise's eyes were dilated, stark against her pale skin. She gulped for air when I had lowered her to the ground but the moment she heard Tyee, she'd gone still as a tree, her mouth slack with relief.

I knew that Tyee's mother was the Queen of the Mists and Mind but this was the first time I was seeing the mind component in action and it was a blunt reminder that I had reasons to keep Tyee at a distance, and the not least of it was this power he could exert over my will. I had been right to throw Bashir's spelled silver chain on him earlier– who knows how things would've gone if Tyee had used his voice to compel me.

I would have ended up a couple pints lighter.

He might dress up with pretty manners that made him

seem different than the Shadow Den, but scratch the surface a little, and he wasn't that different. Though I didn't agree with Marnie, I could understand why she didn't bother to distinguish between vampires at all. They were all equally dangerous to humans.

I needed to wash my hands of this, and them, as soon as possible.

"Let's get you back to Delightful Distractions, okay?"

"No. They'll be watching for me there."

"Who's they?"

Tyee's jaw tightened with anger. "O'Malley."

Whoever O'Malley was, I immediately hated him because he was ruining the rest of my evening. Where could I take a vampire prince and his...employee, to rest up until Tyee could recover?

"Okay, can we take you to your...place of rest?"

Tyee barked a laugh. "Do you think I have a lair or a coffin in a basement somewhere, *ma bichette*?

I had thought that. My face reddened and to hide my embarrassment, I turned back to Eloise. "Do you think you can walk?"

She stared up at me, her face helpless. I held out a hand and she took it. Her hand was clammy in mine but she gamely stood up. Then promptly sagged and I lunged to catch her.

"Merci." Eloise leaned heavily against me and then took steps to walk to Tyee.

This was progress. I wanted to get us out of this warren of caves and somewhere safe. Well, safer anyway. Seattle was never truly safe.

"So we should go to the Night Court, then?"

The Night Court was a grand building in the heart of the Pleasure District where Tyee's mother held her gatherings. Like a queen of old, her courtiers attended her there.

"My mother will kill you if she sees me like this with you."

That would be bad. I definitely did not want to go there.

The three of us limped along and Eloise seemed to grow stronger, which allowed the two of us to lend our strength to Tyee when we had to climb out of the cold rock and dark into the dust and rot of the underground city.

The ripe wet smells of this area coupled with the loose dust made this much worse than the caves had been. The urban camo bandana I'd been given would have been perfect for tonight. I would never forget to wear one again. The bandana reminded me what I was doing all this for. I was going to pass the Trials and be a Slayer. Then I would get my ink and be running on these rogue missions on the regular.

Once I had a Midnight Rose I could smuggle some Cure to my mom. It was the best way I could think of to cure her cancer. Nothing else mattered.

The fact that Marnie had tried to kill me tonight, the fact that I was crawling in dirt and filth, and fetching and carrying like a vampire servant–all of it was worth it. It was a price I was willing to pay to reach for a future where my mom was alive and thriving, and Ava and Jasper could have her back the way she had been.

I kept that image at the forefront of my mind as we trudged through an endless night of climbing and crawling out of the filth of Seattle's underground with two drugged individuals. When we made it topside, I wanted to howl with relief. But we weren't in the safe zone yet.

Tyee had apparently been thinking about this as well, because he had an idea. "You'll have to bring me to your place."

"What?"

"Your threshold will keep out O'Malley's thugs."

"Not happening, Tyee."

"I thought we were friends."

"Professional acquaintances, at best."

He made a show of thinking back. "No... Friend, not food. I recall that quite clearly."

Now he was just messing with me. I grinned at him.

We'd just come out of a rogue's cave and we were all in sad shape, but I realized I was almost having fun. Tyee in this distinctly unprincely state was enjoyable to be around. If I had to pick between spending this evening with him or with Marnie, who could end up being my fellow Slayer, it was no contest.

That was a sobering thought. I wasn't supposed to be enjoying my evening with a vampire. My lips flattened.

"I can take you to the front of the Dojo." That would make this the Slayer's problem instead of just mine.

He shook his head. "You would start a war between our houses."

"I'm trying to help you, but you are making it awfully hard."

I couldn't take him to my place. For one thing, it was too personal for me. For another, I wasn't the only one who lived there. I was just one of six units in the building and the building was owned by Mrs. Chu. I wouldn't bring a vampire into the place where we slept.

Eloise swayed and Tyee wrapped his arm around her waist protectively. He whispered to her in rapid fire French and she nodded. Seeing them like this made me feel strange. Like I was intruding on their intimacy. Had Eloise shared Tyee's blood? Did they share the bond that Mrs. Chu had mentioned?

He turned to me and now he was no longer the haughty prince. "I appreciate all you have done for us tonight. Would you at least provide shelter for Eloise until I can procure more assistance?"

I wanted to say yes. I still didn't understand why we couldn't bring her back to the Pleasure District but my ignorance about vampire intrigue, their various factions, and the mysterious O'Malley was hindering my view of the big picture. It didn't seem right to view it this way but Tyee was a bigger issue for me than Eloise. After all my efforts tonight to save him from the rogues and Marnie, I needed to know that I had buttoned things up so that Slayers didn't get tagged with any wrong doing. Ideally, that the Slayers also got some credit for his rescue.

Actually, I did have access to another threshold. One that didn't risk the co-tenants of my apartment.

"I can bring you to my shed."

Tyee blinked. "Why Roxy, are you going to show me your etchings?"

Very funny. "It should have enough of a threshold to keep them out because it's still part of our household but it isn't where any of us sleep."

Tyee's eyebrows drew downward and he nodded slowly. "Yes, that should work."

What had started out as a Slayer training exercise had somehow morphed into me lugging around a drugged French pastry chef and a vampire prince to stow them in my toolshed. I had always felt that life here in the Veil was interesting but this was the next level. At least the hard part was over now.

25

THE JASMINE BOWER

"You want me to do what?" My voice had risen a tad at the end.

Tyee raised a placating hand. "Roxy, I am more grateful than you can know for your assistance thus far. But I still need you to bring a message to my mother."

"Can't you just, you know, telepathically talk to her?"

"It doesn't work like that." He didn't elaborate and now I was bumping against more of these secrets the vampire royals of Mist and Mind had.

My lips firmed into a hard line. "I'm not doing anything else except going upstairs to tell my landlady that I have brought you onto her property."

"Of course." Tyee gave a gracious incline of his head as if he was in a throne room instead of a tool shed. How he managed to look so regal under these circumstances was a mystery. It was also obnoxious.

With that, I fled across the yard to the main building. The steps creaked reassuringly and the hazy outline of Ernest the ghost bobbed alongside me as I went up to the third floor to knock on Mrs. Chu's door.

When she opened the door, a rush of gratitude swept through me, just for how normal she looked. Her gray curls frizzed to a wide halo around her thin face and she'd pulled on a bulky cream cardigan over red flannel pajamas and fuzzy pink slippers. I blurted out my evening's misadventures in a rush and then apologized profusely for bringing a wounded vampire to her shed.

"Aiya," Mrs. Chu huffed.

In that single breath, I heard exasperation, disappointment, and also a note of curiosity. Tyee was something of a local celebrity I guess, and even older shifters like Mrs. Chu weren't immune.

She hustled over to her counter where a dozen glass jam jars rested, filled with steaming, rich brown liquid. Soup, of course. She screwed the lid on one and then tucked it in the giant pocket of her cardigan. Switching out her pink slippers for tall furry lug soled boots, she shooed me out the door and insisted on going to the shed herself.

In the stairwell Ernest waited. "What is happening?"

"I brought home an injured vampire and his blood servant."

Wow, it sounded bad when I said it like that. "They need our help," I added.

The ghost vibrated in agitation, his cloak fritzing at the edges. "Roxie, you can't help vampires."

Mrs. Chu slammed the door behind her. "Ernest, this vampire is from the Court of Mists and Mind. They abide by the Oceanic Pact and they aren't the ones who hurt you."

The ghost slowed his movement, resuming his usual phantasmagorial state. "Not a rogue?"

I shook my head firmly. "No, not a rogue. He's a prince of Mists and Mind."

That seemed to satisfy Ernest and the three of us went down the stairs and out through the yard. A fighter, a shifter, and a ghost. Sounded like the setup to a joke.

When we got to the shed, Mrs. Chu opened the door and took a deep sniff, her werewolf senses telling her all she needed to know. She clucked in disapproval. I didn't know if it was because I had pulled the camping chairs down for Tyee and Eloise or because she could smell that Eloise had been drugged.

Mrs. Chu strode forward, and Tyee struggled to rise to his feet. She made a dismissive motion with her hand. "Sit, sit."

I realized this was when I was supposed to introduce my werewolf landlady to the Night Prince. I really didn't know what the etiquette was for this occasion.

"Uh, Mrs. Chu, this is Tyee Wilder and his employee, Eloise."

"Tyee, and Eloise, this is the owner of the property, Mrs. Chu."

Tyee tipped his head. "I thank you for your hospitality."

Mrs. Chu hmmphed, her aggravation clear. "Don't thank me, thank Roxy. She didn't know any better, but you do."

A rush of embarrassment heated my cheeks. It was true, I didn't know what I was supposed to have done in the extraordinary events of this evening, but I thought I'd done the right thing. Should have told Tyee to fend for himself back in the cave? Maybe I should have left them there and gone to fetch help? The Slayers hadn't exactly given me a handbook for what to do in the event of discovering a royal hostage.

Tyee's chin lifted a fraction. "I shall repay the debt. I owe Roxy a boon."

Mrs. Chu raised a bony finger and shook it at his face. "And don't you forget it or my sisters and I will remind you!"

Goddess forbid that a pack of angry older shifter aunties were ever unleashed on him. Waves of embarrassment alternated with stunned amusement as Mrs. Chu talked to him like she would pick up a rolled up newspaper next and swat his nose. Tyee did look slightly chastened. It seemed even princes were not immune from the power of the scolding finger.

"Rest assured that I will not forget what Roxy has done for me this evening, Mrs. Chu."

She hmmphed. "Now, I will see to this young lady who has suffered in your employ."

She pulled the jar of soup out of her cardigan pocket and unscrewed the lid. The smell of bone broth, ginseng, and goji berries wafted out, hearty and comforting. She bid Eloise to drink. Eloise cast a wary eye on the werewolf auntie proffering soup and Tyee made an encouraging gesture. Eloise tipped the jar and drank deeply. Mrs. Chu smiled as Eloise finished the jar.

"Merci, madame." Eloise looked better, her cheeks taking on a pinker hue after the warm soup.

Mrs. Chu made a clucking sound and told Eloise she needed more soup.

Tyee cleared his throat. "Roxy, is that a ghost with you?"

I followed his gaze to Ernest, who had come in with us but had been silent so far. "This is Ernest. He lived in my apartment before me until he was killed by a rogue."

Tyee's face hardened. "There's a reason for the Pact, and why we work with the Slayers to control rogues in Seattle. On behalf of the Court of Mist and Mind, and all those who adhere to the Pact, you have my condolences."

When he said this, he sounded like his station–a prince of the Mists and Mind, and with the mantle of authority that came from being a leader. I found myself nodding and then stopped, chagrined. I wasn't one of his subjects. We were not friends, just temporary allies.

Ernest tilted his head. "Okay."

That's all he said, but he stopped vibrating and his expression looked calm.

Mrs. Chu tucked the empty jar back in her pocket. "You need more soup, young lady."

After she went back to the house to grab another jar of soup for Eloise, Tyee returned to his prior line of attack. "Roxy, I know I've asked a lot from you already but my mother needs to know all that has transpired."

My shoulders sagged. I needed to get him and Eloise out of my shed. Mrs. Chu hadn't asked for any of this. And until I had him safely delivered to the Night Court, I hadn't cleared Slayers from possible allegations of wrongdoing. Marnie had likely made it back to the Dojo by now. What was she telling them? What had she told Kotori? My stomach twisted into new and interesting knots.

What a disaster.

Numbly, I nodded. "Fine. Tell me what I'm supposed to say to her."

He reached up to his neck and unhooked a white shell necklace. "Give me your hand, Roxy."

I opened my hand and he placed the necklace in my palm. The shells glimmered with their pearly inlay and the pendant was a Chinook totem, the stylized salmon carved in smooth brown wood. I ran my fingers over it gently. "What's this for?"

"A token for safe passage."

Tyee didn't let go of my hand. I pulled gently but he held fast.

"Are you going to give me my hand back?"

"There's just one more thing you'll need, for Lilja."

What he did next left me speechless.

And then I left to go see the Night Queen.

THE NIGHT QUEEN held court in a grand Victorian called the Jasmine Bower in the center of the Pleasure District. It was a good spot from which to survey all that she ruled over. Despite its name, there was no jasmine planted out front, just rows and rows of majestic cherry trees with glowing pink blossoms, the branches strung with golden fairy lights. The cherry trees and enclosed garden set the Victorian a bit back on its double lot, giving privacy from the busy throng of city dwellers strolling on the main drag.

The Jasmine Bower was three stories tall, painted in cream, teal, and gold trim. The Victorian loomed above me with its ominously steep pitched roof.

I stared at the wraparound porch above me, where the Night Queen had her imposing foot soldiers posted at each corner. They had the high ground and I really did not want to go up those stairs to the porch and try to claim the safe passage Tyee had assured me.

I didn't think he had lied to me. What reason would he have to do that?

The guards all wore what I was coming to think of as the Night Queen's livery–tailored wool suits so deeply indigo they looked almost black. Highly polished black leather boots with tapered toe fronts and hand-stitched seams. I counted three men and one woman, their long hair tied back in neat queues.

While the queen's guard lounged in casual stances against the porch beams, I didn't believe it for a second. She was the Queen of Mists and Mind. It was said she could command her Guard with a single thought and they fought as a cohesive unit. Vamps were fast–these guards together were lethal. These four were likely more than capable of keeping anyone from getting in.

Tyee's disgust had been apparent when he told me O'Malley was behind his kidnapping. Trouble was brewing between the vampire factions. The queen's guard wasn't just for show–they were to keep O'Malley and his ilk out. Unfortunately, they were also keeping me out and I needed to get in to speak with their Queen.

The double doors, a welcoming teal, sported two raven head knockers that looked like solid gold. It made sense. Silver burned vampires and the fae. Gold on the other hand, not only looked nice, it made for a nice magical conduit. The door-knockers were likely spelled.

I narrowed my eyes and let the green lines of the structure fill my inner eye. For all its cosmetic beauty, it was still a centuries old building. There could be deferred maintenance of other oddities that time had pressed down upon and that I could exploit. I exhaled. Ahh. Termite activity. A little wood rot here and there. It might be enough.

Not that I was planning on bringing down the building or anything.

Especially if I were inside.

I strolled up the winding stone pathway and plastered a wide smile on my face and gave a big friendly wave. There was no way I was going to fight my way in. I might as well try the friendly route. "Excuse me, is this where I can find the Night Queen?"

The two guards closest to the front door moved. Really moved. One moment they were on the porch and in a blink they were down on the walkway and in striking range. And this is why Slayers went out in pairs. There was no such thing as a fair fight one on one with a vamp. They had incredible speed and strength. Some could turn invisible. Some could fly. Some could mesmerize you. Some like Tyee could do more than one of those things.

The woman in the back stepped to the right, her eyes studying my hammers. Thor and Loki were unusual to be sure but I didn't think she knew who I was or anything like that. Her face merely registered professional curiosity.

She was a little shorter than I was, but her build had the

heft that told me I really wouldn't like taking a punch from her. Her short blond hair was pomaded back showing off flawless pale skin. Her eyebrows were so fair they were almost translucent and it gave her face a disturbingly emotionless landscape.

The tall guard in front spoke, his voice deep and rolling forth in a startling wave of sound. His face was stern and punctuated with a neatly trimmed beard. He stood ramrod straight with the posture of a drill sergeant. "Queen Lilibet is not expecting visitors. State your business."

If my smile got any bigger, my face would crack. "Prince Tyee sent me, with a message for his lady mother."

The blonde guard gave a huff and her lip curled with disdain. "The Prince comes himself. He does not send servants to treat with the Queen."

She stepped forward and I held up a hand, my fingers spread wide with Tyee's totem dangling, "Wait, he gave me this."

Her eyes narrowed in suspicion. "That is the Prince's token."

"Yes, he granted me safe passage to speak with his mother."

The first guard sneered and moved forward. "More likely you are a thief who stole it."

She held up a hand and he halted, giving a deferential tip of his head. Clearly, she was in charge here for all that he had stepped up first to confront me. This had to be Captain Lilja.

"What has Tyee asked you to deliver to the Queen?" she asked.

"I'm to give her the message myself."

"The Queen's Guard serves as one, and we are all the Queen's eyes and ears." She said this as if by rote and I sensed this was some kind of motto.

If I didn't get this right, there would be bloodshed here in the Queen's garden. My blood, most likely. I lowered my hand slowly, the beads on Tyee's necklace clicking quietly.

"It will just be a moment of her time, and it's important."

The woman's face was devoid of the slightest emotion. "The Night Queen will not be pleased to be disturbed from her festivities."

I let my smile drop, the time for pleasantries gone. I hadn't wanted to do this. With a grimace, I crushed my fingers around Tyee's totem and the sharp edge of the charm pricked my skin. I squeezed harder and blood welled, activating it.

My voice dropped into a lower range, the legacy of Mist and Mind keying off my blood. "Your Prince bids you to grant safe passage to the holder of this totem and this is how you obey him, Lilja?"

Though the words came from my lips, they were uttered in Tyee's voice, amplified by his totem necklace.

Captain Lilja's eyes widened in shock. "As my lord bids."

The guard behind her snapped to and cleared the path to the porch.

Tyee's gambit had worked. When he'd been instructing me earlier, I'd watched in horror as he'd pricked his palm and then mine with the charm, and a black mist had risen from our intertwined hands, obscuring them totally. My arm looked like it had suddenly lost my wrist and hand. He'd spoken a few words so softly I couldn't hear them, then blew gently on the mist until swirled away and revealed our hands, the blood wiped clean as if it had never been. I thought I had known what vampires could do but it seemed that vampire royals had their own forms of magic and conjuration. It had been deeply unsettling.

I hadn't wanted to do it, but this was preferable to being beaten to a pulp by the stalwart captain. So relief won out that I'd gotten this far and I kept my head high as I passed the guards to vault up the steps to the porch.

The double doors awaited me and behind me Captain Lilja followed, her footsteps putting her at my back. I stiffened.

"My Queen, your son sends this messenger with his totem."

I realized she was addressing the doors. Or maybe the knockers? The eyes of the raven knockers glowed white as if hearing my thoughts.

The doors swung open halfway, revealing a hallway strewn with golden fairy lights.

This was a night of revelations for me. I had thought of vampires as beings whose very existence were magical but I had never thought of them using magic. But nothing else could explain the way Tyee's totem had transformed my voice. Similarly the Night Queen's abode seemed layered with enchantments. Which covens did work for the Night Queen?

I looked at the open doors. What would await me within? Would I get a direct audience with the Queen? It was a good thing that Tyee had sent me with his totem, but it had required a show of force before the Night Queen would speak with me. If I had known I would have had a power struggle with the Queen's Guard, I might have been tempted to double back and find another way in.

I raised my hand to push the door wider for me to enter but then I froze in mid motion. A chill raced up my spine–I wanted to turn around, get back on my board and skate back to the Dojo. I thought about all my choices that led me here to the Night Queen's threshold and had an instant of regret that I didn't refuse Tyee and let someone else deal with it. I told myself that I would walk out of here unscathed and that I would live to finish the Trial. Maybe I even halfway believed it.

I pushed the doors wider and strode in.

INSTEAD OF THE home of a deadly vampire enchantress, I somehow ended up in a fairy bower of the night blooming variety. The heavy scent of jasmine hung thick in the air, sweet and dizzying. Lush green leaves fanned out from the seat of her throne with star shaped flowers climbing up the sides.

The throne room was set up to make everyone approach as if a supplicant. Her throne rose above us, the dais a bed of moonflowers, the white blossoms dainty against the dark foliage. Above, the ceiling vaulted up to the roof, where antique glass panels let in the purple light. An ornate chandelier, heavy with candles, hung from the roof casting flickering yellow light over the space.

Courtiers clad in exquisite dress parted as I walked forward.Colorful fabrics swirled and soft chamber music played from hidden alcoves. Dark, hungry eyes followed me on the meandering path to the throne. The hammering beat of my own heart grew louder in my ears as I drew closer.

The Queen of Mists and Mind lounged casually on her flower throne, her long dark hair a riot of shiny curls. Her smooth brown skin radiated youth but her deep set eyes burned with the fires of a millennia.

On the Queen's left stood a petite woman with short salt and pepper hair and razor precise bangs. Her eyes gleamed like black marbles and her skin was brown with sun. She must have been turned later in life. She reminded me of my second grade teacher, Mrs. Yamagami, but with dressier clothes. She wore a sleek pencil suit the color of midnight and her pants had a silky black tuxedo stripe on the sides. Around her waist was a gold chain link belt and an ancient set of keys dangled from them. Mika Inaba, the Chatelaine. She held the literal keys to the castle.

To the Queen's right side stood a tall slender man with chestnut hair and a full mustache and beard. He wore the same deep indigo color blazer as the guards but his was velvet, giving him a worldly air. Gold rings adorned his bony fingers. The jewelry seemed to ooze with power, like the raven door knockers at the front door. Which coven had spelled those rings, and how?. Sebastien Delacour was the Queen's seneschal. When the Slayers dealt with the Night Queen, Delacour was the intermediary. I'd heard rumors that he'd been seneschal for the two prior Night Queens, making him one of the oldest vampires in Seattle.

It felt strange to stand here in front of him as he regarded me, his thin lips in a frown. He had to have interacted with my dad at some point. Could he see the resemblance between me and the late Gabriel Lim?

Sebastien turned to the Queen and intoned, "Roxanne Lim, spawn of Gabriel the Breaker." His voice rang out through the hall.

I guess he did recognize me.

Queen Lilibet interlaced her fingers and the click of polished bone bangles against her slender wrists sounded loud in the cavernous room. The rumor was she'd drunk down a coven of witches and wore the bones of necromancers.

"Ms. Lim. Step forward. To what do I owe the pleasure of this visit?"

By sheer force of will, I kept my knees from knocking together. I had no doubt that she had been briefed on everything there was to know about me, down to my boot size.

I cleared my throat, "Your son asked me to bring a message to you, ma'am. I mean, your highness."

A titter of laughter came from behind me.

Queen Lilibet tilted her head, her face softening with curiosity.

"It is not everyday that we are visited by ghosts from the past."

While some in the throne room were holding whispered conversations, Sebastien had not taken his eyes from me since I'd entered the Queen's presence. His voice was a low rumble that promised trouble. "Indeed, my queen. Given her pedigree I question the veracity of her claim. My sources report the Slayers are--"

The queen cut in smoothly. "Surely this little rabbit is no Slayer?"

I clenched, keeping my back straight. I knew how this worked, with the throne and the dais elevated, making applicants to the queen feel small and inferior. And yes, everyone in this room could probably take me apart with one hand but I wasn't going to act like it.

Sebastien sneered. "Does it matter, my queen? Consider the company she keeps. The weapons she wears so disrespectfully in your presence."

"Hmm. I was under the impression she has been keeping company with my son."

Burn! I clamped down and kept my face calm.

Sebastien's face stiffened. "My queen, I only meant--"

"I know what you meant, Bastien." She waved a hand airily. "And I think I know when I have someone's measure."

"You will forgive Sebastian, Ms. Lim. He sees plots and schemes where I see only simplicity. You are, simple, are you not, Ms. Lim?"

Her eyes bored into mine. The effort to keep my knees straight became a strain that threatened to break me. Creeping tendrils of ecstasy clawed at my mind, pulling me forward, urging me to fall on my knees and debase myself at the Queen's feet.

I clenched my fists until Tyee's totem cut into my palm. The pain sparked like a fire in a dark room and my mind ran for the safety of that light in the darkness.

As quickly as it had appeared, the mental pressure from the queen disappeared. Without the resistance to fight against, this time I did fall to my knees. I gasped for air and found myself covered with clammy sweat and also unbelievably turned on.

Goddess of the moon. Was this what Tyee's power was like?

I forced open my hands. My blood was smeared across Tyee's totem and tracks of red followed the creases of my skin like a river system.

The queen sniffed. "How apropos. My son has ever been defiant. Now, Ms. Lim, the pleasantries are over and I tire of our little drama. You have something for me?"

::WHAT IS IT:: her voice whispered in my mind, an unwelcome intrusion for all its soft tone.

I clamped down on the surge of anger that flushed my neck and face red hot. In this moment, all I wanted was to be as strong of a Breaker as Bashir had predicted, so that I could bring down that chandelier on their heads. Now I wanted to be the Breaker in truth, and more powerful than even my father. Then even the Night Queen might think twice before shoving me down the next time we crossed paths.

My fingers clenched into the fabric of my utility pants, a force of effort for me to avoid touching my weapons. I couldn't make a show of aggression nor could I show weakness here. I had been forced to my knees with vampires to my back and their Queen straight ahead--my situation couldn't be worse.

Tyee had been clear–that no one but his mother was to know about what had happened. I didn't think he would have appreciated all these vampires listening in. It didn't matter if I whispered, their keen senses would pick any smidgeon of sound.

I lifted my head and stared straight at the Queen and let my mouth shape the word "O'Malley" before asking loudly, "May we speak privately?"

Sebastian's jaw hardened and he leaned forward but the Night Queen held up a dainty hand. "Bastien, clear the room."

26

PRINCE RESTORED

S pending the rest of my evening, or dawn as the case was, to lead a small contingent of vampire guards and two of their "employees" to my shed was not something I'd ever imagined doing. I hoped to never do it again.

Ernest bobbed beside us, his cool presence a welcome buffer.

Captain Lilja stuck to my side like glue. Maybe the Night Queen had told her to or maybe she'd spotted Bashir's silver chain looped at my waist. Nothing advertised you were a vampire Slayer better than carrying around a spelled silver chain. Thankfully she wasn't my problem for long. It was with a deep sense of relief that I brought Tyee and Eloise out of the shed.

Captain Lilja barked at the siblings, "Anoush and Davit, attend the Prince."

Tyee's two employees rushed to his side. Thankfully, they didn't call him Master or I would have been even more disturbed by the whole scene. Davit and Anoush looked to be brother and sister, round-faced and with broad foreheads. They both wore their black hair shaved high and tight, with a sheen of pomade across the wave that curved in an elaborate swoosh. Where the guards had the dark midnight of livery, the siblings wore no jackets, just indigo pintucked shirts with an open tab collar. The better to expose their necks I supposed.

The pair got their shoulders under Tyee's arms and helped him limp away from my shed. As he passed me he gave me a searing look. I stepped back in surprise, I was so used to Tyee being nonchalant and superficial. But tonight had changed that dynamic between us. There shouldn't have been a dynamic between us beyond Slayer and vampire but there it was. I'd rescued him and undertaken the extraordinary effort of going to the heart of his mother's domain. He'd given me his token and showed me a bit of his magic that was a closely kept secret among the royals. I'd trusted the token would work.

Somehow we'd gone from two wary acquaintances to whatever this new status was and I didn't know how to feel about it.

Anoush and Davit laid Tyee gently on the ground. They both spoke to him in soft whispers, then Davit opened his collar and leaned over Tyee, exposing his neck. Tyee's eyes went black and his fangs elongated. I turned away before I could see something I couldn't unsee.

I found myself face to face with Captain Lilja who had a knowing smirk on her face, having a laugh at my discomfort. I scowled. "Are we done here?"

Her smirk disappeared and she looked around, taking in the surrounding buildings. "Yes, I believe we no longer require your services. Queen Lilibet thanks you for services excellently rendered."

Right. It was almost dawn. If I was lucky, the Slayers were combing the city for me. I had better make an appearance at headquarters first. If I were really lucky, Kotori wouldn't be around to give me a thrashing.

Ernest fluttered in front of me. "Roxy, would you like me to come with you?"

That was sweet but I needed to be alone to clear my head before heading to the Dojo. "I'll be ok, Ernest. Thanks."

I bolted down the side alley that led to the front of my building, blocking out the soft sucking sounds of Tyee feeding, punctuated by low moans of pleasure from his blood thrall.

OF ALL THE possibilities my mind conjured as I rode my board to Slayer's Dojo, the one that greeted me hadn't even been in the realm of possibility. I rounded the corner to Denny Park and found an honest to goodness coach drawn by four ebony black horses parked on the grass. The horses' coats were glossy black and each animal wore finely tooled leather armor that shielded their faces and chests. The coach was a lavish affair, with exquisitely gilded woodwork decorating the doors and wheels. Even the coachman's seat was upholstered with fine leather cushions.

I kicked up my board and wandered close to the coach. No one was inside and I ran my hand down one of the running boards. The wood was coated in a thick coat of lacquer and polished to mirror smoothness. There wasn't even dust on it. How did this thing exist in Seattle, and not have dust on it?

The sound of screeching metal and clanking gears set a flight of birds up from the trees. The double gates to HQ lumbered open and revealed Sebastien Delacour standing at the head of a small contingent of the Night Queen's guardsmen. His gaze managed to fall directly on me just before I was able to remove my hand from the coach.

He glowered at me.

I snatched my hand back like the coach was made of hot metal and backed away. Delacour strode out of Slayers HQ and his guards filed out behind him in a neat line, marching with near mechanical precision. As they moved out, I noticed a large chest had been left in the courtyard, with intricate woodwork and golden inlay that matched the coach.

Delacour stopped a few feet from me and regarded me as if I was a particularly annoying wad of gum stuck to the soles of his hand-crafted leather boots. His soldiers spread out and took up positions on and around the coach.

After a moment where he seemed to swallow something vile he said, "Ms. Lim. My Queen sends her regards and what she feels is adequate compensation for..."

Again with the look of something bitter caught in his throat. "...your services rendered."

The vampire's eyes fell off of me as if I was as insignificant as a rock and he stepped into the coach, slamming the door shut in one smooth motion. Without a word the coach lurched into motion and the vampire guards moved off as well, in perfect sync with the horses.

When the coach pulled away I could again see the open gate of the Dojo. Standing in the middle of the gate was my uncle, Altan, and Aislinn. Altan seemed to be enjoying a particularly good joke, which Aislinn also seemed to be having none of. Slightly behind the three of them were Bashir, and, cracking her knuckles so loudly I could hear them across the lawn, Kotori.

Goddess save me.

As soon as the vampires were gone Aislinn went for the throat. "She's stubborn, reckless, and nearly precipitated a war with the Mist and Mind!" Her voice rang like a bell across the lawn, as clear as if she were next to me.

Altan seemed to be enjoying himself, much to my uncle's dismay. "Oh, I don't know, Ash. I think she did fine tonight."

The big man pointed at the ornate wooden chest. "And look what we got out of it! This will keep our fighters in top form for a year!!"

Aislinn would not be swayed. "It is not our mandate to save

the vampires from themselves. We are charged with protecting the city. We have specific contracts that define what we do and do not engage in. If the vampires want to eat their own young that is none of our concern!"

Uncle Samuel pinched the bridge of his nose. "Ash, you know it's not that simple."

The tall fae seemed to be vibrating with anger. "It used to be."

In a swirl of her gauzy cloak she spun on her heel and left. My uncle turned to Altan. "I guess we know Ash's vote. What do you say?"

Altan grinned. "It's been a while since we've had someone who could mix things up like this. She's got your brother's eye for trouble."

"That's what Ash is afraid of."

"Ash could use a little fear." Altan looked my way and winked at me. "I like her. I say she stays."

Samuel groaned. "You know I can't be the deciding vote."

"Funny how that worked out. Well, that's why they pay you the big bucks, right?" Altan slapped my uncle on the shoulder and walked off as well.

My uncle waved to me. "Roxy, come here. You're listening anyway."

As I approached my uncle, Bashir and Kotori walked up as well and it felt not unlike presenting myself before an executioner. Bashir looked tired but thoughtful. Kotori's face was unreadable, but there was a coiled tension in her shoulders, and an odd stiffness in her gait. Had she been injured in the caves?

Samuel looked back and forth between me and the other two Slayers. "I can't make the decision on my own because of who she is. I need to know what the two of you think we should do about Roxy's candidacy."

Goddess. My uncle really wasn't going to cut me any slack.

It would be simple for him to vote to keep me in the Slayers, but he wasn't going to let there be even the hint of favoritism. My breaths turned shallow and my chest grew cold. Aislinn's anger made it clear that this wasn't just about ending my candidacy today, it was about blacklisting me from Slayers.

My fate here in the Twilight had suddenly distilled down to Kotori and Bashir's opinion–the very people whom I had disobeyed in the cave.

Bashir spoke first. "If I were this candidate's mentor I would comment on the strength of her resolve, and the clear benefit of her magic as an addition to our dwindling stable of talent. I might mention her skills in combat, or her curious ability to make alliances with vampire royals and fae alike. Alas, I am not this one's mentor, and I shall keep my counsel to myself and defer to Kotori."

He made a face like he was heartbroken and stepped back.

Kotori hadn't moved and I noticed that her hands were clenched into tight fists. What was happening here?

The lines in Samuel's lean cheeks deepened until he looked like he was etched in granite. "Ko-chan..."

Kotori raised her hand now, palm out, and my uncle quieted. With a visible effort, Kotori loosened her shoulders and I could see the tension unwind in her back. I felt my own back relax, only now realizing I'd been preparing myself as if for a blow. Kotori closed her eyes and took a deep breath, letting it out slowly through her nose.

When she opened her eyes, they were clear and calm again, and perhaps a bit red around the edges. She regarded me with clinical detachment.

"She makes enough noise to wake the dead when she walks. She insists on toys instead of weapons. She is reckless to the point of disaster with her magic. She disobeyed my clear orders to refrain from stupidity."

The more she said, the colder my chest got, until my vision

darkened and tunneled down to Kotori's bright eyes. This was it. I was washing out right here, right now. I dimly heard my uncle take a sharp breath. I had failed my dead father and my dying mother in one disastrous stroke. I cursed Tyee Wilder and the day I'd laid eyes on him.

Samuel sighed and then pointed to the Queen's wooden chest. "And this? Isn't this worth something?"

I wondered what the heck was in that thing. I hadn't seen them crack it open and yet they all seemed to know what was in it.

Kotori's upper lip curled in disdain. "I leave the politics to you, Samuel."

I got the feeling that most of them left the politics to Samuel. I wondered how he'd earned that privilege and why they all seemed to treat him like he was in charge. My father had never mentioned how high his brother had risen in the ranks so it was with a bit of awe I watched the other Freaks defer to Samuel.

Samuel grunted. "Fine. Forget the fact that the Night Queen just delivered her son's body weight in crystal to us in gratitude for Roxy's work tonight."

Kotori turned and gave me a tight smile, a sliver of teeth. "I do not feel I have seen enough of this candidate's work to fully evaluate her potential. I expect her to improve. We will start with sparring at five bells, tomorrow."

Kotori turned to Samuel. "She should stay and prove herself."

I sagged with relief, and even my uncle looked like he was ready to fall over. Without another word, Kotori turned and strode back to the dojo. Bashir clucked his tongue and clapped a heavy hand on my back.

"Roxy, you will live to slay another day."

My eyes burned with tears and I bent my head to knuckle

them away. I didn't trust myself to say anything or else I might start sobbing in front of Bashir and Samuel.

I drew in several ragged breaths and when I felt like I could speak, I finally said, "See you at five bells tomorrow."

Then I put my skateboard board down and used my ride home to get my nerves under control.

27

PROVING GROUND

K otori said I'd have to prove myself. I wanted to do that. I was profoundly grateful that I'd gotten another chance to do so. On the other hand, frustration dogged my every kick and bump home as I replayed the prior events after Marnie and I had been given our orders by Kotori.

How was it stupid to save Tyee and Eloise? They weren't rogues. Slayers did business with the Night Court. I forgot to ask but I assumed Marnie got out fine after she'd tried to kill me. The injustice grated and I vacillated between anger and tears all the way back to my apartment.

Samuel hadn't taken my side. I knew he hadn't been there but was it too much to ask that he talk to me first to get my side of the story?

No one at the Dojo had asked me what had happened. No one.

I thought I was joining a team but at the first ride along, Marnie had thrown me under the bus and everyone else had bought it.

I needed the Slayers, but now I knew I couldn't count on

being part of the team or getting the benefit of the doubt from them. I had to stay focused on why I was there, and what I could get out of it. Nothing more, nothing less.

Tomorrow I would be at the Dojo at five bells and show Kotori what I was made of.

I dashed up the stairs to my apartment, and Ernest made his usual ghostly appearance. He hovered near me and his mouth moved but I couldn't make out what he was saying. Finally I stopped moving when I reached my door on the second level and Ernest tried again.

"Slayer?" he mouthed.

"Almost." Then my face crumpled.

"You okay?"

"No, not really, but I will be."

I gritted my teeth. "I'll be a Slayer soon. But I made a mistake yesterday."

"What happened?" Ernest's outline shimmered as he hovered against my wall.

"Just..everything with Tyee. I don't know what else I could have done."

Ernest nodded.

"Then I went back to the Dojo and the Slayers almost voted me out for not following the mission parameters."

I wanted to punch the wall, but that wasn't fair to Mrs. Chu, or the wall.

Ernest patted me, his ghostly arm passing through my shoulder.

Strangely, that did make me feel a little better. For a ghost he was a surprisingly good listener.

"Thanks, Ernest."

I went into my apartment and took a deep calming breath. It felt like years had passed since I had last been home. I put the kettle on and then warmed up some rice for me and Ernest. I sliced some char siu and scrambled some eggs then plated everything up for me along with a smaller plate for Ernest.

Some protein would help me put my life in perspective.

The kettle whistled and I brewed some jasmine oolong, the last of my precious stash. Today merited the good stuff.

I poured out some for Ernest too and then carefully carried his plate and his tea to the hallway. He thanked me and ate silently, the food and tea vanishing with each second. Before when I'd first fed him, he'd eaten, but the food had looked untouched. Now, the food was gone. It seemed like Ernest was gaining more of a toehold on this earthly plane. I didn't know what the implications of that were. But I didn't have time to dwell on it either.

Loud coos echoed from my balcony and I rushed back there. It was Noodle! He was back from the post office.

I cooed back. "Hey Noodle, who's a good girl?"

I filled his water and his treat bowl and gently unwrapped the message canister from his leg. My fingers shook as I unrolled the message. The day's adrenaline was gone and I was running on fumes and prayers now.

I smoothed out the crinkled paper, my eyes scanning the neat blocky penmanship of the postal messenger. "Sis, mom has good days and bad. We miss you. Good luck at the Trials. Love, Ava and Jasper."

My eyes closed in despair. I could read between the careful wording. Mom was getting worse. Today I would deposit the silver Samuel had given me. It should get Mom another transfusion. Give her a little more breathing room. I was closer to pulling off my plan but I needed more time. Once I passed the Trials, I would be an initiate and eventually be trained to do an exsanguination. Using the Midnight Rose, I could get that vampire blood to my mother. She needed the Cure.

That had to be what my dad had been raving about in his last days. The way he'd lamented how the Slayers had a cure for my mom. My dad had been talking about the Midnight Rose–I was sure of it. Because he hadn't gotten specific enough about it, he hadn't broken the geas, but he'd said enough for me to promise him I would get on the Slayers. That I would make sure mom got better. Now my dad was gone and it was up to me.

I wouldn't let them down.

Some days I felt incredibly guilty here because I had so much freedom here in the Veil. I had to hustle hard and often for food and silver but I was only taking care of myself and that had been infinitely easier than managing a household and mom's medical appointments.

But Jasper, Ava, and I were a team. We would pull through. I believed it with all my heart.

I stroked Noodle's head and changed out the paper for Noodle and Dumpling's dovecote. Then I went inside to get a pen and some paper, carefully writing out. "One last Trial. Uncle Samuel has given me silver for mom's treatment. Will deposit ASAP."

Then I wrapped it up and tucked it into a little canister to wrap around Dumpling's leg. I gave her smooth head a little scritch and sent her off and on her way to the post office. I just needed a little more time. Jasper was the older one, and I knew he was doing his best to hold it all together, the same way I had after Dad had passed.

We would be okay. Dumpling's gray wings soared into the purple haze of the twilight and I let my eyes flutter closed and the cool breeze of Seattle wash over my face. I was done with tears. I needed to prepare for tomorrow.

I went back inside and wrapped up the rest of the char siu.

I cleared the empty plate and tea cup from Ernest's spot and took the stairs two at a time to Mrs. Chu's flat.

She answered on the first knock. "Roxy! Done rescuing vampire princes?"

I nodded emphatically. "Never doing that again, I swear!"

Mrs. Chu grunted and stepped back to let me in. "Hmm. You better mean that, Roxy. The vampires are no one to fool with."

I nodded which was apparently not enough for her.

"They may look like you and me, but they are not like us."

She sat me down on her threadbare couch and held my hands. "Most of them have been on this earth longer than anyone should."

"Tyee is only in his thirties--"

"Did I ask for your opinion? I'm giving you advice and you should be listening. He is a member of the royal court. The vampires of the court have existed for so long they have long forgotten what it means to be human. To be alive! To them, we are as inconsequential as insects are to humans. Do you understand me?"

I nodded contritely. There was nothing else I could do, not with her hackles up like this.

Mrs. Chu sighed and dropped my hands. I had a feeling she didn't believe me. Truthfully, I didn't believe me. Kotori had simply told us not to do anything stupid. What I had done wasn't stupid. I knew that in my bones. Letting Tyee die like that wasn't something I could live with. Even if he was a vampire.

A vampire, just like I was supposed to be fighting against if I became a Slayer. A vampire that I needed to exsanguinate if I wanted to save mom.

If I became a Slayer. If. I'd come dangerously close to washing out tonight. If I didn't make it, how could I go back and face mom? Ava and Jasper were holding our family together with strings and prayers. It would break them, break us, if I didn't come through.

I buried my face in my hands. How had my life gotten so confusing in just a few days? The couch creaked as Mrs. Chu got up and padded to her little kitchen. I needed to talk to someone, maybe my uncle, and try to figure out what was going on.

The couch shifted again and Mrs. Chu's comforting weight settled next to me along with the smell of rich broth. She waved the soup bowl under my nose.

"Aiya. Drink. You need your strength for tomorrow, yes?"

Of course she was right. The soup was hot and rich, the broth thick with root vegetables and warming spice. My chest warmed as the soup went down my throat. As I drained the dregs the last of my adrenaline petered out and fatigue crashed over me like a wave. Sleep pulled me down and I was vaguely aware of Mrs. Chu clucking as she tucked me into her couch.

I slept and dreamed of blood and failure.

I WOKE up with a headache but a clear mind. Giving Mrs. Chu a hug, I went through my chores for the building and then gathered up Samuel's silver to take to the Seattle Silver Reserve.

In the last hundred years that Seattle had fallen under the twilight, currency had taken on a different weight here. Crystal was like diamonds, but most of us couldn't get our hands on any, so silver was king.

Ernest floated down the stairs and came with me. I had never seen him so far from the apartment building but since the Herbal College was along the route to the Reserve, I wondered if this was a familiar haunting ground for Ernest. Just how far could he go? Was there some sort of tether for ghosts?

As we approached the Herbal College campus, I slowed.

"Ernest, can you go anywhere in Seattle?"

He looked confused and then he stopped to gaze campus. Students were milling about, a sea of bobbing green cloaks over jeans and boots. Some intrepid students had bare legs under the cloaks so they must have been wearing shorts or skirts.

Finally he nodded. "Yes, I can. But it's only when I'm looking for someone."

"Like me?"

"Yes."

"Why me?" That had confused me. I had seen him for months before I'd finally realized I should do something for him.

"You were living in my apartment."

I guess that was a good reason for Ernest to feel a connection to me. That and I'd been feeding him. Mrs. Chu had warned me against it but I much preferred an Ernest I could talk to than a forlorn hungry Ernest that was haunting me.

"Okay. But what about your friends or your teachers from the college?"

Ernest nodded. "Yes, sometimes I pop in on my lab partner, Ana Victoria."

Then he waved. "I'll go visit her now. She's probably in the greenhouse."

I waved. "See you later, Ernest."

Seattle Silver Reserve's building towered above me, with soaring Corinthian columns and a row of gargoyles on top. The rocky gray stone of the gargoyles seemed to suck all the light and their heads moved with disturbing slowness. Lest anyone try to rob the Reserve, the gargoyles could fly and were impervious to magic. I wondered how the Reserve paid them to work here. It's not like the gargoyles needed silver or credit. Then I realized I didn't know what they ate.

On that disturbing note, I hastened up the steep marble stairs to the teller windows.

Every step radiated a zing of energy under the soles of my boots. Enchantments had been layered all over the building and runes carved onto every visible surface. Absolutely every inch of this building was geared to a visitor getting on with their business and not staying a second longer.

Silver was a lovely conduit for magic and more importantly, toxic to shifters the way iron was to Fae. That made it uniquely valuable to humans here. The Seattle Silver Reserve had the added benefit that it maintained a branch on the other side of the Veil. Silver in, credits out.

Dad had an account here and we drained it all paying for Mom's treatments.

Samuel had given me forty ounces of silver. That was about six thousand credits and would cover one more treatment for Mom. Once I made it through Trials, the Slayers would pay me as an initiate. Slayers paid well. I looked forward to depositing my own hard earned Slayer's wages here at the Reserve soon.

I slid the silver across and the teller worked in silence, weighing, logging and then issuing me a handwritten deposit of account.

"6200 credits."

"Please transfer it to your Boston branch."

The teller nodded.

It was strange to be in such an analog world sometimes, but there was a lightness to my step as I returned home from the Reserve. Even if my harebrained idea didn't pan out, my wages as a Slayer initiate would be able to help my family back home a lot more than anything I could have done in my old job as a short order cook in Boston.

After more of Mrs. Chu's soup and a luxurious warmup routine where I went through a number of my fight forms, I glugged down some demon bone meal and geared up to head back to the Dojo. The demon supplements had seemed to give me endurance during the first trial. I didn't know what was in store today but I suspected an endurance boost wouldn't hurt.

I arrived early, well before five bells. The fight hall was already packed, with Slayers and candidates lined against the walls. I spotted Wen seated on one of the benches, along with Cordelia stretching on the empty fight mat. The two of them looked relaxed and intensely interested in the fight in the next ring. Yvonne stood next to a large porcelain water jug, glugging copious amounts of water. Her dark skin gleamed with the signs of a recent workout. Or a recent fight.

Altan waved me over, his face creased in laughter. He let out an eerie cackle. That was usually a bad sign, for someone else.

"What's going on?"

Altan pointed to the fight mats. "Dario and the Fox having a bit of a spar."

The fight hall had two fight rings which were divided up with benches in between. The fight mats were black with bright orange trim, fitted to the base of the entire ring. Only the back ring was occupied, two bodies in a blur of inhuman speed. Dario and the Fox. Dario and Kotori. Bashir had called her the Fox.

The lightbulb clicked on and I finally made the connection that Kotori was a shifter too.

Leaning against the far back of the room was Marnie. She looked pretty banged up and I wondered if it was from fighting Kotori or from escaping the caves. She'd left me to die in the caves. I wouldn't mind repaying her in the ring today.

Dario and Kotori hadn't shifted, remaining in their human form. Dario had longer reach and his thighs were twice as wide Kotori's entire torso. That didn't seem to matter, Kotori moved like lighting. Striking in bursts faster than the human eye could make out. She hadn't even bothered to take her naginata off her back.

I gestured to the full house. "Kotori told me to come at five bells, but it looks like this has been going for a while."

Altan grinned, sharp canines out. "She must be saving the best for last."

I didn't like the sound of that at all. "I thought we were training today."

Altan wheezed with laughter. "Yes, yes. Always teaching, Kotori is. We had too many of you for the box so we added a bonus round today to score you all."

My lips turned down.

I was on thin ice as it was.

A particularly loud smack brought a collective groan from the crowd. I looked up to see Dario flat on his back. Kotori drew a finger across his neck.

"First cut. Kotori" Altan called out cheerily.

"What are the rules?" I asked Altan.

"Two cuts and you're out. Stay in the orange line."

Simple. Also, totally impossible if your opponent was Kotori.

Dario flipped onto all fours and then bounded at Kotori, resuming their match. Kotori's arms flared out and then in a blink there were five of her. Her illusion magic.

It didn't seem fair but Dario seemed to be game. The five Kotoris circled him, always staying in motion, weaving in and out, playing a dangerous game of Find the Queen. Only in this game the queen could knock you flat on your back.

Dario grinned, his smile filled with joy and the promise of violence. He reared up on his legs and howled. Pale gray fur burst from his skin as layer upon layer of corded muscle thickened his legs. His torso lengthened and his grin stretched until his face looked like it would split in half. Dario's howl faded and he landed on all fours, steam billowing from his silver-gray coat, a massive wolf that had to stand at least five feet at the shoulders.

The onlookers gasped and even the illusory Kotoris seemed to back up a step. Dario was...huge.

I grabbed Altan's arm. "Is that...normal?"

Altan couldn't take his eyes off the massive dire wolf. He laughed. "Oh my goddess, no. Isn't he wonderful?"

Dario's head swung back and forth, taking in the scene. Then he paused and inhaled deeply.

And then to make things even weirder, he laughed and his voice was somehow his, but turned into a basso rumble that shook my feet. "You think I can't find you, little fox?"

Altan whooped and pumped his fist in the air. "Yes! Take it to her, Dario!"

He hardly needed the encouragement. Quick as thought Dario lunged out, his jaws opening wide, exposing massive white fangs and a thick red tongue. He dove unerringly at the Kotori on his right.

Kotori's illusions fell away in the same instant. She knew when to switch tactics. With Dario's nose, the illusions did her no good.

Which was not to say that Kotori was suddenly helpless before the dire wolf.

The Fox bounded to one side, gracefully sidestepping Dario's attack. Her naginata swung up and down in a quick arc, the blade whistling through the place where Dario's neck had been just a moment before. Dario had already dodged the blow and circled back. He planted his paws on the ground and growled, slaver dripping from his fangs. He'd lost the element of surprise and I couldn't see how he was going to find another opening.

Altan's piercing whistle stunned the crowd into silence. Kotori stowed her blade and took a step back. She wasn't even breathing hard. Altan approached Dario. Even as tall as he was, Altan had to reach up to rub Dario behind the ears.

"It was a good effort, son. But you lost."

Altan dug his hand down towards Dario's neck and parted the gray fur. Buried under the pelt, in stark contrast to the fur, was a thin red line where the tip of Kotori's naginata had just grazed the dire wolf's neck.

Altan bellowed, "Second cut, Kotori!"

An even mixture of cheers and boos followed Dario as he moved out of the ring and shifted back to his human form. I made bug eyes at him as he passed and held my fist up to him. He only smiled and shook his head as he bumped knuckles with me. Altan draped a fatherly arm over Dario's shoulders and led him to a distant bench to sit down. I watched them walk off together with a pang of emotion in my chest.

Kotori's voice cut through that emotion like an icy blade. "Roxanne Lim. It is time to prove yourself!"

28

FIGHTING THE FOX

This was it. This was my last chance. I set my hammers down carefully, stood and shrugged off my jacket. The cool air raised a chill on my bare arms but the adrenaline pumping through my system ensured that I barely felt the cold. Kotori prowled back and forth at the other side of the fighting ring, never taking her eyes from me. She looked like a caged animal that desperately wanted to strike out at its keeper.

And I was about to step into the cage.

Hoots and cheers went up from the crowd as I approached the ring. I barely knew any of these people, but nonetheless, they were here to cheer everyone on. There's nothing like getting your butt beat down to build some camaraderie.

Cordelia's voice broke through the din of the crowd. "Go get her, Roxy!" She punctuated her support with a piercing whistle.

I gave her what I hoped was a grateful smile and turned back to face my doom. I'd seen Kotori's fighting skills firsthand last night and I was ludicrously outmatched here. Goddess, we were all outmatched. If a monstrous werewolf like Dario couldn't beat her, what chance did I have?

Looking at things that way, my attitude shifted. I had no possibility of success here. There was no way I was a match for Kotori. Not if I fought like a reasonable person.

This test wasn't meant to hurt anyone. I knew what Kotori was capable of. She was clearly holding back, or else Dario would have lost his furry head just moments ago. My heart swelled as I realized there was a way for me to win this.

I just needed to stick my head into the waiting jaws of death to do it.

No problem.

The grip of the karambit was sticky with my sweat. While the blade was beautiful and sharp, it was pathetically small in comparison to the reach of Kotori's naginata. If I was going to land a cut I would need to be well inside her reach. I rolled my neck, shook out the kinks, and bounced on my toes. Kotori stopped pacing and held her weapon across her body in the high guard position. The massive blade gleamed in the pre-dawn light.

My plan was perfect. I was going to win. Or possibly die. One or the other. But what other choice did I have? The crowd quieted and silent tension fell over the gym like a blanket.

Altan raised his hand and barked, "Begin!"

Kotori came at me in a blur, her body turned into a streak of red and white with a flash of silver in the center. Every part of the lizard part of my brain, the part that kept me alive, screamed in terror as I threw myself at Kotori, aiming directly for that silver streak. In another eye blink, Kotori's naginata would land, and the blade would chop me in half across the torso, spilling my blood and innards onto the floor of the gym.

I ignored my lizard brain and raised my karambit to strike. Kotori's eyes widened and I saw her do the split second calculation, the lightning fast predictive assessment that all experienced fighters are capable of, knowing which punches need to be ducked, and which can be shrugged off, knowing where to be and where not to be.

I was definitely where not to be and Kotori knew it. Did she understand that I was playing a deadly game of chicken?

Kotori flinched and pulled up her blade, turning the motion into a graceful jump that became a forward flip. My karambit passed through empty air as Kotori passed above and behind me. Wow, not only had she avoided killing me, but she'd also seen my blade aimed at her midsection.

Before I could turn to face her something struck my legs and swept them out from under me. The world spun and I landed on my side, the air rushing out of my lungs at the impact. I rolled to find Kotori circling me, her blade held low in front of her.

"What are you playing at?"

I coughed and caught my breath. "Just trying to win some points, sensei."

She spit on the mat. "Reckless. Foolish. Just like your father."

"I've got a few more tricks than he did." The crowd gasped as I went straight for her again, ignoring the naginata, going at her head on. Kotori reversed her weapon and socked me in the gut with the butt end. I went down in a heap but used my momentum to roll towards her and as I got close I swung my arm out, the karambit flashing for her ankle.

Kotori leapt into the air, away from my blade. As she jumped away, the naginata turned, the blade arcing down towards me. I jerked my head back and the tassel tied to the blade slapped me across the cheek. Kotori flipped once, and landed gracefully on her toes on the other side of the ring. It was as pretty as a dance routine. I staggered to my feet, clutching at my gut and gasping. Kotori wasn't even breathing hard.

"First cut, Kotori." Altan pointed at my cheek.

I swiped my hand across my cheek and my fingers came away with blood. I hadn't even felt the cut. The crowd whooped. Cordelia shouted encouragement.

Kotori shipped her blade, stowing it across her back. "Enough of this foolishness."

Her fighting leathers shimmered and her figure blurred, the red of her leathers bleeding like spilled blood until four additional figures burst forth and took up positions around me. I pivoted, trying to keep an eye on all of them. Without a shifter's keen nose, I didn't know how I would beat this particular trick.

I thought Kotori was fast. I'd seen her moves in the caves, surrounded by swarming vampires. I watched her dodge the lightning fast snap of Dario's jaws. It turns out, she'd been holding back.

Last time, I'd seen a blur of color coming at me. This time, there was no such warning. One moment I was warily watching five copies of the Fox circling me, and before the next moment even had a chance to arrive, the first punch landed in my gut. By the time I hunched over the pain in my belly, the next blow landed on my shoulder. Just before my knees hit the tatami mats, the last blow knocked me to my side, sprawling me out on the floor.

The crowd was silent.

Altan sighed. "You made your point, Kotori. Just finish her off." He turned away, a disappointed look on his face.

Meanwhile, I was trying to not whimper in pain. The five duplicates of my sensei approached, right hand raised to deliver the blow. I might be beaten, but I was not going to give her the satisfaction. Since there was no way I could beat her I just closed my eyes and focused on blocking out the pain in my gut and the spreading numbness in my arm. I couldn't feel the karambit in my hands. I supposed I'd dropped it. I focused on my breathing and tried to remember that pain meant that at least I was still alive. If I was alive I could find another way to help mom.

As my mind quieted the pain faded. Behind my closed eyelids a spreading web of lines traced across my vision, showing me the floor and boundaries of the fighting ring. And in the fighting ring, I only saw one solid version of Kotori, sketched in vivid green.

I knew what I had to do. I rolled away from the far illusion, backing myself up towards the real McCoy. I gave a whimper of fear. It wasn't that hard to pull off. I hoped at least one of my arms would be capable of doing something.

I opened my eyes and kept them focused on the furthest illusion. I bit off a scream as five hands descended on me and swung my left arm out behind me. Kotori's hand, the real one, stopped a hairsbreadth from my neck. The other illusions were gone, and her eyes were focused on me, but wide with...surprise?

My hand had landed just above the line of her fur-trimmed boots. My dirty fingernail had drawn a faint white scratch over a bare sliver of her leg exposed between the boot and her leggings.

"Ha!" Altan's laugh broke across the fighting ring and then he was rolling with it, hooting and jumping and pointing. The crowd, confused, cheered belatedly.

Kotori stood and looked down her nose at me. Her face was a storm of emotions. Anger, frustration, and...surprise. Then she turned away and I caught the barest hint of a twitch at the corner of her mouth. Holy cow, did Kotori just smile at me?

But then Altan dug his hands into my armpits and hauled me up to standing. The sudden change in altitude made me dizzy and I swayed when he set me on my feet. Cordelia slammed into me, wrapping her arms around my middle, squealing like a schoolgirl the whole time. By the time I found my footing and pried Cordelia's arms off, Kotori had vanished.

ALTAN ASSEMBLED our group outside the gym. We couldn't have been a sorrier sight. Everyone showed signs of wear, either from last night's missions, or this morning's beatings. Despite the physical abuse, all eyes were bright and eager for Altan's news. I found I was too numb to face the reality of washing out. I was exhausted and everything hurt. I'd tried my best, and if the Slayers wouldn't take me because of my decisions last night, then maybe this had never been my true calling. I'd find another way to get help for mom. And some way to make it up to dad.

The murmur of voices died as my uncle, Altan, and Aislinn stepped out of the gym.

Samuel stepped in front of the others, his bulk conspicuously blocking our view of Altan as he nailed a sheet of paper to the wall.

"The Trials are always difficult. The next step even more so. If you don't pass through to the next round, remember that you can always try again at the next Trials."

Did his eyes rest on me for an extra moment as he said that?

I was still angry about yesterday when I had almost gotten voted off the squad. It was pretty clear to me that if Bashir had not spoken up for me, there would have been no future Trials for me either. Aislinn wanted to blacklist me. Kotori wanted to beat me into a pulp, and she had.

I swayed on my feet. I had given it everything I had and now I had to muster the courage to stand tall on my way out today.

Samuel stepped aside and the group rushed forward as one. I hung back and watched them crowd around the bit of paper on the wall. Kotori had ground me into a pulp on the mat. Hard to imagine doing worse. I didn't want to read confirmation of my defeat on that sheet of paper.

My uncle stood beside me and we watched the others crow about their scores or walk away dejectedly. "Not interested?"

I found myself remarkably sanguine about the whole thing. Had Mrs. Chu put something extra in the soup last night? "I can barely walk after that beating from Kotori."

Samuel only raised an eyebrow at me, the universal look of skepticism practiced by all fathers worldwide.

Before I could say another word Cordelia ran up to me, breathless, eyes gleaming. "Roxy! Come look!"

She grabbed my hand and dragged me into the crowd, throwing fists and elbows to break a path for us.

I dug in my heels. "Cordelia, seriously. You're at the top, I believe you. You don't have to show me."

Bodies parted and Cordelia shoved me into the opening, where the rankings hung on the wall. Altan stood beside them, a smug smile on his face. He winked at me then rolled his eyes towards the list.

The list was eight names in flowing, elegant script. At a guess, it was Aislinn's handwriting, except maybe not because it wasn't sparkling. There, at the top of the list, as expected was Cordelia of the Hinterlands. Harald had placed just below her and Marnie had come in third. I scanned the rest of the list. Dario wasn't on it.

My throat tightened and I looked back to Altan who seemed like he was about to burst out laughing because my name was the fourth on the list. I realized that not only was Cordelia cheering and laughing wildly, but she was also trying to shake my teeth out of my head.

I looked at Altan, questioning. He put a hand on my shoulder, which had the added benefit of keeping Cordelia from breaking my neck.

"You did good, kiddo."

"Good? I got the snot kicked out of me."

He grinned, all teeth, as always. "Sure, but do you know how many times I've seen someone lay a hand on the Fox?"

He held up his right hand. "I don't even need any of the fingers on this hand to keep count! That scratch you put on her leg gave you enough points to go from dead last to top eight. Even Aislinn couldn't argue with that."

Goddess of the moon. I was going through to the next round. I still had a chance to be a Slayer.

29

SWEET REMINDERS

When I got back from the Dojo, I was surprised to see a large cream colored box with a lavish red ribbon tied around it and elegant script that read "La Petite Pâtisserie" sitting at my stoop. I couldn't afford anything that came in a box like that.

I looked at Ernest.

He mouthed the word "delivery" then shrugged.

Mysterious. I brought the box inside and used a Samuel's karambit to slice the ribbon, which fell in a silky pool onto my scarred wooden kitchen table. When I removed the lid I was greeted with the smells of sugar, butter and cinnamon and rows upon rows of delicate pastries and tarts.

Apple turnovers. Cinnamon buns. Bakewell tarts. Croissants. Pain du chocolate.

My mouth dropped open and I inhaled deeply of this treasure trove of sweetness.

Under the box lid was a heavy cream stationery card with a fancy fleur de lis embossed in gold foil. I opened it up and a small insert fell out. I looked at the bold ink scrawl.

"Dear Roxy,

Eloise and I are extremely grateful for your assistance. This gift is from her. I will find another way to show you my appreciation.

Yours,

Tyee"

My mouth went dry. I did not know how I felt about this gift box and Tyee's message. I didn't have qualms about eating the pastries. I would eat as many as I could in short order. But I didn't like the thought of Tyee repaying me personally in some way. The Night Court had paid the Slayers. That was all I wanted–that my efforts keep us in good graces with the Night Court. I was uncomfortable of some kind of personal tally between me and Tyee.

I exhaled and then read Eloise's card.

"Thank you for saving me.

Please come visit so that I may thank you again in person.

Sincerely,

Eloise"

I put the cards aside, lifted the chocolate croissant to my lips and took a big bite of flaky pastry. It gave way under my teeth with perfect crispness to yield a buttery interior, followed by the satisfying bitter sweetness of good chocolate. All the aches and pains of my sparring from the Dojo faded and there was only this moment and this cascading pleasure of taste and texture.

I refrained from moaning but it was a close thing. It was over too soon. I savored the melting chocolate on my tongue. This called for tea.

I set the kettle on, put a plain croissant on the plate and brought it out to Ernest.

"These are from Eloise, the employee with the Mists and Mind Vampires."

Ernest smiled and ate the croissant happily. As always after he ate, he looked more vivid and filled in, the green of his

Herbal College cloak brighter against the paint of the stairwell.

Sitting down with a pot of tea, I ate with a single minded focus, putting away several more tarts and pastries. The bakewell tart had been my favorite, the jammy filling and fragrant frangipane sending me into an altered state of bliss. I rubbed the powdered sugar off my face and looked back in the box. Only then did I realize it was a double decker box. Goddess save my waistband. With some regret, I finally admitted that I couldn't finish it all in one sitting. I packed away some to freeze, then put the lid back on to take it upstairs for Mrs. Chu.

Unfortunately, the trip up the stairs reminded me of every hit and fall I'd taken on the mat. The blood had dried long ago, for which I was grateful. Kotori had so much control that she knew exactly how to terrify her victim, me, while still keeping the cuts shallow.

Mrs. Chu opened the door before I could knock. "Roxy, you're walking heavier than usual."

Wow. I guess to shifters I really did make a lot of noise. Mrs. Chu's comment took some of the sting out of Kotori's critique when she'd excoriated me to Samuel yesterday.

"Yeah, just got back from the Dojo, but look what I got!" I brandished the big box of pastries.

"Come in, come in. My sisters are here."

Uh oh. "All of them?"

"Yes, of course. It's Thursday."

My timing could have been better. Thursday was mahjong night for Mrs. Chu and her shifter sisters. They were nosy and scary and I generally avoided visiting when they were there. On the plus side, they would appreciate my pastry offering.

I toed off my shoes and stepped inside to the scent of whiskey and the sounds of cool tiles clacking against the table.

Grandma caught my eye first. Mrs. Chu and the other

mahjong ladies called her Lydia but to everyone else, she was Grandma, the chief of security for the Zoo's market. In her Kodiak bear form, Grandma was a beast of gargantuan proportions, her hind legs as wide as tree trunks and with a massive chest and impenetrable hide of coarse black and brown fur. She had claws the length of my chef knives and her roar promised waves of blood and pain. I'd heard her terrifying roar one time when she patrolled the Zoo's local market and I never wanted to hear it again. She held a large bottle of Remy Martin XO by the neck and didn't seem to be bothering with anything as mundane as glassware.

Today Grandma wore a red velour tracksuit, looking very fit and put together. Her tight perm of blonde curls was shot through with streaks of gray and stiff as a helmet, not one strand free to move. She gave me a wink and tilted her head back to take a swig of the XO.

On Grandma's left was Malia 'Aukai. She insisted I call her Auntie, which was pretty much par for the course with my upbringing. Any woman who looked at least five years older than me was safely into venerable auntie status. Where Grandma had curly hair, Auntie's hair was long and wavy, black as night, and coiled into a low, loose bun. Her round face was smooth and unlined and her eyes sparkled like moonlight on the deep sea, hinting at deep mysteries and knowledge. I suspected she was much older than she looked and probably older than Grandma despite their respective titles.

Auntie had told me she was a fisherman, which I thought had to be the most dangerous job one could possibly have, what with all that the magic had unleashed. Grandma had wheezed with laughter at that.

"Malia isn't a damn fisherman. She swims around all day and eats fish until it's time for her to take a nap."

Auntie was a mako shark and was over fifteen feet in length

in her shifter form. Even the ocean around Seattle would be a little less frightening for her than most.

Presently, Auntie was tearing into a bakewell tart, her teeth reassuringly human. In front of her was an empty cream box identical to the one I was holding. Eloise had been considerate enough to send Mrs. Chu a box as well. My estimation of her went up.

Across from Grandma sat Beverly Peterson, who lived near the vicinity of the Slayer's Farm. As usual, she wore a flannel shirt, jeans, and worn brown workboots. Bev had a place of her own called River Rock Farm. There were plenty of shifters who weren't interested in life in Seattle and preferred the freedom of the rivers and forests outside the city. Some of them worked at River Rock. Bev drove in once a week to visit Mrs. Chu with a crate of fresh veggies and eggs. I'd always wondered what kind of shifter she was.

That was the thing about most shifters. Here in the Veil, a human would be hard-pressed to know if someone was a shifter, let alone what they shifted into. Shifters knew each other, and they weren't usually interested in cluing in the rest of us. Since Mrs. Chu had more or less taken me under her wing, her "sisters" were relaxed around me, grilling me about my personal life and giving me lots of unsolicited advice. All except Bev. She was polite with me, but she didn't volunteer anything or ask me questions.

Bev expertly racked the tiles, built her the rows, sorted her matches and ignored me, which was fine by me. I wouldn't get off so easy with Grandma and Auntie.

Grandma set down the bottle with the thunk. "Roxy! How goes it with the Slayer Trials?"

I smiled. "I've made it this far. The last Trial starts tomorrow at three bells."

Auntie smiled in return and picked up her tea. "Good for you, dear."

I handed the box to Mrs. Chu. "I don't want to interrupt your game. Just thought you'd enjoy some of these pastries."

Mrs. Chu opened the lid and sniffed appreciatively. "They were very good. So thoughtful of her to send them. Thank you, Roxy. We will polish off the rest of these."

"I'm sure you will." I grinned at her.

In that moment, we shared a look of mutual appreciation and understanding. I was so lucky to have Mrs. Chu in my life. A box of pastries was precious in the Veil and life here had given me a deep appreciation for how much work it took to make things like this. How hard it was to source ingredients. How special these items were. And Eloise had made these for us.

I know Aislinn and Marnie didn't think I had done the right thing in the caves, that I should have let Tyee and Eloise fend for themselves. I'd questioned myself ever since. But standing here in Mrs. Chu's flat, smiling over pastries, reminded me that I was only human and I did things because I wanted things to be better. So I could have moments like this. Connections like these. This is what mattered to me.

"Roxy, how has Dario been doing in the Trials?" asked Grandma, her voice casual.

I shook my head. "He didn't make it after today."

"Pity." But Grandma didn't sound all that sad about it. In fact, she seemed almost happy to hear Dario had washed out today.

I was sad about it. Dario had been cocky but he deserved to continue on more than that oaf Harald. Cordelia had always been a shoe in, and though I wasn't a fan of Marnie, it was hard to argue with how she'd excelled at every single challenge the Slayers had thrown at us.

Replaying my fight with Kotori was surreal and gave me an out of body sensation at the moment I realized my talent could see through her illusion magic. For that briefest moment, I'd seen my future as a Breaker and how much more I could do with my talent, how truly great I could be. Kotori had crushed me anyway, but now I knew there was more for me in the Veil.

I felt like I was hanging in there by a fingernail every step of the way during the Trials. But I was still in it and that's all that mattered.

Finally I said, "Dario would have been a good Slayer."

Grandma's reply was tart. "He'd be an even better Alpha."

So that was her angle. I admit I didn't have a handle on shifter politics but sometimes Mrs. Chu would make statements that told me that shifter dynamics in Seattle were pretty fragmented. I hadn't thought much of it but Grandma's statement suggested that she was interested in a little more cohesiveness and she believed Dario was the key.

I shrugged. "I've got to turn in, so I'll leave you to your game."

Grandma waved and Auntie called out, "Good luck, Roxy!" Bev ignored me and Mrs. Chu gave me a firm hug before I left.

It was so nice that I stood on the stoop for two more breaths and then walked with Ernest back down to my apartment.

"Wish me luck, Ernest."

"You're going to be a Slayer, Roxy."

I reminded myself of that as I drifted off to sleep that evening. I'd had doubts after that match with Kotori, but no longer. After this last Trial, I would be a Slayer.

THE BOX

Laila's workshop was just as crowded and humid as I remembered, but this time the feeling was different. I knew what I was getting this time and I had enough in my pockets to pay for it. It was a nice feeling.

The perky enchantress nearly danced around the counter, my duster draped across her arms like a pristine wedding dress. "It's ready!"

I remembered to close my mouth. It was beautiful. With the excess demon horn Laila had sourced all the necessary materials for my duster. Dark runes flitted across the leather like moving shadows. As Laila turned the garment this way and that, the runes seemed to flow back and forth across the leather. When the engravings caught the light the color of the leather shifted like chameleon hide.

It truly was a work of art. I speared Laila with a skeptical eye. "How do I know it works?"

Laila's eyes widened with hurt. "Are you serious? Look at this thing!"

She held it up before her, spreading the duster out in front of her so I could see the intricate engraving covering the leather. When the duster covered her face I flipped one of my palm-sized throwing knives at her. The blade spun across the distance and thumped into the leather before clattering to the ground.

Laila's head popped over the duster and she looked down at the ground where the blade had fallen. "Rude!"

I picked up the blade. "But, effective."

She made a face at me. "I should charge you extra for that."

"Why don't you tell me what it can do, first."

Her trademark saleswoman 1000-watt smile broke across her face. "What does it do? What doesn't it do! It resists vampire and were-fangs! Swords and arrows will glide off like you're made of melted butter! You can run through an inferno and not even break a sweat! It sheds magical acids and poisons like spring rain!"

I pulled out Thor and hefted it. "What about blunt force trauma?"

Laila frowned. "Really? Are you already asking for modifications?"

I laughed and held up my hands in mock surrender. "No, no. It's fine. It's wonderful, actually. Thank you."

"Excellent. And on the matter of payment?"

Laila made me suffer through yet another round of haggling with her on the final payment. I managed to trap her this time. Given that the duster enchantment was so good, that made my chances of making it through the last stage of the Trials better than most, so I merited the professional discount for Slayers. Since I wasn't inked yet, we split the difference. I paid a little more than I wanted, she got a little less than she wanted. A good compromise. If my pockets were a little lighter than I would have liked, the buttery soft feel of the leather as it draped over my shoulders was more than enough to make up for it.

As I left Laila's workshop she made me promise to come visit again after the Trials and to bring her more business.

"I'm never too busy for your referrals!" she called out.

I vowed to live long enough to send the witch some business.

FOR THE LAST Trial we met at Slayer's HQ and the eight of us piled into a wagon. It seemed a lifetime ago that I had muscled my way past sixty candidates to fight my way to these wagons. That time the wagons had led us to the Farm.

Back then I'd been fighting in the muck and throng of bodies and there had been three wagons. Today, there was just one wagon and there would be only eight candidates. Now I had the leisure to study the wagons. There was a team of mules, and these mules were absolutely enormous. Each one was some fifteen hands high, with long ears and long legs. They had to be over a thousand pounds each and I marveled at their sheer size. Master Akhil hitched the two pairs of shaggy monsters to the wagon and I realized that if I made it through this Trial, someday I might be like him, helping run the Trials. That was a strange feeling and made me eager to get on the other side of this last Trial.

Altan stalked out and gave Akhil a hearty slap on the back, followed by a cackle. Credit to the placid mules, they didn't even flinch at the predator so close to them. I guess when you're a working mule for the Slayers, you're constantly surrounded by predators.

The Dojo was suspiciously empty and when pressed, Altan refused to answer questions.

I was happy to see Cordelia and Wen. Cordelia scooted over and I grabbed the seat next to her. Wen's eyes were closed, probably meditating or resting. Goddess knew we would need every ounce of energy and fortitude we had for whatever the Freaks of Seattle had cooked up for us.

After I sat down, Yvonne showed up. She strode over to Wen, who opened his eyes and smiled at her before making room.

That was good because the other people on the wagon were Axel, Harald, Ulf, and Marnie.

Axel was a giant so he needed the whole bench to himself. Harald and Ulf were sworn brothers so of course the mountain Fae shared a bench. Marnie was alone and clearly, her glare said that was the way she liked it.

I didn't know how the Slayers would split us up today, but I definitely did not want to be in any group with Marnie. However, that meant I would potentially be in a group *against* Marnie which was also an alarming proposition.

I gripped my spear in my hands, the shaft vertical between my knees, and sent my dad a silent prayer for strength. The spear would give me the reach I needed in combat. After yesterday's disaster, I wasn't making that mistake again. For extra luck, I'd tied the Slayers camo bandana around my neck. Dress for the job you want and all that.

A quick scan of the wagon told me everyone else was loaded for bear as well. I knew Cordelia had her whips at her waist and her milky sword across her back. Wen's ability to leap over tall buildings in a single bound made him a threat even before considering his skill with his whip chains. Yvonne had a rather impressive looking staff which I suspected had a number of enchantments layered onto it.

Harald had upgraded, and balanced a two-handed great sword on his shoulder, the guard worked into a set of ram's horns. Ulf was carrying an honest to goodness battle axe that looked like it weighed as much as one of the mules pulling the wagon. If he timed it wrong, he was likely to slice off his nice red braid with that mighty axe.

I tapped my magic lightly and let the green lines cross into my vision. I filed away where folks had weak spots in their armor, weapons or musculature. I also fervently hoped it wouldn't come down to me needing to use any of that information.

"Do you know where the last Trial is?" Cordelia whispered.

"No idea."

Yvonne leaned over. "The dead place."

I didn't like the sound of that.

Ulf snorted. "More like the undead place."

Cordelia slanted him a glance but didn't look annoyed that he'd butted into our conversation.

Harald rubbed his hands together. "We will slay the undead. This is why we are here. This is what we were born to do."

Marnie nodded, and a glint of manic light entered her eyes. "Aye, my brother."

Wait, what? When had those two gotten so chummy?

Then Marnie pointed at me. "Beware Roxy, I will not let you interfere again."

Anger roiled in my belly and it was all I could do not to leap over the bench and belt her. "Look, *sister*. You were supposed to stab the rogues–not me!"

"You're no sister of mine. You laid with vampire filth and you deserved what you got."

Yvonne sliced a hand in the air, her face fierce. "It's not your place to judge. We know you attacked Roxy in the caves and Goddess help you if you try to do the same to me."

Marnie's face twisted. "If you truck with the unholy, you're not fit to be a Slayer."

A thunderous look passed over Yvonne's face and she pointed a finger at Marnie. "Hold your tongue or I will snatch it out of your mouth."

We all stared at Marnie and long seconds passed as Marnie

surprisingly let Yvonne get the last word in. Discretion was the better part of valor when arguing with a warrior witch and Marnie seemed to recognize that.

After that we rode in relative silence, heading south through the city. We passed the Market and I caught just a glimpse of the gaudy lights that indicated the Fangs and the pleasure district. Before I could stop myself, I wondered how Tyee was doing and what he and the Night Queen might be plotting now. I didn't imagine they would let such an affront from O'Malley go unanswered. Was my uncle worried about this as well?

South past the Market the city deteriorated as we passed into the low lying old industrial center. The buildings here were a sodden mess, having been abandoned after the Drowning, and then deemed not worthy of rehabilitation when the city had rebuilt itself. It was rather depressing.

We passed the building that I recognized as the front door for the underground fight club and continued farther south. Even Cordelia was strangely quiet as the horses pulled us through a section of the city that seemed so utterly dead as to be alien.

Ahead, pinpricks of light hinted at torches set alongside the road. Altan turned to us from the head of the wagon. "Pay attention, everyone. We're here."

'Here' was a relative term. I didn't see anything to distinguish this set of dilapidated buildings from all the others we'd passed, other than the torches set into the muddy earth, and the sensation that we were being watched. As we reached the first torch, Aislinn melted out of the shadows and leapt lightly into the wagon.

"Welcome to the Box."

Altan took the wagon on a slow circuit of the building, a massive brick rectangle, possibly once a warehouse, now given over to mud, slime, and who knows what kinds of terrors within. The structure was at least three stories above ground, likely with more buried beneath. At the center of the building a crumbling clock tower rose another two stories, the face of the clock long since lost to time and scavengers. Above the clock, faded lines traced the remnants of a face with eyes blinded by age and the elements. Of all the buildings I had seen in Seattle, this one felt the most like a corpse. Rows of windows, blind and dark, some broken out, stared down at us like funerary statues. Beside me, Cordelia shivered and clutched her arms close to her chest.

Aislinn pointed to the building. "The Box is a zone that is beyond the scope of the Slayer's patrols. This part of the city has become a shelter for a number of rogues, shifters, and demons, all of whom have chosen not to abide by the rules required to exist within the bounds of the city. No Pact, no sanctuary."

We shuffled, uncomfortable. The Pact was what made Seattle a place where humans, vampires, shifters, and fae could co-exist. If parties broke the Pact, they risked the wrath of the Tarim and loss of Veil.

"You will enter the Box in pairs and conduct yourselves in a manner that reflects the values of the Slayers. You should expect all you find within the Box to be hostile and lethal. Do not hesitate to act as necessary."

Again, I felt like someone was speaking about me without saying it explicitly.

Aislinn's gaze passed over me and seemed to settle on Cordelia for a moment. "I have placed three keys within the Box. These keys are what you need to complete your Trials and become Slayers. Those who exit the box with a key in their possession will pass."

Cordelia elbowed me. "What? Only three?"

I hushed her because Aislinn was barrelling on.

"You will draw lots for your pairings. Each pair will enter

from a different face of the building. The keys are hidden separately, so the chances of finding two keys are remote."

Her eyes settled on each of us in turn. "Trust me when I tell you that there is no 'easy' door for this task. Keep your weapons ready and your eyes sharp. Although we are observing, this is a live exercise and candidate deaths are not unheard of. If you are incapacitated we will move with all haste to extract you. Remain true to the tenets of the Slayers and you will do well. Do not disappoint me."

Somehow that last one felt like it was aimed at Cordelia.

Altan and Aislinn divided us up and then the two groups drew straws. Mine had a smudge of blue paint on the bottom. To my dismay, so did Ulf's straw. Great, I was paired with the mountain fae who had an axe that could sever me in half if he sneezed.

I looked up at him, my face grim. "Are you going to pull a Marnie on me?"

The big fae frowned. "That would not be honorable."

Oh good. He had some anachronistic notion of honor. If it saved me from getting chopped by his axe, I was all in favor of his honor.

I watched the rest of the pairings. Axel with Yvonne. Cordelia with Wen. Harald with Marnie. That last pairing seemed like a match made in heaven.

Altan split us up and Ulf and I got the south doors to the Box. They weren't doors as much as man-sized plates of metal that had been hammered over openings torn into the red brick facade. They definitely looked like they had seen better days. Aislinn's light globe rose high above us and I saw the countdown to start trickling within the globe.

I had my trusty hammers and all my knives. A wickedly sharp karambit tucked into my belt. I wore an enchanted duster over my shoulders that would repel vampires and shifters alike.

And in my hands, a six foot spear that had once been my father's. I was as ready as I was going to get.

Beside me, Ulf hefted his axe and cinched his mail vest tight across his chest. Leather bracers covered his forearms, the material covered with familiar runes. Heavy pewter rings adorned each of his fingers, each ring carved with more runes. Whatever he was packing, I meant to stay out of his line of fire. He looked at me and gave me a curt nod.

All right, then. I could be courteous, too. I nodded back and we turned to the door.

"What do you think the keys look like?"

Ulf grunted. "I think we will know when we see them."

"Just remember how to be honorable when we find the key."

He seemed taken aback again. "Honor is not something one forgets."

Aislinn's light saved me from making a crack about his sworn brother Harald when it burst into a shower of orange sparks that rained over the building like a waterfall of light. Hm. Big and gaudy enough so that all of us on all four sides saw it simultaneously. And also bright enough to alert any residents that something was definitely coming for them.

They certainly weren't making it easy for us.

Ulf strode forward and grabbed the edge of the door with his left hand, the axe held ready in his right. I lined up with my spear at waist height.

"I'll clear left. You go right."

The big fae nodded. "It will be done."

Ulf dragged the door open with a scream of protesting, rusted metal. Thick, humid air rolled out of the opening, carrying the rich scent of animal bodies, sweat, and rotting meat. Somewhere inside the building, a vampire screeched, the sound echoing off the bricks. My eyes watered at the stench and even Ulf coughed. The dim exterior light showed me at least six feet of clear space inside the door.

Oh good. An easy start. I said a silent prayer for Cordelia, Wen, Yvonne, and hey, why not, Ulf as well. Time to see what we were made of.

I stepped into the Box.

31

FIRST CONTACT

My heart rate sped up and I wondered not for the first time if it was like a beacon for every rogue vampire in a certain radius.

Entering the Box was like stepping into another world. The air bit down with an unnatural chill that sucked at my exposed skin. I clutched my sister close and tried not to think about anything getting sucked out of me.

It wasn't pitch black, thankfully. There were enough broken windows and holes in the roof that stray light revealed a truly depressing and fetid interior. I pulled the bandanna over my nose to block some of the horrid smells. It wasn't a sewer, but it was a lot worse than the caves. Shards of broken mugs and crushed pens littered the floors. The detritus of Seattle's last age crunched under the heavy lug soles of my boots.

"At least there aren't rats," I whispered.

Ulf shrugged. "Likely something has eaten them."

My stomach rolled. A building full of ravenous vamps and shifters, reduced to eating rats or each other. Lovely.

I tilted my head up to the high ceilings. A century ago the

Box had been some sort of cubicle farm. Now sad tiles dangled from the ceilings, revealing dirty insulation and rusted metal brackets. Anything valuable like copper wiring had been looted decades ago. I pulled lightly on my magic and the green lines told me that unsurprisingly, we were in a death trap. It didn't snow much in Seattle, but even a moderate snowfall would send the roof caving in. In the meantime, the broken ceilings and busted pipes running along overhead gave lots of cover for things that might leap down on us.

I hated it.

On the wall closest to me was a massive sign that might have been white at one point, with crude drawing of a green mermaid. Someone had graffitied fangs on her face, and skulls impaled upon the points of her crown. Very fitting for what could come out of the Pacific ocean nowadays.

It wasn't hard to imagine this place a century ago, with an army of office drones scurrying between computers and mid-month review meetings. Now it was home to a very different kind of resident, though I was sure there was some analogy between corporate blood suckers and rogue vamps.

Ulf was enormous, but he was still fae and he moved silently through the office debris as we scoped out our best approach to find the keys.

In light of the way the first Trial had gone, I assumed there would be a similarly obvious beacon as we neared the key. Ulf gestured to the hallway that headed north. That took us towards the center of the The Box, which was risky. We could possibly converge with the others, but it also seemed the most logical area for at least one of the keys.

A whisper of sound brought my eyes back to the dark ceiling. I stopped and lifted my spear.

Our first customer of the night, a skeletal rogue who might have once been an attractive young woman, crawled across the ceiling, clinging lightly to the battered tiles. She hissed when she saw that she'd been spotted and dropped to the ground. With a clumsy flip she landed hard on all fours, shaking the floor. Ulf roared and charged.

"Wait!"

But Ulf was gone already, ten meters from me, his axe lifted high for a devastating headsman's blow. I cursed and hoped that the rogue was a loner. I hurried after him, keeping my head on a swivel, scanning above us for more climbers, and watching the cube walls. There was too much concealment here, there could be a hundred vamps in here just waiting for us to blunder into their trap.

Ulf's axe whistled down and the vamp dodged nimbly to the side. The great blade sank into the rotten carpet and floor boards with an impact I felt through my boots. The vampire bounced her sideways movement off the wall and pushed herself back towards Ulf who was fixated on working his axe out of the floor.

I ran and leapt forward, covering the last few feet in the air, my spear extended, the butt end tucked tight against my body.

The spear head hit home, taking the vamp through her abdomen with a wet squelch. The blade sank deep and when the orange crystal touched her flesh her scream went up an octave. Smoke curled from the wound as the crystal drained her life essence. She screeched, spraying spittle in the air. A few drops landed on my hands and the spots went numb. My boots hit the floor and I pushed again, leaning all my momentum and weight into it. The vampire might be strong but I had to outweigh her by fifty pounds. Physics for the win. I pushed her back and although she grabbed at the spear with both hands she didn't have the leverage to free herself. I poured it on, aiming for the back wall.

We hit the back wall with a thud, and in retrospect, I got

insanely lucky that we didn't just tear through a sheet of moldering plasterboard. I lost my breath as we jolted to a halt. The vampire screamed and twisted, trying to unpin herself from the wall. Acrid smoke continued to pour from the wound, choking my breathing.

"Ulf! Some help!"

With a roar, his footsteps ran up behind me. Uh-oh. I ducked.

Ulf's axe whistled over my head in a flat arc and cleaved through the vampire's neck, neatly separating head and body. Her shrieks died with a whimper and before her eyes could glaze over she was already dissolving to ash.

The other shoe finally dropped and the sounds of scratching claws and low hissing slowly surrounded us. Because of course it was a trap.

Ulf's head jerked around as he pulled his axe from the wall. A low growl built in his chest as he scanned the darkness. I yanked my spear out and grabbed him by the elbow. He turned, as if surprised to remember that I was here as well.

I tilted my head to the left indicating that we should head in that direction. Ulf merely gave me a confused look over my shoulder. I sighed and began backing up, dragging him with me.

He thrust his axe towards the darkness. "The enemy is there!"

"Right, exactly where they want us to be."

I brought us to a stop next to a massive brick column, what had to be one of the central supports for the entire building. It would make good cover for our backs. I tapped the column with the butt of my spear.

"We pick the fight location we want. Live to slay another day, right?"

He eyed the column with suspicion. "But how will we—"

"HEY!" I screamed into the darkness. "Come and get us you dull-toothed losers!"

The clicking noises grew louder and I released Ulf's arm, pushing him to my left. "You cover that side, yell if you need help."

"I do not nee—"

"Yell. If you. Need help."

The big fae outweighed me, and topped me by a few inches, but still managed to look chastised as I held his gaze. And then the rogues melted out of the darkness and the time for talking was over.

WE GOT LUCKY. Very lucky. I didn't know if our initial kill failed to impress the rogues, or if they were simply over confident, but the rogues tested us by coming at us in singles and pairs. The wide sweep of Ulf's axe kept a buffer zone of relative safety around us.

I thanked the goddess again and again for the longer reach of my spear. It didn't have the heft of Ulf's axe, but stabbing vampires from a distance of six feet was a definite plus.

Over the course of the next ten minutes the rogues came at us and, in ones and twos, they fell to our blades. Our fighting was sloppy and uncoordinated. Several times we caught each other on a backswing, or smashed elbows. We shook off the mistakes and kept our focus on the vampires.

We found a choppy kind of rhythm.

One of us would stop a rogue at arm's length and hold it in place for the other to decap it. I found I could swing my spear like a sword and take off a vampire's head. Well, I would be able to do it eventually, with more practice. I only whacked Ulf twice on the shoulders with the shaft of my spear. He only jabbed me in the ribs with the handle of his axe three or four times.

And just like that, there was nothing but the sound of my harsh breaths and Ulf wiping off his axe on the moldering cubicle wall. The crystal in my spear had drained a half dozen rogues, at least. The gem glowed with fiery orange light and cast dancing shadows around us.

He eyed me skeptically. "Kotori was right, you are very loud. I have seen wild boars mate with more discretion."

Goddess, had everyone heard the story? I yanked my spear free from the wall with a little more force than strictly necessary. "Maybe I just don't want to waste time hunting down all the vamps. I'll let them know where I am and let them all come to me."

"Yes. You are...the...lazy...Slayer."

"Efficient. The word you were looking for is efficient. And why on earth would you be watching wild boars mating?"

"We live high in the mountains, in very dense forest. It can be...boring."

"So you spy on pigs for fun."

He shrugged. "My brothers are in line to rule. I am...extra."

Whatever he was, he certainly seemed to be the polar opposite of Harald and Gorm, which was a relief. He seemed to have inhaled more than his share of his twin Gorm's machismo, though, and I told him so.

"We need to stick together. What if this hadn't been a single rogue? We would have been buried."

I looked around, taking in the maze of tight workspaces. "This place is a death trap. We need to be more careful."

Ulf looked around as well and for the first time I noticed the tension around his eyes, and the way his fingers kept rippling over the shaft of his axe. "This place is not a death trap. It is death. I have never felt so far from the earth."

Well, when he put it that way he was hardly wrong.

As if on cue a chilling scream pierced the relative silence. We both whirled, trying to peer into the distant darkness. Faint sounds of battle drifted out of the inky black. The thunk of metal into meat. Cries and grunts of pain. More unholy screams.

We looked at each other, trying to assess what the other would say. Ulf broke the tension first. "Stick together, yes?"

I nodded. "Let's go."

We ran into the darkness, towards the sounds of battle.

32

KEY

The closer we got to the melee, I thought I recognized Yvonne's voice. Her battle cry. On the plus side, the sounds of battle were loud enough that I didn't feel like the stomping buffalo that everyone accused me of moving like. But short of Ulf cutting a hole through the walls, we couldn't figure out how to get through this maze of offices to where Yvonne and Axel were.

We turned and hit a dead end. Crumbling counters lined the walls, and a battered faucet fixture gleamed in the darkness. Between the chairs and counters, I guessed we had found the employee break room.

Ulf stopped and drew up, his nose in the air, sniffing like a hound.

"I smell Aislinn's magic here."

"Here?"

He nodded.

"You can smell magic?"

Ulf made a face. "We can often recognize another fae signature. Aislinn's is very distinctive."

There was so much I didn't know about the fae. I knew most

of them could cast glamors. But making yourself look different was not necessarily a helpful offensive magic skill for fighting say, vampires or shifters or demons. I didn't know if all of them could cast magic or if Aislinn was unique. From the tone of Ulf's voice, I gathered Aislinn was very powerful.

"Do you have any magic?" I wished I had thought to ask before going into the Box with him.

Ulf stalked within the confines of the breakroom, palm out like some kind of diviner.

"Some. But mostly I prefer to train with my weapons."

I wondered what "some" entailed.

Ulf stopped in front of an ancient vending machine. When I had lived in Boston, those vending machines had smooth digital displays, interactive holograms and an assortment of conveniences. This machine, aside from being sadly dented and half empty, seemed to only hold a couple of cans of soda and bags of stale peanuts. The most amazing attribute of this machine was that the front was still intact.

He sniffed again, his jaw opening and his cheeks drawing back like wildcat about to screech. "Here."

"Really?"

I looked dubiously at the vending machine. Was it hidden in the coils? I thought it would be more obvious. I leaned in for a closer look and wished I had a magical flashlight to peer into the dark crevices of this ancient relic.

"Step aside."

I stepped aside as Ulf took a running leap and raised his axe high. The muscles of his thick arms bulged as he chopped down, like he was felling an oak. The edge of axe hit the polycarbonate front and sank in slow motion. The front dipped from the impact and bulged on the sides.

Ulf grunted and leaned in and I watched in breathless fascination at this display of mountain fae strength versus twenty first century plastics.

The vending machine was dented but unbroken.

Ulf's heavy brows drew together, apparently devoting a lot of brain cells to conquering this opponent. The thing about vending machines is that people have been trying to break them ever since they were invented. It was expressly designed to repel breakage.

"Uh, I don't think the axe will work."

"It will work." Ulf gently patted the handle, like I had insulted it.

"I think we have to use something stronger."

"My axe is mighty."

"No, I mean, like acid or fire."

"Hmmph."

His eyes narrowed in concentration and he stuck out the tip of his tongue as he stared intently at his axe. His lips began to move mumbling something I couldn't make out. Heat flared out from the axe and elvish runes glowed blue as the tip flamed orange.

A wild light glinted in Ulf's eyes and then he bellowed and swung his axe at the offending machine again.

This time, the heated metal pressed further into the glass. My eyebrows lifted as Ulf leaned in with the fire tipped axe and pushed with his considerable strength.

Ultimately, the vending machine gave way and the polycarbonate broke. Ulf looked well pleased with himself and I wondered if he would praise the vending machine for its valor and say it fought well.

"Why didn't you use a fireball or something on the rogue?"

"Can't."

"But you can make your axe flame up?"

"Yes. But I can not conjure something from nothing. This is Little Stjarna of Bål. This axe was forged in flame. It remembers flame."

While Ulf waxed poetic about the mythical origins of his

axe Stjarna, I peered into the gaping hole in the vending machine. Thankfully nothing crawled out.

Ulf went high grabbing snack bags, opening all of them, tossing the well preserved snacks on the floor. I went low, pulling out the soda cans and sport drinks, emptying them into the rusty sink.

I yanked out the last can of soda. It promised lemon lime goodness but was too light. I shook it. It rattled.

"Ulf, I've got something."

Ulf lifted his axe.

"No, no, we don't need to chop it with your axe."

He stared at me, frustrated. "Then how will you open the can?"

I popped the top and instead of the fizz of carbonation, there was only the whoosh of air. I tipped the can upside down and shook gently. A delicate silver chain emerged and with every shake, the silver chimed with a delicate sound.

Ulf's voice lowered in awe. "Spelled silver."

It was the perfect Slayer's symbol–a chain so thin that didn't seem like it should work, yet it was strong enough to hold a vampire immobile. Bashir's chain had worked on Tyee. I was for sure a believer.

This chain also told me how this Trial was supposed to work. Something that has been niggling in the back of my head since Aislinn's instructions finally clicked into place. There were three keys hidden in the Box, but that didn't mean only three candidates could pass the Trial. The chain was forged of many links, a structure that functioned only when every link was strong enough to support the others. Aislinn had reminded us to stay true to the tenets of the Slayers to pass this year. All eight of us should be able to pass if we worked together to bring out the three chains.

I told Ulf this.

He looked skeptical.

I reminded him what Aislinn said, putting emphasis on the pronouns. "Those who exit the Box with a key in their possession will pass."

Ulf was fae so he knew how ambiguous Aislinn's wording was. But he remained skeptical and said only, "If what you say is true, then I can hold onto the chain for the both of us."

I bit my lip. Either I believed in the Slayer tenets or I didn't. Either I believed in myself or I didn't. I had to trust my gut that I was right about this Trial. My father was probably rolling in his grave about now.

"How about double or nothing? If I'm right, you'll give me something. If I'm wrong, you'll have the chain so I got nothing."

Ulf cocked his head. I was counting on the Fae's love of a good bargain.

"And what is this something I give you if you are right?"

I jingled the silver chain. "This is about six ounces. If I'm right, then you'll pay me twelve ounces of silver by three bells tomorrow. "

Ulf's cheeks creased into a pleased smile. I knew he thought it was a cheap bargain. The fae practically dripped with silver. The mountain fae probably had folks who mined it. But for me, twelve ounces would tide me over for two months.

Ulf nodded. "A fair bargain."

I tossed the silver chain to Ulf who caught it in a fist and held it high in the air. His face took on an expression of wonder and for a moment, he looked very young.

Then his craggy face cracked into a broad grin and the two of us shared the elation of being that much closer to being Slayer initiates.

After delight, another flurry of emotions crossed Ulf's face and he turned contemplative. "Gorm was the one who wanted to be a Slayer."

I didn't have the best of interactions with Gorm, what with

me almost stabbing him with a bread knife back at the Farm, so I just made a noncommittal sound.

Ulf hung the chain in a loop on his belt. "I thought we would do it together."

In that moment, I wondered if that was how my uncle Samuel felt–that he and my dad were supposed to be Slayers together. Instead, my dad had made a reputation for himself and then returned to Boston to marry his sweetheart and start a family. Samuel had stayed to become one of the Freaks of Seattle, alone.

I pointed to the hallway. "We should find the others."

I knew Ulf was thinking of finding his sworn brother, Harald. But I wanted to find Cordelia and Wen, or Yvonne and Axel. Maybe we needed to find another key, but I thought the one we had was enough. Of course, none of it mattered right now unless we made it out of the Box alive.

We went back to the hallway. Yvonne's battle cries had faded but there was still plenty of crashing and unholy shrieking going on, which was good and bad. Bad because we would likely have to fight those things too, and I had no idea what they were. Good because it hopefully covered up the sounds of Ulf attacking the vending machine like a berserker.

The sounds of battle led us further into the depths of the dead building. I found the first body by tripping over it--a dead shifter, maybe a jackal by the length of his snout, it was hard to tell around all the stab wounds. The skin around his wounds was burned and blistered, his face battered and swollen.

Silver blades. One of us for sure, most likely Marnie with her crucifixes. We pressed on and found more bodies interspersed with drifting piles of ash. Whoever we were approaching, they were racking up the body count.

I paused as we came upon a blind intersection. The sounds of battle were close now. In the reflection of a wall of cracked glass I caught the glint of silver. Around the corner, Harald roared in pain. Ulf pushed past me and I hurried to catch up.

We found Harald and Marnie knee deep in a peril of rogues. One of them had latched onto Harald's leg and he was desperately beating at its head with his hammer. Ulf ran to his sworn brother's assistance.

Marnie had become separated from Harald and surrounded by four vampires. She had both of her crucifixes out and pivoted warily, trying to keep the vamps at arm's length, but the short length of her stilettos wasn't holding them back. Both of her crucifixes gave off a soft white glow that showed the power of her faith. Marnie's faith was surely strong given this light from her crosses. All the vamps bore the marks of her silvered blades, red, blistered cuts across arms and faces, but none of them looked daunted beyond trying to avoid the light from the glowing crucifixes.

I congratulated myself again for entering the Box with my spear and approached, eyeing which vampire I would stab in the back first.

Marnie caught my movement and whirled, hissing. "Get back!"

Well, yeah, I wasn't going to do that, especially now that the vampires turned and noticed me coming up behind them. What did Marnie think she was doing? I lunged forward, using the strength of my legs to take the nearest vampire in the lower back. It screamed as the spear head exited through his belly. My crystal drank again, its color heating up to near blinding intensity. The vampire went down, writhing. I followed in, pulling my spear back and winding up to take the vamp's head off while it was down.

A body collided into my back, nearly pushing me over. I hop-stepped away from the vampire to keep from gutting myself with the butt of my spear. I recovered and turned to find

Marnie wrestling with the last of her vampires, her arm in a choke hold around its neck.

"Watch out! Friendlies!"

Marnie yelled over the guttural cries of the vampire in her arms. "Leave, donor! The glory of this battle is not for you!"

Goddess in the moon. "Crazy much?! I'm helping you!"

Marnie's eyes were wide enough for me to see the whites all the way around. She calmly drew another of her blades and decapitated the vamp in her arms with the blasé efficiency of opening a can of tomatoes. The vamp dropped to the ground and dissolved. The other two vampires rolled on the floor in agony, twisted up in a length of spelled silver chain.

She jerked the chain, drawing howls of pain from the vamps. Her voice was steady, pitched a little higher than normal and totally devoid of emotion. "Your assistance is neither needed nor desired."

My gaze fell on the silver chain in her hands. So they had already found their key. Marnie kept finding ways to impress and irritate me at the same time. I wondered if Harald had been able to sniff it out just like Ulf had done. Our own personal fae hounds.

Harald limped over, Ulf helping him carry his weight on his wounded leg. Harald's face was a roiling mix of anger and frustration. With a yell, he took the easy shot and brought his great sword down on the vamp I'd speared. The vampire's head exploded like a ripe melon, splattering the other vampire with gore and ash. Harald jerked away from Ulf's help and hobbled away to lean against the wall. His leg was a mess. It looked like the vampire had gnawed him to the bone.

Marnie dispatched the last vampires with quick motions and the building fell quiet again. She coiled the silver chain up and placed it carefully in a pouch at her waist.

She looked at me, a very satisfied smile on her face. "All right, back to work. But let's get rid of some dead weight, first."

33

BETRAYAL

Blood and ash covered us all in equal degrees. But we were alive and the rogues were dead so I considered that an unmitigated victory.

Something in Marnie's eyes bothered me, but I tried to extend an olive branch.

"Good job on finding the chain." I gestured to the loop on Marnie's belt.

She bared her teeth at me.

"What is your problem?" I was sick of Marnie's craziness. She'd attacked me twice. How were we supposed to be Slayers together?

She pointed her sharpened crucifix at me. "You're my problem, Roxy. You ally with vampires and that makes you no different than them."

I pointed to the piles of ash between us. "I'm a Slayer candidate just like you. You don't get to judge me."

Marnie sneered.

My lips flattened with annoyance. None of this was getting me anywhere. This was more conversation than I needed to have with her. I focused on getting out of here.

Harald returned and wiped his sword off on a cubicle wall. "Ulf, you have a key as well. This is good."

"Aye, brother." Ulf's wide smile was a slash of white on his ash covered face.

"'Tis only fitting. You can leave this one behind and we can search for the third one together." Harald waved dismissively in my direction.

"Hey!" I didn't like where this was going.

Ulf frowned. "I cannot do that. She is my sister-in-arms for this Trial. It would not be honorable."

Harald gave a hearty laugh. "She is not worthy of being even your servant."

"My honor is not so whimsical."

Marnie hissed. "She's not fit to be a Slayer. Leave her and we will find the third chain. She can rot in this godsforsaken Box."

I couldn't believe this was happening. It was against everything that the Slayers stood for, and it was not how my team had won the first Trial. My face flushed hot with anger and I drew myself up to unload on Marnie and Harald.

From above, a sound like splintering wood echoed around the room. We all crouched low and stopped moving at the sound.

The ceiling bowed down like an upside down bubble. With a powdery crack the decaying tiles shattered and unleashed a black cloud of leathery wings. Wriggling bodies squirmed through the hole and showered down on us. Real bats were bad enough. Here, you never knew if they were vampire bats. I jumped away, looking for cover.

And then it got dark. Really dark.

Red eyes peered down from the ceiling as the black enveloped us. It was the stuff of nightmares.

The darkness was disorienting but the one sense that worked was my hearing. Yelling voices echoed around me and I couldn't tell if they were Harald or Ulf's battle cries. My instinct was to close my eyes but doing so would have lost me the ability to avoid a frontal attack. My spear went up and I went low, trying to buy myself an extra second.

That extra second gave me the opportunity to witness the blackness parting to reveal the disturbance that had disrupted the bat colony. From behind the smaller bats came the much larger vampire bats behind them. The ones with the skeletal frames and wingspans of pterodactyls.

The first bat transformed into a skinny vampire with leathery skin. I lunged and my spear pierced the vampire's shoulder. The crystal glowed a soft orange and I watched in satisfaction the wound smoked where the crystal touched it. But my satisfaction was short-lived because I'd missed his neck. His fangs drew down and he swiped at me with his claws. I sidestepped and twirled the spear to stab at a larger target. I aimed for the heart but the resistance told me I'd skipped off a rib. The vampire spun back and the dry, dead stench of him hit me square in the face even as his claws missed my neck by inches. My heart thudded, pumping fear-laced adrenaline through me.

I could do this. I was doing this. Muscle memory saved me, burned into my muscles through endless weekends training with my dad. My spear came up, the point steady, my fingers light on the shaft. Time slowed as the vampire reared back for another strike, leaving his chest wide open to me. I yelled, incoherent, flush with terror and exhilaration at the same time. I plunged forward, putting my weight behind the spear. The vampire slumped and dissolved into ash.

With the space before me cleared, I took in the wider battle scene. Five vampires divided me from Harald, Marnie, and Ulf. One of them, stuck in some in-between transformation with leathery webs under her arms, broke off from the group and rounded on me. With a shriek, she opened her jaws wide and jumped at me.

I threw myself left and aimed my spear at her torso. She was quick and my spear head tore through the webbed wing. I yanked downward to finish the job. She didn't seem to care as I tore away the wing remnant. The vampire just howled and her other arm swooped down on my head. Goddess they moved so fast!

She unhinged her jaw like a snake, yellowed fangs extending. My heart pounded in staccato beats as she descended.

I tucked the spear into my gut, front rolled between her legs, and came up behind her. Even as I turned, I knew I was too close, too slow. I'd given her all the time she needed to pivot and grab my neck, easy as plucking fruit from a tree. I drew Loki from my belt knowing I would strike her down even as she drained me.

From the edge of my vision brilliant blue light traced a fiery arc and the flaring runes of Ulf's axe hit home, cleaving the vampire in two. Relief coursed through me. "Thanks, partner!"

"Behind you!" Ulf yelled. I turned and quailed.

My eyes widened in alarm as a figure emerged from the darkness. If the pterodactyl vampires had scared the bats, then this was scaring the pterodactyls. It had to be eight feet tall and where it should have had skin it had an exoskeleton of bone over its ribcage. The vampire's bald head was covered in shiny, leathery skin, eight eyes like glassy black marbles scattered across its face. Grotesque, hairy fangs protruded from an oversized lower jaw. Great, an arachnid vampire. If vampires were bad, this was some next level nightmare fodder. Arachno-vamp? Spider-vamp? What was the naming convention for mutated vampires?

It didn't matter. We only needed to kill it.

I screamed and then Ulf was at my side, screaming berserker curses, his axe in motion. My spear shot out and glanced off the thing's protective bony cage. Ulf's axe didn't even seem to chip the bone. Hitting this thing was like hitting a steel frame. My bones rattled from the impact and my hands went numb for a moment. My momentum carried me to the beast's left, putting it between me and Ulf which improved our odds. Possibly. Our lousy odds.

Vampires were once human but nothing about this monster looked human.

Ulf attacked again, hopefully not in its well protected torso. His trademark blue light shone over the edge of his axe and he swung in alternating arcs, beating back the vampire's arms. With another yell he moved in and took a shot at the vamp's neck. The axe bounced off its clavicle and smoke singed my nostrils from the axe's fiery impact with the undead flesh.

This wasn't going to work. It would take us forever to chip away at this monster. I focused my magic on the vampire, desperate for any edge we could use. My vision clouded with green and I despaired. Not only was it huge and strong, but the carapace of bone was incredibly dense and tough. Thick bands of green light wrapped around the vampire, sheathing it nearly completely from neck to ankle. Even Altan with his shifter strength wouldn't be able to stake this vampire, and I doubted any of us had a sword heavy or sharp enough to decapitate it.

Ulf danced away from the spider-vamp, amazingly light on his feet for such a big man. His axe flitted through the air, blocking strikes left and right, sparks showering down on him. They moved away from me which meant there was nothing I could do as I watched Ulf slip on a patch of moldering carpet and go down on one knee. The vampire plunged into the opening.

Harald melted out of the shadows behind Ulf, his great sword held at high guard in both hands. The vampire's armored forearms crashed into the wide blade and the two forces strained against each other. Harald gave a joyous shout.

"My brother! With me! We will destroy this demon!"

Ulf's eyes blazed with new fire and his grin stretched from ear to ear. He got back to his feet and readied his axe for a two-handed blow.

Marnie appeared beside me, an odd little smile on her face. I jumped when I saw her, then relaxed. "Thank the goddess. With the four of us we might just--"

I never got to finish the sentence because Marnie chose that moment to come at me with both her crosses out, silver blades flashing left and right, her voice rising in a manic scream.

Instinct took over. I didn't consciously drop the spear, it just fell away as my hands dropped to my belt and pulled out my most trusted companions for close up fighting. Thor and Loki jumped into my hands, just in time to catch one blade and deflect the other. I yelled, trying to get through to her, and slowly gave ground, batting away her strikes as fast as they came.

"Marnie! Stop it! We need to work together!"

"Never! You're his thrall! You're better off dead and the Slayers are better off without you!"

I caught one of her blades between my hammers and yanked, pulling her off balance. "I've trained my whole life to be here!"

Marnie bounced back, barely missing a beat. "Well you wasted your time then. You think they want a fang-lover like you?"

"It's not that simple!"

She laughed, the color high on her cheeks. "Oh but it is, Roxy. You are either human, or you are vampire. You are either fighting them, or you are food. Which is it?"

Marnie came after me, blades carving glittering arcs in the darkness.

Behind me, Harald and Ulf bellowed war cries as they fought the beast. They were holding their own, but it didn't sound like they were making any progress. I had to get through to Marnie. It was time for a different strategy.

"They're going to die if we don't help them!"

She lunged in and got under my guard, landing a shallow cut that drew a line of fire across my ribs. Her eyes were fever bright. "Then they are not worthy! Only the chosen will move forward!"

Who was she to decide who was worthy? Anger, fueled by the sudden pain, flared white-hot behind my eyes. Her sanctimonious attitude would leave me, all of us, here to die.

I batted away her follow up and went on the offensive. Thor and Loki dropped back into my belt and my duster flared wide as I pulled the throwing knives at my back. One, two, three, my wrists flicked back and forth and I threw a quick succession of blades aimed right at her face. Shining steel whipped through the air.

Marnie was good. Her crosses came up and she knocked my blades down with tight, efficient moves. She was a good fighter, but she was no Kotori. Blocking my knives had put her on her back foot. I grabbed my hammers and ran into the opening. It was time for Marnie to feel some pain.

Hammers were similar to blades in that no one wanted to make contact with one the wrong way. They were dissimilar in that non-lethal cuts could be sewn up to become scars with a story, something to tell your mates over drinks. If I hit you with one of my hammers, well, let's just say there was no way it was going to be pretty.

Marnie sensed the shift in the fight and pulled back a half step just in time to avoid getting a hammer to the chin. I pressed, bringing Thor and Loki around in quick, brutal arcs, aiming for wrists, elbows, knees. All the beautiful little bendy parts that no one liked to imagine being smashed to a pulp.

As she kept her limbs away from my hammers, she left her core open. I jabbed her in the gut with Loki. Her breath whooshed out as the sucker punch landed and I knew I had her. The church had trained her against starving vampires, optimizing her fighting style for staking and decapitation. I would bet all the silver I had that she hadn't trained nearly as much against other people, much less dirty fighters like me.

I jabbed her again and she nearly retched. Marnie went down coughing and gasping for breath. Seeing her down on her knees, my anger ebbed and I rolled my wrists, willed the tension out of my arms, forced my hands to relax. However crazy she was, I wasn't going to kill her, much less hurt her. I just needed her to see.

My father would have berated me. Never let down your guard, he'd say. A cornered enemy is at its most dangerous.

Marnie leapt at me, her gasping breaths morphing into shrill laughter. "Unclean! Unworthy!"

One of her crosses grazed my cheek and I jerked my head back. Marnie crashed into me and our momentum bore us to the ground. Now it was my turn to lose my breath as she landed on top with her knee on my chest. I felt a crackling twinge in my ribs. A lot of them.

Straddling my chest, Marnie raised her knives, ready to deliver the coup de grace. I dropped the hammers and shot my hands out, grabbing her wrists. I locked my elbows and pushed her back, fighting to ignore the fire in my chest.

Behind me Ulf's war cry took a decidedly different tone. "Roxy!"

Goddess. What now?

Marnie's eyes flicked up and she cackled again. "See! The unworthy!"

I took the opening. Spreading my arms, I forced Marnie's arms apart, and brought her head down to me. I screamed at the pain in my ribs as I curled up and rammed my forehead into Marnie's face. The crack of her nose breaking was the most satisfying sound I'd ever heard. Marnie's laugh turned into a spluttering, gurgling cry of pain and she rolled off of me, clutching at her face.

Ulf and Harald screamed again. I rolled to my knees and spun around. The spider-vamp had the Fae cornered. Both of them bled from cuts to their arms and legs and Harald's limp was noticeably worse than before. He was also clutching his side.

My ribs sang with sympathetic pain.

Most importantly, neither of them had their weapons. I scanned the area and found them, stuck into the spider-vamp's back, embedded into the bony carapace.

The vampire moved in and the shell around its ribs cracked open like a beetle's wings. The bones extended into two chitinous legs on either side that ended at jagged points. Spider-vamp. Maybe Octo-vamp.

The monster stopped and roared, legs--all of them--flailing in fury.

Spider-vamp. Definitely spider-vamp.

Harald and Ulf had managed to do nothing but make it more angry with a great sword and battle axe. What was I going to do with my hammers and spear? I looked around for answers and when I finally looked up, I felt Kotori's disappointed gaze over my shoulder.

"Ulf!"

"Roxy!"

"Get ready to run!"

"I do not run fr--"

Goddess, save me from the fae. "Get! Ready!"

I didn't have time for subtlety, for art. I reached up to where the entrance of the bats had already weakened the frame of the dropdown ceiling. Hundreds of pounds of metal, pipes, and tile hung by a thread. I stretched my magic and Broke it.

The white point intensified until it shone like a tiny supernova. "Now, Ulf!"

I didn't see if they ran. The only thing I saw was the ceiling, all of it, coming down on us. It looked like the entire building was collapsing, crushing us under the weight of the five floors above.

A thundering cloud of dust and debris slapped me in the face.

～

"Roxy!"

The voice was muffled and came from everywhere at once. Darkness surrounded and choked me, like the black was trying to crawl down my throat and fill my lungs. I gasped back to consciousness and when I inhaled, the sharp pain in my ribs reminded me of Marnie. Then the thick, musty dust in my windpipe reminded me that I had brought down the ceiling. More pain as the dust triggered hacking coughs, which triggered more pain as my body tried to spasm even while I was pinned under the rubble.

"Roxy!"

The voice was closer now and then the weight above me shifted. More pain flared as large, unknowable things moved until a dusty bar of dim light pierced the blackness that had swallowed me. Big hands found my shoulders and grabbed, then gently pulled me out of my coffin.

Ulf loomed over me, his face a grisly mix of ash and blood. I hoped none of the blood was my fault. His eyes practically glowed in contrast, the pale blue corneas and white sclera looking eerily bright.

"Leave her!" Marnie shrieked. Her voice was nasally, like she had a cold. I felt perversely good about that.

Harald had one arm around Marnie as he dragged her out from under a pile of rubble. Bright rivulets of blood ran down his other arm as it hung limp at his side. When he offered her a hand to get up she slapped it away.

Somehow Ulf had found my hammers amidst all the destruction. As he handed them back to me I marveled at how much I'd underestimated the big man. I vowed to never do that again. Assuming I got out of the Box, that is.

Ulf levered me up to a sitting position. "She has proven herself in battle and is worthy of being my sister-in-arms. I will not leave her."

Marnie fell silent and her eyes went back and forth between the three of us. When she saw how the new lines were drawing up, her mouth flattened with displeasure.

The floor was...no longer a floor, but the twisted wreckage of the dropdown ceiling, including all the support structures, air ducts, and yards and yards of decaying ceiling tiles. The junk heaped up to a largish mound in one corner where I assumed the spider-vamp was dead under the pile. Good riddance.

Ulf got in front of me, his eyes intent on mine. "Can you stand?"

Amazingly, nothing felt broken. The recoil from using my magic was a dim shadow of what I'd expected. Maybe I'd missed the worst of it by being unconscious. Lucky me. Otherwise, I hurt, but no worse than I'd been hurting before. My leather duster glowed faintly, an aftereffect of Laila's enchantment. The intricate pattern of glyphs, engraved into the leather, shone with pale blue light. The light faded one glyph at a time until the leather was dark again. My whole body was going to be a giant bruise tomorrow, but beaten and bruised was a clear winner over dead as a doornail any day. I was definitely giving Laila a 5-star review when this was all over.

I nodded. "Let's get out of here. I still need to win that bet."

He held out his hand and we clasped them together, my smaller hand almost buried inside his big one. I'd never had a brother-in-arms. It felt pretty good. He leaned back and helped me to my feet. Whatever happened to Marnie, I knew Ulf would have my back if we became Slayers. It was a good start.

Something that hadn't seemed right finally twigged as we hobbled off. "Where's your axe?"

Ulf smiled ruefully and tipped his head towards the garbage pile. "Still buried with the vampire. It did not seem prudent to go digging for it."

My jaw dropped. "But you put all that time into it. Your years of training. The runes."

"I can craft a new weapon."

He seemed to consider for a moment and spoke again, completely deadpan. "Or perhaps, when you are feeling better, we can return and search for it. Perhaps fight another spider-demon."

I didn't know which was more astonishing. The fact that I would gladly return to the Box to help him, or that Ulf had just tried to make a joke. That was more than enough to lift my spirits, even with Marnie glaring daggers at me as Harald held her back with his good arm. Being nearly crushed by the ceiling seemed to have taken some of the fight out of her, reducing her to tolerable levels of annoyance.

When I let go of Ulf's hand I found I could stand on my own, albeit a little wobbly. I needed a lot more practice if I was going to fill my dad's shoes as the Breaker.

I scanned the room. "Which way out?"

Ulf did his magic nose thing for a moment before pointing to the south. "That way."

Between us we had two keys. I knew in my bones that we just had to get out of the Box and we could all be Slayers. Maybe not Marnie. Samuel needed to know what Marnie was capable of. But Aislinn's rules had been just vague enough so even my human mind could drive a truck through the loopholes.

We made our way across the wreckage, carefully picking a path that appeared the most stable, Marnie and Harald leading the way. We skirted around the main pile burying the spider-vamp and were nearly to the far end of the room when Harald stopped short, his eyes focused off to our left. Ulf noticed and stopped as well.

"What is it, brother?"

Harald stood silent for a moment, then turned to Ulf, a fierce grin on his face. "Fate smiles upon us, my brother!"

He dashed onto the pile of twisted metal and junk, a look of utter glee on his face. Ulf took a step forward and nearly fell into an open hole. I grabbed at his arm as he yelled.

"My prince! No!"

And then I realized exactly what Harald of the Reach, son of Sten, Guardian of the Northern Pass, and colossal idiot, was going for. By then, he'd reached his goal and had his hand on the hilt of his great sword. The curling ram's horns barely protruded above the junk.

He crowed. "Ice Storm has returned to me!"

Harald yanked at the hilt and everything moved. A low, scraping sound filled the room and the floor shifted under our feet, sending Marnie to her knees. Harald, unperturbed, kept pulling on the sword.

The fool! "Harald! Leave it!"

He laughed, an ugly sound. "A human would not understand. This was passed to me through ten generations! From my father, and his father--"

I never got to hear his sword's storied lineage because at that moment, the spider-vamp, most definitely not dead, ripped through the mountain of junk that buried it. Still grasping the hilt of his beloved sword, Harald was tossed ass over tea kettle to the far end of the room. He did not get his sword back.

The spider-vamp stood, junk and debris falling away as it dug itself out. Its ribcage flared as it roared and the sound filled the room with vibrating horror. Marnie scrambled back, mouth open, crawling away on hands and knees. The vampire's head swung around until it found me.

Goddess. I had dropped an entire ceiling on this monster and hadn't even scratched it. How were we supposed to defeat something so powerful? The vampire threw itself at me with hooked claws out, mouth open, fangs extended, and a blood chilling screech. I stood, unable to move, unable to draw my weapons. What was the point?

"No!" Ulf leapt in front of me.

Time slowed to a crawl. Ulf's body slewed sideways in front of me. He was a big man but not big enough to block my view of the spider-vamp. The vampire closed in and its ribs opened wide like another mouth, the leathery skin beneath smooth and moist. The extra legs pulled out and back, ready to strike.

The vampire's hands snapped out and grabbed Ulf by the head and neck. The extra legs rammed home, all four plunging into Ulf's gut. He gave a pained grunt of pain as the talons pierced him through. Ulf's blood sprayed and warm droplets landed on my face. Harald screamed.

Ulf groaned and slid downward, blood pouring from the wounds in his gut. The vampire flung his body and it cartwheeled through the air, landing at Marnie's feet. The vampire advanced on me and through its legs I watched Marnie drop to her knees and pull the silver chain from Ulf's belt.

The little snake!

Harald roared at the desecration, his eyes bright with murderous fury. Marnie held out the chain like a talisman to ward him off. "He's dead! She's dead! Do you want to be dead, or do you want to be a Slayer?"

Ulf groaned, his head rolling. The fire in Harald's eyes died. He looked like he'd been kicked in the crotch, his face pale and damp. I kept backing up, praying I wouldn't trip on anything, trying to circle my way back around to Ulf. If I could stop the bleeding, maybe I could stabilize him until one of the Slayers saw him and extracted him. They had to be watching, right?

And then the bottom dropped out as Harald reached out with his one good hand and grabbed the key from Marnie. His fingers trembled as they clutched at the fine chain.

I couldn't believe it. "Harald! He's your sworn brother!"

A pained look crossed his face, and he turned away from me and Ulf. Marnie shot me a smug look as the two of them ran for the exit.

They didn't matter now. None of this mattered. I had to get to Ulf, had to stop the bleeding. I dodged and ducked, working my way closer to him. I dithered for a moment and the vampire took the bait, coming hard for me. I juked left and beat it, sending the vampire into the hole that had nearly taken Ulf earlier. I ran for my partner.

Ulf's face was waxy, his beard matted with sweat, his breaths coming fast and shallow.

"Hang on!" I pressed my hands into his gut, trying to staunch the blood.

Warm fluid squirted out around my fingers and he gave a pained gasp. He was dying. He was dying right in front of me and I wasn't going to be able to help him.

The floor rocked again as the vampire dug itself out. It found us in a second. I pulled on Ulf but he was too much dead weight. There was no way I could move him.

His voice was paper thin. "Leave...me..."

I grabbed his hand and clamped down hard until I felt him squeeze back. His eyes managed to focus on mine. "No. We will live to slay another day."

Ulf closed his eyes and his breath rattled in his chest.

The vampire advanced slowly, sensing cornered prey. As it approached its rib cage opened once again and I cursed myself for a fool. Of all the ideas I had had in the last few hours, this one was by far the stupidest. If I kept resetting the bar like this, Kotori would have a hard time keeping up with my lunacy.

I laid Ulf down and gauged the distance. My spear was gone, lost somewhere under the broken ceiling. The only play I had left was the wicked little karambit under my armpit, which was coincidentally the shortest blade I owned. Lucky me.

When the vampire was a few feet from me I made a half-hearted lunge at it. Just for show. The creature dodged easily and followed me as I retreated from my miss.

Only, I didn't retreat. I stepped into it, getting nice and close to the soft inner section of the vampire's ribs, conveniently exposed with the bone carapace opened, and shining brilliant white in my magic vision.

My karambit flashed out and I drove it in low, deep, then up, piercing the bottom of the vampire's heart, the sharp steel opening it like taking the bottom off a paper cup. The vampire screamed and hot, sticky black blood fountained over my arms. I grabbed the vampire and leaned back, dragging the monster with me to direct the spray of its blood over Ulf's body.

Black blood dripped down my arms and off my elbows, splattering over Ulf. He moaned as the hot blood made contact. The vampire writhed, even as I felt its strength waning. With a spasm, the vampire clenched and its ribcage snapped shut. I nearly bit off my tongue as the bones cracked me across the face and mashed me into the vampire's body. Spiny ribs crushed into my neck, the rough bone like broken glass on my skin.

Hot lines of agony flashed across the front and back of my neck. The vampire screamed and its arms clamped down until I felt like my head would burst. I might have been screaming, too. I wasn't sure.

The vampire's scream petered out as it dissolved into ash. I hung, motionless for half a heartbeat, then fell to the floor. My knees buckled and I collapsed on top of Ulf.

Ulf coughed as I hit him. "Oof. Roxy. Get off me."

I moaned and pressed my hands to my neck and chest. My shirt and duster were soaked. My hands came away wet and sticky. Most of it looked like the black blood from the spider-vamp. Maybe half of it? Hard to tell in the dim light.

"Roxy? Roxy?"

Ulf sat up and I rolled bonelessly off his body. This section of the floor was gloriously flat and unmoving. Finally the big fae was thinking along the right lines. A nap sounded like a fabulous idea. I'd had a hard couple of weeks. I deserved it.

A big hand grabbed my shoulder and shook me gently. Why couldn't he leave me alone? The hand pulled insistently until I rolled onto my back. Ulf's face swam out of the darkness, lines of worry creasing his forehead. His color had improved considerably. I wondered distantly if Kotori would still think my plan has been stupid. I bet that Ulf didn't.

Ulf's once stand-offish demeanor had become very intrusive and annoying, though. What had happened to the quiet, brooding mountain fae? His eyes darted back and forth, and his fingers pressed into my neck. Ow.

"Goddess. Roxy, stay with me. Say something."

"...tell Koto...wasn't a bad idea after all..."

Darkness swallowed everything and I went away.

34

BALANCING THE SCALES

The utter peace and darkness didn't last quite as long as I would have expected.

Sound returned to the black first, a shouting voice, much too loud and yet far in the distance. A brief wave of euphoria hit me and I wondered if I was about to see a bright light at the end of a long tunnel. A pang of emotion speared my chest, like a stake through a vampire.

Dad, I'm so sorry. I tried.

Then the world started shaking and the dim, dank, and stinking reality of the Twilight crashed into me like a freight train.

"Roxy, you need to drink from me." Tyee's voice was low and urgent. How had he gotten here?

Ernest hovered behind Tyee's shoulder, the pale ghost vibrating with agitation. How had they gotten here? Was Tyee having me followed?

Another shake. "Roxy!"

Mrs. Chu's warning swam out of memory along with the tantalizing smell of soup. Tied for eternity. I didn't want that.

"No! No ties." I put a hand on his broad chest and pushed

him away. Or rather, I tried. It felt like trying to move a build-ing. When had Tyee gotten so big?

I tried shaking my head, which only made the room spin. Tyee's face stayed front and center. I stared at those midnight dark eyes, trying to focus, willing the room to stop moving. I grabbed his fancy shirt and my fingers curled into the silky fabric, leaving bloody tracks under his collar. I pulled him down until our eyes were inches apart. "Won't drink."

Frustration was evident on every line of his face. "You are dying, Roxy."

"I'll be okay." I whispered.

Tyee held out his wrist. Blood had dried on his forearm. "I opened a vein to heal your neck. But you've lost too much blood. If you drink directly I can heal you."

He'd saved me. My emotions spiraled from relief that I was alive to despair that we had lost the chain. This Trial was over for me and Ulf but we still had to get out of the Box. Tyee was our best shot.

I twisted my hand tighter into his shirt. "You owe me."

"And I'm trying to save you."

Focusing like this was taking too much out of me. The world blackened around the edges. I moved my head until Tyee's face came back into the light. "No...ties. Take us... through the Mist. To the Slayers."

It was Tyee's turn to clutch at me. "You fool. You didn't want my help before. And now you only want your precious Slayers? I don't see them running in to help you."

I blinked, adjusting to this new vantage. This close, his eyes were not as black as I'd thought but shot through with gray sliv-ers. Like starlight. "Ulf, too."

"He's not my concern."

"You owe me for Eloise as well. Two lives."

Tyee's jaw hardened. "Fine. Now there will be no more debts between us."

"Deal."

He reached out and grabbed the edge of Ulf's armor. Cool darkness consumed us, like a thousand yards of silk sliding around me. It smelled like midnight in the forest, and I closed my eyes to sink into it.

The darkness lifted and the rotten scent of the Box evaporated. I forced my eyes to the beautiful purple hues of the Twilight. Tyee propped me up against the wall of the Box. Ulf slid down next to me and I nearly cried from the peace of simply not moving.

A flutter of green crossed my vision. Ernest floated before me, his eyes wide with concern. I blinked, confused. Ernest didn't usually visit me so far from the apartment.

"Hey, Ernest." My voice was faint.

"Roxy, this place is bad. Very bad." Ernest vibrated in agitation, a blur of motion.

"Yeah. Totally agree."

Even Ulf grunted assent.

The Box had been bad. Very bad. But we'd made it out alive. But that was about the only good news we had.

As if reading my mind, Ulf mumbled. "We don't have the chain."

My body ached everywhere. The acid burn of disappointment made each moment in my body worse. We'd failed. I'd failed. Tears burned in my eyes and I blinked hard to avoid crying in front of Tyee and Ulf.

Ulf looked up at Tyee. "Your assistance was timely."

Tyee nodded, apparently used to circuitous fae thank yous. "Ernest saw Roxy go in and thought I should know."

So that was how Tyee had shown up. I guess he wasn't having me followed after all.

Ulf shook his head, his face rueful. "When I considered the Slayer Trials, I did not imagine I would be helped by a human, a ghost, and a vampire."

I looked up at Ernest. "Thank you, Ernest."

He nodded, his transparent face relieved.

I turned to Tyee and opened my mouth to thank him, then thought better of it and stopped. He caught the brief movement and his cold starlight gaze pierced through me, as if he sensed what I'd been about to say.

My heart swelled with emotion, too full to put into words. I had saved him. He had saved me. We were square. Or at least, he didn't owe me anything. I'd never wanted him to owe me anything.

Fatigue pulled at me, weighing down my limbs and my thoughts. I had failed the final Trial, but Tyee had ensured that I would live to try again. The need to express myself properly to Tyee burned in me, a tiny flame at my core, but my mind refused to make the words. I opened my mouth again, trying to make him understand what even I couldn't yet grasp.

Before I could speak the doors burst open and slammed against the wall. Marnie and Harald stumbled out, both of them limping. She had a silver chain looped and hanging at her waist. Harald had his slung around his shoulders.

A new jolt of adrenaline burned my fatigue away like morning mist and I reached for one of my throwing knives. I owed Marnie. Without taking his eyes from me, Tyee tensed and his fangs lowered.

Anger roiled in my gut and anchored me solidly to my body. Every pain, every ache, all of it served to focus my rage on Marnie. She'd betrayed us all and defied the Slayer's credo. Given the chance, she chose to leave us to our deaths, and yet she'd slithered out of the Box with Aislinn's key. I might not be a Slayer but there was no way I was letting Marnie present her key to Aislinn.

Harald spotted us first and limped over, breaking my eye line with Marnie. "Ulf, my brother!"

Ulf shot to his feet and spat at Harald. "You are no brother of mine! You are forsworn."

Harald halted. Even I stopped short at Ulf's outburst.

Ulf raised his voice. When he spoke, his voice was pitched to carry. "Harald, son of Sten, Guardian of the Northern Reach, your blood is not my blood."

Harald's eyes widened and his jaw slackened. "No, Ulf, don't--."

Ulf continued, his voice growing louder. "Your blood is not my blood. Your vows are not my vows. Your path is not my path."

Harald sank to his knees. "Ulf...forgive me."

Ulf's eyes were the cold blue of ancient ice, his voice the relentless swing of the headsman's axe. "I abjure our blood oath. I abjure our brotherhood. I abjure our sworn vows."

Harald looked like Ulf had backhanded him.

Ulf held out his hand to me. I acted on instinct and slapped the hilt of my knife into his palm. Beside me, Tyee had gone very still, his sharp eyes watching the fae melodrama playing out before us.

Ulf raised his hand, brandishing the thick white scar in the center of his palm. He slashed at the scar. "Harald, you are as nothing to me."

Blood welled from the cut and the world slowed as the flow cut a wet crimson stripe across Ulf's palm. Tyee's nostrils flared and even I caught the faintest scent of salt.

Ulf slashed again at the center of his palm. "Harald, you are as nothing to me."

I held my breath because I finally understood what was happening.

Ulf made a third cut, turning his hand into a bloody, crimson star. His voice grew hoarse with pain, but remained loud enough to carry down the street. Ulf's eyes glittered with unshed tears. "Harald you are as nothing to me."

Thrice named and thrice shamed, Ulf severed his blood ties to Harald Stenson, Guardian of the Northern Reach.

Ulf wiped the blade on his tunic and turned away from Harald. He handed me back the knife and I tucked it in my boot. His choice made, Ulf folded to his knees, his eyes now glassy and distant. He still wasn't fully healed, and the effort of his actions must have taken a toll on his body.

My anger with Marnie had lowered to a simmer as I watched Ulf shun Harold. Harald flexed his own hand as if each cut in Ulf's hand had had cut him too. Maybe it had. Who knew how their fae blood oaths worked?

When Harald moved, his movements were slow and brittle, like he'd aged a century. His head drooped, his beard folding against his chest and then in slow, deliberate movements he unwrapped the silver chain from his shoulder and tossed it at Ulf's feet. It chimed as it landed and lay in a sparkling pool of silver between me and Ulf.

THE NEXT FEW things seemed to happen all at once.

Cordelia and Wen rounded the east corner and rushed over to me and Ulf. Unsurprisingly, Cordelia had a silver chain looped at her waist. She and Wen were also clean, as if their garments had been freshly laundered. It figured.

Behind Cordelia, Altan lugged Axel on his back, Axel's massive frame making the werejaguar look small. Axel was covered in blood, his eyes swollen shut and his right arm sagging limply. Yvonne limped at Akhil's side, the warrior witch leaning heavily on her knobkerrie. Yvonne's left leg was badly wounded and blood matted the hair on one side of her head.

Cordelia knelt at my side. "Roxy, you don't look so good."

She poured some water onto a handkerchief and wiped my

face. Her eyes locked onto my neck. I knew it was bad. Tyee's blood on the outside had sealed up the worst of it but since I hadn't drunk from him, my internal injuries hadn't been affected. I was trying not to think about it. The upside was I couldn't see my own neck.

Wen had two fingers deep in Ulf's leg applying pressure along a meridian. After a moment the big man seemed to relax a little, and his breathing slowed.

Altan was all smiles, seemingly unfazed by Axel's weight on his shoulders. He looked over our group and appeared to be inordinately pleased with himself. "I knew this was a good crop of candidates this year. Not one death!"

The fact that he was saying this while carrying Axel, bloodied and unconscious, the biggest and strongest candidate among us, was more than enough to put my escape from the Box into some bleak context. I owed a lot to my dad for preparing me to survive the Twilight, but in a lot of ways he had not prepared me for the Slayers.

Akhil set Yvonne down next to me. The warrior witch groaned as she settled her injured leg. She patted my shoulder. "Glad to see you made it out."

"Same to you."

We shared a sad smile. Her leg looked bad but it wasn't anything the Slayers couldn't fix with a dose of vamp blood. Of course, that was poor consolation for washing out of the Trials. To come so close to the finish line, only to stumble at the end. The thought hurt almost as badly as my neck.

Cordelia stood to make room for Akhil to kneel next to me. Akhil reached into his vest and pulled out a Midnight Rose. I tipped it back and the coppery taste coated my tongue and the thick blood stuck in my throat.

My eyes met Tyee's above the edge of the Rose as I drank. His mouth was a flat, angry line. I had refused to drink from him. To drink from a vampire, a prince no less, was a rare privilege, one that he undoubtedly did not offer lightly or often. I doubted he had ever been turned down, either

I held his gaze as I swallowed the Cure. The Slayers were my life now. I would not start my new life tied to Tyee with a blood debt.

He stood, abruptly. "I see you have things well in hand now. I will take my leave." Tyee tipped his head curtly to me and Ulf and pivoted on his heel. He strode away from the broken ruins of the Box without looking back. A swirl of dark mist wrapped him in darkness, and then he was gone.

My heart squeezed and I didn't even know why. He had looked angry and disappointed in me and he had no reason to be. We were nothing to each other. It was confusing and I was too tired to sort it out.

A flutter of fabric drew my eyes up. Aislinn floated down towards us, her cloak rippling around her like a living thing. She touched down, graceful as a butterfly, her boots right next to the silver chain Harald had tossed at us moments earlier.

She scooped up the chain, her slender fingers running over it as she coiled it loosely.

"The Trials are concluded," she called out.

My heart sank. Ulf closed his eyes and let out a pained breath. He had to be feeling just as bad as I was. Maybe his reasons for attempting the Trials were different than mine, but we had survived this crucible together and we were changed forever.

Marnie stood alone, watching us with her hands on her hips. The knowledge that Marnie was going to be a Slayer with Cordelia and Wen burned me with the injustice of it all. She couldn't be trusted. She didn't know what it meant to work as a team. She'd stolen Ulf's key rather than help us fight that unholy spider-vampire.

The Slayers needed to know. Uncle Samuel needed to know. They couldn't let Marnie join their ranks. I leaned forward, ready to say something when Aislinn stopped me with a glance. Her golden eyes seemed to see through me and my throat locked up. Panic surged in my belly, hot and liquid. Was this her magic? Did she know my thoughts? Aislinn's eyebrow twitched up, ever so slightly, and then she turned away.

She leaned down and placed a hand on Cordelia's shoulder. "Congratulations, Cordelia of the Hinterlands and Wen from the Brooklyn Temple. You two fought with grace and skill that speaks to your rigorous training and preparation. You worked together and made it out of the Box with a key in record time. The Slayers are pleased to invite the two of you to join us as initiates."

Ulf turned to look at me, the resignation on his face clear. I had been right. It hadn't been limited to three keys for three candidates. Pairs or groups returning with a key resulted in all members passing the Trial.

Yvonne lowered her head to her chest. I wondered if she would try again the next Trials or return to her coven.

Aislinn took a step closer to where Ulf and I sat propped against the wall. She lifted the chain Harald had tossed at us and draped the chain over our legs. It was heavier than I remembered, and sent a tingle through my pant legs, into my skin. She held my gaze for the briefest moment before addressing us both.

"You two," she sighed.

My muscles tensed as I braced to hear about how poorly we'd fared in the Box.

"You two fought as a Slayer pair, and you fought against the most foul of creatures that claims the Box as its territory. We were impressed by your fortitude and your bravery...despite your...unorthodox methods."

Wait, what? I mean, this was nice, but where was this going?

Aislinn whirled and pointed at Marnie. "We were disappointed to see you take a key off your fallen comrade. As Slayers, we must count on each other to defeat the rogues that stalk this city, and that requires trust. That is how we live to slay another day. You violated that most sacred trust."

Akhil nodded, his face solemn. Altan grunted in assent. In fact, all of the Slayers were frowning at Marnie.

It wasn't exactly a victory, but I tried to enjoy it as Aislinn chastised Marnie. Marnie was a deadly fighter and she had all the skills to be a fierce Slayer but at least they had been watching her. That was something.

Aislinn's voice rose and the air grew thick, like a brewing storm. The hairs on my arms stood up and latent power crackled through the air. When Aislinn spoke, the air trembled with her breath. "Marnie Black, you are barred from the Slayers, now and forever more."

Lightning flashed, a sizzling bolt of blue-white that forked down from the clouds and slammed into the next building. A frisson crawled across my scalp as the energy washed over our group. A moment later, thunder clapped, the sound reverberating through my bones.

Cordelia gasped but I was too shocked to react. I had never heard of a candidate getting blacklisted from the Trials. Everything was a test. I shouldn't have been surprised.

Rain fell, softly at first and then increasing to a steady drumbeat that filled the silence. Marnie clenched her fists, holding them tight against her side. Her mouth opened and closed but she said nothing.

Finally she tilted her head back and gave a loud undulating trill.

Whatever I thought she might do, that hadn't been it.

Then she pointed at me, her face pinched and red with anger. "You speak of trust. This one betrays all of us. All of you. You do nothing as she allies with vampires. I used to think the Slayers were righteous. You are all weak! Even as you pretend to hunt them you secretly lust for their power."

From the heavy clouds above us, came the thrum of heavy wings, as loud as a helicopter. A massive bird swooped down, its wingspan the size of a boat. Its talons descended and grabbed Marnie by her vest. That thing looked strong enough to lift elephants. The proud crest of its head had black and brown markings trimmed with gold. As it turned to fly away, Marnie flung down the silver chain at Aislinn.

"We will meet again, Slayers, and then I will show you what righteous fury looks like."

I couldn't believe Marnie had just summoned a roc to bail her out.

Altan grunted, surprisingly sanguine. "Saves us the trouble of taking out the trash."

With a sigh, Akhil just shook his head. "Let us not dwell on this further. We have new initiates to welcome."

Altan beamed at the stablemaster, his mood switching with dazzling speed. "Oh yes, let us welcome the new initiates. Finish up, Ash!"

Aislinn lifted her hands high in a parting motion and the rain slacked off to a drizzle. The sky lightened once more into the Twilight's familiar purple hue and I shivered in my duster. I was exhausted and the cocktail of adrenaline, relief, sadness, and anger had drained me. The Cure had healed my wounds but my body still needed rest. I needed to lie down for about ten years.

Aislinn bent down to peer at my face. I blinked at the breach of personal space.

"You are not what I wanted, nor what I expected. But I was wrong to let my feelings about your father cloud my judgment. Harald has cast his key back at you and Ulf, which fulfills the terms of the Trial. We welcome you two to join us as initiates."

Ulf's head thumped back against the wall and he gave a short bark of laughter.

Samuel had given me an odd look when he had given me

my father's spear. Aislinn had that same look now, searching my eyes for something. I could only wonder what they were looking for. When my father had walked away from Slayers, he had broken much, that much I could tell. Aislinn was telling me not to do the same. I tried to swallow but my throat still hurt too much. It turned into a cough and then I managed to whisper, "I'm not my father."

Aislinn's eyes were bright and hard like gems. "See that you don't follow in his footsteps, breaker."

I closed my eyes finally, unable to stop the tears that had pooled there from running. The tears streaked down my face, hot and furious–a reminder I was alive. I had made it. *For you, Dad.*

35

INITIATES

I had no idea what was coming next. Dad had been unusually tight-lipped about Slayer rituals beyond passing the Trials. Maybe he'd thought I wasn't ready to hear it, or he'd been under another geas to keep the Slayer's secrets. While Yvonne and Axel were carted off to have their wounds tended to, Wen, Ulf, Cordelia, and myself were taken by wagon back into the city. My uncle drove the cart and resisted all our attempts to wheedle information out of him.

In the absence of information, the four of us fell back on the time-honored tradition of baseless speculation and gossiping.

I punched Ulf in the bicep. "Hey, you owe me twelve ounces of silver."

He grinned, his red mustache stretching wide across his face. He reached inside his vest and pulled out a small leather pouch. He dropped it into my palm.

"A debt happily paid."

I smiled at the pleasant clink of silver and the comforting weight in my hand.. This was rent, groceries, and maybe a little extra for the next two months.

As the wagon pushed north we fell into the comfortable silence of comrades who had not only cheated death, but also completed the Trials. We ate hard bread and cold jerky, and drank cool water from canteens that Samuel had laid out for us. It was a glorious feast. My emotions see-sawed between bone-weary exhaustion and giddy elation. I had done it. We had done it. I even hoped that I had dodged the final bullet.

Of course, Cordelia was far too observant to let Aislinn's comments pass unanswered. She sidled closer to me and pitched her voice loud enough so that Wen and Ulf were certain to hear. "So...what was Aislinn saying about your father?"

Suddenly the wagon felt too confined and I struggled to find an articulate response. I hunched my shoulders defensively but I wanted to come clean with everyone. I hadn't felt right about keeping quiet before, but I was proud to be a Lim. Proud that my father had been a Slayer and that I was following in his footsteps. Samuel had urged me to keep under wraps and I hadn't wanted to cause distractions for myself. The Trials were hard enough without the other candidates thinking I had some edge.

"My dad was a Slayer. Samuel is my uncle. They were brothers. I didn't want to say anything before because it wasn't like any of the Slayers were going to cut me any slack."

Wen nodded, his expression thoughtful. "If anything, perhaps they had higher expectations of you."

Relief rushed through me at Wen's insight and my shoulders sagged. "I worried about that too. Honestly it just made me uncomfortable because it was all before I was born. My dad passed away a few years ago so I couldn't ask him anything anyway while going through these Trials."

Cordelia patted my back, her small hand giving me a comforting thump. "That must have been hard."

I nodded. Tears pricked at me again and I pressed my hands

into my eyes. It didn't seem appropriate to be sad when we should all be celebrating.

Ulf put a big hand on my shoulder. "The spirit of your father watches over you and knows you have triumphed."

This time the tears fell and it felt like a door opening in my chest. In a different way than Ava and Jasper, these people were my family now. We were all Slayers, but I felt in my bones that our group was special. Maybe this was the reason Samuel never left. Because his comrades gave him something he had never found elsewhere in his life.

"Why'd she call you a breaker?"

Ah, I should have figured Cordelia would miss nothing. Well, these fine people would be fighting by my side. It was only right they should know. "I can see weaknesses in things. Structures. My father could break things using those weaknesses. I think I can too."

Ulf grunted. "Like you did with Sven's sword?"

That felt like a million years ago, when I had broken Sven's sword and earned Harald's undying enmity.

"Yeah. Like that." Maybe even more than that. I'd have to learn just how much more anyway.

The wagon rolled to a stop. We were back at the Dojo. Before, I'd been just one of many candidates. Kotori had wiped the mats with me. She would likely continue to wipe the mats with me. Still, pride swelled in my chest. I wasn't a candidate any longer—I was a Slayer and this was my place of work.

The gates cranked open. Six figures greeted us in a loose semicircle inside the gates. Altan, Kotori, Bashir, Aislinn, Akhil and someone we hadn't seen much of during the trials, Tanner Matsui. Instead of armor and weapons, the Slayers had cleaned up and wore matching blue tops with loose sleeves and an overlapped front closure. When the wagon stopped, Akhil tossed a blue jacket to my uncle, who quickly doffed his armor and donned the blue top to match the others.

I realized that together with Samuel, these were the Seven. The Seven Freaks of Seattle. All of them were here to initiate us to the Slayers.

As we climbed down from the wagon, Bashir handed each of us a creamy white candle. "Follow me, initiates."

We stepped into the dojo and I yanked off my boots. I didn't want to think about what kind of things were now caked onto them. Soon we were all barefoot. Akhil held out a plate of wet towels and I wanted to groan in relief to wipe the grime off my face, neck, and hands. The heat of the towel and the fresh scent of lemons did a lot to refresh me. It wasn't a hot shower, but it would do for now.

Tanner gave us a big smile, one that suited his square head and square frame. His salt and pepper hair said he wasn't a young man, but his brown skin was smooth and unlined. He looked like he could lift a truck and arm wrestle a crocodile at the same time.

"Welcome to the Dojo, Slayers."

His rich baritone voice put me immediately at ease.

"Today you will see part of what we defend and you will take the vows that bind us together."

He slid open a wooden screen, revealing a row of indigo fabrics, neatly folded in stacks. Tanner handed one out to everyone.

It was the same jacket the Freaks had donned. An indigo dyed samue jacket, the linen fabric soft from many washings. On the back of the jacket, orange thread stitched out the outline of two raised arms, one hand clenched over the fist of the other. It was a powerful image, and one that confirmed what I believed–Slayers were not solo fighters. They worked together. *We* worked together. I was a Slayer too now.

I tied on the loose jacket, smoothing the fabric diagonally across the right side. I watched my fellow initiates do the same and Cordelia's eyes sparkled in delight as she held out the sleeves of her jacket.

Tanner stepped into the closet and slid open an inner door. I leaned forward, curious, but Kotori pulled me back.

"Wait," she hissed.

Then all the lights in the Dojo went out, revealing a faint orange glow that emanated from the closet.

I knew only of one thing that glowed that particular shade of orange.

Tarim crystal. A lot of it.

Akhil snapped his fingers and our candles lit with a gentle flame. He gestured for the initiates to follow and we followed single file into another hallway that led down narrow stairs to a basement.

With each step, it grew colder, and the orange glow grew more intense. The stairway fit only one person at a time then opened into a surprisingly wide and empty room. Except for a massive outcropping of glowing Tarim crystal in the center.

A crystal chamber. The chamber wasn't a room, so much as a cave hollowed out of the ground. The Tarim crystal jutted out from the very earth itself, its rocky structure rugged and raw.

The crystal was massive, gnarled and twisted like the roots of an ancient tree. It was hard to tell if the structure burst from the ceiling and reached into the earth, or the other way around. Either way, it seemed to continue beyond the reaches of this small hollow. Bright motes of orange light flowed through the structure like blood through arteries. The points pulsed to some arcane rhythm, and each pulse bathed the chamber in glowing light.

Around the main crystal, several smaller outcroppings of crystal seemed to grow out of the floor and ceiling. These smaller structures pulsed with their own light, to their own rhythms.

This was the stuff of legend in Seattle.

Like me, the others had been awed into silence as well. I'd always done my trading in silver, but I knew that crystal could be traded as well. I just never rolled in such wealthy circles where they traded chips of crystal as big as my finger. Now I was standing in front of a crystal the size of a redwood.

Aislinn broke the silence. "You will never speak of this room, and you will never speak of what you see, hear, or do here today. Swear it."

The four of us repeated the oath and just like that, I felt the geas lock into place.

Tanner leaned casually against the central crystal and smoothed the overlap on his samue jacket. "The Slayer's Credo is 'Live to Slay Another Day.' It is this way because of what Seattle became after the Rift. We are surrounded by those who are stronger, more powerful, more deadly. Those with the power to eliminate us like that." He snapped his fingers for emphasis.

He paused for a moment. The first Slayers had all been human, vulnerable to all the glamors, enchantments, and sheer physical speed and strength of shifters, vampires, fae, and otherworldly beings that had swarmed Seattle after the Rift. They had banded together to survive. Did those first Slayers anticipate this? How the Slayers would transform into the group it was today with fae and shifters fighting side by side with humans.

Tanner smiled, his teeth very straight and white in the glow of the crystal. "I want to impress upon you that Slayers value valor and loyalty above all. Our world is one that values strength of arms. We train to be the best. This is how we live to slay another day. Slayers fight back to back."

The rest of the Freaks picked up the chant. "...back to back!"

"Unity in the face of the enemy!"

"Unity!"

Tanner's words soothed the ragged edge of my emotions.

This is why I was here and Marnie wasn't. I had trained my entire life to be strong enough to become a Slayer. It felt right, like I had found my place at last.

When I'd lived in Boston, it had been us Lims against the callous world that didn't care if we had enough to eat, or enough for my mom's medicine. My hardscrabble life there had been fraught with desperation but tempered by the love of my family and knowing we were a team.

My dad's death had torn that apart and when Samuel had asked me to cross the Veil, I'd struggled with the guilt of leaving Ava and Jasper behind to take care of our mom. Samuel had made it possible by sending a hundred ounces of silver, and giving my family a modest level of security to replace my earning power and then some for the last six months.

Now I'd be earning ten times what I had made as a short order cook in Boston. I could send most of it home. Even if I never figured out how to send home a Midnight Rose, the money would buy all the medicines mom needed.

Tanner took a step away from the crystal and pointed to the smaller outcroppings from the earth. "You all know about the Tarim crystal and the importance it plays here in our lives. You see the pyramids rising out of our ocean. But what you may not realize is the crystal in this chamber is alive."

I blinked. I mean, I knew it was organic. But did Tanner mean the crystal was sentient?

"On Crossing Day, these crystals are seeded again by the Tarim. Between each Crossing day ceremony, we uphold the Pact and we protect this room. Aislinn, if you would."

Aislinn strode over to him, her long legs outlined in the light of the crystal. She made a fist and Tanner did the same. When they bumped their fists, sparks lit the air between their knuckles, gold and orange. Okay, not the usual casual fist bump.

Aislinn turned to face us. "This is how you may know a

fellow Slayer though our patrol territories may be far apart. Every Slayer has undergone an exchange with the crystal here, and it knows like to like."

Apprehension coiled in my gut. What kind of exchange?

"Cordelia, please step forward." Aislinn made room for Cordelia next to the largest pillar of the crystal.

Cordelia walked up to Aislinn and standing side by side, the height disparity was obvious. Cordelia really was pretty short for a fae.

"Strike the crystal three times. Each blow must be harder than the one before."

Cordelia bit her lip but turned to face the pillar and bent her head. In rapid succession, as if she couldn't bear to stretch it out, she punched the crystal with her fist. She punched so hard that on the third blow she cried out and her blue fae blood splattered across the crystal.

The pillar turned red and pulsed. Any alarm I felt at Cordelia's wound disappeared as her blood was steadily absorbed into the crystal.

Just how alive was the crystal? Did Slayers feed blood to the crystal blood? In my wildest dreams I never imagined the crystal might be carnivorous. The crystal clearly changed us, as shown by Tanner and Aislinn's fist bump. Did we, in turn, change the crystal?

Cordelia looked down at her right fist. The cuts from the crystal sealed together, healed by the crystal itself. Aislinn held out her own fist and when Cordelia bumped it, the golden and orange shower of sparks lit up her face with childlike wonder.

Then it was Wen's turn, Ulf's turn, and mine.

I wasn't fast like a fae, or a precision martial artist like Wen. I was a street fighter the way my father had trained me to be and I punched that pillar like it was a thug trying to take my lunch money, then twice more to send a message.

The pain was excruciating. The crystal felt like ice where it met my skin but radiated through my bones. The skin of my knuckles split and my blood smeared across the pristine crystal.. The pillar glowed red and absorbed my blood. Was part of me in there now? An itch built across my hand until only a faint white crisscross of scars covered my knuckles, looking like a decade old scar. Just below the surface of the skin I felt the chill of the crystal. I'd known the experience would change me, I just hadn't expected...this.

Cordelia grabbed my hand and bumped her knuckles against mine. Sparks flew and elation washed away my reservations.

At last, I was a Slayer.

36

SWEET BEGINNINGS

S amuel sent us all home just as the violet sky over Seattle began lightening into the Twilight's version of dawn.

"You have two days to get your affairs together. We have dorms here in the Dojo if you need them. Spend your two days wisely."

His steely eyes found us all, quelling our euphoria. "The Trials are over. Now the real work begins."

I had no recollection whatsoever of finding my way into my apartment but I managed to shower and then collapse into my bed. My plan was to sleep away half of my two day reprieve. Noise of clattering dishes tugged me out of sleep and then the rich aroma of steaming bone broth dragged me into the waking realm.

My landlady bustled about in my small kitchen, a cute apron over her dark blue track suit. Steaming pots and pans occupied all the burners on my stove. My stomach protested loudly that I needed to be in the kitchen. Now.

Mrs. Chu turned at the noise and smiled. "I used my key to open the door. Hope you don't mind."

I inhaled deeply. "As long as whatever that is, is for me, you can come in any time."

Mrs. Chu's laughter was a series of high pitched hiccoughs. She made a tray and brought it over. I scrambled out of bed to meet her at my kitchen table and found the tray laden with bowls of soup, each one swimming with chunks of meat, carrots, and daikon. She sat across from me and pushed the tray in front of me.

"So? You passed?"

I nodded and dug into my soup, my body nearly singing in pleasure. Between bites and slurps I related what I could of my experience in the Box, leaving out some of the more gruesome details.

Of course, the gruesome details were exactly what she wanted. All through my story Mrs. Chu nodded and smiled at the right parts, and her eyes went big and round when I told her how Ernest had helped me.

"Looks like you had the right idea all along."

"Ernest watched over me but it was Tyee who got us out."

She went still. "You didn't drink from him, did you?"

I shook my head. "No. That was too...permanent...of a solution."

Her shoulders relaxed. "Smart girl. The Court of Mists and Mind is powerful. Alliances are good, but they aren't like us. A blood tie is a dangerous path."

Tyee's face rose out of memory, his eyes locked on mine when I drank the Cure. We barely knew each other, but the expression on his face had been pain, maybe anger. It had made me feel awful, like I'd betrayed him.

Mrs. Chu narrowed her eyes at me, as if she could tell what I was thinking. I shook off thoughts of Tyee. I would be a Slayer and that put an end to any kind of relationship I might have with the vampire prince, no matter how innocuous.

Loud cooing floated in from the open kitchen window and I

dropped my spoon with a thunk. "Excuse me for just a minute, Mrs. Chu, I have to feed Noodle and Bao!"

She waved me off and I dashed out onto the balcony to check on my pigeons. Noodle's beady eyes stared at me reproachfully. "Sorry, boy."

I ran a gentle finger over his head and then made sure to refill all their supplies. Mrs. Chu had checked in on them periodically so it hadn't been dire, but of course, I felt terrible that I'd slept so long.

After taking care of them, I wrote a note to Ava and Jasper. There were only so many words I could squeeze onto the little scrap of paper that the pigeons carried. I couldn't tell them about my harebrained plan with the Midnight Rose. Aislinn's geas prevented me from writing any of that.

I also didn't want to get their hopes up about Mom. Not yet.

Finally I settled on, "I made it. I love you all and thank you for cheering me on."

With a final scritch on Noodle's head, I tied on the message capsule and set him off. Ava and Jasper didn't understand why Dad wanted this for me, but I had gotten this far. I was so close to getting my ink I could taste it.

I went back inside and chatted further with Mrs. Chu. When I mentioned the dorms available for initiates at the Dojo her eyes took on the flat look of disappointment deployed by Asian grandmothers the world over. I quickly reassured her that I would be staying in my apartment and continuing my handyman duties. Her eyes sparkled as she smiled, all teeth.

"Have some more soup, dear. You're going to need your strength."

～

I walked over to the Pleasure District and stood there in front of La Petite Pâtisserie for a long time before I reached for the door. Mrs. Chu had already gone to visit Eloise and had admonished me to do the same now that I was no longer on my deathbed.

La Petite Pâtisserie was a bakery cafe that bustled with the hum of carmelized sugar and commerce. Their pastries were very high end--special occasion goods. The window displays were spectacular works of art, stacked high with tiered cakes draped with gold ribbons and candied fruits.

My emotions were still ragged from my brush with death, and I wasn't ready to see Eloise or Tyee again.

But my initiate schedule with the Slayers was sure to be demanding. This lull before the storm was my only chance to get as much of my to do list checked off as possible.

Also, it was not Eloise's fault that I was uncomfortable around Tyee or anyone affiliated with him.

I straightened up my shirt and smoothed my hair. I pushed the door and a little bell jingled pleasantly. The bakery was warm and smelled of sugar, butter, and happiness. There were two full display cases about chest high and to the right, a long wooden counter with cutting boards, knives and above that, shelves with the fancy boxes and ribbons.

Eloise bustled around behind the displays, loading up the cinnamon buns and raisin breads. My mouth watered at the memory of her bakewell tarts. Maybe I'd save up to get those for the other initiates when we got our ink.

"Roxy! Welcome, welcome!"

She rushed forward and enveloped me in an effusive hug, kissing the air by my cheeks. I patted her back awkwardly. I was fine with hugging, but the air kissing confused me and I hardly knew this woman. Although to be fair, we had shared a rather harrowing evening, and I had lugged her around like a runaway bride so maybe we were close by that standard.

"Hi Eloise, it's nice to see you looking better."

"Oui! All thanks to you." She beamed, her cheeks apple round and shiny from the heat of the bakery.

A door closed in the back and Tyee strolled out. He wore the Night Court's trademark indigo blazer and he moved like an animal on the prowl, incongruous in this cozy pastry shop. He looked so handsome my eyes wanted to linger on his face and I almost took a step closer to him. My heart pounded a touch faster and I exhaled slowly to get it under control. His vampire senses would tell him my reaction, which annoyed me.

"My lord, look who has joined us."

Tyee propped an elbow on the display counter and gave me a lazy smile that didn't quite match the intensity of his gaze. His eyes flicked over my neck and I resisted the urge to touch the scars. The scars were a reminder that he'd saved my life and he'd spilled his own blood to do it. I wondered if he could smell it still or if by taking the Cure after, I'd masked it. I wasn't about to ask him, though.

"Roxy, I see you've recovered from your Trials."

I nodded. "Thank you for getting us out."

"Only fitting given our long standing personal relationship," he drawled.

"We don't have a personal relationship," I huffed.

I gestured back and forth between us for emphasis. "We can't have a personal relationship."

"We already do, Roxy."

"No, I'm a Slayer and you're a vampire. That's a bad combination."

Tyee gave a slow smile, revealing a hint of fang. His dark eyes danced in amusement. "I don't see any Slayer ink."

"I'll get my ink."

And I would. The Slayers had their secrets but I would be learning them now. I knew the ink came after a successful exsanguination run. This was yet another reason I couldn't be having cozy coffee chats with Tyee—a vampire. I had to keep a distance between us so that I could do my job and see them as what they were, apex predators of humans and fae.

Eloise slid open the display doors. "Milord, I need a box for Roxy."

Tyee stood to do her bidding and I watched in amusement as the little baker bossed around the Prince and he dutifully stacked pastries into a double decker box. He even tied a ribbon on it. His movements were easy, as if he had done it many times before. Did the Night Queen know her Prince was moonlighting as a bakery clerk?

Eloise dusted her hands off on her white apron and picked up the box from where Tyee had set it. "Roxy, for you and Mrs. Chu. Enjoy it with my compliments."

I grinned. "I will enjoy it. A lot. Thank you, Eloise."

She waved at me. "Milord, aren't you going to say goodbye to Roxy?"

He tipped his head. "Until we meet again, Roxy."

I shrugged. "Seems unlikely. The Slayers will keep me pretty busy."

Tyee leaned forward, both elbows on the counter. His starlight eyes seemed to look through me. "Don't worry, *ma bichette*. I will never be too busy for you."

I clutched the pastry box tighter to my chest and ducked out of there, my face flaming. It was a good thing I was headed back to the Dojo tomorrow. I had to make sure that I was busy enough to dodge the prince. Anything to avoid a situation where Tyee might be on the other side of my stakes. It had already gotten too complicated but I couldn't change the past. I could only look to the future.

This was the life I'd chosen and the life I would lead. A Slayer who was loyal.

I promise, Dad.

∾

BRICKS AND MURDER

Coming soon in late 2022! Pre-order Bricks and Murder now to read about Roxy's Initiation into the Slayers!

Read on for an excerpt of the second installment in the Seattle Slayers series, Bricks and Murder:

Chapter 1 - THE DOJO

The muggy summer heat sat thick and heavy in the air and sweat drenched the back of my shirt as I fought in the court-yard. It didn't help that my opponent was my sensei, Kotori the Fox, and that she was three times faster than I was. Every time she smacked me with her staff I would have a bruise there for days.

And yet, I wouldn't trade a second of it. The thwack of bamboo bo staffs striking against each other, the twist of bodies and grunts of exertion felt like home.

When I'd been a kid in Boston, I'd played a lot of basketball and there was something about the squeak of shoes on the gym floor and the swish of the net and the thump of basketballs that always sounded right. Now I was a Slayer initiate in a city drip-ping with vampires and shifters and fae and the sounds of fighting, in or out of the Dojo, was the soundtrack that made me feel good. Made me feel strong.

And I needed that. Being a Slayer made me a target. I didn't carry the Midnight Rose yet but I'd earned my ink, exsan-guinating my first vampire last month. My inking ceremony was tonight and I needed to burn off my nervous energy. Kotori had been more than willing to help.

Earning the Midnight Rose was why I joined the Slayers, part of my plan to save my mom from further decline. But I had been kidding myself. I'd almost washed out of the Trials on my way to becoming a Slayer initiate and only then did I face the truth–that I'd been doing it all along to live up to my dad's ideals. To step into shoes and be as great, if not greater than Gabriel Lim, the Breaker of Seattle.

I still wanted that, but now it was tempered by something else–the loyalty I felt to my fellow Slayers. Even my sensei who was currently beating me with a stick.

Kotori's staff found my shin with a crack. I grunted at the pain and was forced to dance back a step. She moved smoothly into the opening, a swirling mass of brilliant red leather, the other end of her staff coming around at somewhere in the vicinity of the speed of sound. It didn't matter that I was a full head taller than Kotori, the petite woman could always get inside my longer reach. I gave up on grace and simply fell to the mat to avoid the follow up strike.

With a grunt of annoyance Kotori elbowed me in the ribs, pushing me into the fall. I brought my staff around as I hit the mat, just as my sensei stopped with her feet straddling my chest, the end of her staff next to my neck. The end of my own staff was just under her armpit.

Kotori's lip curled. "And what did that get you, *neh*?"

I tried to control my breathing, to speak as evenly as she did. It still ended up coming out between panting gasps. "Strike to the axillary artery. Exsanguination."

She rapped the end of her staff against my head. Ow. "But you are dead. So your exsanguination isn't happening."

Kotori stepped back and I rubbed my head. I didn't think I would have a lump there tomorrow. Maybe. As I rolled back onto my feet, Kotori flicked her fingers at me in a dismissive gesture. "Go work on the mat. I will spar with Wen so I can get my own workout in."

I was insulted and relieved at the same time, which was par for the course when I dealt with my feral sensei. I bowed to her and racked my bo staff on my way to the mats.

Truthfully, Wen was a better fighter hand-to-hand fighter than I was. He had an economy of movement that made his sparring look effortless. Even when fighting the Fox, Wen didn't seem to break a sweat. Not that he beat her. None of us ever beat her. As part of my Trials, I had rapidly concluded that she would crush me but she didn't want to actually kill me and I'd fought accordingly. That was the only way I'd gotten even a scratch on her.

I wasn't so foolish as to repeat that.

A soft puff of air brushed my hair as Wen stepped by. And by stepped, I mean in that ethereal way he moved, as if traversing an invisible staircase. It would have been even cooler if Wen had long flowing hair to go with his gray monk's robes, but he shaved his head to spotless perfection daily.

My floor routines beckoned, but I couldn't help stopping to watch Wen spar with Kotori.

Wen wasn't tall, but with his robes and musculature, he looked like a giant next to Kotori. They made a striking tableau, the slight Fox in red, and the big monk in gray. All we needed was rain and some mood music.

Their staffs struck against each other in a staccato of hits the human eye could barely follow. That made sense since Kotori wasn't human. But Wen was. His staff speeds were the envy of the rest of the initiates. I'd asked him about it, assuming there was some ten thousand hours type of reason for his skill.

"I know where the next strike will go so I just try to get there," Wen explained.

As far as I could tell, Wen had decades of training *and* his magic here in the Veil gave him a preternatural sense of what would happen next–like fighting clairvoyance. It seemed extremely useful to me, especially for a Slayer.

Behind me, Ulf Skardeson of the Reach, stumbled and then grunted with annoyance as Bashir whacked him on the ribs. "Why this stick? Why not let me train with my axe? Or a sword, I ask you?" Ulf complained.

Bashir laughed. "Sometimes all you have is a stick. What then? You must master all the weapons at your disposal."

"Bah." Ulf shook his head, his long red braids moving in emphasis to his annoyance. He set his bo staff next to mine and came to stand next to me. He slapped my back with what for him was probably a companionable tap but practically knocked me forward.

Bashir gave a sharp whistle, and a swirl of leaves circled around Cordelia. With a cheerful smile, she waved at Bashir and he tossed her a bo staff.

Cordelia, perfect at everything, leapt in the air and caught the staff in one smooth motion. She launched into a front roll with the staff to land in front of Bashir. Bashir's handsome face split into a broad grin, white teeth flashing against his dark beard. She was his favorite and it was easy to see why. Cordelia was a natural, and she was good-natured to boot.

Somehow, her fae robes didn't get a smudge of dirt on them. I wondered if they were spelled to repel dirt. It would explain how Cordelia managed to stay so clean even after rolling in the mud. I always came out of these workouts a hot sweaty mess, my samue jacket usually sporting a rip or tear.

Cordelia had taken a shine to me at the first Trial and I'd never understood why. I was a grubby street fighter who favored hammers for my weapon of choice. Cordelia harkened from a noble fae family and wielded a milky sword that gleamed like moonlight. She'd earned my loyalty and my friendship, and I'd learned to ignore her critiques of my messy fighting style.

The only time I'd ever seen her smile fade was when she dealt with the mountain fae. Like our first encounter with Ulf and his brothers.

I'd grown fond of Ulf, which was a far cry from how we'd started out. His former sword brother, Harald Stenson, was a prince of the mountain fae tribe Ulf hailed from. Harald had taken an instant dislike to me in the first Trials to become a Slayer. The battle lines had been drawn that day, with me and Cordelia on one side, and the mountain fae on the other.

Then the Trials escalated. We were forced to put aside old blood feuds, petty grievances, and just plain annoyance to work together and survive those Trials. Ulf and I had made it out of the Box. His sworn brotherhood with Harald had not survived.

Ulf and Cordelia had never explained to me what happened on their Trial together but they had reached an uneasy truce, with the millennia old blood feud no longer at the forefront of their dealings. They were Slayers now, and their fae politics had taken a back seat. At least, that was how it looked to me.

I was still relatively new to the Veil. This intersection of Tarim magic and powerful factions like the fae, the two vampire courts, the various churches, and the Slayers often confused me. But I tried to keep it simple, like cleaving to my identity as a Slayer.

Sometimes things got messy for me, like my interactions with Tyee Wilder, the Night Prince. He was a vampire that I was better off avoiding but couldn't help thinking about. I appreciated that Slayer training kept me busy. Busy enough to avoid wandering by the Pleasure District to bump into Tyee.

Especially after tonight.

We were getting our ink. I would be a Slayer, like my father before me. Cordelia, Wen, Ulf and now Finn would be by my side. If that meant I had to avoid a certain flirtatious vampire prince, it was worth it.

"We should go celebrate tonight." I said to Ulf.

"Aye." Ulf was always up for a party.

"Anywhere you want to go?" I asked.

"Here is good."

Ulf bunked here at the Dojo. Wen did as well. I kept my cozy studio apartment in the old international district, or risked my landlady's displeasure. Also, I liked having that bit of personal space. It was me, my pigeons, and my side hustle projects, which was just the way I liked it. Slayers was too consuming otherwise and I kept my space to remind myself that I still had to follow through on my promise to my dad. It meant becoming a Slayer but betraying the geas that kept

Slayer secrets. Away from Slayers, I could look at that picture of my family and remember that my work wasn't done. *Soon.*

"Yield." Kotori had maneuvered Wen to the wall, her staff pressing into his neck.

Wen had lasted three times longer than I had. While Kotori often expressed her irritation at my candidacy, I could tell she approved of Wen's addition to the ranks. That she thought he was what Slayers needed more of.

I wanted to be like that, but earning Kotori's approval seemed impossible, so I aimed to avoid her wrath.

Kotori released Wen and he bowed to her. She bowed back and gave him a punch on the bicep. I'd never seen her do that with anyone other than Bashir. I guess after our ink, we would all be equals, but some of us were more equal than others.

Ulf gave Wen a fist bump and then we moved through some stretching routines together and I asked Wen if he had a preference for celebration festivities.

Wen's eyebrows drew down and he frowned. "I wanted to tell you all together."

"Tell us what?"

"I will not be getting the ink."

"What? Why not?"

Wen looked at me, his dark eyes solemn. "Roxy, you should ask more questions about the effects of the ink."

Wen's words hit me like a punch in the gut.

All of us were supposed to get our ink tonight. We'd survived the Trials together and it had made us stronger. And now Wen was telling us that he didn't want the ink.

It was also strange that he should direct that only at me and not Ulf. I hadn't thought about the effects of the ink at all. We all had the scars of our last interaction with the Tarim crystal. When I cut myself on the crystal, it had drunk from me, then healed me. Until that ceremony, I'd always thought of the crystal as inert. But now I knew better.

And Wen was telling me the ink was why he wasn't going to be Slayer.

Now I had to ask myself, did I want to know?

Would I do it anyway?

Pre-order your copy of Bricks and Murder today! Patrons receive chapters weekly on our Patreon:

THE FANGS

To read Tyee's perspective when seeing Roxy in the Fangs, scan below to get your complimentary copy of The Fangs:

EBONY GATE

Julia Vee and Ken Bebelle bring you a female *John Wick* story with dragon magic set in contemporary San Francisco's Chinatown

Emiko Soong belongs to one of the eight premier magical families of the world. But Emiko never needed any magic. Because she is the Blade of the Soong Clan.

Or was. Until she's drenched in blood in the middle of a market in China, surrounded by bodies and the scent of blood and human waste as a lethal perfume.

The Butcher of Beijing now lives a quiet life in San Francisco, importing antiques. But when a shinigami, a god of death itself, calls in a family blood debt, Emiko must recover the Ebony Gate that holds back the hungry ghosts of the Yomi underworld.
    Or forfeit her soul as the anchor.

What's a retired assassin to do but save the City By The Bay from an army of the dead?

Pre-order your copy of Ebony Gate Today!

TROLL DUTY

Roxy has a lot to learn. Between Stakes and Bones and the next book, she gets troll duty. Of course, nothing goes as planned.

"I moved to Seattle to get my dream job with the Slayers. So far my work duties risk getting my throat ripped out on a daily basis. My sensei at the Slayers is sending me out on a job to deal with a rampaging stone troll. Even better, my backup is the new kid from Ireland who doesn't know which is the pointy end of the knife. If we fail, the Caravan can't cross the bridge and the citizens of Seattle who are counting on the life-saving medicine on the Caravan will suffer.

I'll get the job done, no matter what it takes, because I haven't come this far to wash out of Slayers now."

Roxy's adventures continue when the Slayers assign her Troll Duty! To read about how she earns her ink, buy this novelette direct from us here:

ACKNOWLEDGMENTS

First of all, thank you to my wife and kids, for humoring me on my writing journey. It's taken a while and I hope it keeps going for a long time!

Thank you to my co-author, Julia, for keeping us on track, especially when I tended to branch off in new directions we didn't need yet. (Don't worry, those new directions will get out there eventually.)

And lastly thank you to my mom and dad for helping me rediscover a part of the Asian myth I had learned as a child but forgot as I grew up. So I guess thanks for helping me re-find part of my childhood. ~Ken

A book doesn't happen without a lot of people. I'm putting down the words with Ken, but my husband and kids give me the space I need to make this happen.

Thanks to dear friends who listen to me blathering on about writing: Kevin, Karna, Teenuh, Katie, Casey, and Wendy. Thanks for always cheering me on.

The product you're holding started while we were deep in lockdown. Ken and I spent countless hours on the phone and on the page to bring you this version of magical Seattle. Our wonderful cover artist Christian Bentulan really brought Roxy vividly to life. A big thank you to my writing accountability partners Kendrai Meeks and Tracy Cembor for keeping me focused. Special thanks to our early readers Penny and Michelle who read this with the speed of light, gave us valuable feedback and identified the typos and formatting issues so we could make this the best product possible for you!

Then there's you–the readers. Knowing that I can share stories with you is the best feeling in the world. ~Julia

ABOUT THE AUTHORS

Ken Bebelle - Ken turned his childhood love for reading sci-fi and fantasy into a career in prosthetics. After twenty years he came back to books, writing about plucky underdogs and ancient magical artifacts with deadly secrets. He grew up in northern California and now lives in southern California with his wife, two kids, and too many tomato plants.

Julia Vee - Julia likes stories about monsters, money, and good food. Julia was born in Macao and grew up in Northern California, where she studied at UC Berkeley and majored in Asian Studies. She is a graduate of the Viable Paradise workshop.

Ken and Julia have written together since middle school. Their forthcoming trilogy has been acquired by Tor and debuts with Ebony Gate in the Spring of 2023. Ebony Gate is a contemporary fantasy with Asian elements and mythology set in the Pacific Rim.

KEN BEBELLE AND JULIA VEE

Made in the USA
Middletown, DE
28 August 2022

72574575R00215